FUTURE

Best wishes

Katrina Mountfort

FUTURE PERFECT

BOOK 1 OF THE BLUEPRINT TRILOGY

KATRINA MOUNTFORT

Elsewhen Press

Future Perfect
First published in Great Britain by Elsewhen Press, 2014
An imprint of Alnpete Limited

Elsewhen Press, PO Box 757, Dartford, Kent DA2 7TQ
www.elsewhen.co.uk

British Library Cataloguing in Publication Data.
A catalogue record for this book is available from the British Library.
ISBN 978-1-908168-45-0 Print edition
ISBN 978-1-908168-55-9 eBook edition

Printed and bound by CPI Group (UK) Ltd, Croydon, CR0 4YY

This book is a work of fiction. All names, characters, places, authorities,
media shows and online services are either a product of the author's fertile
imagination or are used fictitiously. Any resemblance to actual services,
shows, organisations, sites or people (living or dead, *Vile* or *BodyPerfect*) is
purely coincidental.

For Ayaz

CHAPTER – 1

5 March 2171

Newsfeed: Marked citizens to be ejected from Citidomes.

Latest figures suggest that the incidence of TJB virus is on the increase. The permanent Marks left on the skin by the virus are recognisable to all, as well as the recurrent debilitating sickness. From next month, legislation will be in place to eject all Marked individuals from Citidomes and detain them in outdoor correction centres, to discourage virus spread.

That was ridiculously harsh. How would anyone survive outdoors? Of course I kept my mouth shut – I didn't want to be reported as a subversive thinker. After all, I barely knew Von and Jem. But I didn't have time to dwell on it: a door slid open, revealing a vision in shimmering lilac who floated into the room with the words, "Hey, everyone!"

So this was the famous Uma. Her voice was every bit as irritating off-screen as on. But I had to admit, she was dazzling; lean even by BodyPerfect standards, her hip bones jutting out like the handgrips on an OmniTrainer.

"Hey, kitten, so you're the new girl," Uma said. "Let's connect!"

We exchanged smiles and each other's details.

"Wild hair colour – where did you get it?" Uma said. I glowed; my thick black hair was the only part of my appearance anyone ever complimented. Her eyes dropped to my chin – I had a ripe spot – but thankfully she didn't comment.

"It's natural. I love yours."

"Cray-cray crazy, isn't it?"

Uma's hair, matching her body suit, was metallic lilac, and scraped back so tightly it no longer looked like hair. Together with her translucent skin and steely eyes, she looked barely human and didn't so much walk as glide. I stared at her with envy; elegance is pretty much impossible when you're as short as me and I never quite mastered the art of walking with anything close to grace. But 'kitten'? 'Cray-cray'? 'Wild'? Had the residence team gone mad? Why on earth did they think we'd be compatible resmates? Uma glanced up and down at my ochre tunic and black pants, no doubt thinking the same. I chewed on a nail. Jem and Von didn't seem any more inspiring, their eyes flickering with the images on the virtual screens of their DataBands. So much for the scintillating adult conversations I'd hoped for.

"Not much welcome for Caia, is it?" Uma pouted. "Our first night together and you're watching a boring newsfeed about – euw – the Mark."

"Caia's been living here three nights now but you haven't been in for long enough to meet her." Jem smiled, almost allowing himself a laugh.

"Odd that the virus is on the increase, though, isn't it?" Von rubbed his smooth chin and I raised my eyebrows. It was the first time he'd spoken about anything other than exercise. His expressionless eyes made it impossible to guess what he was thinking, or even if he was thinking at all. "Why would anyone want to do something so creeving ... animal?"

"It's too gross! I don't even want to think about it," said Uma, tapping her DataBand, which caused the newsfeed to be replaced by an ever-changing array of virtual images and ambient music. I gasped as the room filled with iridescent bubbles so realistic I wanted to reach out and touch one. As the bubbles appeared to burst, a swarm of glittering butterflies replaced them.

"Oh ... it's magical," I said.

"Wild, huh? Guess you never lived in B2 residences before. You fresh out of a development centre?" Uma gave me a patronising smile as though I was about five years old.

"Academic centre – I just graduated. I've never even had my own room. I still can't quite believe I'm living here; it's beautiful." That was a bit of a lie. Stylish would be a better word. The décor was minimalist, all white except for the expansive scarlet seating unit.

"Yeah, this place is so cool. I've been living here for –"

A buzzing at the door interrupted us.

"Delivery for you," Jem said, handing me a garment on a hanger.

"Thanks. Ooh, my Ministry uniform." I held up the black pants and white tunic bearing the Ministry logo.

"Poor you." Uma said. "Not exactly superstylish, is it? What's your job?"

'Superstylish'? I grinned. Another word I'd never felt the need to use. "I start tomorrow as a researcher at the Ministry of Biotechnology. I'll be developing new biopolymers." Uma's eyes were blank. "That's plastics."

"Ooh, aren't you clever!" Uma glanced at her DataBand.

"I've seen your show," I lied. "You're great on it." Did that sound sincere enough? I guessed *Truth or Dare* wasn't any different to any of the other media games that passed for entertainment. I outgrew them years ago, but it looked like I may have to start watching them again if I wanted to fit in around here.

"Thanks, kitten," Uma said with a tinkling laugh. "Isn't it immense? Hey, have you personalised your fashion program yet?"

"Not yet."

"What, are you mad? Let me see. You doofus, you haven't scanned your skin tone yet. How did you expect to get the right colours?" I proffered the DataBand on my wrist, swallowing a laugh. No doubt the wrong shade would ruin my life. "You did a body scan for the fit?"

"Yeah." Well-fitting clothes were the only things that interested me about my fashion program. Before, all my clothes had been a standardized short length, which were still too long.

"You're the smallest person I ever met." Not bad, Uma had taken – what – five minutes to mention it? "You don't look old enough to be a graduate."

"I was fast tracked; I'm nearly seventeen." I tried not to sound too defensive.

"Aww!" What would she do next – pat me on the head? She selected more options on the DataBand. What else could there possibly be? "Let's check out your unique outfits."

"I wondered what they were."

"They're the best – the ones you only wear once. That's odd, you're only allowed two a year. Must be a mistake. I get thirty-five." Uma sniggered again. It was already starting to grate on me. Why would I even need two? Weren't my standard party outfits enough? Better not admit I wasn't a party sort of girl. But Uma seemed to have worked this out for herself and started chatting to Von about a launch she'd been invited to.

"Good job we're bright, huh?" Jem said to me, his eyes taking in Uma's never-ending legs before a disparaging glance at his own, altogether less-perfect, body. I swallowed, unsure of what to say. So far, Jem hadn't said much to me. He was a health worker, and so ought to be more on my wavelength, less intimidating than the other two. But, like them, he was in his early twenties and constantly dropped names of people I'd never heard of. I was used to being the youngest in my peer groups – most of my fellow graduates were nineteen or twenty – so why did these guys make me feel so … unsophisticated?

"Does not being BodyPerfect bother you?" I asked.

"Course it does, but I'll get there." Jem ran his hand through his coarse hair, which despite the barrage of gels he'd subjected it to, refused to lay flat against his skull, like Von's. "I had my eyebrows done last month – Beki at the Western leisure centre – she's outstanding. You should think about it."

"Mmm, they look good. Maybe I will when I've been paid," I said, though I wasn't keen on the fashion for ultralighting away eyebrow hair and replacing it with a tattooed line. My own eyebrows may be on the heavy side but they were mine. Unthinkingly, I quoted the words of my preteen youth development centre. "'Be satisfied with what you have.' That's what they said to me when it was obvious I wasn't going to reach a normal height." I blushed and then sniffed. "Of course, in the next breath they told me to do stretching exercises for the rest of my life." My eyes met

Jem's and a flash of understanding passed between us.

"They diagnosed me with Dissatisfaction Syndrome," Jem muttered.

"Hey, you two. Getting a bit serious, aren't you?" Von frowned.

Jem's tone changed and became uncharacteristically chirpy. "Hey, it's no big deal. I have therapy and I'm coming to terms with it. I quite enjoy my work."

"Only 'quite enjoy'? Medicine must be so rewarding. What you do really *matters*!" I winced. Had I offended Uma and Von? No, they hadn't noticed.

I just didn't get Jem. No-one got to be a health worker without having a high brain score, so why was he so fixated on being like Von and Uma? Dissatisfaction Syndrome – how did therapists dream up such stupid titles? How could such a complicated guy be summed up in two words? Apart from that attachment business, I'd never had therapy. It didn't seem to help anyone, but I guess people found it comforting to have a label to put on their problems.

Uma and Von – now they were easy to understand – cheerful and carefree. Why wouldn't they be? After all, they were the beautiful people, so similar-looking that from a distance it was difficult to tell them apart.

"Yeah, my work matters but I worked fifty hours last week," Jem grumbled.

I saw his point. BodyPerfects had it easy. Endless parties, glamorous and well-paid jobs: sport stars, exercise trainers, leisure co-ordinators, and models. It must be galling for Jem to work long hours while Uma was paid the same for shrieking on one weekly show and Von only had to work mornings – he devised fitness regimes for celebrities. But I'd hate their lives. Anyone with half a brain would.

I went to the kitchen and heard Uma say, "She's a nice little thing, isn't she?"

"Yeah, seems a sweet kid," said Von. "No looker though, is she? Couldn't she lighten her skin?"

"Yeah, maybe I'll get her some better facebase. And something for that spot. Did you see it? Gross!"

I tried to shrug off the comments about my looks – I'd heard them all before – but they didn't hurt any less. The assessment of my personality stung too. Why did no-one describe me as charismatic, vivacious, mysterious even? Huh, who was I kidding? Nice and sweet seemed to be my lot in life. Still, it was better than the way I'd heard myself described at a party last year: 'geeky brainiac freak'. What was wrong with wanting to learn things? Uma followed me and glanced at her shelf in the cooler. Several of the packets had turned red.

"Not again." Uma tossed them into the waste disposal. "I order food every week and then go out so much I forget to eat it. I'm going to order nutribars from now on, it's easier."

I screwed up my face. "Really?"

"I'm not into food. Ooh, you've chosen the healthy options haven't you? I guess you're on fat control food." She cast a critical eye up and down my body.

"Yeah. I'd give anything for a protiburger," I said, ogling the food on Jem's shelf.

"You should get Von to do you an uberfitness program."

"Oh, I should, I know, but apart from racketball, I'm not a sporty type."

At the mention of his name, Von joined us. "It's all about energy balance, Caia. You have to give out more than you put in. Why don't I make up a program for you? My latest one burns seventy fat units an hour." He patted his taut stomach.

"Maybe I'll give it a try." How would I get out of this? Why did anyone want to push themselves to the point of near-death? But maybe I should give in; I'd get more health credits. Besides, it'd give me something to talk to Von about.

"Running's great too." Von persisted. "I'm doing the terathon at the Pleasuredome next month."

"I've entered too," said Uma. "The beach party afterwards should be kicking!"

Their talk turned to parties again. Now I knew they were mad. Who in their right mind would run 60 km on a resistance track? No, they weren't the like-minded resmates I'd dreamed of. But they had something that intrigued me: a sort of lightness, a gaiety, I guess. I'd never had that. Last week I'd been living with students who spent their evenings revising for exams, playing VirtuChess or doing brain puzzles.

A cacophony of voices outside made us all turn around.

"What's going on?" Jem moved to the residence entrance. "Oh, veez, it's the CEs."

I followed the others and my hand flew to my mouth. Two correction enforcers were dragging a guy and girl by the hair. The guy struggled and yelled until they stunned him into catatonic submission. The girl, tears streaming down her face, looked anywhere but at us. A third CE pressed something to their forearms. I frowned and looked at the others, but the action had been so swift and covert that no-one else seemed to have noticed. What was it? Behind them, another woman was hurling insults. Then she spat on them.

"Hope they keep you in forever, you creevil viruses!"

"Hey, Shyna, what's happening?" asked Uma.

"I caught Toc and Fay ... coupling."

"Euw, gross, and they came to my last party."

Uma and Von joined Shyna in spitting on the couple. Jem, after a minute's hesitation, gave a mock spit. I stood away; there was something ... brutal about the whole scene.

"I'm going to have to get someone in to disinfect the whole place." Shyna turned to me. I resisted the temptation to point out that spitting was pretty unhygienic too. "Hey, you're new. Woah, aren't you small? I'm Shyna. Sorry you had to see that; let's hope we get some decent resmates next time."

The show over, we went back inside.

"You never know about anyone, do you?" said Von. "Toc and Fay ... thought they were straight up. Oh well, I guess Shyna's pleased, if she turned them in ..."

"Yeah ... But knowing they've been doing that in her res," said Uma with a dramatic shudder. "Filthy creevs. Anyway, let's forget it. I've programmed some banging music, so let's get Blissed."

"Good idea," said Von.

I giggled; no-one had ever said "let's get Blissed" to me. Should I admit I'd never taken Bliss before? At the same time, I couldn't believe that Uma and Von could brush aside what we'd just seen. Dragging by the hair? Spitting? Knowing their neighbours might be banished to an outdoor correction centre? And all for coupling? I just didn't get it.

Coupling was gross and indecent – I understood that much – but was it really such a hideous crime? Oh, why worry? Perhaps Uma had the right idea. I'd 'get Blissed'.

Uma handed over a packet and I gaped at the purple pill. I swallowed it before my nerve deserted me. What would it do to me? But I didn't have long to worry: a minute later my muscles relaxed; I could feel my jaw loosening. Soon it was like someone had filed all the hard edges of anxiety from my mind. It didn't even bother me that the conversation had turned to a celebrity I didn't know. Hmm, I should take these more often.

Two hours later, when I went to my room, I was still Blissed but not sleepy in the slightest. I looked at the new Document feature of my DataBand, its light dazzling me – must be the Bliss. I read the words "Privacy Settings" and hugged myself. For the first time ever, I could input documents that only I could read. Some Ministry work would be secret. Privacy – I'd been longing for it my entire life.

Without thinking, I found myself saying, "Title. My first private history entry." What was I doing? "Delete."

"Are you sure?" a synthetic voice asked.

Well, why not? As long as I logged out after every entry, who'd find it? Then again, what was the point? Why record history that no-one would ever read? Perhaps because the only history I knew of was the Knowledge Fountain, which recorded very little before 2065. Huh, Knowledge Fountain, what a contradiction in terms. I once asked my development leader why the history on the Knowledge Fountain had so many gaps.

"Most history is an accumulation of pointless facts," she'd replied. "Everything you need – things we can learn from to improve society – can be found on the Knowledge Fountain."

I wasn't happy with the answer. Plenty of other things we'd learnt – like advanced logic and nanoionics – had no obvious point. Why couldn't I find out how ordinary people used to live before the Citidomes, rather than vague references to wars and discontent? Did it matter whether it was useful or not? It'd be interesting. That sealed my idea. I'd record my history, details of life in the Citidome, for future generations. That newsfeed on the TJB virus was still running across the screen, so I pasted a Knowledge Fountain entry into my document. If I was going to illegally record history, I needed references to support it.

> **TJB virus**: A <u>virus</u> identified for the first time in 2118. It is transmitted by <u>coupling</u>. The infection causes severe nausea, fever, dizziness and fatigue, and skin disfigurement in the form of between one and three large crimson Marks up to 10 cm diameter, the face being most frequently affected. The Mark never disappears, and the sickness recurs at regular intervals, causing degenerative health changes and lowering life expectancy by ten years. The TJB virus can generate spontaneously and anyone who couples runs a high risk of becoming Marked. <u>Ultralight</u> cannot remove the Mark. The Citidomes, in an attempt to eradicate subversive behaviour, offer citizen points to anyone who reports a Marked individual.

I'd never understood how a virus could generate spontaneously but my development leader told me off at preteen when I asked.

"Too much curiosity is a dangerous thing," she said.

And there was that word again: coupling. I wish I understood exactly what it meant. I got the basic idea, but why would anyone run the risk of getting Marked? I asked about that in preteen too. I cringed at the memory.

"You disgusting girl; you should know better than to ask," the development leader barked. "Decent people don't indulge in animal behaviour, nor do they talk about it. Come to the front of the room."

I crept to the front of the classroom, where she took my DataBand from me, and projected the words, 'I am an indecent girl who questions too much' above my head.

I stopped asking questions after that.

As the Bliss wore off, I started overanalysing the evening – the way I always did. Had I fitted in? Kind of, but not comfortably. Should I have shown more enthusiasm over the clothes? It was always the same. Whenever I found myself in a group, it was as if a circle had been drawn around them, which excluded me. What was wrong with me? Why did I always have to be so … different?

I stopped myself, of course. Mustn't give way to negative thoughts. Maybe it'd all happen tomorrow, my first working day. Maybe there I'd find people I connected with? I programmed my RestPod and a peculiar feeling overcame me … that tomorrow would be the day when my life began.

CHAPTER - 2

As my DataBand reminded me of my day's schedule – like I could possibly forget – I held my head and groaned. Already my stomach was a tangle of knots. I was pinning so many hopes on my first day at work that I was setting myself up for disappointment. The usual doubts swirled in my brain: what if I didn't fit in? But even worse, I started worrying that I might not be up to the work. That was a new one for me. Must be a comedown from last night.

They'd told me to arrive at 9:30 but I was pacing up and down outside by 9:20. The street throbbed with people returning to work after the weekend. Some, anxious to cram in as much exercise as possible during a working day, ran or cycled in the fast lanes. In the central lanes, the occasional TravelPod passed by. I glanced at the time again – 9:22. Oh, this was silly; I'd just go in. Two rounds of security checks later, the team leader, Kit, met me at reception.

"Caia, welcome." His smile loosened the stomach knots. He'd interviewed me and seemed an approachable guy: not too tall, not too intimidating. "Come and meet the rest of the team."

I followed him into the office where two guys and two girls stood up.

"This is our new graduate trainee, Caia," Kit said.

Each of the team said "hey" and held their DataBands to mine in turn. First, I craned my neck to smile at Jana. Great, just great: a BodyPerfect. Then Dal – oh, he was a guy not a girl – gave me a huge smile. Phew, he was short too. Ren was kind of ordinary-looking as well. Perhaps I wouldn't be a freak here. Then I looked at Mac, and for some weird reason couldn't stop looking. Even worse, my heart had sped up as if I'd done an hour on the OmniTrainer. What was this – more after-effects of Bliss? Stop staring, Caia, do you want the shortest career on record? I forced my eyes downwards.

As Kit carried on talking, I stole another glance at Mac. What was it about him? He looked to be the closest in age to me but there was something else. Most people would focus on his imperfections. His mouth was too large, his fleshy lips tweaked into an expression of permanent amusement, as if he was enjoying a private joke. Then – oh no – his eyes met mine, his gaze penetrating, as if he could see right inside me.

My eyes wandered to what people would have found most shocking about Mac – the hint of stubble that darkened his chin. Why didn't he get rid of it with ultralight? But then again, why should he? I'd imagined facial hair would look weird, disfiguring, but now I felt the opposite. He was also broader in the shoulder and chest than the other guys in the team. That's when it clicked. The reason I couldn't stop looking at him. I'd never mistake Mac for a woman.

I shivered. This wasn't attraction, was it? No, it was just appreciation of his looks. I liked the way Jana looked too – all legs and long, copper hair. So why did my heart give a strange little flip when Kit said, "Mac went through the graduate trainee program two years ago, so I've assigned him to be your mentor. He'll help you settle in."

"Hey Caia," Mac said. "I'll give you a quick tour." He showed me my workstation and the rest of the office. "That room's a private meeting room." He raised an eyebrow and I grinned. The transparent walls offered little actual privacy. "And through here is the good stuff." I followed him into a sleek laboratory, heaving with instrumentation.

"Woow, just look at this! I've never been in a lab as big as this before. All this equipment. Two positron analysers!" I stopped myself before I revealed any more of my inner geek. But the truth was, I could happily spend my life in a lab like this.

"Don't get too excited. We share them with two other teams. Have you used a PA before?"

Science, think about science. I took a breath, wondering how honest I should be about my experience, or lack of it.

"I'm not assessing you, so you don't have to be on your best behaviour." The skin at the outer corners of his eyes puckered, as if his whole face was smiling. Why was that smile setting fire to my pulse? Did I want a one-way ticket to a correction centre?

"That's a relief. To be honest, I've never used one but I talked about them so convincingly in my interview that Kit thinks I have."

"Don't worry. We all did that." His grin was boyish, more co-conspirator than mentor.

"I'm not sure what a mentor does," I said.

"Oh, I'm not your boss. I'm meant to help you settle in and, after that, if you have any problems you can come to me first."

You've no idea of the problems I'm having with you right now. I swallowed the thought.

"And you can admit things to me you might not want to say in front of Kit, like all the other skills you exaggerated in your interview." He grinned. "Work can be daunting after academic centres – you graduated young, didn't you?"

I nodded, bracing myself for the patronising comments.

"I was pushed up three grades too, so I know how you feel," he said.

"How old are you?"

"Nineteen. Pretty weird, being fast-tracked, isn't it? I'm technically senior to Dal, and he's thirty."

"How old are the others?"

"Ancient." That grin again. "Jana's in her forties, Ren over fifty and Kit's seventy-two."

"You're kidding? What will I talk to them about? "

"Actually, they're OK. Nothing like development leaders."

We finished the tour of the lab, and I settled at my desk to start on the tedious preliminaries: risk assessments and a heap of rules to read.

"Caia, do you play sport?" asked Jana.

"Only racketball."

"Cool, let's book a court soon."

"I play too; I'll give you a game," said Dal. "Did you see that gross stunt on *Truth or Dare* last night? They injected something into the girl's cheeks that blew them up. By the end of the show her whole face was covered in skin bubbles."

I shook my head and inwardly groaned, wondering if I should voice my opinion. But Mac beat me to it. "Can those shows sink any lower? Caia, tell me you're not hooked on media games too."

"Can't stand them." Did I imagine it or did his lips twitch in response? "But I'm going to have to watch *Truth or Dare*. My resmate, Uma, is one of the presenters."

"You live with Uma?" Dal said. "Woah, can you introduce me?"

"Yeah, come over some time." My spirits sank. So even the so-called intellectual elite weren't immune to celebrities.

Mac rolled his eyes. "Let me guess. BodyPerfect, metallic hair, squeaky voice, good at whooping."

"Spot on." I laughed.

And the morning carried on that way: plenty of chatting, my tasks not too demanding, and the disconcerting effect Mac had on me.

"Coming for lunch, Caia?" Dal said. "We usually all go together."

As we walked to the food centre, Kit asked, "Has the morning lived up to your expectations?"

"Yes, thanks." Knowing he was so old intimidated me, made me more self-conscious than ever. "Everyone's been so welcoming."

"It's good to have a newcomer, and I think you're going to fit in well. We've always been a tight team. You realise that we're a lucky society. Before Mind Values, loneliness became a major social problem. Individuals were less open and accepting."

I nodded, my mouth fixed in a polite smile. Here we go again. Time to have Mind Values rammed down my throat. It was the same at development and academic centres, always telling newcomers how wonderful society was. I didn't disagree, but why did we have to keep reminding ourselves?

We passed a huddled figure on the side of the walkway, her red-stained cheek betraying her status. Without a word, Mac, who was walking ahead of me, took a nutribar from his belt and dropped it at her feet so inconspicuously that no-one else appeared to notice. What a strange and, at the same time, lovely thing to do. At best, people hurried by and pretended not to notice the Marked. At worst, they spat or kicked at them. And that woman looked so sick. But at least for now she had shelter from the elements. Next month she could be sent to an outdoor correction centre. Surely she'd freeze to death out there? But, inconspicuous or not, Mac had taken a crazy risk by helping her.

Once back in the office, Jana said, "Can I have a quiet word, Caia?"

I followed her into the stark, white, private room. Had she noticed me staring at Mac earlier? When she spoke, it was in a whisper. "You saw what Mac did at lunchtime, didn't you?"

Oh no. Was this a test? I chose my words carefully. "Yes, I was … well, shocked, but I didn't think I should say anything."

"Thought so," Jana's mouth was set in a hard line. "I need to warn you about him. He's the team maverick and I suspect he has sources of illegal information. One of these days he's going to get himself into trouble. And it's frustrating because he's a genius. He has the most brilliant mind in the Ministry. I can't prove he's a subversive thinker but …" She raised her finger. "Be careful. I don't want him to be a bad influence on you."

"Thanks for the warning. I'll keep my distance as much as I can." I bit on the inside of my cheek. That was all I needed. But at the same time I couldn't help being even more intrigued. Illegal information?

When I returned to the Residence, Von was pounding at the OmniTrainer, his skin glistening. Uma lay draped over the sofa watching a media game. She stretched and turned to flash me a dazzling smile.

"Hey kitten, good day?"

"Yeah. I like my workmates."

"Are scientists all odd-looking?" Uma's tone suggested she didn't consider her words to be remotely offensive.

"You'd think so, apart from Jana, a BodyPerfect. One of my work team even has facial hair." Why did I tell her that? Heat rose from the back of my neck.

"Veez, that's gross. What does it look like?"

"There isn't much. I guess he shaves it. It just makes his chin look darker."

"Sounds revolting." Uma screwed up her face and immediately drew her fingers across the lilac line of her eyebrows to smooth any hint of wrinkles. "Why would anyone not get it ultralighted? He should go on this show."

I glanced at the screen and cringed. I hated *Vile Bodies* – the presenter was interviewing a morbidly obese Marked citizen, the folds of his flesh glowing under the studio lights. How had he become so fat when no-one would serve him at food centres?

"You fat, disgusting blob!" Uma yelled at the screen.

The audience were laughing and shouting, too. I turned away, sickened, and wondered whether I dare ask Uma about illegal information. She'd already told me she had 7,400 contacts, making my own 300 or so, puny by comparison. Uma's celebrity status meant she was invited to the best parties in the Citidome and knew everyone, from models to Ministry. Surely she heard snippets of conversation?

"We were talking about illegal information today. Do you ever hear anything?" I tried to sound casual.

"Yeah, all the time, but it's usually dull, dull, dull. People have mad ideas about life outside the Citidomes." Uma examined a minuscule blemish on her chin in a magnifying mirror app. "Oh look, the blob's going to balance on a beam. This should be funny."

"What sort of mad ideas?" I asked, my heart racing. This was exactly what I was hoping for. Life outside the Citidomes – my thoughts always returned to it.

"They say whole communities can survive out there but they've regressed. They're like savages. Ha, look, he's fallen. Still, all that fat should give him a soft landing." Uma sniggered. Von almost fell off his OmniTrainer from laughing.

"But how do they survive without food centres? Water? Electricity?"

"No idea." A bleep drew Uma's attention to her DataBand.

I sighed. That girl had the attention span of a microbe.

"Anyway, I have a media launch to go to," she said.

"Me too," said Von.

Once they left, I switched off the screen. Guess I'd never get anything useful out of Uma. Maybe I should forget it and take a hit of Bliss. I remembered the headache. Maybe not. Jem came in.

"You OK?" he asked.

"*Vile Bodies* was on. I can't stand that show."

"Me neither. Sick, isn't it?"

I raised my eyebrows. Would he have said that if Uma and Von had been in?

"Who did they have on today?" he said.

"A Marked citizen, but hideously fat."

"Oh, that. Sometimes they pump them full of steroids, supposedly as a treatment but it makes them bloated. Stigmatizes them even more." He rubbed his nose, as if realizing he'd said too much.

"Don't worry, I don't earn my citizen points by telling tales." I murmured. "Do you have to do that sort of thing?"

"Yeah. Still think what I do really matters?" He changed the subject and I let him. It was enough for now, a breakthrough. Now Von and Uma weren't around, he seemed more relaxed, no longer endlessly smoothing his hair. We talked about our days, and relaxed with insubstantial chatter, until he said something that made me sit upright.

"One of my work team disappeared last week. They told us he'd moved but there's rumours he's run away from the Citidome – outside, I mean."

I took a deep breath. Finally, someone wanted to talk about something real. But how much should I say? "Really? Veez, why would anyone leave a comfortable residence to live in somewhere that's probably uninhabitable? I wonder how cold it is out there."

"I've heard it varies from minus-thirty up to forty degrees, depending on the time of year."

I whistled. "We have refrigerated storage rooms in our labs that get to minus thirty, but I wouldn't set foot in them without protective gear."

"Yeah, and forty degrees would be like a SteamPod. No-one in their right mind would stay in one all day."

"And even if the body could adapt, how could anyone survive without all the things we take for granted?"

As we chatted about the odds of a person surviving outside, my curiosity mounted. Just what lay out there? Were Citidomes like this throughout the world? Why couldn't we travel? I'd seen animals in zoos at the Pleasuredome but dreamed about seeing them in the wild, and knew that most of them weren't native to State 11. Most of all, I dreamed of seeing the sea and the remains of ancient cities. They were crazy fantasies, but in my imagination I saw the whole world and uncovered its mysteries. Maybe I wouldn't admit all this to Jem yet.

But the evening boosted my optimism. Maybe I had one resmate I could connect with. He'd be a safer friend, if any friendships could be safe, than Mac: one whose looks didn't have any effect on me. At the same time, I wished Mac could be part of this conversation. Just what did he know? But how could I find out, if I wanted to keep my job? I stopped my thoughts before they took root. Why take unnecessary risks?

***

Newsfeed: New standards for stem cell donation changed.

New standards for stem cell donation published.

Maximum five donations per female, ten donations per male, under the following limitations:

Minimum height:
men 1.72m women 1.61m
Maximum body fat:
men 19% women 25%
Minimum <u>brain score</u> 100

"Looks the same to me," says Jana as the words flashed across our screens. What's changed?

"The minimum heights," I said, swallowing the bile that was creeping up my gullet. It was the end of my first week at work and I was getting used to the constant interruptions of newsfeeds. As Ministry workers we were supposed to read each one.

"Ah, right. What did it used to be?"

Of course, statuesque Jana wouldn't notice. "1.60m," I muttered. "It was 1.57m when I donated almost three years ago, so I made the grade – just. When I tried to donate again a few months ago I assumed I'd be OK – I've grown a little since then – but they'd raised the standards and I wasn't eligible any more."

"You donated young, didn't you?" Dal said.

"Yeah, just after my fourteenth birthday."

"Huh, you were an early developer." Dal grinned.

I felt the heat in my face. Fat, that's what he meant. I folded my arms across my breasts.

"You were lucky you could donate at all," he continued. "I've always been too short. The money comes in handy when you're a student, doesn't it?"

"Yeah, shame for you guys. I've already donated four times. It's a nice extra income," Jana said, with more than a hint of smugness.

"You ever donated, Mac?" asked Dal.

"No," he said.

"Why not?" asked Ren. "There's always a demand for young people with high brain scores. What's yours again?"

"955."

I raised my eyebrows. That was off the scale. Irrationally, it annoyed me; I'd never met anyone with a higher score than my own 934.

"Don't need the money. I'll keep my non-perfect genes to myself." He shrugged.

"I have to admit; it's a blow to the self-esteem when you're not chosen. Only half the pay, too," said Ren.

I sympathised; we'd discussed this in the res. Von's stem cells were always selected; he'd almost reached his maximum donation limit. Jem, on the other hand, donated regularly and had never been chosen. But how could Mac be so self-possessed, so unconcerned about his "non-perfect genes"? I wished I could shrug it off so easily. When they told me I couldn't donate any more, I'd been devastated. It made me feel substandard. I still felt it. Stop it, Caia. Don't give way to negative thoughts.

But money hadn't been my motivation for donating. I found the whole process fascinating. There was something special about being able to produce a healthy offspring, a kind of validation of my own existence. I'd played as active a role as they'd allow, reading every development report, scrutinizing the genetic screenings and size measurements, until they confirmed that my offspring had no disease tendencies and wasn't likely to be unnaturally short. Only at this point did I get the first instalment of my payment. The rest came after the baby came out of the secondary breeder. I wondered about the baby, of course. Was it a boy or a girl? Did it look like me?

Then, two weeks ago, something brought my thoughts into sharp focus. I earned citizen points by working as an adult mentor at the development centre one weekend a month. The points bought me an extra week a year at the Pleasuredome, so were well worth the effort. And I enjoyed the work; I loved children.

I noticed her as soon as she entered the room. I tried to avert my eyes in case anyone noticed, but it was hard not to stare. It was her colouring – the black hair and brown skin, only slightly paler than mine. Later that morning, I had to supervise the kindergarten kids in brain training. When I asked them their names, she answered in full, in the literal way kids have, "Suna 121968." For a minute I forgot to breathe. So she was born on the 19th December '68, nine months after I donated. It had to be! I assigned another puzzle, giving me a chance to look at her more closely. Her height and weight seemed normal but she wore an amber badge, meaning she'd been assigned fat control food. Poor thing. Even in the kindergarten, the chant "Fit is better than fat" rang from every child's lips.

Forcing thoughts of Suna out of my mind, I spent a productive day in the lab until Mac once more threw me off-balance.

"Is it all going OK?" he said in a loud voice.

"Fine thanks," I said.

He looked away and his voice dropped to a mutter. "Ridiculous, isn't it? What right has anyone to say you're not fit to donate? Don't let the system get you down."

Our eyes met in a long, even gaze. Heat flooded my face and I looked away. But in that moment, a connection between us had been sealed.

CHAPTER – 3

As the days passed, I couldn't get Mac and Suna out of my head, and cursed my own weakness. Any sort of relationship with either would have me flung into a correction centre. Instead, I started to enjoy the safer company of Jem, who was starting to treat me less like a kid and more like an equal.

"You're late this evening," I said.

"My therapy session," he muttered.

"Does it really help?"

"I sometimes wonder." He stared at his feet.

"If it helps, you could talk to me sometime."

"Thanks. What about you? Are you as well-balanced as you seem?"

"Slight tendencies to timidity and anxiety. Tendencies to pride and attachment were corrected." I rolled my eyes. "That's what my last emotional health report said, anyway."

"Pride and attachment?"

"Uh-huh." I scowled. "What's wrong with being pleased when you do well? I'd just found out I was top of my peer group for a third year running. Then my development leader called me in for a meeting, said I was getting conceited."

"That happened to me. Did they fix your marks?"

"Yeah. At the next assessments I came third, then second. I felt cheated." My jaw tightened at the memory.

"Me too, but it's for your own good, you know. A sense of superiority's a bad thing."

I raised my shoulders in an exaggerated shrug. That was the trouble with Jem. For a while he'd seem like a questioner, then he'd parrot some brainwashing doctrine straight out of Mind Values. I opened my mouth to comment that no-one seemed to consider Uma and Von's conceit about their appearance a bad thing, but thought better of it.

"What about the attachment?" His voice dropped. "You

don't have to tell me if you don't want."

"Oh, it was a friend … a girl, two years ago," I said, suddenly overcome by that peculiar melancholy I got whenever I thought of Sharee. Why was what we did so bad? She'd been the only real friend I'd ever had. "All we did was talk – you know, personal stuff about our feelings – but someone must've decided we were getting too close. They told the others to join us, 'to prevent any inappropriate intimacy'." I chanted the words. "We found ways to shake them off. Then, last year, for no apparent reason, they moved me here and forced me into attachment counselling. So I had to start again: a new academic centre, not knowing anyone."

"Ah, where were you before?"

"Rho-2."

"Was it like here?"

"Identical," apart from the fact that I wasn't lonely there. Why did I start this conversation? Oh, I know why they did it, to teach me a lesson. All contacts are temporary. No-one knows when they'll be moved to another city sector or even another Citidome. Attachment is pointless; it only makes people unhappy. But if anyone was able to see my innermost thoughts, the ones the Citidome couldn't control, they'd know that the yearning for a confidante had never left me.

My thoughts turned to Mac. I told Jem about him and even suggested that we invite him over one evening.

"Hmm, best not," Jem said. "I came across that type at my academic centre; one was expelled for saying the wrong thing. The authorities may already be watching him if he's a possible subversive thinker. Being associated with him may be bad for my career. You should be careful, too. It's easy to question everything at your age – I did the same – but it gets you into trouble. Do you want to end up confined to a correction centre? I was called to a medical emergency there once. It was a subversive thinker, in a cell on her own, a red plastic tag attached to her ear. She'd tried to tear it out. Looked painful. Relax and accept things as they are."

He curled his lips upwards in a sanctimonious sneer that infuriated me – I hated it when he spoke to me in that condescending way – but his words chilled me. What happened to subversive thinkers? I'd better be more careful.

I started rationing one-to-one chats with Mac and making sure I talked equally to the others. But sometimes, he was his own worst enemy. He seemed to get a kick out of starting controversial conversations.

"I heard something interesting about BodyPerfects," he said one lunchtime. "Turns out they're not as perfect as you'd think. Can't reproduce, for one thing." I fought to stop my eyebrows from rising.

"Not that old myth again." Dal curled his lip. "The donation program started because people were getting too fat to conceive like animals. The BodyPerfect cult was a good thing. It wiped out the obesity problem."

"Besides, I heard that the hormones in the water supply caused the drop in fertility." Ren added. "Now we don't eat animals, that's improved too."

"Can you imagine eating animals?" Dal added with a scowl.

"Well no, but that's not the whole story," Mac said. "BodyPerfects are actually unhealthily thin, you know, especially women. It's causing a crisis, because they're usually the ones whose stem cells get chosen. But their stem cells are less likely to produce mature ova. The success rate of the whole program has plummeted, but they're keeping it hushed up." He drew in his breath. "Carry on at this rate and the human race could die out in a few generations."

"It does seem contradictory, doesn't it?" I couldn't help agreeing. "They're meant to be the ideal, but Uma can't donate because her reproductive organs never matured." I'd discovered this last week; it was the one blemish in Uma's otherwise golden existence. Passing on her beauty through procreation had appealed to her, but she'd never even had a monthly bleed.

"I don't know where you get this rubbish from, Mac. And you're missing the point," said Jana. "Maybe stem cells from people with more ... primitive body shapes have a higher success rate, but can you imagine children looking like Alda?"

Dal and Ren sniggered. Alda, a data processor, had round buttocks, wide hips, and huge breasts, and everyone laughed at her behind her back. I sucked in air through my teeth, almost bursting with the effort not to speak. I liked Alda. Any teasing bounced straight off her. She carried her flesh sensuously, and her infectious laugh made her whole body shake.

"Actually, I don't think Alda's bad looking." I wanted to take the words back as soon as they left my mouth.

"Neither do I, and she's a good laugh." Mac shot me a smile that not only made me lose my train of thought but the ability to think at all. I turned to read an incoming message and hoped that when I turned round again, the redness in my cheeks had subsided.

"Oh come on, she's repulsive! There's no excuse for obesity these days."

I flinched at the cruelty in Jana's voice.

"Anyway, time to get back," Jana said.

"She needn't worry; you'll never see children like Alda. The way they choose stem cells … eventually we'll all look identical," Mac muttered almost inaudibly, leaving me twitching with intrigue.

No-one was in when I got back that evening, and my thoughts turned to Mac's tantalising comment. He'd touched on one of a million things that puzzled me about Citidome life – skin colour. While most people under forty had skin tones ranging from pallid to cadaverous, I'd seen older people with skin the colour of dark vegelate, and coarse black hair. My own was somewhere between these extremes and it made me stand out; dark skin was rare in younger people. Did they really gear stem cell selection towards a more homogeneous look? How could I find out the answer? There must be some reason that dark skin had died out. Jem's voice returned to me: why worry? What value would there be in knowing? But I recorded the conversation with Mac in my history. It was becoming a catalogue of unanswered questions.

***

"Caia, you're to have a one-to-one training session with Mac in the private room, at 14:00," said Kit. My heart surged. This was my chance to ask him some of those questions that jostled for priority in my brain.

"Ready for our session, Caia?" Mac said after lunch. I took a slow, deep breath. The door closed. "We're going through the whole approvals process today. Sorry, it's not exactly thrilling."

"Ah well, guess it's got to be done," I said, trying not to look directly at him. Now that I was on my own with him, coherent thoughts seemed to have tumbled out of my brain.

"Are you settling in OK?" he asked.

"Yeah, I'm really enjoying it."

"Don't look so panicked; I'm not about to tell you we're a lucky society. No problems you want to talk to me about?"

"N-no, thanks." None that I could give voice to, anyway.

As we started the training, Mac became guarded, professional, then I realised that his eyes occasionally darted to the office outside, sizing up opportunities when no-one was looking our way. Without looking directly at me, he spoke in a murmur. "I was glad you stuck up for Alda. You know, she's had an official warning at work about her weight."

"That's ridiculous!" I followed his lead and kept my outraged voice on a low simmer. "Like it's any of their business. It doesn't stop her from doing her job."

"Anyone who's that little bit different and happy with it – it scares them." Was this how subversive thinkers operated? How many people around the Citidome were having ostensibly ordinary conversations and then dropping in inflammatory thoughts and ideas? How should I react? This was no sanctimonious Jana. This was a test of a different kind. Seeing Ren walk across the office, he returned to the task in hand.

Kit entered the room, making me jump. "Sorry to interrupt," he said. "I just needed to check your availability on the tenth of May. There's going to be an official visit from the Minister and I need everyone to be in."

"I'll be here," said Mac, after a glance at his schedule.

"Yeah, me too," I said, suppressing a frown. It didn't seem such an urgent request that it needed to be made in person. Was Kit making a point that there was no such thing as privacy? Were we already under surveillance? Jana's warning returned to me.

Kit left the office and Mac returned to the training without comment. It was several minutes before his voice dropped once more. "Private office. Huh. But if you ever want to talk to me about anything – you know, not just work – these sessions are our best shot. Just keep your voice down and pretend to be doing something else while you're talking."

This was my chance. But as I opened my mouth, heat flooded my face. What if Kit walked in again? What if Mac was trying to recruit me into a network of subversive thinkers and illegal knowledge? Even worse, what if he sensed my attraction? "Er, thanks, I'll bear that in mind," I said. A silence, punctuated only by my own heartbeat, lay heavily between us until I glanced towards him. "There's nothing, for now." Did I imagine it or did a flicker of disappointment pass over his face? Oh, why was I such a coward?

"OK, let's get on." He returned to the training, his voice taut, unsettling me for the rest of the day, knowing I'd let him down. But at the same time I couldn't help thinking that I'd saved myself from treading on a precarious path.

***

"Hey, kitten, you're not going to waste your leisure day, are you?" Uma said. "Why not come and watch a recording of my show?"

"Er, yeah, why not?" How annoying; I'd hoped for a restful day. I was certain I wouldn't enjoy it but, at the same time, flattered to be asked. Uma hadn't dismissed me as dull or serious. I had the regretful feeling that Mac had already written me off. Our second training session had passed without any low-voiced comments. And, ridiculous though it was, I craved Uma's approval in the same way I used to long to be part of the popular set in preteen. Whenever I saw a group of BodyPerfects, I was intimidated by their high-pitched laughter, assuming that they were having a better time than me. So I approached the studio with a mixture of trepidation and excitement, which quadrupled when Uma introduced her co-presenter.

"Caia, I'm sure you know Masa. Sit over there and you'll

be able to watch all the fun."

"Hey, Masa," I said with a flutter of excitement. I hadn't realised that Uma worked with Masa. He was one of the biggest celebrities in Sigma-2. His prominent cheekbones could have been sculpted from marble, like the statues in the park, his golden hair clinging to his skull like a gleaming helmet. Even though I liked to think myself above celebrity worship, I couldn't wait to get back to work and tell Dal and Ren that I'd met him.

"Good to meet you, Caia." Masa flashed me an impeccable smile, his teeth almost fluorescent under the studio lights.

Half of the Citidome would give anything to meet Masa, yet, as I looked at his flawless features, I wondered why he didn't have the same effect on me as Mac. Sure, Masa was beautiful, conventionally much more so than Mac, but the way I'd felt when I first met Mac had come from somewhere deeper. I couldn't make sense of it.

When the recording began, lasers bounced across the studio.

"Hey, citizens! It's time for *Truth or Dare!* Uma, are you ready?"

"Woow, it's going to be cray-cray-crazy tonight, Masa!" Uma's internal volume control had risen by several notches.

I soon realised that Masa was the backbone of the show. All Uma had to do was whoop in the appropriate places. After Masa introduced each set of contestants, she rushed out of view to where a dresser ripped off one outfit and put on another. The show was every bit as bad as I'd expected. Even the truth component – the only part that threatened to be interesting – appeared to be nothing more than a true-or-false question about a celebrity. If the contestant answered incorrectly, the other contestant dared him or her to perform a self-mutilating stunt. One contestant had a wart grafted onto his nose; another had something injected into his face that caused one side of his mouth to jerk upwards, the other side to droop. The overall effect was grotesque and kind of upsetting, but not to the audience, who roared hysterically. Thankfully, it was over within two hours.

Uma glided over. "What did you think, kitten?"

"Brilliant. You were stunning. Will that guy's mouth

recover?"

"That was cray-cray, wasn't it? His smile was just gross! Yeah, the effects wear off eventually. Anyway, I'll see you later; I have to meet the producers now."

An assistant called, "Over here, Uma," a tray of lurid drinks in his hand. None for me, I noticed. Right now, I could understand Jem's bitterness. Uma's working day was hardly arduous. And yet I'd never change places with her. Surely someone as intelligent as Jem would hate to inhabit this empty world?

***

"Time for training, Caia," Mac said.

I looked up. Last night's *Truth or Dare* had featured an older woman with skin even darker than mine. They'd decorated her back by injecting some sort of bleach that revealed white marks with every pass of the needle – a sort of reverse tattooing. It had been playing on my mind all day. Surely one question would be safe?

"Before we start, can I ask you about how they select cells for the fertilization program?" I muttered. "I know about the minimum height and brain scores, but what about skin colour?"

"Finally." He let out a slow breath, and his lips pulled into a warm smile. "I was beginning to think I was wrong about you. Sorry though, I don't know for sure. I guess they either don't select many dark-skinned people's stem cells or, when they do, they match them with cells from pale people. Look this way so it looks like we're working." He pointed at the screen, his attention seemingly fixed on it, and I followed his gaze.

"But why? What's wrong with dark skin?"

"Pale complexions can't cope as well with the sun's ultraviolet rays. The Dome shields us from them. If you don't have much pigment in your skin, you burn up if you go outside. So people are less likely to survive out there, and that's what the authorities want."

I had to ask, I couldn't stop myself. "Do you think it's possible to survive on the outside?"

He paused. My head spun – what was he about to say? "I've heard rumours but nothing's been proved. But yeah, I guess so."

I slumped in my seat. Was that it? Of course he didn't know everything but I'd hoped for more. I chewed on a nail. Inside my head, the riot of unanswered questions erupted, knocking my caution aside. "Why did people have different skin colours in the first place?"

"Funny, isn't it? No-one ever asks the basic questions. At least you've asked one I know the answer to. It's to do with geography. Originally, people from hotter States, like the United States of Africa, had dark skin and people from Northern States were pale."

I screwed up my eyes, trying to grasp this concept, embarrassed to admit that my understanding of geography was shaky. I knew that State 11 was an island, but had no idea which of the United States it belonged to, or even where it was in relation to the rest of the world. He carried on talking about the mobilisation of societies and ethnic mixing. I reeled. Where was he getting this information from?

"The Knowledge Fountain says that racial mixing doesn't work and that's why no-one moves from country to country any more, but the Knowledge Fountain only tells you what it wants you to know." He sniffed. "They said that's what caused the Thebula Virus Tragedy, but I'd better save that for another day or we won't get any work done."

"How do you know all this?"

He rubbed his nose. "Don't ask. Sorry, didn't mean to give you such a lecture. I just can't stop when I get going. I wish I had darker skin, like yours."

"No need to apologise. I could listen to you all day … I mean, it's really interesting." I raised a hand to my cheek, which was burning from my careless words. "One more. What's religion?"

"You don't ask easy ones, do you? I don't quite get it, to be honest. It was a kind of moral code for people to live their life by, like Mind Values. There was one called Buddhism, kind of like Mind Values. From what I've heard it was all about acceptance and eradication of negative thoughts, but also something else, something we've lost. Compassion. You know what that is?"

I shook my head.

"It means caring for other people's feelings." His words were heavy. "Mind Values – huh, total hypocrisy. Acceptance? What about the Marked? What about the so-called obese like Alda who get passed up for promotion time and time again?" He brought down his hand against the table. I held my breath. His eyes had darkened so much that the pupils were almost indistinguishable from the iris, something untamed in him barely suppressed. Then his face reddened and he rubbed his mouth. "Sorry. It gets to me, that's all. Better get back to this database. But ask me anything. I hardly ever get a chance to talk about anything real."

"You ought to be more careful," I whispered. "Jana warned me that you're dangerous. I'd hate to think of them spying on you and marking you down as a subversive thinker. Don't say controversial things to them; say them to me instead."

His smile sent a ripple of happiness through me.

"Thanks. You're right – I should keep my mouth shut – but sometimes I get this urge to shock them all out of their complacency. Nice to know someone cares, though. The guy you replaced got moved to a different Citidome for 'personal reasons' that no-one knew about. And after a day or so, no-one mentioned his name any more, like he'd never existed. Seems wrong that people are so disposable, doesn't it?"

Oh yes, it did. I remembered the guy and the girl next door. Would anyone care if I suddenly moved? Could it be right that a human life had so little impact on those around it? We settled to the database but I came out with a glow that lasted all day. It had been the most thrilling conversation of my life.

I returned to the residence to find it empty, so decided to indulge in a long session on the Knowledge Fountain. I started with that word Mac mentioned – Buddhism.

Buddhism: An ancient religion associated with the East, though it became popular in the Western States in the late 20th and early 21st century. Died out in the mid-21st century along with other religions.

36

Typical Knowledge Fountain, neither useful nor informative. Without hope or expectation, I selected the word religion.

> **Religion:** A term defining a number of traditions characterised by belief in and worship of entities that do not exist. Religion was characterised by intolerance and was the cause of <u>wars</u> and acts of <u>terrorism</u> for many centuries that culminated in a number of terrorist atrocities in the early 21st century and, ultimately, the Thebula Virus Tragedy. Since <u>Mind Values</u> promotes a healthy mindset, religion, war and terrorism have almost been eradicated.

So religion died out for a good reason. After reading that description, I couldn't believe it was ever popular. Why would anyone worship entities that don't exist? The more I read, the less I understood. But Mac seemed to think that Buddhism was a good thing. I sat back, bemused. I didn't suppose that the section on Mind Values would tell me anything I didn't already know, but decided to look anyway.

> **Mind Values**: A system that promotes healthy mental development and is taught to children from the age of four: Mind Values encourages the following:
>
> - <u>Non-attachment</u>: Attachment to another person is unhealthy. Before Mind Values, people tended to live only with one other person but these unions were largely unsuccessful. This led to social problems, particularly in the raising of children.
> - <u>Acceptance</u>: Intolerance and racial hatred led to the <u>Thebula Virus Tragedy</u>. It has since been recognised that multi-racial societies do not work. However, children are taught the importance of accepting others and are trained in welcoming newcomers.

- Eradication of negative thoughts: Negative thoughts such as dissatisfaction, hatred, envy, greed and jealousy are responsible for social unrest. Citizens are encouraged from childhood to eradicate negative thoughts. <u>Therapy</u> is available for those who fail to achieve this.

Negative behaviour leads to <u>war</u> and <u>hate crimes</u>. Mind Values have abolished much of the evil that used to exist in the world.

I had to admit that the aims of Mind Values seemed decent and, much as I hated agreeing with that tired old cliché, we were lucky to be living in a peaceful society. Apart from seeing people dragged to correction centres, I'd never seen any violent acts or social unrest. As for the old ways – they didn't make any sense. Why would anyone commit themselves to living with just one person for the rest of their lives? Of course that wouldn't work; any fool could see that.

My eyes rested on the words in front of me. Then I remembered my conversation with Mac and my stomach clenched. He was right. Why had I never noticed? There was a huge seam of hypocrisy running through the core of Mind Values. Society only accepted those who complied with its norms. The Marked were ostracised. Obese people were only ever offered the jobs other people didn't want to do. Dal and I weren't accepted as stem cell providers. No-one ever chose Jem's stem cells and he couldn't get the glamorous jobs he craved. In preteen I once went on a training day at the breeding centre and watched perfectly healthy embryos being destroyed, just because they didn't conform to certain standards. So much for acceptance.

And why were multi-racial societies such a bad thing? Maybe I should read the entry on the Thebula virus. At that point, Jem trudged into the room and flopped onto the sofa.

"Hey. Bad day?" I asked.

"Exhausting. We had an emergency. A girl came in unconscious – she'd taken pills. We pumped her stomach but it took the lab forever to identify the drug and it was almost too late to administer the antidote."

"Attempted suicide?"

"It'll go on the record as accidental poisoning but, between me and you, yeah."

"How sad. I wonder why? Hard to imagine desperation so great."

"You really are a bleeding heart, aren't you?" He smirked. "Just as well you never went into the healthcare profession."

"Do you think many suicides go unreported?"

"I suspect so. They don't look good on health reviews." He paused, then reset his voice tone in that way I was getting used to, as if reprogramming himself. "But if that's the worst that happens, we're lucky. For the last ten years the Citidome has had no reported disease, and accidents have dropped for the sixty-seventh year in succession."

"I guess so." I wasn't convinced. How many of the foundations of our existence were built on lies and suppressed facts? A chill settled over me.

"What've you been up to all evening?" Jem asked, looking over my shoulder. "Typical you! Can't just relax in front of the media console like everyone else. Thebula virus, eh? I did my final year dissertation on it – have to admit, it's terrifying. Can you imagine the stench of all those bodies left to rot in shallow graves?"

He sat next to me as I read the entry.

Thebula Virus Tragedy. In 2065, following an increasing incidence of terrorist attacks, missiles containing the Thebula Virus in aerosol form were simultaneously launched on the ten most populous cities in State 11. Citizens that originated from the United States of Central Asia were responsible for this atrocity. The virus proved impossible to contain and the fatality rate was estimated at 18 million. Due to the rapid spread and high fatality rate, bodies were buried in mass graves and the cities became uninhabitable. As a result, the combined forces of the rest of the world launched military strikes on the United States of

Central Asia. Aid to State 11 flooded in, causing
the escalation of the <u>Citidome project.</u>

"Horrific. How can a virus kill so many people so quickly?" I
shuddered.

"That's why it doesn't do any good to question," Jem said
with a shrug. "Look at the alternatives. We have peace. We
don't have disease."

I couldn't exactly argue with that, so took advantage of the
opportunity to ask the question I couldn't ask Mac for fear of
showing my ignorance. "Which of the United States are we
part of?"

"I'm not sure. I think we're in the USE – that's Europe."

"It seems something fundamental we ought to be taught."
Another question leapt out. "If the TJB virus can
spontaneously generate, surely the same can happen with
Thebula?"

"No, TJB's the only one that can generate."

"But how?"

"I don't know – I'm not an expert. It's something to do
with mingled body fluids." He folded his arms across his
chest in a way that suggested that the conversation was over.
He was lying, I was sure of it. Mingled body fluids producing
a virus? It wasn't possible, surely? "I'm going to have a
VirtuSlam and then a long sleep. You should try the
VirtuSport league. It's way more relaxing than the
Knowledge Fountain."

I watched as Jem played VirtuSlam, which turned out to
involve him curling his hand into a ball and slamming it in
the face of a virtual opponent, who reeled backwards as if
hurt. I flinched.

"Yesss! It's always best to get them on the nose. Fifty
points," said Jem with uncharacteristic savagery.

"Good slam." What a bizarre game. If Jem did that in real
life he'd probably spend the rest of his life in a correction
centre.

As I entered my history that night, I knew Jem's words
made sense. Imagine the streets filled with scenes of genuine
violent attacks. Imagine people treating me as an inferior
because my skin was darker than everyone else's. Actually –

I remembered Von's words – I didn't have to imagine that one. No-one exactly treated me as an inferior but I wasn't one of them, that much was sure. Maybe the homogenization of society was deliberate, and maybe it wasn't such a bad idea. I was safe here, so why did Mac's voice echo in my brain, drawing me down a road that could only lead to disaster?

CHAPTER – 4

On Monday morning I barely spoke to anyone at work, still chewing over the events of yesterday. As soon as I'd entered the development centre, I reminded myself to squash my excitement. No-one must notice my interest in Suna. I'd stopped to look in the playroom first, but she wasn't there. I loved infant playrooms. The kids, all in lilac playsuits, bounced around on springy flooring and three-dimensional climber sets. Oh, I longed for a go on that climber set. A girl from my development centre got expelled once. I've never forgotten the words that caused her to be hauled out of the room.

"Once upon a time, children were allowed to have fun," she'd said. "They'd play – proper play like in playrooms – until they were ten, twelve even. Not spend all their time doing puzzles."

Of course, she couldn't possibly have known this. She'd never been very good at puzzles and was just frustrated, I guess. But I'd liked the image of older children playing. Now I watched the little ones and tried to remember how it felt to be that age.

Then the happy scene was shattered as a stone-faced man called Mari started yelling.

"Hands off each other!" he shouted at two children who were shoving each other. Girls? Boys? It was impossible to tell.

"Leave him alone!" Mari screeched.

I flinched. What now? Oh, I saw. One child had put an arm around a smaller one who'd started crying. Mari separated them and said a few words to the little one, whose sobs turned to sniffs. I clenched my teeth. That was so harsh. Surely the urge to comfort was a basic human instinct? But where was Suna?

"Caia, come in here," said the section leader.

I followed him into the office and saw a tight-mouthed girl next to him.

"Gal's going to be shadowing you today," he said, without further explanation, though I didn't need it. They were keeping an eye on me. I went through the motions of a routine visit with growing despair. There was no sign of Suna, and I couldn't exactly ask what had happened to her. Someone must have seen me looking at her and moved her away. I knew I'd never see her again, and it tore at me. That's why attachment gets you nowhere.

I had to bite the inside of my mouth for the whole visit, to stop myself from crying. The only bright spot of the day was when I stopped outside a classroom and listened to a group of five-year-olds being taught.

"And long ago, children didn't live together like this; they had to live with two adults and usually only one or two other children. Imagine how lonely that must have been. And since it wasn't natural for just two adults to live together, they'd fight, sometimes hurting the children. We're a very lucky society."

For some reason, even though they ended in that irritating phrase, the words gave me a rush of nostalgia. I loved kindergarten. My jaw relaxed. It was hard to imagine adults hurting children. And yet I still wanted to scream and shout at the unfairness of it all. Suna was my daughter. Sure, I wouldn't want to look after her, but why couldn't I even see her?

***

"Ready, Caia? We've got a more exciting session today; time to use the PA." Mac interrupted my thoughts.

Oh, that was annoying; I hadn't realised we'd be in the lab. I'd been hoping for another good talk. But I was in luck. The lab was almost empty; the only worker within earshot was using a noisy sonic disperser and wearing ear defenders. The dazzling lights of the lab highlighted the strong line of Mac's jaw. A weird impulse gripped me – to reach out and trace the contours of his face with my fingertips. What was wrong with me? I held my arms rigidly against my side, willing them to behave.

"First, we need to autotune it." His voice dropped. "You OK?" He had quite a talent for speaking almost inaudibly while barely moving his lips and ostensibly doing something else. I needed to practice it.

"Fine, thanks." But my words were too hasty.

"I'm your mentor; you're meant to be able to tell me things."

"I will if there's anything to tell."

"Fair enough. But you look like you've had something on your mind all morning. And you've hardly spoken to me since you bombarded me with questions in the last session. You can trust me, Caia."

It was the way his voice lingered over my name that undid me. "I thought I'd found my daughter but I've lost her." The words came out in a jumbled rush.

His head snapped up. I cursed my stupidity, but his expression was one of understanding not condemnation. With one eye constantly scanning the room, I told him a condensed version of what happened yesterday.

"Unnatural, isn't it?" He paused, then whispered, "Since you've told me a secret, I'll tell you one. My biological mother found me. She worked in the birth centre and hacked into the records. When I was twelve, she told me who she was."

"You're kidding! What happened to her?"

"Disappeared, like everyone does."

He lowered his eyes and it was the saddest sight I'd ever seen. The strangest feeling passed through me, as if his unhappiness was mine. That couldn't be healthy. Maybe it was just as well I hadn't got to know Suna.

And so Suna disappeared from my life without ever becoming part of it. My following month's visit to the development centre passed uneventfully, as if nothing unusual had ever happened. Had Suna been moved to another development centre or another Citidome? I'd never know. The pain eased to an ache.

As the weeks passed, Mac stopped making any contentious comments in the office but I only had to look at him to know what he was thinking – a raised eyebrow here, a curl of the lip there. In fact, our muttered conversations during our training had been fairly tame, until our final session.

"Ever had any attachment counselling?" he asked.

"Come on, you must know. Surely as my mentor you know everything about me?" I said with a hint of irritation and a stab of fear. Why was he asking?

"OK, you got me." That boyish smile. "I peeked at your records; I know you had it in your teens. Just curious, that's all."

"I had a friend; apparently I spent too much time talking exclusively to her." I told him about Sharee. Dare I ask him the same question? "How about you?"

"Yeah … once. I used to live in Tau-2. When I was fifteen I met a girl I … liked. More than liked, if you know what I mean." He shot me a sidelong glance. I fixed my gaze on the screen, trying to keep my face cool and my breathing even. Why was he telling me this? What did he expect me to say? "Long story … let's just say she didn't feel the same. Six months of counselling and they forced me to move. That's how I ended up here."

The walls were moving inwards. How much more was he going to reveal?

"That's awful." I released the breath I'd been holding. "I hated having to start somewhere new."

His eyes sought mine. I sensed he wanted something more from me, but what else could I say? In truth, I was shocked. It must have been terrifying for him to lose control of his feelings to that extent, and even worse to have the girl betray him; at least I assume that's what happened. And yet he'd sounded so young, his voice had betrayed a touching vulnerability that I couldn't ignore.

I shifted in my seat. "Sometimes it's hard to be yourself in the Citidome, isn't it?"

"I struggle with it all the time." He bit his lip. "I know life would be easier if I just became a clone like everyone else … but I can't."

"Me neither." My shoulders slumped with the admission.

"Caia …" His voice was measured. "Most of the information I get comes from an illegal knowledge base. Do you want me to tell you about it? It's dangerous. If anyone caught you using it you'd lose your job, be flung in a correction centre, and who knows what else? But it's safe if you shut it down each time you use it."

I held my breath, not knowing what to say. Part of me glowed, flattered by his trust. At the same time I shrank from him. Exactly as I feared. He wanted to draw me into his illicit, subversive thinking world.

"I'm ... not sure. I'm interested but ... terrified. I've never broken the law. D-dunno if I'd ever dare use it." On impulse I added, "But tell me anyway."

"It's a place where anyone can say things – you know, the sort of things we're not meant to talk about. You can only access it with a code that scrambles your user records so it's undetectable. You can read anything that other people have said or take part in discussions yourself. You can even send private messages. The guy who set it up is an IT wizard – told me it's foolproof. But it's best to use it in your room and face the door. That way, if someone walks in you can close it down in a hurry. I'll give you the details to memorize, then it's up to you."

With the code lodged firmly in my brain, I dithered for a full week. What pearls of knowledge lay inside? Maybe there were theories about life on the outside. Maybe more history. On the other hand, why take the risk? I'd already revealed far too much to Mac. Was it worth ruining my life to find answers? Mantra-like, I repeated what they told us in preteen. "Questioning leads to unhappiness. Acceptance leads to a tranquil mind."

The words became less convincing with each repetition.

My resistance crumbled, of course. The next time I was alone, I input the forbidden words. Immediately, a discreet logo appeared with the words, 'Truth Exchange', and under it a mass of text. I exhaled in a huge rush. What had I expected – flashing lights, sirens and a CE at the door? The design was subtle; from a distance it could be the Knowledge Fountain. I read from the top:

Are you tired of only finding on Knowledge Fountain what the State wants you to know?

Do you want to learn genuine history, not just the few facts that are made public?

Join the following discussions:

History of the Citidome project: a huge experiment in social control.

Why did technology stagnate after the year 2065?

Attachment: why is it wrong?

The ten biggest lies we're force-fed since infancy.

The TJB virus: how it's used to manipulate us.

I nearly jumped out of my seat. I hadn't even dreamed of asking some of these questions. Where to start? I wanted to read them all. I pointed at the *ten biggest lies*, but my trembling hand missed, hitting the option below, and a block of text appeared.

Did you ever wonder how the TJB virus originated and spread so quickly? Sexually-transmitted viruses generally take a grip on a population gradually, and they rarely have a visible sign. Apparently, the virus is rife throughout every Citidome in the State, and was first reported in each Citidome in the same year. But how can that be when less than 5% of citizens are moved between Citidomes? And as for the idea of the virus spontaneously generating, an eminent virologist has confirmed to me that this is impossible.

Could it be that laboratory scientists artificially created the TJB virus to shame us, to finally make sex, or coupling as we now call it, taboo? To keep us in a state of fear; to make us more easy to control? Did we deliberately infect people? Sexually-transmitted diseases don't spread quickly enough unless coupling is a common activity, so either it's more widespread than they make out, or someone's artificially speeding up the process. I also believe that the virus has no long-term health consequences. Once more, a false fear. Why do you think they're throwing them out of the Citidomes now? They're scared that the truth will come out, that the TJB virus really isn't as bad as we all think. But oh, that Mark. Really scares the beautiful people, doesn't it?

Is it any coincidence that thrill pills became so popular at the same time that coupling was outlawed? The same sensation, but none of that dangerous attachment. There was also a surge in the prescription of hormone suppressants for anyone daring to admit to natural feelings. And why the cult of BodyPerfect and intense exercise? Scientific research shows that excessive exercise subjugates the sexual urge. Why do we all think coupling's disgusting? Because we're taught to. But why is the sexual act forbidden? Neutral, unemotional people are easier to control. They won't team up and challenge the system. It's hard to have sex without messy emotions becoming involved, so they've invented a way to prohibit it.

I read in a feverish rush, then in a moment of panic shut down the page. The adrenaline rush was like nothing I'd ever experienced, like talking to Mac but more dangerous, my blood pulsing with illicit excitement. I took a hefty swig of water. It was the truth. I realised that straightaway. Is that what the CE did to the guy and the girl next door – deliberately infected them? Now I thought about it, it did seem unlikely that a TJB outbreak could happen simultaneously in all forty-five Citidomes. But as for the lack of long-term health consequences, I wasn't sure. The Marked always seemed so weak. And was it really so wrong to make coupling taboo? The idea of it made my flesh crawl.

So coupling gave you the same sensation as thrill pills? I'd tried them, of course. Someone got hold of a packet in my academic centre. I can still remember that packet making its clandestine journey around the lecture room; they were meant to be for over-sixteens only. But I could take them or leave them. I got a kick out of the hot, pulsating sensation. Who wouldn't? But afterwards I always felt kind of low – that vague sort of unhappiness you can't quite pinpoint the cause of. The thrill that lasted seconds didn't seem worth that hollow feeling that lingered for hours.

I heard movement and laughter outside; some of Uma's contacts were looking for her. Too scared to log on again, I selected the Knowledge Fountain instead. How could the Citidomes be an experiment in social control?

The Citidome Project: The concept of Citidomes was first conceived in the United States of the Americas in 2025 and the first domed city built in Houston in 2041. The United States of the Orient soon followed, with ten Citidomes in place by the end of the 21st century. The first Citidome in State 11, Alpha-1 was completed in 2057, precipitated by two catastrophic events; the East Coast Storm Surge of 2047 and the London Flood Disaster of 2051, which led to the mass evacuation of London and ultimately necessitated the relocation of 5 million people over 10 years. By this time, the average surface temperature of the planet had risen by 5°C in a century, and extreme rainfall and localised floods had become common occurrences.

Citidomes comprise an ethylene tetra fluoro ethylene (ETFE) dome supported centrally by six ten-storey office blocks, laterally by smaller residential blocks and steel cables. Air is brought in from outside by large fans and heated and cooled as necessary to maintain a constant 20°C during the day, 14°C at night. The air is passed through filters, which remove bacteria and other airborne contaminants. Each Citidome houses 500,000 inhabitants. Citidomes are arranged in groups of five, each linked to warehouses and a <u>Pleasuredome</u>.

The project accelerated following the <u>Thebula Virus</u> tragedy of 2065. The entire population of State 11 is now housed in forty-five Citidomes.

I'd never heard of London or the East Coast Storm Surge and, by the time I'd looked them up, my head was spinning. Finally, the Knowledge Fountain had told me something interesting. I couldn't picture villages with less than a hundred residents teetering precariously at the point where the land ended and the sea began. In fact, I couldn't even picture the sea. And State 11 used to be bigger, much bigger. London had been vast and it took an hour to get from one side to another. Oh, I wish I could have could have seen it, experienced it. Why did all Citidomes have to be identical?

And then I was lost, off in my own world. Imagine relocating to Australia. Even on the fastest jet, Australia was sixteen hours away. Sixteen hours! How could people have wasted fuel travelling such vast distances? I knew I'd never see these places but why couldn't I even know what they looked like? And yet the wider world was the least of the questions swirling around in my overactive brain. Had I been force-fed lies since infancy? Surely the Citidomes were built to protect us and for no other reason? And I knew I'd never think the same way again. The Truth Exchange would always be lingering darkly in my mind, teasing and luring me.

CHAPTER - 5

Newsfeed: dissidents incarcerated.
Hal 230648 was detained indefinitely in a correction centre last night after entering Citidome Tau-2 from the outside. He was reported missing a month ago. Hal, a suspected subversive thinker, is said to be weak and emaciated. When asked of the whereabouts of Mei 081148, his resmate who disappeared at the same time, he reported that she had died.

I shivered. Conditions out there must be appalling if the guy was trying to get back in. What had the girl died of? Starvation? Exposure? The words 'suspected subversive thinker' made me think of Mac. How did people get classified that way and at what point did it get onto official records?

After my first try, I'd been too jittery to access the Truth Exchange, and the newsfeed further fed my fears. The risk of being caught was just too great. Doors in the Residence were constantly opening and closing almost silently, and Uma had fallen into the habit of wandering into my room to ask my opinion on party clothes. She never took my advice; she just wanted me to admire her. It seemed unlikely that she'd have the curiosity to look at my screen, but I felt compelled to be cautious. But I couldn't get it out of my head. It had invaded my brain, tempting me, like an itch I knew I shouldn't scratch. A deep, agonizing itch.

Uma had a reputation for hosting the best parties in the Citidome, but I'd been living at the Residence for nearly two months before she held one.

"It's my birthday next week so it's party time," she said. "Bring ten people each."

"Wild," I said with a sinking feeling. I loved dancing, but the only parties I'd been to before had been restrained academic centre parties – exotic fruit juices and not-too-loud music. I'd be well out of my depth with the celebrities whose names Uma casually dropped at breakfast. No, not out of my depth. I wasn't sure I could keep up conversations shallow enough for them.

I cringed as I sent the invitations on Monday morning on my way into work.

"Reach for the stars with Uma's intergalactic spectacular!!! Saturday 10 May 21.00 till late, late late!!!! Dress to impress!!!!!!"

How could I possibly send that to my team leader? But I didn't want him to feel left out. Of course, he turned it down immediately.

Mac and Dal followed me in, laughing.

"Won't it be the wildest thing!" squealed Mac in an impressive imitation of Uma. "How many exclamation marks has she managed to cram in? Thanks, Caia, but celebrity parties aren't my thing."

"Oh no, you have to come!" I said and quickly added, "You've all got to be there. I need some friendly faces among the beautiful people."

"You saying we're not beautiful?" Dal stuck out his lower lip.

How much hotter could my face burn? But Dal grinned.

"Hey kitten, I think we're the coolest team in the Ministry!" I said in Uma's helium voice. "Seriously though, I need some people I can look in the eye without standing on a chair."

"You don't have to persuade me," Dal said.

"Guess I can't let the glamour team down," said Mac with mock reluctance.

"Great." I tried to sound casual although my stomach was doing cartwheels. Why? What did I expect to happen? What could possibly happen?

That evening, wanting to be able to tell Mac I'd used the Truth Exchange, but knowing I wouldn't be able to discuss the TJB virus and coupling without blushing, I logged on.

World experts in technology, but we don't get any of it. In the space of a hundred years, man flew to the moon and Mars, and computers evolved from something the size of a house to the DataBand. World travel used to be a daily event. State 11 was designed as a self-sufficient state from which the main export was scientific and technological advances. Each Citidome specialises in a different area of expertise. But what happens to our findings? We don't see them, that's for sure. Did you know that the TravelPods and DataBands we use are identical to the ones our ancestors used a hundred years ago?

I heard a noise outside and closed the screen, pulse racing. Straightaway I needed another hit of information; it beat Bliss hands down. How much had been kept from us? But that was the last time I had to myself all week.

Saturday finally arrived. I returned from the exercise centre and flopped into my chair, exhausted and sweaty from two hours of Von's fitness program. I hated it, but I'd lost three kilos. I rubbed my eyes – had I come back to the right res? The wall separating the kitchen and leisure room had disappeared and a glowing dance floor stood in the centre of the expanded space. The remaining walls were silver and clouds of ultrahaze swirled around the room. Excitement swelled inside me. It would be the first time I'd seen Mac outside work. What would he look like when not in his Ministry uniform? Ridiculous, if he followed the dress code – "intergalactic". I'd decided to use one of my unique outfits. What else would I use them for?

"Hey, Caia, your clothes arrived; I put them in your room," said Jem.

Silver shoes with a ten-centimetre heel. That's all I needed. I'd have to do something about my preferences. The balls of my feet would be throbbing after an hour of those. Then I looked at the dress and frowned. It was shot through with silver, and turquoise, one of my so-called key colours, according to Uma. I had to admit, it did seem to flatter my skin tone. But what had gone wrong with the size? It wouldn't fit a preteen. The fashion program rarely made mistakes, so I squeezed myself into it. Ah, it stretched. Hmm, it hugged my curves perfectly; it even flattened that horrible little bulge on my stomach that Von nagged me about. What was this fabric? Then I looked in the mirror and sighed. My breasts and hips still looked enormous. Let's face it: no fabric could shrink them.

Was I about to make a fool of myself by wearing this in public? I'd better see what Uma thought. I walked into her room and found her sitting in front of a mirror, naked except for her briefs. Now I felt even more enormous. Her hips were the same size as her waist, her stomach concave.

"Kicking!" said Uma. "I love it!"

"Really? It's not what I expected. You don't think it's too small?"

"It's meant to be tight, doofus! Maybe something underneath to flatten those?" – Uma waved her hands at my breasts – "You'll have to dance later."

Easy for her to say. Nothing would flatten them. Perhaps I should wear one of my sports bras. They were humiliating at the best of times; most women didn't need them.

"I programmed two unique outfits so I can choose. What do you think?" Uma asked.

I raised my eyebrows – I couldn't imagine wearing either. One was a short bodysuit, black with a matrix of flashing red lights, slashed to the waist, the other an almost translucent dress that glowed.

"They're … both great," I murmured.

"I'll go with the bodysuit, better for dancing. Hey kitten, let me do your face art. Haven't you been using that spray I gave you? Looks like you've got a new spot coming up there."

I goggled at the mountain of face paints and glitters. "OK, thanks. I don't usually bother."

Returning to my room, I barely recognised Jem, his face art transforming him into something grotesque, comical even. He scratched at his silver bodysuit, which had a flashing light panel on the front. I'd have a headache by the end of this party.

"Caia – woow – you look fantastic. Veez, I hate metallic

fabrics."

"Looks good though. Seriously, is this OK? Uma said it was, but I feel ridiculous. I look so fat next to her."

"Everyone looks fat next to her. You're fine, I promise." His smile reassured me.

An hour later, I made a less-than-glamorous entrance, wobbling on the impossible heels, tugging the hem of my dress down; my entire face was a kaleidoscope of shimmer and sparkle. What a lot of effort for one evening. At this early stage of the party, anyone could work out who'd invited whom. Uma and Von's people exuded allure and charisma, Uma collecting contacts onto her DataBand with nonchalant smiles. Jem's and my guests, fidgety in outfits they weren't used to, huddled in corners in small groups, awed and starstruck.

"Hey Caia, fabulous dress!" Dal arrived.

"You look great," I said, though he looked ludicrous in head to toe gold, including his hair and false eyelashes. I didn't have a clue what an intergalactic resident would look like – space travel was the stuff of movies and had ended in the mid-21st century – but I was certain they wouldn't look like Dal. BodyPerfects could carry that sort of look more successfully.

"I have to pinch myself to remind myself this is real," he said. "I've just seen Uma over there, talking to Masa."

"Come on, I'll introduce you. Just don't faint." Masa was a regular visitor to the res and by now I wasn't remotely starstruck by the shambling mass of vanity that could barely function without Bliss. But, to his credit, he chatted to Dal, even though he'd hardly be a useful contact.

Most eyes were turned to one of the walls, onto which images of Uma were being projected. But where was Mac? Surely he'd turn up? It was a full hour before he arrived and, by then, the room was full. It wasn't until he moved closer that I could see him properly. His only concession to the theme was a tiny silver flash on his tight black top. He looked stunning.

I held my breath as he moved towards me. But no, Jana stopped him and started chatting.

"Hey Caia, great party. Will you introduce me to Uma?" It

was Ren. I suppressed a sigh – I guessed that's what everyone had come for.

Soon Mac was circulating around the room with an ease I envied. Why hadn't he even said hey? How could I approach him without making my attraction too obvious? Instead I spoke to Jem.

"Hey, having fun?" I said.

"Yeah, are you?" We chatted for a few minutes, and then he said, "Look, that's the new presenter on *Extreme Hairstyles*. Catch you later." I cringed as he fawned over the beautiful people. Just look at him, proffering his DataBand with the eagerness of a small child who'd found a new source of trading cards. I decided to stay on the sidelines and let Mac approach me. The party was large enough to let me be anonymous, which I preferred; I felt fatter than ever among the throng of BodyPerfects. I took a Bliss and watched the party swell with new arrivals, the bodies and personalities melding into a montage of faces, voices and colour.

"What are you doing, hiding in the corner?" Uma said. "Come and meet Tia."

I had the obligatory conversation but struggled to make it last. Uma and Von's contacts were as bad as I'd expected. Everyone appeared to be talking but no-one was actually saying anything.

"And what do you do daah-ling? Oh isn't that interesting?"

"Woow, Fifi's here – her new show's getting awful ratings."

"Look, that's Vida, must say hey. Catch you later."

Why wouldn't Mac come over to me?

Then I saw Alda, another of my guests, and took a step backwards. Her dress was cut low, her enormous breasts pushed together and spilling out of it, a deep groove between them. Didn't she care? My dress was lower cut than I was comfortable with and I'd been horrified to notice the hint of a crease between my breasts. I pulled the dress up so it wouldn't show.

"Hey Caia, you've got great curves! Dance?" she said.

"I'd rather not, thanks. I haven't got a bra on – the straps on my sports bra were too visible."

"Neither have I. Come on, let's bounce together."

Alda wasn't taking no for an answer, so I let her drag me into the centre of the room, but immediately regretted it. The dancing pairs parted at the sight of us, nudging each other as if to say, let the freak show begin. And even though I could see that most people were looking at Alda rather than me, I longed for the dance floor to swallow me up. But what could I do? It would hardly be fair to abandon Alda.

"Hey Caia, you can really move."

"Not as well as you." Alda was a natural, unselfconscious dancer, her hips swaying in perfect rhythm, and I struggled to match her movements. I glanced around. Others had stopped dancing, but their expressions weren't the mocking ones of a few minutes ago. It was impossible not to admire the way Alda moved. When the music faded, applause rang around the room.

"Hey, another dance?" a BodyPerfect asked Alda.

I slunk away, but a BodyPerfect blocked my path. I looked up and my eyebrows shot up at the sight of Masa.

"Hey, Caia, isn't it? Dance with me?" he said.

By the time I left the dance floor, I still hadn't worked out whether the attention Alda and I were attracting was genuine admiration or amusement at the novelty fat women. All I wanted was a corner to hide in. Head lowered, I almost bumped into Mac. I looked up. His face art consisted of a simple line of black eyeliner, which made it difficult for me to stop staring at his eyes. But he didn't look directly at me.

"Hey, look at you, dancing with the celebrities," he said, his expression unreadable. "Having fun?"

"Actually, I can't shake the feeling that everyone's laughing at me."

"They're not. You looked … great out there." Still his eyes didn't meet mine. His Adam's apple bobbed up and down in his neck. My heart sank. He was obviously lying to protect me. I tucked a stray strand of hair behind my ear, suddenly unsure what to do with my hands. After waiting all evening to talk to him, I wanted nothing more than to be on my own.

"I'm going to sit down," I said. "These shoes are killing my feet."

He looked at my feet and laughed. "I'll join you. I'm impressed you can even stand in them. My fashion program chose stupid heels for me too. Why don't they get that not everyone wants their head to touch the ceiling?"

I giggled at the five-centimetre chunky heels on Mac's black and silver shoes. "They don't fool anyone either. Uma's friends keep looking down at me and saying, 'Hey, aren't you the cutest thing?'"

We found chairs against the wall and sat down. "Ah, that's good." He sighed. "Don't think I can face any more inane chat from the in-crowd." This was better; he seemed more himself.

"I know what you mean; aren't they dire? All Uma's friends have the same conversations over and over and never get bored with them."

"Uma's really something isn't she? What is this place, a temple of narcissism?" He nodded his head in the direction of the wall, from where the image of Uma wearing nothing but minuscule sapphire shorts now projected out into the room. "She wants the world to look at her but not to touch – it's crazy. I must admit though, she's even more striking than I remembered from the one time I saw her on a media show. The face and body of a marble statue with a personality twice as hard and cold."

"That's harsh. Have you even spoken to her yet?" I tried to sound outraged to mask my annoyance that he'd called her striking. "She's generous-spirited and fun to be with."

"I guess so … but there's something about her I don't trust. Hope you don't confide in her."

"She's never in for long enough for me to get to know her well. The only person I really connect with at my res is Jem, the guy on his own over there."

"Oh, the wannabe who keeps hanging around the celebrities? I met him earlier but he ditched me the minute Uma walked past. Guess I'm not glamorous enough. Is he the guy that donates stem cells and always gets rejected?"

"Yeah, it's sad. He's an ultra-bright health worker and all he wants in life is to be BodyPerfect. He's wearing shoes with six centimetre lifts tonight."

"Can't be that bright, then. Why would anyone want to talk to those lamebrains all night?"

"That's what I tell him. It's a shame he didn't talk to you;

you'd be good for him." I lowered my voice. "He steers clear of so-called dangerous people but I'm sure deep down he thinks the way we do. Did you see the newsfeed this morning? That guy barely survived one month outside and his resmate died."

Mac paused. What did he know?

"I'm not so sure," he muttered. "Didn't you think it was odd that there were no pictures of him? Maybe they told us he was in a bad way to perpetuate this image of the outside as a frightening, inhospitable place. You know, a warning to anyone who's thinking about escaping."

"Escaping? Strong word. The Citidome's hardly a prison."

"What else would you call it?"

"But he obviously wanted to get back. His friend died."

"Again, did you see any pictures of her body? Maybe he reported her as dead to protect her. I knew them, Hal and Mei, in Tau-2. Mei was the girl ..." He rubbed his nose.

"The one you liked?" Why did my guts twist at the thought? "Oh ... that must be weird for you. But he wanted to get back. You can't deny that."

"Maybe he'd just come to steal supplies?"

"Yeah, never thought of that ... don't suppose there's much out there."

"Have you been on the Truth Exchange?"

I grinned. "Yeah, but I always panic and shut it down after a minute. I read something on how our technology hasn't advanced at all since we all moved into the Citidomes."

"I read that. Makes you wonder what other countries are like, doesn't it?"

"Yeah ... do they even have Citidomes? I was reading about the Citidome project and the London Flood Disaster on the Knowledge Fountain. Hard to imagine a city the size of London, isn't it?"

"Yeah, so huge. Have you ever noticed that the population figures don't add up? Look up 'Missing Millions', you know where."

I smiled. This is what I'd wanted from tonight. But then Uma joined us.

"So this is the famous Mac," she purred, swishing the ice in her drink, which was purple and glowing, "Caia never stops talking about you."

Heat prickled the back of my neck. I didn't realise that I talked so much about him, or even that Uma remembered a word I said. I'd better be more careful.

"I've heard a lot about you too, and you don't disappoint in the flesh." Mac smiled. "What's that drink?"

"Mil brought it. It's called cyber violet. Totally cray-cray, huh?"

"Yeah, I'll have to try one later. You want to dance?"

"Hey, I live to dance!"

They turned their backs on me and I found myself alone, every muscle taut. What was he playing at? How could he be such a hypocrite? He was as shallow as the rest of them – couldn't resist the chance to dance with a celebrity. Well he was hardly likely to ask me to dance, was he? I couldn't compete with Uma; it was only my mind that appealed to him. I was the freaky fat girl, my dark face brooding and severe among the spectral elegance of the BodyPerfects. Not someone to look good with on the dance floor. My spirits plummeted once more. Here I was, at a party full of Sigma-2's most glamorous residents, a party that would be talked about long after the ultrahaze had evaporated, and I'd never felt lonelier.

I stood up, unable to resist the temptation to watch Uma and Mac perform a mesmerising dance together, both moving with a fluid grace. I had to admit, they looked amazing together. Mac was shorter than Uma, but his rugged looks complemented her ethereal beauty. I stretched my hands, realising they'd clenched.

"What's up?" Jem joined me.

"Has it ever occurred to you that there's something inappropriate about the way we dance? Look at them all, dancing in pairs, gyrating their hips, mirroring each other's movements. It's ... I don't know ... primal, almost animal, like an ancient mating ritual."

"You sure it's not the fact Mac and Uma are dancing that way, that bothers you?"

Oh no, he'd noticed! "No, it just seems odd, that's all."

"Too many questions ... remember? It's only a dance. It's what people do. You danced that way with Alda. You're a great mover; I saw you. Anyway, it's not like anyone touches each other."

"Guess so. You want to dance?" I didn't feel like dancing any more but he'd unnerved me.

"Yeah, why not?"

By now the dance floor throbbed with an oppressive mass of tall bodies. I feigned enjoyment.

"You're a great mover," I lied.

When we danced to a second track, Mac and Uma came into view. I couldn't help glancing at them. Uma said something to Mac and he threw back his head in laughter. My jaw tightened. As the music faded Jem leaned over and whispered in my ear, "You're dancing with me, so stop looking at him."

My face flamed. How was I going to talk my way out of this?

"Come on." He led me away. "We're not Blissed enough."

I followed him, weaving my way through the massed bodies to Uma's Bliss dispenser, and took one.

"So that's Mac. You like him, don't you?"

"I w-work with him … he's a nice guy."

"Don't act stupid. You know exactly what I mean." His voice softened. "You don't need to lie to me. It's attraction, and you know how dangerous that is. Don't worry, your secret's mine. Just be careful. I'd hate to see you get into trouble."

"I don't know what you mean," I said ineffectually.

"Don't insult me."

I sighed. "You think anyone else has noticed?"

"No chance." He laughed mirthlessly. "Everyone's too self-absorbed to notice anything."

I reached for a drink. In a way it was a relief. The truth I hadn't dared acknowledge was out there. I was suffering from attraction. But I didn't want to talk about it with Jem. Not here, anyway.

"Are you having a good time?" I said.

"Yeah, but I haven't got as many new contacts as I'd like."

"I don't know why you bother. You're worth ten of this lot. But if it means that much to you I'll introduce you to my workmates."

I introduced him to Dal, then danced with Ren, determined not to talk to Mac again. I managed to get through the rest of the night without seeing him. As the last guest left Uma said, "I thought your hairy workmate was going to be boring but he was a good laugh. Great mover, too. He's weird-looking, but there's a sort of primitive animal appeal about him isn't there?" She giggled. "I can't believe I said that!"

Uma had taken far too much Bliss; her pupils were dilated and her eyes unfocussed. I seized the opportunity to deflect attention from my feelings.

"That's gross!" I mimicked Uma's confiding tone. "I don't see any sort of animal appeal in him."

"So who was the hottest person at the party?"

"You, as always." My laugh rang hollow in my ears. What did it matter how people looked if they weren't allowed to feel attraction towards each other? "But Masa's ultra-cool," I added; he was a safe target.

"Goodnight, kitten."

Through the wall separating our rooms I heard Uma giving a little squeal. She must have taken a thrill pill or maybe something illegal – I saw some packets being passed around. I selected a mind clear program on the RestPod. It failed. I wouldn't, couldn't dwell on Mac. Nothing made sense tonight – the way everyone watched me dancing, the way Mac behaved. I was never going to a party again. Then I remembered our interrupted conversation. Look up the Missing Millions, he said. No one would burst in on me now. I'd have a peek at the Truth Exchange.

The Missing Millions: Have you ever thought about the population of State 11? 45 Citidomes, each containing half a million inhabitants, that's 22.5 million, right? I've found census data from 2049 that estimated the population at 65 million. The London Flood accounted for a loss of around 120,000 accounting for emigrants. Thebula knocked off around 18 million, maybe a few more million emigrants afterwards, let's call it 20 million. Well, you do the math. That's almost 25 million people who don't make it into the Citidomes. What happened to them? Are they still out there or did most of them perish? And most sinister of all, how were the chosen few who did make it into the Citidomes selected?

I shut the page down. So not everyone relocated into the Citidomes? Surely that couldn't be right? Why would people be deliberately left out there? This was wild speculation, scaremongering. How could I believe anything I read?

On Monday morning the office was buzzing with gossip about the party, in particular Uma.

"She looks even better in the flesh than she does on screen," Ren said.

As Mac agreed, I silently fumed. On the one hand I was relieved that no-one mentioned my embarrassing dancing, but at the same time I was already sick of this new Uma Appreciation Society.

Inadvertently, I looked at Mac and, as our eyes met, he winked. What was that supposed to mean? I looked at his mouth, still slightly upturned. Was he teasing me? Had he sensed my attraction to him and was ridiculing it? No, surely he wouldn't be so cruel. He'd confided that he'd felt attraction towards a girl. He couldn't have noticed the way I felt.

I'd have to work to keep it that way.

CHAPTER – 6

Newsfeed: job satisfaction at all-time high.

A recent study shows that job satisfaction has reached its highest recorded level, with 82% rating their job satisfaction as "high" or 'very high".

I couldn't argue with that; I'd been in the job five months and loved it. My latest project was the development of SolarPlas, a lightweight flexible polymer with integral photovoltaic technology, which could be incorporated into the structure of a Citidome. It was everything I'd hoped for – intellectually challenging but not too stressful. And the work team, if not quite that longed-for group in which I belonged, accepted me, provided good company. Even better, I'd managed to put a lid on my inappropriate feelings. Mac sometimes winked at me when the others weren't looking, and I still didn't know whether to interpret the gesture as friendly or mocking, but I'd stopped stressing about it. And although my pulse still didn't behave when he walked into the room, I ignored it. Besides, I still hadn't forgiven him for dancing with Uma.

It was the conversation with Jem that had changed things.

"So, this … attraction, you want to talk about it?" he'd asked, soon after the party.

"There's nothing much to say." I swallowed. "I have … feelings for him that I've never had for anyone."

"Would you ever act on the feelings?"

"Of course not! I'm not stupid. He fascinates me; that's all. He's funny. He's the most intelligent person I've ever met, and he makes me question things."

"You'll never learn, will you? Why bother? It doesn't get you anywhere. And I guess you like the way he looks."

"Yeah." I lowered my eyes. "I've never looked at anyone

that way before. It's quite different to the way I look at you or Uma or Masa. Does that make sense?"

"I'm sorry, it does." He put on the serious expression that health workers have when they're about to give out bad news. "It's a hormonal imbalance; I once had something similar myself. Don't tell anyone, but I had a lot of spots and these weird … urges, when I was around your age. It's curable; you might even outgrow it in time. But I could prescribe something for you. I'd keep it off the record."

"Thanks. I'll think about it." I remembered the article I'd read on the Truth Exchange about the rise in the prescription of hormone suppressants around the time coupling became outlawed. Was that what my feelings meant? I felt sick.

"I hope you do. No good can come of it – you and Mac – you know. To be honest I don't like the guy." Jem narrowed his eyes. "Don't get too close, you'll end up getting hurt."

Hormonal imbalance – it made sense. And my life would be easier if I didn't suffer from it. I asked Jem for the medication – maybe it would at least clear up the few spots that still plagued me – and a few days later he handed me a box. In the privacy of my room I listened to the information that came with the hormone suppressants and reeled at the side effects – mood swings, hot flushes, cold feet, high blood pressure, anxiety, insomnia, headaches, and irritability. Not an appealing prospect. I'd keep them in reserve for now. I could handle this, couldn't I?

"How's it going with the pills?" Jem said a week later.

"Brilliant. Those weird feelings – they're definitely going away."

He smiled. Why had I bothered to lie? I guess I wanted to please him; we'd become close. I'd even call him a friend if I dared. On the other hand, Uma and Von increasingly grated on me. I worried less about what they thought of me and was happy to spend more time alone in my room. My only contact with Von came when he adjusted my fitness program, which had burned off so much fat that I was able to eat some of the tasty things I craved.

"Pizza? Caia, do you know how fattening that is?" said Uma. "You're still carrying extra fat. If you stayed on fat control dishes you'd lose a few more kilos."

I bristled, my hands moving defensively to my waist. There was barely anything to pinch. "I'm happy with my weight, thanks. I just want to be fitter."

"Fit is better than fat," she chanted.

I'd never be thin enough to get their approval – why bother? I went back to my room for my weekly session on the Truth Exchange. I was now hooked on that illicit kick, and it was hard to limit my sessions. But it gave me more questions than answers.

> Be warned, anyone who lurks around the Citidome gates, planning escape. The South Gate isn't safe. Last week I was watching it at three in the morning, when the quiet was shattered by a group of around ten citizens being marched to the gate by an armed CE. Half of them were Marked; the others had discs attached to their ears. And some of them had freakish deformities. Just what do the authorities do to subversive thinkers? I watched them leave through the gates where they were herded into a large vehicle. Has anyone seen these discs before?

I drew in my breath. Didn't Jem say something once about a red plastic tag on the ear of someone in a correction centre? I'm sure he said it was a subversive thinker. Were subversive thinkers taken outside? Guess they never came back; I'd never seen anyone with freakish deformities, or with tagged or scarred ears. And that word again – escape. How many people fled the Citidomes to live on the outside?

The Truth Exchange heaved with theories about communities outside the Citidomes. Someone said they'd seen the recaptured runaway and said that he wasn't as emaciated as reported in the newsfeed. Others suggested that the large cities devastated by the Thebula virus were abandoned and once the risk of infection from decomposing bodies had passed, people outside plundered the resources of those cities for years, sustaining outdoor communities. But for a hundred years? Hard to believe.

There were suggestions, like Uma mentioned, that outside communities were full of savage creatures, almost unrecognisable as humans. Others said there were organised communities and transport networks. One person claimed to have seen a horseback rider from the shuttle train to the Pleasuredome. It seemed unlikely – how could the speed of the shuttle train and opacity of the windows allow such a detailed observation? – but these ideas fired my imagination. I wondered what Mac was reading and even if he'd written some of them. More than one bore his hallmark.

"You realise that we're a lucky society," How many times have you heard that tired old cliché? Too often, I guess. From early childhood, we're drip-fed eternal gratitude. It's not the only way our minds are manipulated from childhood. All our desires and decisions are influenced by the State. Have you ever wondered why we're not taught more facts as children? Because facts lead to questions and questions lead to the truth. Anyone bright enough to question gets fast-tracked through education and put onto graduate programs – sometimes as young as sixteen. What use does it serve us to solve countless logic problems and mathematical equations from an early age? Do we overdevelop that side of our brain to the extent that we're not capable of feeling emotion?

I shifted in my seat; anything involving the word emotion made me uneasy. So far I'd avoided any criticism of Mind Values on the Truth Exchange. They left me confused. I preferred postings about the outside world. But I increasingly questioned what I read. If anyone could post ideas, this so-called knowledge was no more than conjecture. Nothing I'd read had been backed up by evidence. It wasn't my only disenchantment with the Truth Exchange. I accidentally stumbled into an area called a chat room.

To Dreamgirl from Hardguy. Hey, you looked hot today. You know how much I want you right now? Meet me at my place at 20:00 tonight; everyone should be out. I'm going to peel off your clothes and kiss you all over.

I shut it down, nauseated and confused. Was that the way I'd been heading, with Mac? Then something new grabbed my attention:

Cancer: the secret epidemic they don't want you to know about.

Did you know that cancer isn't a new disease? It was prevalent in the twentieth and early twenty first century but, thanks to advances in gene therapy and targeted drug strategies, by 2040 most cancers were preventable and/or curable. It should have joined the list of diseases eradicated in the last century, which includes most heart disease, infectious diseases and liver disease. But cancer has returned in a new form that is resistant to most known treatments and is reaching epidemic proportions, a health worker told me. Considering how genetic screening ensures that no hereditary predispositions to cancer exist, and how our food and air are modified to be free of all known carcinogens, this seems a curious finding, until you consider what cancer is. A tumour is a mass of undifferentiated cells: conformity on a cellular level. A place where everyone is forced to conform is the perfect environment for cancer to flourish.

But what happens to cancer patients? Most people know someone who was diagnosed with cancer and then mysteriously disappeared. Where do they all go?

Conformity on a cellular level. I felt sick. But I didn't know that cancer had once been eradicated. Surely Jem knew something? I approached the subject tentatively.

"A woman at work was diagnosed with ovarian cancer last week. Yesterday we replaced her. It seems odd; she'll recover won't she? Isn't cancer curable?"

"Yeah." His eyes dropped.

"You know more than you're letting on, don't you? Come on, you can trust me."

"If I tell you, you can't repeat it to anyone, especially Mac. I could lose my job." The tremor in his voice betrayed genuine fear.

"I promise."

"The new forms of cancer are resistant to the old treatments, so patients go to one of the Citidomes dedicated to medical research. They get the newest treatments available in the world."

"But that's fantastic, exactly the sort of propaganda the newsfeeds generally tell us. Why the big secret?"

His voice lowered. "None of the treatments are approved. It's the same with most medical research; all patients with chronic illnesses or disabilities in the Citidomes get transferred to the medical centres and enrolled in clinical trials. They use them, to test new therapies at the pre-approval stage."

"Really? How do you know that?"

"I saw a report at work, one I wasn't meant to see. That's what I mean about questioning not getting you anywhere. What good is knowledge like that, other than to be a burden?" He scratched his head. "It upsets me. State 11 does most of the world's clinical trials these days because it bypasses all the ethical issues. The treatments have been tested on tissue cultures, but patients don't give their permission to be experimented on. Some pretty aggressive therapies get to early clinical trial stages. A lot of people die of the side-effects."

"I see your point. I'm kind of sorry I asked." Jem was right; that sort of knowledge was a heavy load to carry. I couldn't share it on the Truth Exchange without betraying Jem. In fact I hadn't yet made a single entry. A voice inside me said that if I did, I'd become one of them: a dissident, a subversive thinker. At the moment I was nothing more than a curious spectator: just looking, not participating.

Poor Jem. How much more was he keeping to himself? He seemed more stressed than usual, and increasingly obsessive. He'd started a body alignment program.

"I was given exercises like this to do in my teens, but gave them up years ago. It doesn't seem worth the effort." I watched him groan while grasping a bar attached high on the wall, his body hanging beneath.

"It's meant to give me an extra two centimetres of height," he grunted between clenched teeth.

"Aren't you more than two centimetres short of the BodyPerfect mark?"

"Yeah, I'm five and a half short. Femur implants add only a maximum of five centimetres so I need those extra two to be safe."

"Femur implants? What are they?" I frowned, not sure I wanted to know.

"I forgot, you missed the program last week. Actually this might interest you." He dropped from his bar and tapped his DataBand.

"Attain BodyPerfect status!" a gaudy advertisement announced. "We offer the following: ultralight hair removal, jaw surgery, skin bleaching, liposolubilisation and femur implants."

I groaned. Was he really so gullible? "You're not serious? I've seen adverts like this before. How do you know it's not a scam? Is this a registered clinic?"

"I doubt it, but these seem like genuine testimonials."

"What happens if they don't reset your bones properly? You don't get another pair of legs. Why is this so important? Mac's a similar height to you but he's OK with it."

"Maybe I don't have Mac's charms." Jem curled his lip. "And you can't pretend looks don't matter. You know being BodyPerfect's a passport to instant social success. Look how few parties we get invited to, compared to Von and Uma. How many contacts do you have? I have only 521."

"Social success? Huh, I'd rather be a social failure. This is so stupid. I can't believe you know the exact number of your contacts. I'm sure I don't have that many. Why do you want more? It's so superficial and meaningless. Who cares about Uma and Von's collection of names? I don't even like their parties that much."

"You've got to try to act like them, even if you don't feel it. Uma said last night that you're not as much fun as when she first met you. You're playing a dangerous game with your attraction and your illicit knowledge."

"I've got the attraction under control."

"Yeah, maybe, but you spend too much time alone in your room. You turned down Von's Bliss last night. And you haven't even started watching the new series of WildLife. They'll get suspicious."

I fought the urge to slap some sense into him. "I thought you of all people would understand. Shows like WildLife have been running for centuries. Why haven't we moved on? I've been watching them all my life and I'm getting bored. The contestants all have identikit personalities. At the end of the day it's just a beauty contest, and I'd have thought you'd despise that as much as I do. Oh, and I've found out how they started, with a show called Big Brother at the turn of the millennium. The term Big Brother comes from an ancient story about a society where all thoughts were controlled. Sound familiar?"

He tutted. "That's exactly the sort of cynical talk that's going to land you in a correction centre. Why do you have to look down on everything? Don't you have a good life? You think I'm taking unnecessary risks to become BodyPerfect, but at least when I get it I'll have a glamorous life and maybe even get a more exciting job."

"So you'd ditch a good career? What would you do instead, be a media presenter? Whoop when someone pulls their fingernails out just to get their moment of fame?" I could hear myself shouting and took a breath. "Von and Uma aren't important at all. Wake up to yourself. You think the same way as me. You're just fighting it."

"But look how happy they are. They don't waste their time worrying about stupid things. Uma doesn't have to fight a dangerous attachment the way you do – I don't believe you're over it. Why would she? Everyone thinks she's wonderful. I just want to have more fun. Why don't you try to lighten up, instead of hiding in your room, obsessing over someone you can never have?"

"I'm not obsessing. I don't want him; I'm happy. Uma and Von don't worry about anything because their minds aren't capable of deep thought. Everyone wants to be with Uma because she's glamorous. No one actually cares about her. If she died tomorrow there'd soon be another minor celebrity to host the best parties in Sigma-2. I like Von and Uma but has either of them ever said anything you remembered more than five minutes? If you plunge into their world you'll die of boredom."

"It's you that's boring. When I first met you, you knew how to laugh, chill out and party. Now you're intense and nagging. Oh, you know how unproductive arguing is so let's not bother." He turned away from me.

"Maybe I want to argue! Maybe, just once, I want a conversation that's real!" I was on my feet now, my body tense, but at the same time my anger was vivid, exciting even.

"And maybe Uma will walk in on you right now and report you for subversive thinking. Anger's one of the worst negative behaviours."

"Maybe I want to be negative! Maybe it's natural to admit that, hey, life's not always great. Maybe we should just accept that we're all flawed, imperfect, glorious human beings."

He shook his head. Oh, why was I bothering?

"OK, let's be 'normal' and watch a media show." I sighed, defeated.

We sat silently in front of the media console and my shaking subsided. The argument had been upsetting, destabilising, yet at the same time, exhilarating. Now I felt deflated, stung to hear myself described as intense and nagging, but at the same time I understood why he said it. I used to enjoy WildLife. Perhaps I did spend too much time on the Knowledge Fountain and Truth Exchange. Perhaps I wasn't fun any more. I guess I was the one who hadn't woken up to myself. I needed to decide what I wanted to be, "normal" or a subversive thinker.

I pretended to enjoy the media show and afterwards

feigned tiredness and went to my room. With the now familiar tremble of anticipation, I logged on to the Truth Exchange, where my eye was immediately drawn to the first sentence.

BodyPerfect: the sinister truth about this dangerous cult

I sniffed. That sounded like something I ought to read, if only for Jem's sake.

Our State never ceases to promote the cult of BodyPerfect, claiming it leads to a healthier Society, but here's some facts you might not know.

The dangerously low body fat levels promoted are unhealthy for women. This has led to a dangerously low level of sexual maturation that threatens the whole State fertilization program and ultimately the future of our Society. Before this cult a body fat percentage of up to 30 was considered normal for women.

Up to 30? Outrage flooded each cell in my body. For years everyone had told me I was too fat but my body fat percentage had never been that high. At my last health check it had gone down to 24, and the health worker told me I should stick to fat control food. I read on.

By encouraging the feminization of men, the lack of breasts in women (once a desirable attribute) and the lack of distinction between the sexes, the state is able to suppress natural urges in men and women and discourage coupling because it believes society is safer this way.

The social pressures to become BodyPerfect are the cause of a growing incidence of mental illness, especially among those who fail to meet the height requirements. Illegal procedures such as limb lengthening and femur implants have a low success rate and can lead to permanent disability. It is physiologically dangerous to add more than 5 cm to the height other than under controlled surgical conditions over time and with careful monitoring. Failure to be BodyPerfect is becoming a leading cause of suicide.

We believe that the State promotes this harmful cult to encourage conformity, which is all it ultimately cares about.

At the sound of footsteps, I shut down the site and rested my chin in my hands. Was there any point in warning Jem or should I let him continue on his path of self-destruction? He wouldn't listen to me anyway. I looked at the breasts I'd spent so long trying to flatten, with new appreciation.

"Hey, you used to be a desirable attribute." I giggled. What would Uma say if she walked in on me right now?

Oh, I was glad I didn't take those hormone suppressants. There was nothing wrong with me. I wasn't fat; I was normal. But it was a new definition of normal. It was the truth, not the distorted norms that the Citidome imposed. And in that moment I couldn't deny the truth any more.

I was a subversive thinker.

CHAPTER – 7

Newsfeed: Ministry project reports expected soon.
In what is expected to be a record year in productivity at the Ministry, we await the end-of-year project reports from several key departments, which are expected to reveal exciting developments in technology.

Exciting for people who read them, perhaps. Not for those who write them. My workload had doubled, forcing me to work late most evenings. Even worse, my Pleasuredome visit was scheduled soon and I'd be livid if I had to cancel it. I poured all my energies into meeting my targets. With so many reports and new project proposals taking up my time, I was doing a good job at being "normal." At the end of the day I was happy to flop in front of the media console. Then came the day that messed with my head again.

"We need to go outside this afternoon, to examine the exterior construction of the Dome." Kit announced, as if this was no big deal.

"Outside? Really?" I squealed.

"Wild! It'll be my first time too," said Dal.

"What, the rest of you have all been out before?" I scanned their faces. Each nodded nonchalantly. "Why did no-one tell me? What's it like out there?"

"Before you go, you have to sign a secrecy agreement, saying you won't talk about it," said Jana. "It's OK to give vague details, but no more. There's some beautiful scenery out there but the climate's usually so awful that it isn't the big treat you expect. We'll need to put on the heavy coats – it's cold out there in October, you know."

"I don't care. I'm still excited. The only glimpse I've ever had has been from the shuttle on the way to the Pleasuredome," said Dal.

"Me too." Finally, I'd get to see what was out there! The dome material itself was neither opaque nor transparent, but an intermediate state that allowed the observation that the sky was blue and the ground was brown and green, but little else.

We left the office and made for a group of three TravelPods.

"Is it OK if I don't drive?" I asked. "I'm not very confident with TravelPods." I tended to walk everywhere, and if I was running late and had to take them, set them to autodestination.

"Hop in with me then," suggested Mac. "I could even give you a little driving lesson outdoors. That's OK isn't it, Kit?"

"Why not?" Kit said. "Take her for a circuit around the Dome."

I leapt in beside him; I hadn't spoken alone to him for weeks. He set autodestination for Gate Four and turned to me. Our gazes locked, and my pulse was out of control once more. Oh no. So much for putting a lid on my feelings.

He spoke with urgency. "At last. I never get a chance to talk to you these days. Are you still using the Truth Exchange?"

"Yeah, I've been dying to tell you. I'm completely hooked. Guess I really am a subversive thinker."

His face erupted into smiles, and a peculiar feeling gripped my stomach: thrill mixed with terror.

"I knew it! What's wrong with being a subversive thinker anyway?"

"How about being locked up in a correction centre? Every time I go on it I panic that someone's checking up on me."

"I've got to admit, I'm a bit like that too, but it's worth it. It's like the only sane voice in an insane world. You could send me messages in the chat room, you know. My user name's Walkunafraid."

"I'm not sure I want to. I went in there once and it freaked me out."

He laughed. "I know what you mean." He rubbed his chin. "But you know, for some people it's their only outlet. Society's conditioned us to believe that any sort of emotion is wrong, perverse even. But what's wrong with two people loving each other?"

I squirmed in my seat, still struggling to define my feelings for him. Attraction, yes. But love? I didn't even know what it meant. Did I want all that possessiveness and jealousy that used to come with marriage? No way. Best keep it safe.

"Oh come on, that's basic stuff. What about the suffocating intensity of relationships? The hate crime? We don't have any of that any more."

"Yeah, none that's reported, but how much do they keep from us? And what's the payback? Sure, we don't have much stress and plenty of leisure. But the loneliness – don't tell me you never feel it. Even talking like this is pretty near impossible most of the time. And do you ever feel excitement, passion?" His eyes burned with an intensity that unnerved me. This conversation wasn't going the way I'd hoped.

"I get lonely, course I do. And yeah … I wish we could talk more often. But the rest of it scares me to death. Passion sounds like a dangerous emotion and a one-way ticket to a correction centre." I could hardly bear to look at the disappointment in his eyes. I knew how wooden, how prim, I sounded, but my hands had started shaking and we were almost at the gate. I couldn't handle this, not when we were meant to be working.

"Listen to yourself; you're talking like an automaton. So you're going to spend your whole life in a neutral emotional state? That's not a life; it's an existence."

"I'm not neutral; I'm happy," I said automatically. But was I? Had I made myself a misfit, no longer satisfied with this life but not ready to make the leap that his words demanded?

"Huh. You think you are, but have you ever known joy?"

Joy? I didn't even know the word. But we'd reached the gate. We cleared security and drove out.

Mac shrugged. "OK, I'll lighten up and let you enjoy the outside. Just remember that I'm here if you need me. Let's change places and give you a go at driving."

He stepped out of the TravelPod and I shuffled across to the driving seat. A biting wind rushed through the Pod, making my eyes water. So this was what fresh air tasted like!

Then I looked around with dismay. The sky was a dingy grey-white, with no sign of the sun. A desolate wasteland stretched for as far as the eye could see – bare earth scattered with rubble and weeds. Clusters of nondescript shrubs lay here and there. A rough track of gravel and stones led away from the gate but there was nothing promising on the horizon.

"It's not what I expected." I accelerated the vehicle.

"I didn't want to burst your bubble, but I knew it was grotty around here. I think they do it on purpose – make it look as unappealing as possible. That way, if people peek through the Gates they assume that they're not missing out on much. I've been out on a couple of missions and believe me; once you get away from here, it's stunning."

"Really? What's out there?"

"The whole of nature. I went on an assignment with Jana last year. Honestly, it's incredible. Rivers and hills, flowers and trees, not manicured like the ones in Sigma-2 or the Pleasuredome but wild … uncultivated. Nothing untamed survives in the Citidome." His eyes gave that thrilling flash, then he smiled. "You're doing fine with the driving."

"It's easier than I expected." And it was. A smooth road ran around the perimeter of the Citidome. "How long do you have to work here before you get sent out on missions?"

"Well, I wasn't going to tell you, but the SolarPlas pilot studies start in January. And in my last assessment, Kit promised me I'd lead the next mission if I stop making controversial comments." His tone became playful. "Have you noticed what a good boy I've been lately? Toeing the line, saying the right things? I even told the student from the academic centre that we live in a lucky society!" His eyes twinkled with mischief.

"Hang on, so you're leading, but we don't know if I'm going with you."

"Course it'll be you. If I'm leading, it could only be you or Dal, but you're the new star. Everyone thinks so, and you've done more work on this project than Dal has. Besides, I heard Ren saying that they always sent the younger ones out in winter. Imagine the two of us together for two or more days, all the things we can talk about." He winked at me.

"What does that mean? I can't work out whether you're poking fun at me."

"Oh no, is that what you think?" His face fell, and then I saw something new in his eyes: an expression of such tenderness that I had to blink away tears. "It means I like you."

His hand briefly covered mine and I shivered at the unexpected contact. I opened my mouth but couldn't speak or make sense of my feelings. Pleasure. Pain. Confusion. The other TravelPods came into view.

"I'm sorry." What was I sorry for? I couldn't resist adding, "What's joy?"

"It's a state of happiness so intense it seizes you up. Stop fighting what comes naturally, and you'll feel it." My eyes met his once more, and I couldn't bear to see the sadness in them. I fought that craving to trace his jaw and instead brushed my hand lightly against his.

I climbed out of the TravelPod slowly, my head spinning. I hated it when he was overly intense. All that dangerous talk about passion. But what was I doing, chanting Mind Values like a silly preteen? Oh, but I might be going on an outdoor mission with him. I could hardly focus on Kit's demonstration, furious with myself. Why had I wasted a valuable opportunity to have a real conversation? I didn't have any these days. Why couldn't I make sense of the emotions that Mac talked about? He said he liked me. What did that mean? Did he feel the attraction I did?

The rest of the day was an anti-climax. But, once back at the residence, a new hankering seized me. I needed to make sense of Mac's words; to understand love, joy, excitement and passion. Automatically, I chose the safer option, the Knowledge Fountain. First I searched for the word 'joy'.

There was no entry.

The definition of 'passion' didn't help much, either.

Passion: A dangerous mental state caused by an excess of emotions. Consequences include obsession, nervous exhaustion and insanity. Isolation and enforced rest can cure the condition.

I massaged my temples, as if trying to rouse my brain into understanding. That can't have been what Mac meant. Instead I opened the Truth Exchange and had a peek at the chat room.

To Dangergirl from Dangerguy: I want to be with you, to feel your skin against mine, to smell you, to touch you, to fuck you.

I closed the page with a shudder. I had no idea what fuck meant – presumably coupling. Maybe the Knowledge Fountain was right. Passion was dangerous. But why did I feel stirred? A sudden fear gripped me – did Mac exchange these sorts of sick messages with others? What was his user name – oh yes, 'Walkunafraid'. I searched for it. Hmm, he used this a lot. I read through each message, knowing as I did so that this was obsessive behaviour. But with sweet relief, I found only impersonal conversations, usually about Mind Values. Oh, why had I wandered into this perilous place? I'd go to the leisure room. I needed some mindless entertainment to calm myself.

I walked in with a sigh; only Jem was in. Things hadn't been the same between us since that argument. I'd hoped for light, easy banter with Von or Uma. He turned to face me and I gasped. His cheeks and forehead were red and shiny, his jaw encased in a plastic brace, from which protruded a swollen purple mass.

"Veez – what happened?"

"I had a skin peel and jaw corrective surgery," he mumbled. He could hardly part his lips and was drinking a liquid meal through a straw.

"Oh … I wish you hadn't. I don't see what's wrong with a prominent jaw line." I thought of Mac's jaw with a delicious shiver.

"In a week's time, my skin's going to be as smooth as yours and my softer jaw's going to make a huge difference to my looks."

I read last week that men's skin wasn't meant to be as smooth as women's, but what was the point of saying so?

"You're not still thinking about limb lengthening are you?"

"No." His eyes looked anywhere but at me. Oh, let him do it. I couldn't face another argument.

"Isn't WildLife on tonight?"

"Yeah, just starting."

I tried to focus at the screen, but a stab of yearning pierced me. What would the stubble on Mac's chin feel like against my skin? I should never have gone into that chat room. My thoughts spiralled out of control for the next few days. I read the chat room posts and imagined what it would be like to say those words to him. This was unhealthy. This was obsession, the consequences of passion, like the Knowledge Fountain said. What were the cures? Isolation and enforced rest. Huh, fat chance of that. Oh, but wait. I checked my scheduler. My week at the Pleasuredome started in ten days. Perfect.

***

I boarded the shuttle train with a warm glow of anticipation. The charms of the Pleasuredome were entirely predictable – it would clear my head. Each group of five Citidomes shared a central Pleasuredome roughly 50 km away, from which tracks radiated out in a star shape to each Citidome. I looked out of the semi-opaque windows of the shuttle with a new cynicism. Why did the authorities want to obscure our view of the outside if there was nothing more to see than a barren wilderness? All that was visible was a blur – could anyone really have seen a horseback rider? Besides, why would a rider be so close to the Citidomes? Surely outside communities, if they existed, were far away?

Fifteen minutes later the shuttle stopped at the Pleasuredome where an army of identical greeters stood in a line.

"Welcome to the Pleasuredome, Caia." A BodyPerfect with a fixed smile scanned my DataBand. "You'll be in unit 52, room 313. Follow the blue line. Your leisure suits should be laid out for you. Enjoy your stay!"

An illuminated stream of blue dots appeared at my feet. I reached my room and exhaled slowly and luxuriously. I looked at my activity menu. Garish displays advertised beach parties, clubs, sporting events and concerts. It all looked exhausting. Why did people have to schedule every moment of their day? I wanted peace of mind but that didn't seem to be an option. I selected the spa menu and scheduled a massage: Von had increased my weights yet again and I ached all over. Personal grooming and pampering ... yeah, maybe some of that too. But first: my favourite place. I selected the zoo – oh, good – a visiting slot was available in fifteen minutes.

I strolled through the handsome iron gates and saw the hordes of children. I guess I should've outgrown this by now. I took a protective coat and stepped into the Ice World. The unfamiliar chill stung my cheeks. I thought of being outside with Mac. No, got to push him out of my head this week. Oh, there it was, the animal that enchanted me most. The polar bear's vast paws prowled the snow. What was it about the bears that always got to me? They perfectly combined raw power with gentleness and beauty. I gazed into its eyes, wondering what it was thinking. Was it happy here, or should we have let nature take its course? They were extinct except in captivity.

I shed my coat and found myself in a tropical rainforest and encircled by birds and butterflies. A kaleidoscope of colour in every direction. Sweet aromas assaulted my nostrils while water from the warm, humid air condensed on my chin. Birds sung to each other, as if in conversation. Oh, this was wonderful. I felt happy again. I adored the Pleasuredome. Who needed the outside world when all its wonders were contained in a safe environment?

"Hey, I thought I was the only adult in here," said a girl with pink hair and an infectious grin.

"I always come here. I love plants and animals."

"Me too. My name's Kiki. Let's connect."

Exchanging details, I discovered that Kiki was an eighteen year-old junior healthcare assistant from Upsilon-2. Together, we explored the African plains, the Desert Zone, and then the Sea Zone.

"I always wanted to see the sea," I said.

"Have you been to Splash Zone? The waves are

enormous."

"Not for years. I got knocked over by one and it put me off going back."

"You should try it again. Come with me, I'm scheduled for 15:45."

Kiki was so bubbly and persuasive that I couldn't refuse, and that's how I found myself at Splash Zone, buffeted by waves and screaming like a child as I whizzed down twisting tubes. I had to admit, it was fun. Eventually, exhausted, we relaxed on the synthetic beach under the glow of an artificial sun.

"See you at dinner around 20:00?" Kiki asked.

"OK."

So much for rest and solitude, but maybe I should let myself be carried along on Kiki's relentless tide of enthusiasm. I wouldn't have to make any decisions and, more importantly, I wouldn't have time to think. The way I'd been feeling, that had to be a good thing. Kiki was one of those people who drew others towards her without even trying and by the end of the evening I was part of a lively group.

"Who's up for the Thrill Zone tomorrow?" she asked.

I kept my mouth closed. The idea of Thrill Zone just didn't, well, thrill me. But I bowed to peer pressure, and the novelty of new experiences turned out to be exactly what I needed. We rode virtual rollercoasters that spun us in all directions, experienced virtual space flight, racing cars and deep sea diving. As I leapt up and down at the Bounce Party, the turbulence tumbled out of my brain and was replaced by pounding dance rhythms. Afterwards I was so exhausted that I slept without any input from the RestPod. I hadn't had so much fun for years. But was fun enough? I remembered that strange, unfathomable word of Mac's: joy.

And the week passed as it had started. The conversations were trifling, the people unmemorable, but everyone was so focussed on the present, so engrossed in the activities that it didn't matter. I'd never enjoyed a visit to the Pleasuredome so much. And while my subversive thinker brain told me that I'd been filling myself with artificial stimulation to prevent myself from feeling anything genuine, it was what I needed. My new reality was too frightening.

On Saturday my new contacts said goodbye.

"So long, kitten, it's been the greatest fun," said Kiki.

"So long," I kissed the air around her cheek, and then boarded my shuttle, my DataBand heaving with new contacts that I was unlikely to meet again. This was normal, the way things were meant to be. I'd forget Mac and rediscover peace of mind before it was too late.

CHAPTER – 8

Newsfeed: BodyPerfects reach an all-time high.

An annual survey has found that 40% of the Sigma-2 population has now attained BodyPerfect status. This positive finding has important implications for health and longevity, a spokesman said.

I arrived back at the res that evening, my step light and my heart even lighter. From now on I'd be the fun-loving resmate the others wanted me to be. I'd take up more activities and stay away from the Truth Exchange. Jem would be pleased. I looked forward to telling him all about my week, but I felt deflated when I found the leisure room empty. Odd, he was always in on a Friday. I went to his room and pressed the 'Open' button.

"Go away," a faint voice slurred.

For a second I couldn't make sense of the scene in front of me. Jem was lying inert on a sofa, his legs dressed with polymer bandaging.

"Oh no, you didn't." I couldn't move, rigid with disbelief. He'd obviously had the limb lengthening treatment and judging by the state of him, it hadn't been professionally done. His face was an unnatural colour, like uncooked pizza base.

"I did, but it didn't work. I measured myself afterwards and I'm still 1.5 cm short." His voice was indistinct and his eyes half closed.

The realisation hit me like the chill of the outside. "Jem, have you taken something?"

"Yeah, but don't call medical emergency yet. It's too late anyway; it's irreversible. It shouldn't take long. Stay with me."

Panic stampeded through me. What were you meant to do? Induce him to vomit? Force him to drink salt water? Ram my fingers down his throat? I took out my DataBand to call medical emergency, but he pleaded, "Please, not yet. Let me go peacefully."

I looked at his unfocussed eyes and knew I was too late. Jem would have known exactly what to take. I slumped onto the floor and knelt beside him, trembling inside and out.

"Why?" I whispered.

"I'm nothing. I hate myself. No one can be happy in this Citidome except BodyPerfects. There's ... only one other thing that could have made me happy."

"What?"

"You." His eyes bored into mine, before returning to their half-closed state. "Stupid, I know ... impossible. Even then, you wanted someone else."

"Me?" I tried to keep the incredulity from my voice.

"Yeah, you. I shouldn't have told you to hold back what came naturally ... but I couldn't bear to see you suffer like I did. Hold my hand."

I grasped it, cool and clammy. This was a nightmare, surely. I'd wake up in a minute.

"No one was ever as kind to me as you were ... Uma's party ... you were so hot," he murmured dreamily. "Two men desperately wanted you ... you couldn't see it."

Jem's voice faded and his words became unintelligible. The Pleasuredome evaporated. Pain spiked through me. Why didn't I notice? But what could I have done? I could never, ever, think of Jem the way I did about Mac. I guess that was the tragedy of attraction and love. It really did destroy people. Clutching his hand as if the contact would make him cling on to life, I leaned over and kissed his forehead, tears dropping from my eyes to his skin.

"Thank you," he mouthed, his final words.

Soon afterwards, his breathing slowed. Time to call medical emergency. I sat with him, stroking his hand as his life ebbed away. By the time the health workers arrived I was sobbing. I'd never felt anything like it – a grief so intense that I felt I was being torn in two. I took a hiccuping breath. Pull yourself together, Caia. What would they think? The senior health worker glared at me.

"Jem 170846, time of death 18:38," she said into her DataBand, and the team efficiently zipped him into a body bag.

Was that it? Was human life really so expendable, so easily disposed of? A convulsion of nausea gripped me and I rushed to the restroom where I retched long after my stomach had voided its contents. When I walked back, Jem's body was already on a trolley.

"Seeing someone die is disturbing, but you appear to have had an extreme reaction." The health worker's lips were tightly drawn in. "I won't report it, but you might want to think about attachment counselling."

"N-no, it's just the shock." My words were fast, urgent.

The team were wheeling him out when Von and Uma arrived.

"Oh, don't tell me, he's done a Lian," Uma said, using the slang expression that referred to a high-profile celebrity suicide.

"Woow, I don't believe it! How did he do it?" Von asked, his eyes wide as if he was watching a media game stunt.

"They ... found pills in his room."

"That reminds me; you know Cheyna?" Uma asked.

I shook my head.

"Veez, Caia, keep up, she's the singing gymnast on last month's TalentTime. After she got knocked out she tried to top herself with nutripills! What a doofus!"

Von's laugh caused my nausea to return. Would Jem's tragedy just become another entertaining anecdote to them?

"I'll miss him." My voice cracked in my throat. Someone had to inject some humanity into this conversation.

"Don't be silly. People come, people go; we'll have another resmate in days," said Uma. "He hasn't been much fun these days anyway, and he was ultra-embarrassing at my last party, practically begging my contacts for their details. Not cool. Hey, look at you; you've been crying, haven't you?" Her hand went to her mouth. "Veez, you and him – you were always together. There wasn't anything creevish going on, was there?"

"Euw, gross." Von had taken his DataBand from his

pocket. Was he about to report me?

"Me and Jem?" I widened my mouth, forced my lips downwards. "Course not … revolting. It was just … do you know why he did it? Because he desperately wanted to be BodyPerfect. It's so sad."

"Loser. He'd have never made BodyPerfect. Either you've got it or you haven't."

Oh, the callousness of Uma's words. I guess it was the appropriate response, but it no longer felt normal. I'd been a useless friend to Jem, worse than useless. How must he have felt when I confided my feelings about Mac? But why the obsession with becoming BodyPerfect? He knew it wouldn't impress me. Were his desperate attempts at conformity just to suppress his feelings? Too many unanswerable questions rioted inside my head and once in my RestPod I let my tears flow. I passed Sunday in a state of torpor, while the others continued life as normal, their routines undisturbed by the tragedy.

Soon it was time for work and I wasn't sure I could face it. Mac rose to his feet when I walked into the office.

"Hey, Caia, hope you're not too chilled out. I've got some urgent updates to run through with you."

He walked towards me, his posture relaxed, not constantly straining to appear taller, at ease with his so-called physical imperfections. To me, he was perfect. Just who was I trying to kid at the Pleasuredome? I'd never get him out of my system and, after Jem, I wasn't sure I wanted to.

"Did you have a good time?" he asked.

"Yeah. B-but … Jem killed himself." I burst into tears; I just couldn't help myself. What had I done? I'd be sent to therapy, labelled deficient in emotional health, put the mission with Mac in jeopardy, and yet I couldn't stop. I leaned on the desk for support.

Mac rushed to my side, while Ren, the only other person in the office, brought me a chair. Mac knelt beside me, so close I could smell him. Hopefully Ren would think it was the grief making me tremble. I craved the comfort of another body like never before, and fought the urge to fling myself against Mac's chest. But they both acted appropriately, without any physical contact.

"Was this the first time you witnessed a suicide?" Ren asked.

"Yeah, I found him after he'd taken pills and by then it was too late. I watched him die."

"How awful for you," Ren's voice was warm with sympathy. Mac said nothing but he didn't need to: his eyes said it all.

Kit and Jana arrived.

"What's happened?" Kit asked.

It seemed that Uma and Von's reactions weren't typical. If Kit, Jana and Ren thought my reaction inappropriate, they didn't say so.

"I forget how young you are; witnessing suicide is always a shock. Would you like the day off to rest?" asked Kit.

"No, thanks. Being busy will take my mind off it."

The updates with Mac didn't take long, and the tenderness in his voice made me want to cry even more. Afterwards, I tried to focus on my report but my mind refused to fix on any subject for more than a few minutes. Halfway through the morning Mac called me from the lab.

"Caia, could you give me a hand? The UMS is playing up and I know you're a genius with it."

As we pretended to look at a screen, his voice was a caress. "Pretend to explain things to me; we should be safe for a couple of minutes."

Pointing at the screen occasionally, I whispered, "I daren't talk here. I might cry again."

"Then talk to me on the chat room."

"I want to but –"

"Be brave. Or do you want to end up the same way as Jem? Dare to dream, Caia."

I swallowed my gasp. His words resonated with me so strongly; I couldn't keep my feelings bottled up inside any longer.

"I'll send a message after work," I whispered.

That evening, with trembling hands, I selected the "Register" entry, my first active input into this clandestine world.

Input Username a prompt asked.

Mac's words flooded my brain. Daretodream I input.

Taking a deep breath, I spoke my message.

> To Walkunafraid from Daretodream: I had to
> talk to you, because of what J said to me
> before he died. He said that apart from being
> BodyPerfect, only one thing could have made
> him happy – me. I had no idea. And I'm
> overwhelmed with guilt because I never felt
> that way for him. In fact, I'd confided to him my
> biggest secret. It's you I'm attracted to. I think
> you've figured that out. And I wanted your
> arms around me today for comfort. Why would
> that have been so wrong?

I'd been chewing it over in my head all day. I had to tell him.
But as the words glared back at me, I swiped my hand over
them, ready to delete, my nerve deserting me. Was I making
the biggest mistake of my life? Had I even phrased it
properly? I noticed from the other posts that no-one used
words like attraction. No, I had to. I couldn't let myself
become as unhappy as Jem. A valuable life had been lost and
to make up for it I needed to find value in my own life.

"Send," I said.

How did this work? When would he reply? I moved away
from the screen, trying to steady my now out of control
breathing, and gasped as a block of text appeared.

> To Daretodream from Walkunafraid: If it's any
> comfort you've made me happier than I've
> been for ages. You keep giving me mixed
> messages; I sometimes wonder if I was wrong
> about you. And, of course, I feel the same. You
> know that, don't you? This morning – it wouldn't
> have been wrong; it would have been the
> most natural thing in the world. It killed me to
> see you looking so sad and not being able to
> do anything that actually helped. I wanted to
> take you in my arms and never let you go. Trust
> your feelings, and trust me. Stay strong,

sweetheart.

I shut down the page, my pulse galloping. Sweetheart. I'd never heard the expression before. I repeated it over and over. I read the words until they were embedded in my brain. The next day when he winked, I winked back with a new understanding.

A new resmate replaced Jem within a week. His name was Mik, a BodyPerfect with the same outlook on life as Von and Uma but with more sarcasm. His eyes were grey, his chin small and sharp, like the rodents in the zoo.

"I know you, don't I?" asked Uma.

"I should hope so; I present *Extreme Pressure*." His whiny, high-pitched voice oozed arrogance.

I suppressed a groan. Another show I loathed. *Extreme Pressure* was one of the most sadistic media shows, humiliating people with endurance stunts that were no more than torture. Usually the contestants were Marked. I guess they were the only ones desperate enough to appear; they needed the paltry currency prize.

"Woow, you spend a lot of time in your room don't you," Mik sneered. "What do you do in there?"

"I have to do extra research, for work."

I told the lie that usually satisfied Uma and Von. Mik snorted and turned away.

To Daretodream from Walkunafraid: Was that it – one message and then nothing for a week? Did you scare yourself by writing it? I dare you to write another. Go on. I knew you were a kindred spirit from the start.

To Walkunafraid from Daretodream: You know me too well. Scared? I half expected the screen to explode and CEs to storm the building. What does kindred spirit mean?

To Daretodream from Walkunafraid: It means

we see the world through the same eyes. You looked cute today.

To Walkunafraid from Daretodream: Kindred spirit. I like that. When you were bent over your screen this morning, your hair fell in front of your eyes, and I had this really weird impulse to smooth it back. Can you imagine what the others would have said? Actually, another reason I didn't reply is because we've got a new resmate. He's vile and he makes sarky comments every time I go to my room, so I'm limiting my time here. He's a minor celebrity and obsessed with exercise so he fits in perfectly. I've been going out more. Could we do something together one evening? Do you play racketball? I used to play with J.

To Daretodream from Walkunafraid: Racketball? I don't really go in for public sports – haven't played for years – but for you I'll give it a go. It couldn't be less fun than the OmniTrainer. Be gentle with me though. Tomorrow?

The following day Mac arrived at the residence, racket in hand. I barely looked at him, terrified that my face would flush and the others would see.

"Ready to destroy me?" he asked. "Hey Uma."

Uma raised a hand, and then visibly recoiled. What was wrong with her? Oh, I see. In his sportsuit, Mac's legs were exposed and they were covered with a dusting of dark hair. Don't stare, Caia. Don't blush.

"Hey, didn't know you played." Uma recovered her composure.

"Caia talked me into it. I think she's planning her revenge for all the reports I keep foisting on her."

"Go easy on him, Caia." Uma turned to Mac. "She's good, you know."

"I will. See you later, guys."

"Woah, who's the freak? Did you see the creeving hair on him? They should put him on *Vile Bodies*!" I heard Mik's jibe before the door closed. Had Mac heard? He gave a hollow laugh.

"Charming new resmate you've got."

"I warned you. Sorry you had to hear that."

"I've had worse." His expression changed to that one of boyish vulnerability that got to me every time. "That's why I don't play public sports. I know I should get it ultralighted but …"

"Why should you?" I said and then in a whisper, "Besides, I like it." And I did. In fact, I liked the sight of him in his sport suit almost more than I could bear. I remembered a word from the chat room. He looked hot. Red hot.

"Not as much as I like you in that outfit," he whispered back, eyes looking ahead so that no passers-by could have imagined we were having this conversation. "We'll have to start playing more racketball. Anyway, I've been dying to tell you. Kit's finalising the details of the mission. Act surprised when he tells you, but it's definitely going to be me and you."

"Fantastic!"

The five-minute walk to the racketball court gave us little chance to say anything else. I beat him easily in the first game.

"You were meant to go easy on me," he protested.

"No way. I play to win." I smirked. He always seemed to have the upper hand on me: more intelligent, more self-assured, more knowledgeable. Beating him had given me a smug satisfaction. But, annoyingly, he soon improved. In truth, neither of us was focussed on the game. When he asked me how to change his grip, I surreptitiously stroked his wrist.

"This is my sort of game. Your breasts bounce up and down when you run," he whispered.

I opened my mouth to apologise for my inadequate sports bra but the expression in his eyes told me that he hadn't meant it as a criticism, rather the opposite. On the next point, I ran for a shot and accidentally crashed into him. When he took my hand to help me to my feet, his thumb caressed my palm, slowly and deliberately, sending jolts of longing through me – longing for what? I increased the pressure on his hand, thrilled by my boldness.

"So there is a bad girl in there after all," he murmured.

His face glistened. I inhaled his aroma of fresh sweat and exertion, my body responding in a way that made no sense to me. I leaned against the wall, light-headed.

"We could do this once a week without it looking too suspicious, couldn't we?" I asked.

"Don't see why not. Do you play other people?"

"Yeah, I'm in the league. I usually play on Saturday and Sunday."

"I'd better join too. Otherwise my resmates might think it's odd."

I returned to the res, flushed and happy for the first time since I came back from the Pleasuredome. The odd illicit message, a weekly game, and the mission outside. How did life become so good, so quickly? Even Mik's company became tolerable with these treats to look forward to. I made an extra show of fitting in. The next day, Uma burst in.

"Hey, Caia, even you'll be interested in this; it's a kicking piece of gossip! It'll be on the newsfeed tomorrow but here's an exclusive. Guess who's got the Mark!" She paused for dramatic effect as if about to reveal the name of the latest reality show winner. "Masa!"

I shrieked, genuinely shocked. This scandal would be headlines for weeks.

"How did you find out?" asked Mik, eyes almost popping out of his head.

"He took all last week off sick, and then asked to do his own facebase. The cosmetics assistant called in the producer. We caught him trying to cover up a huge Mark on his cheek. I always suspected there was something off about him. He patted me on the ass once, creev. They've thrown him out of the Citidome. He's gone to one of those outdoor correction centres."

"Who'd have thought he was like that?" said Von.

"Gross! To think I liked him," I grimaced in what I knew would be the expected response.

"Have they lined up a replacement?" Mik's voice was even

higher than usual.

"I don't think so; shall I put in a word for you?" Uma said.

As they revelled in every salacious detail of the story, my shock was mixed with a new understanding. The way Mac and I were, during the racketball – that must be at the root of what caused people to do the disgusting act. But could I imagine coupling with Mac? No! I wanted to hold him, to feel the warmth of his body, touch that jaw line, but nothing more. Why didn't Masa control the urge? He'd sacrificed his fame and lifestyle for a mad impulse. It just didn't make sense.

To Daretodream from Walkunafraid: Bet your res is buzzing with the scandal. Poor Masa – he was obviously more human than he looked. I see they've thrown him out pretty quickly, but not before plastering pictures of his Mark over every newsfeed.

What sort of response did he expect? Some sign that I understood Masa's behaviour? I'd better choose my words carefully.

To Walkunafraid from Daretodream: Vile M has already put himself forward as a replacement. Have to admit I was shocked. Seems harsh to send him outside though.

There, that was suitably neutral, wasn't it?

The next week, Kit asked to speak with me in the private office.

"As you know, now we've perfected SolarPlas, we need to test it in real-use situations for a year, to see how it withstands the full range of climate. The mission's going to involve being outside for three days in January, and I'd like to send you and Mac. But I wouldn't force anyone to go outside in winter. If you'd rather not go, I could send Dal instead."

"Er, no, I'd like to go. I've always wanted to see what's out there. I was disappointed that there was so little to see when we went out in October. But just how cold will it be?" I tried to inject a note of caution into my voice and not betray the excitement that was exploding inside me like a laser show.

"It may get as cold as the minus-twenty freezer, though most likely not lower than minus-ten. You'll need to acclimatise yourself by going in there every day. You'll also need some shots and take extra nutripills. We don't want you catching any diseases out there."

"Diseases?" I pretended to look alarmed. Who cared about diseases? Three days alone with Mac!

"Outside of the Citidomes, there are all sorts of airborne bacteria and viruses. Don't worry; some people come back with rare strains of flu but you should be protected against most things. And there'll be plenty of travelling so you'll get to enjoy the scenery too." He smiled. "I've been impressed with your input on the project so far; I'm sure you won't let me down. Mac has done a full risk assessment so he'll brief you more fully. I'll allocate you both an hour a day in here to make plans."

"Thanks," I said in as calm a voice as I could manage.

To Walkunafraid from Daretodream: I can't believe our luck! Three whole days!

To Daretodream from Walkunafraid: It could be even better. I've got something to tell you in the planning session. Don't scream or jump out of your seat when I say it.

To Walkunafraid from Daretodream: Is that it? No clue? That's not fair.

To Daretodream from Walkunafraid: Trust me.

The next day, swaddled in protective clothing, I braved the minus-twenty room.

"Try a minute at first," said Mac.

After forty seconds I stumbled out, coughing and spluttering.

"No way! My lungs have frozen."

"Lightweight. OK, try again tomorrow. It's not likely to get that cold, anyway. Want to sit in the warm office and go through the schedule?"

"Yeah, right now."

"What's the big secret?" I muttered once he opened the schedule.

"OK, don't react. Or at least do it quietly. This is going to kill you." He smirked.

"Stop torturing me. Out with it!"

"When we're on the mission we'll be mostly outside. The official schedule is: night 1 at Upsilon-2, night 2 at Tau-2, return that evening. But no-one's likely to keep track of our movements. They'd never track us as long as we report in on schedule. Our permits give us free access in and out of the Citidomes."

"Yeah, yeah, get to the point."

"Patience is a virtue. Who's been forgetting their Mind Values?" Oh, he was infuriating. "Just look at your face." He grinned. "Well ... if we work quickly, we could finish in two days. There's a community not too far from Tau-2. It's risky –"

"What?" I hissed. "You mean people actually survive outside?"

"Tau 2 is due north," he said in a louder voice, projecting a map onto a wall. "Close your mouth," he muttered. "Told you it was huge. I've known for years but you're the first person I've told."

"I knew you were hiding something when I asked you months ago. But why tell me here? Why not a message? Why haven't you posted this on Truth Exchange?"

"I swore I'd keep it secret."

"So how long will it take to get from Upsilon-2 to Tau-2?" I said in a normal volume then whispered, "What sort of community?"

"About an hour." Then, quietly, "It's an old village."

"Villages ... I always assumed if people survived outside it would be in villages. They had their own photovoltaic generators and wind farms on high ground. All the cities were connected to the state grid and'presumably their supply got cut off."

"How do you know that?"

"I did my final year thesis on photovoltaic technology. I researched the history of solar power." I couldn't keep a hint of smugness from my voice – so rarely did I know anything that he didn't. "But how do you know about this village?"

"My biological mother lives there."

"*What*?" I put my hand to my mouth; the word had come out more loudly than I intended.

"I warned you you'd have to be outside for up to four hours at a time," he almost shouted, scowling at me, then, "Ssh! Jana's looking this way. Sorry, I didn't want to say anything until we got outside but I had to make sure you were up for it, then we can use this time to work up an alternative schedule –"

"Yes!" The response was automatic. Then came the panic. I'd agreed to something so criminal that the Truth Exchange sessions were tame by comparison. Of course, curiosity won the battle in my head. Three weeks to go. How could I wait that long?

"She's not going to last five minutes in the cold," Mac said to Jana as they left the office.

"Why did I ever think a trip outside was a treat? Give him a sniff of power and he turns into a slavedriver." I played along.

At our next session I whispered, "You're torturing me. All these questions keeping me awake at night."

"Revenge. Thinking about you always keeps me up at night." He smirked.

"Just answer one. How did you keep in touch with your biological mother?"

"She escaped. Two years ago she sent a message. It's risky to use DataBands outside, so she said she'd only try once. She gave her co-ordinates so I could find her if I got the chance. But I never have until now. It's not far from Tau-2."

A cold tingle of fear crept up my neck. Did he plan to run away with me?

"You're not planning on staying there, are you?"

"It's crossed my mind." He paused. "But it'd be madness to escape on official business. They'd track us down. I just want to see what it's like."

"How do you know she's still there?"

"I don't. But there's a community. Has to be worth seeing, doesn't it?"

I stopped bombarding him with questions, satisfied that soon I'd know the full story. We spent the remaining sessions dutifully, scheduling our time officially and unofficially.

In the meantime, the Citidome fizzed with talk of New Year parties. I didn't think I could stand another party with Uma's crowd, but felt dejected when I found out that Uma, Von and Mik were all going to a party to which I hadn't been invited.

"I can get you an invitation if you want," Uma had said, "but it probably won't be your sort of thing."

"Why don't you sit in your room playing with your DataBand like you usually do?" Mik had sneered, with one of the collection of snorts he reserved for me.

"What's everyone doing for New Year?" asked Dal, and as everyone told tales of lavish celebrations, I had to shamefacedly admit that I had no plans.

"Come to our res party," said Mac.

"Are you sure? I don't want to intrude."

"My resmates will be pleased. They're worried that no-one's going to come."

To Daretodream from Walkunafraid: What are you wearing tonight? Hope it's a little tight number like the one you wore for Uma's party. Don't be offended if I don't spend as much time talking to you as I'd like (which would be all night). Got to be careful.

To Walkunafraid from Daretodream: Can't wait to see you too. You liked that dress? You were really off with me that night; I wasn't sure. I'm wearing my second unique outfit. Glad they're good for something. Hope you're wearing black. I like you in black.

To Daretodream from Walkunafraid: Are you kidding? You were so hot you practically sizzled. When I saw you dancing, I wanted you so badly I could hardly stand it.

"Hey, you made it," Mac said, his eyes moving up and down to take in my outfit – another tight-fitting dress – and mouthing the word, "Nice." I nodded appreciatively at his black bodysuit. "Come and meet Wenda; she organised the party."

I enjoyed talking to Wenda. Mac was lucky; his resmates were all academics. But she was forced to circulate and so I followed her lead, pasted an animated smile to my face and talked to strangers while sneaking glances at Mac. Eventually I made my way over to him.

"Dare we risk a dance?" My eyes pleaded with him.

"I want to but I can't."

"Why not?"

"If you danced like you did with Alda, I'd enjoy it so much I wouldn't be able to hide it, if you know what I mean."

He glanced downwards and grinned. What did he mean? I could hide my excitement; why couldn't he? One of his resmates asked me to dance and I swayed in time with him, imagining Mac in front of me. But my dancing had attracted others, and I danced with one person after another, stopping only to take Bliss, until a hushed anticipation fell across the room.

It's nearly midnight!" someone shouted.

A giant countdown covered the wall.

"Happy 2172," declared a huge virtual firework.

Everyone air-kissed each other. I found myself caught up in a whirlwind of festivity until I found him. Instead of the tiny peck around a centimetre from the cheek that was customary, his lips made brief, thrilling contact with my skin.

"Happy New Year, sweetheart," he whispered and turned away, leaving me breathless, open-mouthed, and tingling from the touch of him, but disappointed the moment had been so fleeting.

To Walkunafraid from Daretodream: So how did I look? You looked so hot, and that kiss was incredible. But you owe me a dance.

To Daretodream from Walkunafraid: Like a woman. Perfect. Kiss? That wasn't a proper kiss. It was nothing compared to what I want to do to you. Veez, it was a rush though. You smell amazing.

I couldn't sleep, didn't want to. He'd left me teetering on the threshold of danger, but I couldn't stop myself from plunging into the unknown. Whatever 2172 held, it promised to be a memorable year.

CHAPTER - 9

January 2nd. I crept into the rugged TravelPod, eyes downcast in fear of revealing our illicit plans to anyone. I felt sure the guard could read my mind and was about to report me. The gate opened and the cold took my breath from me.

"It's freaking freezing! But we're out! We're really out!" I clasped my hands together.

"So much I want to say. I don't know where to start," Mac said.

"Work now, talk later?"

"Spoilsport. Who's the boss here? But let's be sensible."

The first part of the mission involved placing test samples and monitoring devices on the outside of Sigma-2, but I was distracted. As well as the anticipation, icy air bit into my cheeks, tightened my chest and penetrated deep into my core.

"How can anyone live in these temperatures?" I said.

"It's way colder than last time I was out. Here, pass me that sensor. Keep your fingers moving."

We could only wear thin gloves because we had to manipulate the samples, and my fingertips soon became numb. When Mac put his hands on mine, there was no electric jolt of excitement, just relief from the chill.

"Your lips are going blue," I said. "It's not a good look."

"You'll have to warm them up later." He winked.

It took us almost three hours to set up the studies. When we returned to the TravelPod, my body was so rigid with cold that any excitement had faded.

"I'll turn the heat up. You OK?"

"I will be when I thaw out."

As we left the Citidome the immediate surroundings were bleak – bare shrubs, trees, meadows overgrown with weeds, but within half a mile the rough stone track that led out of the Citidome became a concrete road. I looked across at him.

Was this the moment when we had the big conversation about the way we felt? I didn't know how to start. Judging by his unnecessary focus on the driving, neither did he.

"I assumed there were no roads," I said.

"Yeah, but they're pretty old. You'll see why we need the rugged TravelPod."

Soon I saw. The road quickly became cracked, potholed and overgrown with long-term neglect. As the TravelPod plunged into another hole, my stomach lurched.

"It's so forbidding."

Sinister tree skeletons glowered against the white sky, leaning into the road. I was half intimidated, half riveted by my surroundings. Then a fleck of white hit the windscreen and briefly lingered before melting away.

"Stop!" I squealed.

"What?"

"Look, snow! I want to catch a snowflake."

"You're right. Brilliant! I've never seen real snow."

He stopped the TravelPod and we stepped outside. A tiny snowflake, perfect in its symmetry and delicate beauty, landed on my palm. But unlike the artificial snow in the Snow Zone, it disappeared in seconds.

"They say that no two snowflakes are the same," he said. "Unique and infinitely complex, like people used to be."

We started catching and comparing them. He was right; none were identical to the other.

"This is magical!" I flung my arms outwards, cast my eyes towards the sky, and spun around. And then his arms encircled me. He lifted me off my feet and swung me round and round, both of us giggling. When he put me down, he opened his mouth to speak, his breath forming frosty clouds, and then closed it, as if unsure what to do next.

"Caia ..." He brushed the hair from my face, leaving a streak of heat. Then both of his hands framed my face, drawing it towards his, and his mouth touched mine. Who would have thought that his lips would be so soft, so yielding, and would set my heart crashing all over the place? The cold, in fact the whole world around us had evaporated. I leaned closer into him. So this was what he felt like, hard and lean beneath the coat. And then his arms were around my back, pressing me closer to him. Instinctively, my arms reached to hold him. And once more we were kissing, the pressure of his lips increasing, until I pulled away. Part of me never wanted him to stop. The other part of me froze with fear. This was more, far more, than the heady rush of close contact in the Citidome. This was something dangerous. I tried to swallow but couldn't.

"Sorry, I can't do this." I'd broken the spell. The world reappeared and the cold stabbed through the seams of my clothes.

"Coward." But his smile didn't reach his eyes. "Guess we'd better get back in the TravelPod."

I followed him, teeth chattering.

"You want to, I know you do. Don't fight it," he pleaded. "This might be our only chance to be together." The desperation in his voice gave me a peculiar feeling, of being powerful and at the same time in his thrall. The shiver that passed through me had nothing to do with the cold.

"I'm scared." Oh, just listen to me, a snivelling child. But my chaotic mind couldn't cope with the bombardment of my senses, much less express it.

"Suit yourself." His head and shoulders drooped.

"It's not that I don't want to. That kiss … oh, it was amazing. And … I want to talk about my feelings; I just don't know how. I haven't even got the words. People on the Truth Exchange talk about wanting each other. How can you want someone? Makes them sound like a possession."

"It's about – oh, how can I put it – desire. Don't tell me when you kissed me just then, you felt nothing, I mean … physically."

"Course I did. That's what freaked me out. It felt like my body didn't belong to me. Yeah, I guess I … desire you."

"It's a start." His face relaxed. "It's hard to explain, but there's all these natural things go on in your body, that Citidome life doesn't let us feel. Sometimes it's physically painful for me to be around you."

"But it's … wrong. Sometimes I can't concentrate on my work if you're in the room and I'm petrified that someone will notice and I'll be moved and I'll never see you again." My words accelerated.

"Surely by now you get that it's not wrong?" He gripped my hands.

"But how can we live like this, wanting to be together and not being able to?"

"We'll find a way."

"What way?"

In reply, his lips curled into that secret smile that infuriated me. He drove on and within a mile turned onto a vast road, much bigger and better maintained than the other.

"What do they do to subversive thinkers?" I asked. "I've seen so many rumours: sent outside, discs attached to ears, people freakishly deformed ..."

"No-one knows, because no-one gets back to tell us the truth," he said. "Don't think about it."

I tried not to.

"Tell me more about your biological mother."

"She got to know me when I was twelve. She'd deliberately got a job as a supervisor at my development centre. She was funny, made me laugh, and it took me a while to realise that she singled me out from the others, always finding excuses to talk to me. I got to like her; and then one day she just came out with it." He sighed. "I guess someone noticed, the way they did with you and your daughter, because the next day she was gone. She's lived outside the Citidome for five years."

"Uma told me that people on the outside had regressed and live like animals."

"She would. Actually, from what my biological mother said in her message, they're pretty civilised. There's around thirty of them in an abandoned village. Some of them were born there and can trace their ancestry back to the first people to establish the community, almost a hundred years ago."

"Born there? People can give birth?"

"Yeah, some can."

"And communities have survived for so long? Where does their food come from?"

"No proti products." He grinned. "They eat meat from animals. They grow grains, get milk from cows and goats, make butter, yoghurt and cheese, grow vegetables."

"Eating animals? Gross." I wrinkled my nose. "So they're

organised societies? Surely the authorities know about this? Why don't CEs go out there and arrest people?"

"I wondered that too. They must know they exist. I guess once people are out it's easier to leave them to get on with it than to round them up, throw them in correction centres and risk them telling other people what's out there."

"Hmm, makes sense. How do people travel?"

"I've no idea. Her message didn't go into much detail."

"Not good enough! I expect you to know everything."

"You're hard to please, aren't you? Well, you know as much as I do now."

As the next Citidome loomed ominously ahead, my mind struggled to contain this new information.

"Before we get too close to so-called civilization, how about another try at a kiss?" His voice was tentative.

I nodded. He stopped the TravelPod and leaned across. The kiss was soft, short and sweet. Immediately afterwards he set off.

We stopped for the next set of studies. Disappointingly, the snow had stopped, but the frosty air gnawed at our flesh. Our illicit schedule meant a ferocious work rate and there was no more time to talk. I winced at the pain between my shoulder blades as the muscles of my neck and shoulders tightened.

"So much for the great outdoors," I muttered.

"And if I even rubbed your back I'd be flung in a correction centre."

Evening fell early, forcing us to stop and spend the evening at Upsilon-2.

"I don't want to go in. I want to talk to you all night, but I wouldn't mind getting some feeling back in my hands," I said.

"Just think of tomorrow. Three hours" work then off to the community."

Once inside, I sighed with pleasure, letting the comfortable temperature envelop me. We cleared security and went to the ResLodge for visiting workers. I wanted to scream with the effort of acting as if the day had been like any other. After eating, Mac said, "I've hired a private room to input the notes for today."

A wave of melancholy overcame me. I didn't want to

spend a minute away from him, but private rooms were strictly for work, and only one person was allowed in.

"OK. See you tomorrow. I'm going to jump into a hot tub."

I went to the bathing and sanitation facility, climbed into the tub and leapt straight out again. The water burned my still chilled skin. I inched my way in. Only after twenty minutes did my flesh thaw and my body relax. If only my mind could do the same. I sent my clothes for overnight cleaning, and summoned a RestPod. I'd have a long sleep tonight and then tomorrow would come more quickly.

The next morning we worked demonically on the outside of the Citidome.

"Think I worked out what's wrong with attachment."

"What?" He frowned.

"Last night, when I left you, I was miserable. This is how it's going to be from now on, isn't? Suffering when we can't be together."

"Ha, now you know what it's like for me all the time." He opened his mouth as if to say more, then paused. "I think we're done here. Ready to go?"

"Yeah ... I can't believe we're actually going to do this."

I drummed my fingers on my knee, unable to keep still, and the Citidome disappeared from view.

"Why have you stopped?"

"Why do you think?"

He leaned towards me and once more we kissed, a longer and more lingering kiss than yesterday. Once more it was me that pulled away, terrified of feeding the fire inside. I had to give voice to my worst fears.

"I think what's unnerving me about all this, is that it's leading to ... coupling." I could hardly look at him, blushing to the roots of my hair.

"I won't do that to you, I promise," he said, his eyes avoiding mine, "I ..."

At the fading of his voice I felt a hardness inside, like a stone lodged in my stomach. "Have you ... done it before?"

"I ... haven't told you anything yet about the guys who got me into the Truth Exchange. It was a group of students in Tau-2. They were like us, the sort that questioned things, but they called themselves rebels rather than subversive thinkers.

I was fifteen; they were around eighteen, nineteen and they dazzled me, especially one of the girls, Mei. You remember, the one who escaped, who was on the newsfeed. And Hal was one of the guys; he's the one who started the Truth Exchange."

When was he going to get to the point?

"Mei took me under her wing, told me most of the things I know. They invited me to a party, and there was wine. That's alcohol."

"Alcohol?" All I knew about it was that it was an ancient intoxicant that caused lack of self-control and liver damage. Nothing tempting about that, as far as I could see. "What's it like?"

"Sour, musty, but people take it because it does weird things to you. At first you feel happy, chilled out, a little like taking Bliss. Kinda fun, actually. But then … I got dizzy. Then – well let's say it makes people lose their inhibitions."

"Go on." The bile crept upwards.

"Give me a chance; I'm getting to the tough bit. I told Mei I liked her and she laughed at me. She said she didn't go for children. I slunk into the corner. Then another girl, Gini, wrapped her arms around me and pressed herself against me and" – he rubbed his nose – "Well, I felt rejected, and she wanted me, and I'd had all this alcohol, and …"

He stopped again. I'd never seen him lost for words. Silently, shaking, I willed him to stop there. He didn't. He couldn't …

"She led me to her room. I guessed what we were about to do … I was terrified but I'd got past the point where I could stop and by then my head was spinning and … it didn't even occur to me that she had the virus. She had no Mark, you see."

I clasped my hand to my mouth, overcome with nausea. Had I ever really known him at all? But something else gnawed at me … the image of him with someone else. Why did it bother me so much? I certainly wouldn't … Then came the worst thought of all.

"So you're … Marked?"

"Well … these guys all had the virus, but they knew a surgeon. As soon as it appeared on my chin, I got it ultralighted. The sickness ... well, that was harder to explain. I ate some out-of-date food and gave myself food poisoning to mask the symptoms. But I only ever had one bout of it."

"I thought ultralight couldn't remove it?"

"Huh, Knowledge Fountain lies again."

"But how could you – coupling, the animal act? Especially when you liked someone else?" My voice was brittle.

"I told you, I'd had too much to drink and she was leading me on and I could hardly think straight." He met my gaze and cast his eyes downwards, as if unable to bear the pain he'd caused me. "Don't look at me like that. I wanted to be honest with you. But you needn't worry about ... you know. I wouldn't try anything on you, no matter how much I want to. Couldn't have you getting it, could I?"

"Don't say any more. I can't even look at you right now." I turned away, tears smarting in my eyes.

"If it's any comfort I felt sickened the next morning. Talking to the others helped me put it into perspective. Please don't hate me for it," his voice pleaded.

"I don't hate you." I forced out the words.

"You know ... people outside live as couples and it doesn't cause all these social problems they warn us about at preteen. Ever since then I've questioned the whole concept of Mind Values. Is it to make society better or is it just to control us?"

"I can't take this," I muttered. "Don't say any more."

"We can turn round if you'd rather not face it."

"No. I've got this far; I have to see this place."

But my instinct told me to run back to the nearest Citidome.

We carried on in silence, and the churning in my stomach was only partly caused by the holes in the road. I tried to concentrate on the landscape unfolding before us, which was becoming captivating. We were driving through rolling hills coated with vast swathes of moorland unlike anything I'd ever seen. I hadn't realised there were so many different shades of green, and this in winter, when the landscape was at its most dull. The Citidomes could imitate nature but not convey the scale of the outdoors. From the hilltops, infinite views stretched out in all directions. Late afternoon sunshine had burst through the clouds, bathing the hillsides in an amber glow. I glanced across to Mac, who looked so unhappy that I softened.

"It's stunning," I said.

"It is, isn't it?"

"So it's true that the virus doesn't do any long-term damage?"

"Apart from the first time, I've never had any symptoms." His voice was heavy. "Used to freak me out, thinking I'd end up like the Marked people you see lying on the streets. I asked one of them once if he was ill, but he said he was just hungry, hadn't eaten for a week. That's why I started giving them nutribars. Mind Values, huh."

"I've wondered about Mind Values too. Is attachment such a bad thing? Even before you, I've felt it … for Sharee, for Suna, for Jem. I hated Uma and Von's heartlessness when Jem killed himself. I don't want contacts, I want friends."

"I knew from the start that you were like me, saw that place for the sham it was. So, Caia … what do you want from me?" His words were challenging.

"I don't know what to say." Unthinkingly, I raised my hand to my breast, and then dropped it, feeling the rush of heat to my face. "It's more but I don't know what. But what's the point of wanting it? What could we have? And now, with what you've told me … you're asking me to throw off years of conditioning at once and it's doing my head in."

"I'm sorry. I knew it'd upset you. Oh, I hate this. We can't get to know each other properly. I had to throw it at you all at once; we haven't got much time."

"So what happened with you and the … girl in the Citidome?"

"Nothing. Soon afterwards I got sick. But Gini kept hanging around my res, and one of the development leaders noticed. He hauled me in for questioning."

"What happened?"

"I said I was confused. They told me that if you're ever questioned, it was the best thing to say. And next thing I knew I was moved to Sigma-2, and I had no-one to talk to."

"You never met any more rebels? Or girls?"

"No, just on the Truth Exchange. And girls … most of them are too thin. They don't look like women. I was starting to think that I wasn't capable of feeling attraction again until the day you started work. You're lovely, beautiful. You do know that, don't you? And the way I feel about you … it's way more than I felt for Mei. With her it was more … admiration, hero worship I guess." He inhaled. "I've got to say this, and I know it's going to mess with your head even more, but with you it's love."

Love. The word lay between us, too delicate to be touched. And yet I glowed, feeling cherished in a way I'd never felt.

"Thanks," I whispered, because it was all I could think of to say. His warm eyes sent surges of longing through me, together with a fresh wave of confusion. How was it possible to feel so giddy with happiness and yet disgusted and desperate at the same time?

CHAPTER – 10

As the rugged hills gave way to signs of human habitation, we read the sign "Welcome to Ashford-in-the-Water".

"*In* the water? I hope not." I giggled.

Though still early in the afternoon, the light was dim and the cottages were sprinkled with small yellow squares of light from the white-framed windows.

"Oh how pretty!" I said, and then winced. Articulacy, it appeared, had abandoned me today. Pretty didn't come close to describing this wonderland. We gazed out of the windows, hardly knowing where to look, each building more steeped in history than the last. At first glance the village appeared to be uniform; everything constructed of the same grey stone, but, on closer inspection, I noticed that each cottage was unique, with different roofs, windows, doors. It was endlessly fascinating.

"Ooh, look. What's that?" I pointed to an imposing stone building, with a tall square tower and an expanse of grass in front, from which sprang stone slabs. A garden of grey stone. Strange.

"No idea. Fantastic, isn't it? Look at that tower." Mac glanced at his DataBand and pointed up the road. "According to the co-ordinates, her cottage should be up the road."

We walked up the street until he stopped and turned to face a tiny cottage.

"This is it." He swallowed.

"You OK?"

He nodded, but I grasped his hand and felt his tremor. Only at that point did I realise that I was shaking too. I wasn't sure what was causing it, the cold or the anticipation. Uma's words rang in my head – people here live like savages. Mac knocked on the wooden door, multicoloured from the wearing of many layers of paint. After a few moments, the door opened a fraction. An emaciated, elderly woman wearing a tattered woollen jacket peered at us then pulled the door wide open. "God almighty!" Her hand flew to her mouth. "It can't be! Mac?"

While I was trying to decipher her strange way of speaking, she ushered us inside, flung her brittle-looking arms around him and burst into tears. Didn't Mac say she was about forty? Surely not – she looked older than Kit. Her skin was an amber tan, two furrows carved between her eyebrows. I stood back, feeling like an intruder. The display of raw emotion was part shocking, part compelling. When they drew apart, the woman smiled, revealing a missing tooth. But she was respectably, if shabbily, dressed, a long way from the feral scavenger of my imagination.

"I'd given up hope of ever seeing you again. Let me look at you properly," she said. As mother and son held each other at arm's length, I noticed that Mac, too, had tears in his eyes. Something swelled in me – it tightened my throat and, bizarrely, filled my eyes with tears. "Look at you – my little lad, all grown up. You escaped?"

"No, we're on an official mission. If we're not back at Tau-2 by the time it's dark, it'll look suspicious."

She sighed. "You can only stay three hours then. Night's drawing in soon after four-thirty. Aren't you going to introduce me to your friend?"

"Sorry, this is Caia."

The woman put her arms around me. I stiffened. Not wanting to appear standoffish, I placed my arms on her back, shocked at the protrusion of her shoulder blades and trying not to recoil at the odour that emanated from her; a heady mix of what I later realised was wood smoke and something else, pungent and fusty.

"I'm Anna." There was something compelling about her smile. Despite her frailty, her eyes glowed with a kind of vivacity, a vital spark I didn't see in Citidome dwellers. With a start I realised that I'd only seen such an expression in Mac.

"Anna, I brought you a present." Mac took a bag from his pocket. "Toothbrushes and medicines. You've lost weight. Have you been ill?"

"You can call me 'Mum', y'know. I've had the flu,

influenza, that is. Took blooming ages to shake off. Ooh, thanks, a million, sweetheart. Proper treasure, this is." She peered into the bag.

So she wasn't usually as skeletal as this. I released my breath.

"Just look at your faces; you can tell you've never been outside before," Anna said. "I'm sure you're dying to have a look round the house. Go ahead."

Keeping our coats on – the house was mostly glacial – we wandered round, goggling at everything.

"Look at that – a fire, in a house!"

"Are those wooden doors?"

"What are those things on the shelves?"

"They're books," Anna said.

"Books? You mean words written on fiberstone? They still exist?"

"Yeah. Most of these are even printed on paper – it's like fiberstone but more fragile." Anna said. "Proper relics, these are. We found boxes full of them in the stores. But it's what's written in the books, that's the real thrill. It's fiction, fantasy, y'know? Love, hate, things that actually make you feel something."

I ran my fingers across the spines of the books, and pulled them out at random, caressing each, admiring the cover designs. I read one of the titles – *The Time Traveller's Wife* – and my imagination ran riot. I don't know which tantalised me more: 'time traveller,' or 'wife'. I opened it and inhaled the sweet, damp smell. I stroked the page. So this was paper! As smooth as fiberstone! I rustled it in my fingers. Reading used to be such a multi-sensory experience. Then – oh no – I made a crease that I couldn't smooth out. Not that the book was in any way pristine – the spine had split open in the middle and several pages had detached; others were loose.

"Don't worry, happens all the time. Guess that's why folks stopped using paper, too fragile. Have a look upstairs too," Anna said.

At first it was hard to drag myself from the low-ceilinged room and the glorious heat from the fire. Daylight streamed through the windows, illuminating a thousand tiny particles in the air. But I had to see it all.

"There's no toilet," I whispered to Mac. The restroom was otherwise primitive but functional.

"Maybe they go outside?"

We both put our fingers in our mouths, miming a vomit. The other two upstairs rooms contained beds, like those I slept on as a kid but larger, big enough for two people.

"Be weird to sleep in the same bed, wouldn't it?" He linked his fingers with mine.

"Yeah, but I'm not sure I'd ever sleep with someone else next to me." I swallowed my shock. Sleep seemed to me the ultimate privacy; hard to imagine it being invaded.

"I'm freezing. Shall we go back to the fire?"

Staring at the dancing flames had a hypnotic effect, and soon my face and hands were burning. If it hadn't been for the draught sending a chill from the back of my neck, I could happily have fallen asleep.

"Isn't it fabulous? Until now, I've only ever seen fire on media shows."

"Me too," said Mac. "So you burn wood?"

"That's right," Anna said. "We're not short of trees out there. Fancy a coffee?"

I blinked.

"You have coffee?" I said.

"I make my own from barley and dandelion root but, for you, I'll break open the good stuff. Got it from a Citidome trader."

"Traders come from the Citidome?" How much went on that I didn't know about?

"Yes, they either live inside or break in."

"I'm amazed things get across the gates," Mac said.

"Happens all the time. Security's not as tight as you'd think. They only guard the four official exits, and most of the guards take bribes, or used to."

"But what do you have to offer traders?" I asked and immediately regretted my tactlessness. But looking around the dark, shabby room, still chilly despite the fire, I couldn't imagine what anyone in the Citidome would want from here.

"Don't look like that, you haven't offended me." Anna smiled. "Illegals, that's what we trade in, d'you know what I mean?"

I shook my head.

"Alcohol, mostly, but plant drugs too. Hallucinogenic mushrooms – they always go down well – and cigarettes. D'you know what cigarettes are?"

"I've heard of them, but they've been banned for centuries, haven't they? Are they things you put in your mouth, set light to, and inhale?"

"That's right."

"It sounds so bizarre; I thought I'd got it wrong. What's inside them?"

"Dried plants. The best stuff's called tobacco. A community not far from here grows it. I'm not so keen myself, but there's plenty that are. And our village has something special to trade, or rather someone."

"Sorry, I don't understand."

"Sex. You know, coupling. That's what drives a lot of traders out here in the first place, the chance to try it. No-one born outside is Marked you see, unless they've been with someone from the Citidome. And one trader, Shin, took a fancy to Mary."

"A fancy?" A horrified thunderclap of realization. "You mean ... she sells herself?"

"You could put it like that, but she's happy to do it for the good of the village, and she likes Shin."

"So the virus really was artificially introduced in the Citidomes?"

"Seems so," said Anna. "It's not a big deal out here. Loads of us have it; people have been escaping the Citidomes for years, so it soon spread on the outside. It's just a mark, for heaven's sake."

"Huh, it's a big deal in Sigma-2," Mac's confession invaded the riot of thoughts swirling in my brain. I shivered. "What do you do here, as a job?"

"Help on the farm mostly, and I brew beer and wine. Fancy a try?" Anna took two plastic bottles from a cupboard. I gave Mac an anxious glance, too polite to refuse. "Go on, be brave. You'll like this. It's strawberry wine, sweeter than most I make."

I took the tiniest sip; what would it do to me? Then I smiled. The wine, though musty, had captured perfectly the ripe sweetness of strawberries, but also had an unfamiliar flavour. I followed with a hefty swig. It warmed all the way from my throat to my stomach.

"Woow. That's delicious."

"Don't knock it back too quickly; takes you by surprise if you're not used to it. Now, Mac, you should try beer. Proper man's drink, that is."

Anna poured a cloudy liquid, which formed foam at the top.

"That's really safe to drink?" Mac's eyebrows almost hit the ceiling. The brown sludge at least had an appealing aroma, like the yeast cultures we used to make in bioscience. Still, rather him than me. He took a sip and lurched backwards, then smiled.

"Weird ... bitter but kind of smooth, rich. I like it. Try it, Caia."

I took one sip and couldn't stop myself from pulling a face. I could only taste bitterness, which lingered in my mouth. I sipped the wine to take the taste away. "Sorry, I really don't like that."

"No need to apologise; everything's an acquired taste after the Citidome," Anna said. "Once you get used to it, the food and drink here's much better. Have you eaten?"

"No." With a shock I realised that I hadn't eaten since breakfast and became aware of the gnawing emptiness in my stomach.

"You're in luck. I just ate but there's plenty left. I made a rabbit casserole yesterday. I'll put some potatoes on for you; it'll be about half an hour."

"Rabbit?" Mac mouthed to me. I don't know which of us was more nervous.

Together we watched Anna peel some gnarly tubers, boil them in water then pound them with butter and milk. She put the peelings into a bucket outside.

"What happens to that?" I asked.

"The kids collect it every morning and take it to feed the pigs."

"Kids? You mean children? How many?"

"Three, all in the same family, but there's a few around."

Families. My imagination soared and projected into the

future. Was it possible that Mac and I could produce a family? I extinguished the deviant thought. This house was fogging my brain. While we waited for the potatoes to cook, my stomach rumbled. I'd never waited more than five minutes for food.

"Why did you leave the Citidome?" I asked Anna.

"Couldn't stand that life any more. Didn't see why wanting to know my son was such a huge crime. And I don't know what happened ... someone must have thought I was inappropriately attached to him, or some such rubbish. They moved me to a health centre. Christ, I hated it there. They made me go to a correction centre every week for counselling. I resisted at every turn; I didn't want my mind to be manipulated."

"How awful for you. I traced my daughter but they moved her. Not that I wanted to look after her myself but ..."

"Only natural that it tugs on your heartstrings, isn't it? Soon after that I caught the cleaner at work stealing some of the health centre supplies. I promised I wouldn't tell, but only if he told me what he was up to. That's when I found out he was a trader. One night, he took me with him out of one of the unguarded doors. Gave me away at the market."

"Have you ever regretted running away?"

"Sure, it was tough at first, but once I got used to it, no. I'd have had an easier life in the Citidome, but out here you make genuine friends. Hell of a lot better than all those superficial contacts I had there. Best of all, I've got my freedom."

Freedom, such an evocative word. For a moment I imagined what it would be like to live here, then the chill drew me back to the fire. Mac leaned forward and planted a tender, unthreatening kiss on my forehead.

"Glad you came?" he asked.

"Oh, yes."

The firelight cast shadows over his face, accentuating his cheekbones. Finally, I gave way to the urge I'd fought for months and traced my fingers along the strong line of his jaw, fighting to reconcile this beautiful boy, my friend, with the animal who'd given way to his primal instincts. Why did he have to tell me? He took my fingers and pressed them against his lips, with exquisite tenderness. If only someone could reprogram my brain and tell me that this wasn't wrong.

The next culture shock was the toilet. Anna led me out of the back door into the yard where the stench of the cubicle made me want to retch.

"We're lucky," said Anna. "We have well-designed toilets. They make fertiliser for the land, and they don't reek like some do. Just put in a scoop of that," – she pointed to a wooden box containing what appeared to be a mixture of dried leaves and sawdust – "when you've finished."

Still shivering, I tried not to gag and made admiring comments. I dreaded to think what a bad-smelling toilet must be like. How could anyone live like this? And yet the rest of the cottage, for all its shabbiness, impressed me. It felt personal in a way that a residence never could. I returned and finished the glass of wine, which became more delicious with each mouthful, and my eyes feasted on the books on Anna's shelf.

"I wish we had more time; I'd love to read a book."

"Let's have dinner and then I'll choose one for you to take back to the Citidome and read tonight. Hire a private room at your ResLodge; it's the only way you'll be able to be alone."

"But surely that's dangerous? Besides, I can't return it to you."

"I don't mind. It'd be worth the loss to know you'd had the pleasure of reading it. Honestly, books transport you out of the trivial world of Citidomes. Once you've read one, your imagination starts to work and nothing's ever the same again, d'you know what I mean? Oh, what am I saying; course you don't. Keep it hidden, though. If anyone finds you with it you'll be in trouble. Throw it away outside of the Citidome. But first, let's eat."

We ate the grey-brown stew at a rough-hewn wooden table. Thankfully, it tasted better than it looked. The rabbit, denser and chewier than proti products, had an incredible full flavour, as did the sauce, rich with herbs and wine, served with a creamy mash, tomatoes, carrots and hunk of dense bread with a delicious nutty flavour. Apart from the toughness of the meat, this was the best meal I'd ever eaten. I ate slowly, relishing the unexpected awakening of my sense of taste.

"This is delicious. You grow all this yourself?" I asked.

"Rabbits and squirrels are all over the place; any fool can catch 'em. They're bottled tomatoes – no fresh ones at this time of year. And we make bread with wheat and barley."

"Are all animals edible?"

"Yes, even humans." She chuckles. "Sorry, couldn't resist the chance to freak you out. We don't eat human flesh. But some animals make better eating than others. Sheep, cows and pigs – they're the best."

"How do you cook this?"

"In an electric oven." Anna showed us.

"Where did you get ovens and refrigerators from?"

"When people moved to the Citidomes, they left everything behind. Such a waste. So we still have heaps of spares and, over the years, people have gone and scoured abandoned cities and Citidome dumps; got all sorts of useful things – spare parts and the like. You'd be surprised how long these things keep going if they're looked after properly."

"Surely, eventually you won't have any working appliances?"

"We try not to think of that." Anna narrowed her lips.

Anna continued to tell us about life outside. Encouragingly, none of those who had escaped the Citidomes for a life here had been recaptured, but neither had anyone seen Citidome people with discs or strange deformities. Presumably they never escaped.

When Mac left for the toilet, Anna took my hand in hers, dry, calloused and broken-nailed.

"Mac told me you're struggling with all this – the emotional side I mean. Would it help to talk to me?"

I took a slow, deliberate breath. What could I say to this woman I hardly knew? But the sincerity in her voice made the words spill out. "Now I'm here, words like 'attraction' and 'attachment' sound silly but they're the ones I'm comfortable with. The way I feel for Mac, it's ... like nothing I've felt before. It's so powerful it scares me. When I'm with him, all common sense and reason evaporates. But everything we're doing's so dangerous. On the journey here, he told me he had the virus, and the idea of him doing ...

that, revolted me." I sighed. "Now I feel I hardly know him any more."

Anna smiled. "I know which book you need. In my third month here, I fell in love with a man. After a lifetime of Citidome conditioning, Mind Values and all that rubbish, I couldn't make sense of my feelings at all. This'll help. It's about love, passion, jealousy and hatred: all the stuff the Citidome doesn't allow you to feel. I can see why you're shocked, but Mac didn't do anything disgusting or wrong."

I wanted to believe her but my mind had reached its elastic limit for one day. Instead I turned my attention to the battered cover of the book, which portrayed a dark man standing on moorland, his cape blowing out in the wind. The image roused me – wild and untamed, reminiscent of Mac himself – as did the title: *Wuthering Heights*.

"How can I throw this away? It's so precious."

"I've kept it in here" – she placed her hand on her heart – "and you will too. Let someone else find it and enjoy it."

"Thanks. I can't wait to read it." I paused, wondering if I dare ask a personal question. "What happened to the man you fell in love with?"

"We were together for three years. Didn't work out though. He died in an accident last year. Oh, it's OK. No regrets and all that. Who knows, I might find someone else. I'm not quite past it yet." She chuckled. "Don't fight your feelings. And maybe … think about coming here permanently. If not now, then later."

Live here? I couldn't … could I?

The time passed too quickly and soon it was time for us to go.

"What's that amazing building down the road?" Mac asked as we left.

"It's a church, an ancient place of worship. Parts of it date back to the thirteenth century. Have a look – it isn't locked."

We wandered down the path to the church entrance. Two trees with needle-like leaves and contorted trunks framed the gateway. Their roots bulged from the path.

"They look as if they've been there as long as the church," I said.

"Yeah, I never saw trees so old. Look at those stone slabs –

looks like they commemorated lives."

Inscriptions were carved into them, most so worn that they were almost illegible.

"In loving memory, in affectionate remembrance, cherished," I read out loud. "So much love. And look at the dates – they're centuries old: 1883, 1869. And this word, 'sacred'." A stone cross by the entrance stated, "To the Glory of God, those who laid down their lives in The Great War, 1914-1918."

"Imagine, a war lasting four years," Mac said.

"I wonder if there are still wars going on in the world? Don't you hate the fact that we don't know?"

"Drives me mad. I never accepted that there's any point in suppressing history. Oh, look at those wooden crosses in the corner. Must be more recent deaths."

"Yeah, guess so. Shall we go inside?"

We pushed the door open – so heavy – and entered a tiny porch. A faintly spicy perfume filled the air. Two more doors took us into the cool, dark interior. My eyes were immediately drawn to huge, coloured windows that formed pictures. The number of wooden benches hinted at the substantial community that once lived here. I took a long, deep breath; the soft scent had infused the entire building. We sat, my hand resting in his, and I became overcome with serenity for the first time since I'd left the Citidome. If I could sit in this wonderful place longer, I felt sure I'd find peace of mind. Such artistry, all lost now. How could it be right to deny people this beauty?

"Breathtaking, isn't it?"

"Like something out of a dream."

"I'm glad I came," I whispered, finally certain that I'd done the right thing; that I'd treasure the memory for the rest of my life.

As birds swooped in front of us and the sun disappeared behind the hills, we made our way back to Tau-2.

"You first," said Mac. "I can see you're bursting."

"Where do I start? Anna's lovely, and her standard of living's better than I imagined. But I'm dying of cold. I can't imagine how people cope with it. How was it for you? Must've been emotionally disturbing – sorry, is that the right expression? – seeing her after all these years, and then leaving, not knowing if you'll ever see her again."

"She looked so old ... frail, too. She's aged a lot more than five years. To be honest, it's killing me to leave her ..." He closed his mouth and rubbed it before continuing. "Were you tempted to stay?"

"I ..." How did I feel? That today I'd breathed in real life for the first time, but it was an alien life, one that demanded a quantum leap. "Let me think about it tonight."

It seemed to satisfy him.

Back at Tau-2, my fat control proticurry and Mac's chilli were soft in texture, insipid in taste and differed little in appearance from each other. Other visiting workers chatted to us and I couldn't help contrasting the food and the trite conversations with the precious discoveries I'd made during the day.

On the pretence of inputting the day's notes, I hired a private room. Once alone I sobbed, needing to vent the pressure inside. What was I expecting from this visit? My mind had been broadened more than I'd have ever believed possible, my curiosity being satisfied at a dizzying rate. I had a feeling that my old way of living would never satisfy me again. And yet, part of me longed for the security and peace of the Citidome.

Anna's words – don't fight your feelings – reverberated in my ears. But how could I not fight them?

I turned my attention to the book – creased and yellowed. I flicked through the pages and savoured the smell, then immersed myself in the world of *Wuthering Heights*. I was pretty good at speedreading, but the language was unfamiliar and the novel wasn't an easy read. I devoured each page until my eyes would no longer stay open, fascinated and shocked by the savagery of emotions in the tempestuous story.

Soon I was lost. The image of Cathy and Heathcliff running wild as children on the moors thrilled me. When I came to the point at which Cathy declared, "I am Heathcliff," my spirits soared higher than I'd have imagined possible and, at the same time, tears flooded down my cheeks. I was devastated by the concept of a love so intense it consumed and destroyed. How could a work of fiction seem so real? As the story developed, Heathcliff perplexed me.

To Daretodream from Walkunafraid. What are you doing? I'm watching a deadly media show and missing you.

To Walkunafraid from Daretodream. Missing you too. Reading Anna's book – you should read this after me. Passion, hatred, revenge, it's a sort of anti-Mind Values. I can't decide whether I love or hate the main character. But, oh, it makes me feel alive. I want to feel like this with you.

By the end, I skimmed through pages, desperate to finish. In truth, I felt disappointed. It wasn't the ending I wanted. If that's what passion did, no wonder society used to be in such a mess. And yet the book had lodged itself in my brain. The idea that Cathy and Heathcliff could live neither with nor without each other haunted me, and I couldn't get the image of them out of my head. Oh no, I'd only left three hours to sleep. I returned to the RestPod, and gratefully selected UltraSleep.

***

Was it really morning already? Dazed by the sudden change from intense sleep to wakefulness, I climbed out of the RestPod and lumbered over to the sanitation facilities.

"You look like you had UltraSleep," a cheery voice said.

I raised my head, catching my breath. Mac was wearing only a towel, revealing a smattering of curly dark hairs on his chest. I stared at him for what seemed an infinite time, fighting an urge to touch his chest, stroke it. What would the hair feel like against my smooth body? What was wrong with me? These were sick, perverse thoughts, but I couldn't stop myself. Finally, I had the words for the feelings I'd suppressed for months. I loved him, wanted to be with him always. He beamed, as if he could see into my core and recognized the change in me.

"See you at breakfast." He winked.

My skin feverish with hope, I dressed quickly. What now? I'd glimpsed a magical new world. How could I return to the old one?

CHAPTER – 11

As we prepared to complete the final checks, my hands fumbled in fastening my coat. Once outside, I pressed my hands to my eyes, almost blinded by the reflection of the sun against the glistening frost, distracted by my thoughts. I couldn't return to the Citidome yet. Not now. It was as if the book had caused a shift in my brain. My mind was beginning to grasp that the dangerous attraction I'd fought was in fact, the most natural of emotions.

"Mac –" I stopped. What did I want to say?

"Sorry about yesterday," he said. "I threw too much at you. It wasn't fair."

"But I'm starting to get it. I love you. Let's not go back yet. I don't care what risks we take." The words hurtled out.

"I love you too." Mac placed a hand on my arm then snapped it away, with a glance at the Citidome. He said nothing for a minute. I could almost see his thought processes. "But why go back at all? We could escape now, live with Mum."

"After what you said about not throwing too much at me, you hurl a giant boulder like that!"

But a voice nagged in my brain.

Could I?

Right now I wanted nothing more than to be with him forever. But a logical voice answered. How could I live out here, in these freezing conditions? I'd die!

"I've got an idea." He called Kit. "We didn't have a very productive day yesterday. It was colder than we expected. Caia looked like she might be getting frostbite so we didn't get all the samples and instruments in place."

A pause.

"No, her hands seem fine today. A few more hours should do it; we could stay here tonight and return tomorrow morning."

Yet another pause. Would he really get away with this?

"No, don't worry. I'm right outside the entrance of Tau-2; I'll make the arrangements."

After what seemed like forever, he put his DataBand back in his pocket. "OK, I've bought us one more night. Let's finish here and go back to Mum's. We'll spend the night there."

I gave a shiver that had nothing to do with the cold. What had I agreed to?

Once more, we worked wordlessly, with fevered intensity. Two hours later, we drove back towards the hills. After fifteen minutes, the Citidome disappeared from view.

"I need you to stop," I said.

Frowning, he stopped the TravelPod at the side of the road. I flung myself into his arms and our mouths locked together. We kissed with a new urgency, and I found my lips parting under the pressure of his. Then his tongue probed my mouth. I stiffened, the unexpected invasion taking me by surprise. But it felt good. My tongue joined his in a long, lingering dance. That kiss engulfed me; I poured into it all the feelings that were gushing out. And, amidst the explosion of sensation, something changed in me, never to be reversed. The taste of him lingered long after we stopped. He held me against his chest, his hands twisting into my hair.

"I can't stop shaking," I whispered.

"Me neither. That was something else, wasn't it? Bet that peck on the cheek at New Year doesn't seem so thrilling now."

All the new thrills of the last months paled in comparison to the flood of longing that had swept away the conditioning of a lifetime. I wanted more, desire crushing any thoughts of safety. Common sense returned just in time.

"I know what you're doing," I said. "You think that'll persuade me to stay."

"Wasn't it good enough? I'd better try harder next time." He grinned, then his smile slipped, the now-familiar intensity darkening his eyes. "But why not? Life would be an adventure. We could live fully and passionately, experience new things. Find the truth. And, most importantly, we'd be together."

"Being with you … of course I want that, but oh, I don't know. We both have jobs we love. Once we're back, we can work out ways to see each other in private. What would there be for us out here, other than just survival?"

"After this, how could we go back to furtive little winks and brushing hands? I don't want to carry it all inside any more. I want to show you how I feel, all the time, wherever we are." His eyes flashed black. "I want to live, Caia. Don't you?"

"But you said yourself, it'd be madness to escape on official business. If we don't return tomorrow, Kit might think we've had an accident and send out a search party. They might track the TravelPod and find us here."

"It's worth the risk. We could hide for a few weeks. Come on, don't back out on me now. Dare to dream, remember?" His voice was low, persuasive.

Dare I dream? Dare I start a new life with Mac? To live without him in the Citidome would be torture, but at least it was comfortable. What if I couldn't stand it here? Once out, we could never go back. Our arguments spiralled round and round.

"We're wasting this precious time. Let's treasure today and make a definite decision tomorrow morning," I said.

"OK." His lips twitched into a smile, as if already plotting ways to make me stay.

By lunchtime we were back in Anna's cottage.

"I just couldn't destroy that book," I said.

"You've escaped!" Anna squealed.

"Not quite," said Mac. "We've got the rest of the day to persuade Caia to live here."

Anna was brewing in the kitchen and the air was heavy with a peculiar aroma: sweet with a hint of sulphur.

"Nothing I'd like more than for you to stay," she said. "But it's not for everyone, y'know. You've got to be sure, both of you. Tell you what – why don't you start by exploring the village?"

We strolled around the village, which appeared to be deserted, and stood at a beautiful stone bridge, watching the river.

"Just look at that clear water." I said. "When I look at a scene like this, and realise I could be looking at it every day, I want to stay here forever. But it's not as simple as that, is it?"

"I know; there's things I'd miss about Citidome life. The job, for one. But look around. Everywhere you look there's something exciting to discover. Look, I think they're sheep." Mac pointed to an area of grass uphill, where animals with bodies like dirty clouds were chewing the grass.

"Bit vacant-looking aren't they? I wouldn't feel bad about eating them." I grinned. But he was right. Every time I took in a scene for the second time I noticed something new. My eyes wanted to drink it all in and dwell on it. What was there in the Citidome to surprise and delight?

Once back, my feet were icy; the cold had penetrated my padded boots.

"Put them on my lap; I'll warm them," Mac said.

"That sounds like an offer I can't refuse. I don't think anyone's ever touched my feet before."

He stroked the base of my feet and I flinched. "Ooh, that's weird."

Anna rolled her eyes. "Looks like someone's ticklish."

"Ticklish – what does that mean?"

When Anna explained, Mac's eyes twinkled. "Let's see if you're ticklish anywhere else."

"I'll leave you kids to it," Anna said, smiling and shaking her head.

Soon we were rolling about the floor, hands grabbing each other, giggling like infants in kindergarten. Our hands slowed and once more we kissed. His hands moved to stroke my hair, my back, my hips. Heat had started to rise from low down inside me, so much that it set up an ache between my thighs. My hands explored his buttocks and thighs. His whole body tensed.

"Better not get carried away. Mum's in the next room," he whispered.

"So this is still a secret, furtive behaviour, even out here?"

"Well, everyone knows it happens, and people hold hands in public, kiss, hug, but I think anything more is kind of a private thing."

"There'd be a whole new code of behaviour? How would I know what's appropriate?" My voice rose.

"But we'd be in it together. Remember, around half the people here once lived in the Citidomes. They've all had to learn a new way of living."

Over lunch, Anna told us just how this strange world worked: all about the farm and trading arrangements with neighbouring communities at Bakewell, the nearby market town, and I realised how much I took for granted in the Citidome.

"Am I putting you off?" she said. "I want you to be certain what you're letting yourself in for. Tell me honestly what you're thinking. You won't offend me."

"Oh, I'm no closer to making my mind up than I was this morning," I said. "But I can't help wondering if my brain would turn to mush. I didn't spend half my life being fast tracked through education to become a farmer."

"That's what they all say at first." Anna smiled. "You want books? There's stacks of 'em in the stores here, not just fiction. You could learn all sorts – stuff they'd never put on the Knowledge Fountain. Teach me some of it while you're at it."

"Guess so." The thought intrigued me.

"Well, food for thought. Anyway, I'll give you a few hours to yourselves. I'll pop in on a few friends and neighbours too and try and arrange a gathering for this evening. Do you good to talk to some others."

Anna left the room, leaving Mac, for the first time, looking as confused as me.

"Makes me realise that I've had an idealised image of it all. Truth is, I don't fancy farming either," he said. "The books – yeah, they sound tempting. But why are they still in the stores? Why's no-one reading them?"

"Seems to me that there's so much to do; everyone's too tired at weekends to read. And there's all that housework she talked about. Washing your own clothes – I wouldn't know where to start. Could you believe that Anna didn't even care about how many other communities there were in the country?"

"But me and you ... we'd be different. We'd find the truth.

Come here. I want to kiss you again."

We fell into each other's arms. His lips sought mine once more, our tongues intertwining. And there it was again. That terrifying heat and hunger that took over my whole body. My mind melted. His hand cupped my breast. My nipple stiffened, my whole body trembling.

He pulled away, his voice hoarse. "Veez, this is killing me. But we can't."

I allowed myself to relax against his body, absorbing his heat, my body loosening in reprieve from the assault on my senses. "It's as if there's a voice in my head roaring, screaming for release."

"You can see what drives people to do it now, can't you?"

"C-coupling?"

"Yeah."

"What ... what was it like?"

"To be honest, I was so drunk I hardly remember. As a physical sensation – unbelievable. Beats thrill pills hands down." His head dropped. "But with her, no better than doing it myself. "

I frowned.

"Oh yeah." His lips twitched. "That's something else those guys told me. You know how they taught us in preteen that you should only wash yourself down there with a disposable wipe and it's unhygienic to touch it? Total crap. Turns out it's the most fun you can have in the Citidome."

"What on earth does that mean?" I screwed up my face. He explained and I gagged.

"I'm sure you're making it up to gross me out."

His laugh faded. "I wish I hadn't done it that way; with her, I mean. I wish it had been with someone I loved, like it's meant to be. I wish it had been with you."

I slumped against his chest, overcome with a sudden melancholy, both of us seemingly having run out of things to say. The question of escape still hung heavy in the air. An idea came to me.

"I've thought of a compromise. Your mum said that it was easy to get out through the gates. Perhaps we could go back to the Citidome and escape in spring when it's warmer. Then we can acclimatise more gradually. And it'd avoid the risk of

Kit looking for us."

"That's not a bad idea," Mac said, rubbing his chin. "If we went back we could make plans, maybe bring a few comforts with us when we do escape. Things for the village, too. More medicines. We could plan it properly. It'd take a long time to get from Sigma-2 to here, but if I could get hold of a navigator ... yeah, it'd be possible."

As we talked, the idea gathered momentum. This plan was perfect. Most importantly, it bought me more time to decide whether this was what I really, truly wanted. Eventually a loud slam of the door drew us apart.

"We've got ourselves a party this evening," Anna said.

"And we've got a plan." While Mac told Anna, my mind continued to whirl.

"It makes sense." She nodded. "I sometimes wish I'd prepared myself better. Get that dental treatment – the UltraCoating one. It's expensive, but your money's no good out here. I had to have a tooth pulled out last year – it wasn't fun. Talk to Daniel – he's our leader – this evening. He'll advise you what to bring out with you."

That evening, we strolled down the street, but it seemed an entirely different place. The houses had been swallowed up. Darkness. I'd never experienced it before. The Citidomes were bathed in perpetual lights. Residences had daylight and a dim nightlight setting. Even in a RestPod, lights pulsated at varying speeds, which slowed the brain waves. Over the day I'd marvelled at the subtleties of the different qualities of sunlight: the blinding brilliance of early morning; the way the late afternoon sun set the landscape on fire; long, sinister evening shadows; the soft haze of twilight and now total blackout, except for that compelling glow in the sky.

"Look, a full moon."

It was huge, and I swear it winked at me, as if saying, go on. Do it. As my eyes acclimatised, I noticed tiny pinpoints of light sparkling in the void. Part of me wanted to keep on looking, but a shiver propelled me forward. It wasn't so much the bone-chilling temperature, but something else. A feeling of disorientation, of constriction. If the outside world was daunting by day, by night it was truly fearsome. I reached for Mac's hand.

We pushed a heavy door and the room fell silent as around twenty people turned to look at us. I put my hand to my hair, suddenly shy. I'd never been under such obvious scrutiny before. But, although I felt I was being judged, I sensed a sort of mutual empathy that made the atmosphere unthreatening. Daniel had a beard, which took me by surprise. I'd never seen one before. Anna had told me he was forty-two but, like her, he looked older than Citidome dwellers of that age.

"Hey, you must be Mac and Caia. After Anna came to see me I spoke to the council – that's the group of elected members that makes all the decisions. You're welcome to join us. But everyone out here has to pull his or her weight, and that includes working on the land. We'll make use of your technical expertise at some stage." I suppressed a giggle; I couldn't see how positron analysers or ultrasonic microspectroscopy would be much use out here. "But in summer we need everyone under fifty to do outdoor work – farming and so on. It's tough work. I don't want you to be under any romantic illusions. And once you're out of the Citidome, there's no going back, so don't stay unless you're sure."

No going back. The words seemed to echo around the room.

"Thanks. Actually, we've had a change of plan. We thought we'd go back to the Citidome tomorrow and return in the spring with supplies for the village," Mac said. "Our team leader thinks we're at Tau-2; he might try to find us here if we don't go back."

"That'd be amazing." Daniel's smile softened the severity of his scary, hairy face. "Give me your DataBand; I'll input a list of things we need. And talk to Daisy; she's the most recent escapee so she'll be the best person to tell you how to get through the gates. In fact, talk to everyone. Ask plenty of questions. Make sure you know what you're letting yourself in for."

"If we ever escape, fill your bag with razors," I whispered to Mac. "Can't picture you with a beard."

"Me neither. I always wondered what it'd look like. Veez, it's so bushy. There might be wildlife in there." He grinned, rubbing his chin. "Anyway, better not talk to each other all night. Let's check out the social life."

As I peered at this technicolour patchwork of characters – patchwork being the operative word, judging by the frayed state of their clothes – I noticed that few of the villagers were as frail as Anna. Most were wiry and spare, but they looked healthier than BodyPerfects. Only their skin, darkened and scarred by the sun, betrayed their lifestyles. I'd have no difficulty recognising these people again; Citidome people were identikit in comparison. All dressed imaginatively, in bright woollen jackets, animal furs and scarves. I felt underdressed in my Ministry uniform, my colours muted in this vivid composition.

"Hey, Caia, I'm Vanessa," a young woman said in a strange accent, "What d'you think of the outside world?"

"Mindblowing, but cold. How long have you lived here?"

"Since I were a kid. You Citidome lot are all soft about the cold at first. You toughen up."

I was soon engrossed in Vanessa's tales of village life and became used to her peculiar flat vowel sounds. But as she talked, I noticed her stealing a glance at Mac. In fact, all the younger women were doing the same. Out here, it appeared, everyone saw him for what he was – the best-looking guy in the room. A cold, hard knot formed in my stomach. This was how life was going to be from now on. When you threw open the doors to your inner being, you let in pain. The self-control imposed in the Citidome served a purpose: it was a protective coating, and I'd lost mine. The knot tightened as I noticed him talking to others with a confidence that I'd never have. I'd always be in his shadow.

At that moment, a terrifying thought pierced my brain. He'd been attracted to someone before me. Anna's relationship didn't last. I remembered the words of the Knowledge Fountain: long-term relationships never lasted. What if I stayed here, only to lose him to one of these girls who were so obviously attracted to him? I'd rather live the rest of my life in the Citidome without him than out here in the frozen wilds, watching him with someone else. I gazed at him now, chatting to a BodyPerfect girl who was laughing at his every word, and felt sick with fear.

"Caia, come and meet my closest friend," Anna said and,

as I approached, her voice lowered. "You doing OK, sweetheart?"

"Not really." I chewed on the lining of my mouth. "Look at Mac. He's so funny and charming, and I'm not. That beautiful girl he's talking to looks like she's attracted to him. He'll leave me for someone else. I know it."

"Hey, no more of that," Anna said, putting an arm around me. "That's Daisy, and she's with the big guy over there. He'll be getting advice about escaping. But I know how you're feeling. Jealousy goes hand-in-hand with being in love, I'm afraid. Mac wouldn't leave you; he absolutely worships you. He told me so. Have a glass of this plum wine and come and meet Kate."

I chatted to Kate, who was absolutely fascinating. She was older than Anna, but fleshier, which suited her. Her white hair was the curliest I'd ever seen, and her face sprinkled with tiny brown flecks.

"Curlier than pig's tails, me mam used to say," said Kate. "And it used to be the colour of carrots. I'm the spitting image of me grandmother. I get me freckles from her too. Kisses from the sun, they are. Bet you can pick out me children a mile off."

"The big guy and the woman over there?" I pointed at Daisy's guy and a woman who bore a striking resemblance to him. Both had red-blonde hair. Daisy's guy also had a beard, but a more controlled one than Daniel's.

"That's right. Peter and Margaret. They're twins. Bet you don't know what that means."

Soon I was absorbed by the details of Kate's family and her job as a weaver, and Anna topped up my glass. As Anna introduced me to more people, I found myself immersed in life stories so diverse it was hard to take in. Margaret had given birth to three small children, and was a member of the village council. The level of organisation staggered me – how was it possible that outside communities had thrived for over three generations and no-one in the Citidomes knew?

"Come and meet my granddaughter, Mary," Kate said. "Though she's more like a daughter. Her mum, God bless her, died just after she was born and her father were a Citidome guy who took off as soon he got her knocked up, so we brought her up."

Mary was less than two years older than me but much more knowing.

"What job do you do?" I asked.

"I look after the horses. But – you'll probably hear from the others so I may as well tell you – I get luxuries from the trader. I trade meself, if you get me meaning."

"Oh, er … yeah." I fumbled with my words, anxious not to offend, but could feel the heat in my face. I remembered Daniel's advice to ask plenty of questions. "I can see how the village does well out of it, but what's in it for you?"

"Popularity. I grew up without any friends me own age. Last year, I wandered over to the Citidome trader stall in the market and this guy called Shin asked if I wanted any candies. They looked so tempting but I had nowt to offer. He stroked my hair and asked if I'd ever been with a man. When I told him no, he said that if I met him in half an hour behind the market square I could have the candies."

"Weren't you scared?"

"Yeah, but … it was the first time anyone had made me feel important, special, y'know? Grandma and Granddad were bloody livid, but they came round. Now I get extras for everyone. I get to go to the market every week and Shin's a good guy, so everyone's happy."

"I guess so." But it sounded sad to me.

"Anyway, you've got to come and live here. We could be mates." I glowed. Was it really so easy to make friends out here? "There's Daisy now, as well. She escaped last year; she's nearly twenty."

"Hey, did I hear my name mentioned?" Daisy joined us. "I've just been talking to your lush guy." Lush? An icicle pierced me. But Daisy continued, unperturbed. "He told me you're planning to escape in spring. Great plan; the cold's a bloody killer isn't it? Pack your bags full of vegelate and coffee. Smuggle me out some Bliss and you've got yourself a friend for life. Even Mary can't get 'em." Daisy's words didn't so much flow out as bubble. Although her build and accent were recognisable as originating from the Citidome, her cheeky grin belonged here. I'd have liked her instantly, if I hadn't seen her laughing with Mac.

141

"You don't regret escaping?" I asked.

"Never. Best thing I ever did. Piece of cake getting out, honestly. Bribe a guard with all the currency you have, if you have any hassle. It'll be no use to you once you leave. Don't think about it too hard, Caia, or you'll talk yourself out of it. Anyway, come and meet my Peter."

Peter was heavyset and rugged. He unnerved me, not that he was unfriendly, but less effusive than the others. He looked me up and down in a way that made me feel uneasy, reminding me that these people were more bestial, less civilized than citizens. But clearly his behaviour wasn't considered abnormal, as Daisy continued to talk with an openness that shocked me.

"How did you get together with Mac?"

"We work together." I'd hardly got my head around the fact that I'd 'got together' with Mac, let alone talking about it. I liked these people, but I wasn't comfortable with the way they talked.

Armed only with strange stringed objects, two men sang and played.

"Lovely music – ancient tunes, I guess?" I asked.

"Yeah, some of it centuries old. The small round thing's a banjo, the bigger one a guitar. It beats that digitally generated shit hands down, doesn't it?" said Daisy.

"Yeah, way more intimate." The music was gentle, melodic. It matched the feel of the village.

I lost count of how many glasses of wine I'd had but it had taken effect. I was talking more, less worried about what everyone thought of me. Mac flung an arm around me, his face flushed.

"Having fun?"

"It's wonderful!"

Right now, everything was wonderful. The band finished playing. I noticed someone programming what looked like a DataBand, then familiar rhythms pounded around the room. Daisy and Peter started to dance.

"How on earth do they get current music?"

"The traders. Better than Uma's party, isn't it?"

"Huh, don't remind me. I still haven't forgiven you for dancing with her."

"Don't forget, you danced with Masa. Anyway, what was I supposed to do? When she said that you talked about me all the time, I thought she'd get suspicious. So, fancy that dance I owe you?"

We started dancing the way Mac and Uma had danced in the Citidome, our hips swaying in unison. Then, in a move that would get us flung straight into a correction centre, we drew together until our bodies pressed against each other's, my arms around his neck, his round my waist. Our hips locked and rotated with the rhythm of the music. My body burned, licking flames of desire that craved release.

After another dance, I noticed that the party was starting to break up.

"Mum said that if we wanted to go early, she'd give us some time to ourselves before she got back," he whispered with a wink. "Can't think what she had in mind."

"Let's go, now."

We said our goodbyes and ran back to the cottage, no longer able to keep our hands off each other. I couldn't hold back any more; my body had taken control and was screaming for satisfaction.

"Not all the way. We can't ... the Mark." He pulled away.

"I don't care. I want this."

Giggling and fumbling, we took each other's clothes off.

"You're ... breathtaking."

"S-so are you," and he was, but as I took in all of him, I had to stop my jaw from dropping to the floor. Not that I hadn't seen a penis before: Mik and Von rarely bothered to wear towels on the way in and out of the shower, but theirs were soft, small and unthreatening. Now I stared aghast at this huge, hard, protuberance, more weapon than benign anatomical part. And he had hair down there too! In this moment, he barely seemed human.

"Don't be scared ... I'll try not to hurt you. Tell me if it doesn't feel good or you want me to stop."

Hurt? My body froze; what exactly was he going to do to me? His fingers and tongue flickered over my breasts then slowly travelled downwards. Lower, to that place where I'd never been touched. Veez, what was he doing now? Something urgent grew and throbbed inside me. I gasped.

The feeling was incredible, exquisite, but at the same time tormenting. I wasn't sure whether I wanted it to go on or end. I was falling, no, not falling, soaring ... then everything was shuddering sensation, as if something had burst inside me.

"Better than a thrill pill?"

"A million times better." I giggled.

He pushed against me. Ah, I realized what he was trying to do. Finally, I understood what coupling involved. When I tensed at the shock of pain, he stopped, his eyes warm with concern.

"I'm OK, don't stop," I murmured.

He was inside me. Actually inside me! And we were no longer two people. We'd combined into one glorious, burning entity, moving together in ecstatic frenzy. Woow. And afterwards, the breathless euphoria of lying in his arms, my body spent but still twitching.

"That was ... oh, I don't have the words," I whispered.

"Mindblowing." He planted kisses on my cheeks, my forehead and then – oh – on my eyelids.

The whole scene was wondrous: all entangled bodies and shared heat, my head rising and falling with the rhythm of his breathing. In a matter of minutes, everything I believed about the world, about myself, had been flipped inside out.

At least, that's how it felt at the time. When I woke to the terrifying darkness, it was a different story. Disorientated, my mouth dry, overwhelmed by nausea and a full bladder, I held my throbbing head. What was that raw soreness between my legs? Mac lay beside me, his breath coming out in alien snorts. The room was icy. I flicked on the lamp beside my head. As I rose, the room started tilting and spinning. Oh no – where was I going? Ah, there it was – the bucket in the corner. I urinated into it and the vomit rose in my throat – sour, gross. It spilled out of my mouth before I had chance to lean over the bucket.

I woke again on the floor, my body numb with cold, to the stench of vomit. It was all over the floor and caked to my face. As I eased myself upright, I flinched. There was a rank stickiness between my legs and running down my thighs. It smelled, of heat and salt and something else, something I remember from my early days in the laboratory, an almost deviant smell of uncleansed, mingled bodies. Look at me, lying in my own filth, worse than any animal. There was a towel by the bed. I scoured the carpet with it.

Light was beginning to peek through the holes in the ragged cloth that covered the window. I climbed back into the bed and saw a smear on the sheet. Blood. It must have been from when Mac tore into me. The stupefying horror of what we'd done struck me with full force. The animal act! I'd be Marked. He stirred and looked at me, and kissed my forehead.

"It wasn't a dream. Hey, you're absolutely frozen." He sniffed. "Oh no, did you throw up? We had a bit much, didn't we? I had the spins just before I fell asleep, and – shit – I've got a stinking headache now. How about you?" He rubbed warmth into my frigid body.

"What have we done?" I whimpered.

"Something pretty amazing, if I remember rightly." He grinned, then his voice became tender. "Don't torture yourself. Did it feel unnatural? Disgusting?"

"No, it felt good, unbelievably good. But we shouldn't have done it."

He reached out to draw me towards him but I held back.

"We can't. The Mark ..."

"Too late to worry about that. One more time won't hurt. We'll have to stay here now."

I turned away. "No. I have to go back. We'll have to find someone, get it removed."

"Are you mad? I knew someone, remember? No, it's way too risky."

"Surely there's other people that do it illegally? We could ask on the Truth Exchange. Anyway, we're not safe if they find us, nor is anyone else here. Kit's bound to send someone out looking for us."

"I talked to Daniel last night. They can take the chip out of the TravelPod."

"But this is the closest settlement to Tau-2. They know we were there this morning."

"Remember the latest directives. If you get the Mark, they take you somewhere outside of the Citidome. We can't risk that."

"I don't want a horrible Mark on my face!" I wailed like an infant. "How long will it take to appear?"

"About a week. Don't think about it. You'll always be gorgeous; a bit of discolouration won't change that."

"A whole week? Then can't we try and find someone? My skin's so dark it won't show as much. I could hide it with facebase. We could pass the sickness off as a virus I caught outside. If we don't find anyone in a few days, we'll leave again with all the supplies for the village; how's that?"

"I guess … if you're sure. How about a hug instead?"

I moved towards him but couldn't relax, my body rigid with shame. I felt gross. I needed to shower. The stink of my degradation – a mix of sweat, vomit and mingled body fluids – clung to me. I scrubbed myself with soap and water, but I wasn't sure I'd ever feel clean again. Anna was already in the kitchen making breakfast when I came downstairs. Her knowing smile made me feel even worse.

"You don't have to say anything; your face says it all. Just remember, you've nothing to be ashamed of."

"As well as – you know what – I was sick. I've messed up the bedroom." I started crying again.

She drew me against her and I relaxed into her embrace. Oh, I wish she was my mum. This was exactly what I needed right now.

"We had a thick frost last night. Come and see," Anna said.

Yesterday, I'd have been in raptures at the transformation of the back yard to a crystalline palace. But this morning I could only nod and murmur, "It's lovely."

"You have to stay now. You'll be Marked."

"I want to, but we still run the risk of being found if we stay now. Mac got his Mark removed. I'm sure I can do the same. We'll come back but, for now, I need the Citidome."

"If you're sure." Anna sighed. "Wait a minute; I heard one of Margaret's kids came down with the flu. Let's go see after breakfast. If you get infected with something else, it'll mask the symptoms."

Mac came down, not looking me in the eye, but moved forward to hug me. I put my arms in the right place, rested my head against his chest, but my body didn't mould to his the way it did yesterday.

"Come on, you two," said Anna. "No-one died, did they?"

"My head hurts," I moaned.

"That's called a hangover, sweetheart. Try this bacon sandwich. Kill or cure."

I ate the bacon sandwich mechanically, almost failing to notice that the smoked bacon had a stunning flavour and texture, nothing like the rubbery protibacon I was used to. As I stared at the sandwich, as if it was the cause of all my problems, I heard the low rumble of voices from the other room. Then, as if I didn't feel soiled enough already, I had to face the stinking toilet again, cringing at the alternative to the bidet function. Before plunging my hand into the bucket of water by the door, I had to break through its icy crust. Once back, Anna took me to see Margaret. Sure enough, her daughter was tucked up in bed.

"Put your mouth close to hers," Margaret instructed, as if this were an everyday occurrence. "Now, breathe in."

Inhaling the child's stale, germ-laden breath was the final indignity, killing the remnants of my fantasies of living here. Back at Anna's house, a cloud had descended over us all.

"Time to go," said Mac.

I hugged Anna. "Thanks for everything."

"Good luck. I'll see you soon." Anna's voice was unconvinced.

Our journey back was so sober, our conversation so prosaic.

"You'll see the Mark a day or so before you get the sickness," Mac said. "You'll feel nausea, dizziness and faintness at recurring intervals for a few weeks. It'll be severe at first but it's not uncommon to get infections on your first time out of the Citidome. Pretend you're feeling ill as soon as we get back. Don't worry about finding someone to remove it. Leave that to me. We'll communicate by the Truth Exchange."

The magic that had bound us dissolved. I could barely manage a smile, and was almost relieved when the landscape became increasingly bleak and Sigma-2 loomed ahead of us.

"Will you stop looking at me like I'm creevil?" His voice was tight.

A wave of remorse washed over me. This might be my last

chance to be alone with him for months, and I'd been so cold.

"I'm sorry. Whatever happens, I'll always love you," I whispered.

He stopped the TravelPod, grasped my face and we kissed, a last, exquisite memory to treasure. I wished I could take his breath and solidify it; a token of our time together, so that when time had dulled the memory of the week I could look at it and remind myself that it really happened. I felt certain it was destined to stay that way, a memory.

CHAPTER – 12

The Citidome gates opened, we passed security clearance, and checked in at the Ministry. How strange. It was as if nothing had changed, and yet everything had.

"How was it?" asked Dal, his voice eager.

"Freezing! You didn't miss much. Go stand in the minus-twenty room and try and manipulate sensors and SolarPlas samples, then you'll get a good idea of what it was like," I grumbled, and if Dal had spotted a change in me, a new knowledge and shame in my eyes, he didn't comment.

"Good to have you back," said Kit. "Did it all go well?"

"Yeah," said Mac. "The cold was vile – the worst I've ever known out there – but we managed to get everything in place."

After a debriefing, Kit dismissed us early.

"You both look exhausted, you especially, Caia. I don't want you getting ill. Go back to your res and rest."

"Thanks, that'd be great. I must admit I feel lousy," I said, remembering to prepare the lie.

"I'm going straight for a hot tub. You should too, Caia. See you tomorrow," said Mac as if it was just another ordinary day.

My hand moved; already it felt instinctive to reach out and touch him, but I stopped myself. I trudged along the well-trodden route past offices and residences while around me the peaceful life of the Citidome continued as normal. Every cell in my body rebelled against the artificial calm. I fought the urge to shout, "This isn't normal! There's a whole other world out there!" Soon I was back at the residence, and remembered a word that Anna had taught me: home. Anna's house was a home, filled with love. All I had was a RestPod, a chill in my bones, a handful of memories and a pit of shame in my stomach.

As the door to the leisure room slid open, I crept in, my shoulders tensing. I felt so altered that surely the others would notice? But Uma was out on one of her rare working days. Mik, staring at the media console with empty eyes, only acknowledged me with a grunt, and Von was on the OmniTrainer so barely glanced in my direction.

"Hey, kitten, how was the big wide world?" Von said.

"Horrible. So cold I lost feeling in my fingers and toes and I'm sure I'm coming down with something." I told him tales of snowflakes and trees, the sort of things he expected to hear, but he was soon distracted; the climax of the WildLife series was approaching. I glanced round the leisure room that had once impressed me and felt stifled. Had it always been so narrow, so constricting? I remembered with longing the sunlight streaming in through Anna's windows. This room was windowless, its light artificial.

"Hey, I have snacks and Bliss for the big night!" Uma arrived. "Woow, kitten, you look like death!"

"I feel like death. It was creeving cold out there; I'm still chilled. I'd better go to my room in case I picked something up; I don't want to infect you all. What I really need is a good soak in the hot tub then a long sleep program."

The relief of being alone engulfed me. I edged into the tub and soaked until I couldn't take the heat any more. Returning to my room, I climbed into the RestPod. It was too early to sleep so I selected a mind clearing program. Almost immediately as my head hit the headrest I reached out, remembering Mac's warm body next to mine. A physical craving seized me, like an itch I couldn't scratch but worse. Much worse. This was torture, as if a switch had been flicked inside my body, and I couldn't control it. My hand reached downwards and I touched the part of myself I'd never before touched. I snatched it back. No, I just couldn't. My memories of the evening were still hazy but as I tried to reassemble the events, clarity returned with a thud. Oh no. I'd started it. Poor Mac. How must he be feeling now?

I rose from the Pod, ended the program and recorded my adventure on my DataBand while still fresh in my mind. My hands trembled as I entered the words. Twice I stopped and deleted what I'd written. Surely the memories of the week were so etched into my brain that I should let them stay there, safe. If anyone read this ... but I felt compelled to continue, if only to try and make sense of it all. As an afterthought, I logged into the Truth Exchange and my pulse quickened at the sight of a message in the chat room:

> To Daretodream from Walkunafraid: How does it feel to be back? I'm miserable and missing you like mad. Let's get you well and head back to where we belong. I hope you don't regret what we did. I'll treasure the memory forever.

Immediately I replied, though my words seemed foolish – insufficient to carry the weight of feeling behind them.

> To Walkunafraid from Daretodream: I'm miserable too. No regrets, except for how I was this morning – cold, snippy. You're part of me now. I'll never wake again without longing to have you next to me, for your face to be the first thing I see each morning, for your body touching mine to be my first waking feeling. I love you. I love you. I love you.

I relived the night in my mind, the dancing, the music, the way our bodies had moulded together. I tried to recapture the sensations, the taste of his mouth on mine, the smell of the fresh perspiration of our entwined bodies, even our mingled fluids. But now the fire that blazed had gone out and in its place was a cold, lifeless pile of ashes. That's why Mind Values tried to suppress passion, nagged my rational voice. It's a destructive disease.

I slept badly, resisting the best efforts of the RestPod, and returned to work heavy-eyed the next day, after dulling my skin with some of Uma's facebase I found in the restroom. Only Jana and Mac were in, and he looked as dejected as I felt.

"Hey, Caia. Have you warmed up yet? Even last night I felt

chilled to the bone."

"Hey, Mac. Hey, Jana." I tried to mimic Mac's casual manner, but every muscle fibre tensed with longing. "I'm the same. I'm not sure I'll ever feel my toes again. And I still feel like death."

"You look awful. Hope you're not coming down with something."

"Yeah, you do look pale. You really drew the short straw, going outside in January," said Jana.

I let out a long, unsteady breath. The air around us was fizzing. Could Jana see it? Could I really be in the same room as Mac, treating him exactly as I had before, when all I wanted to do was inhale the air around him, dance with him and – yes, I admitted it – couple with him. Somehow I survived the day, fell into the familiar routines, and was happy to be back at work. I needed to tax my brain, find a point of focus.

To Daretodream from Walkunafraid: Someone has recommended a surgeon so I'll contact her. I nearly forgot myself and touched your hair this morning. You don't know what it does to me, being near you and not being able to touch you. You should come with a health warning. I might spontaneously combust one day.

To Walkunafraid from Daretodream: Thanks, you're amazing. It's the smell of you that does my head in. And when you leaned over me to help with my frozen screen I felt your breath on my ear. Part of me wanted to grab your hand and run straight out of the place, but this has to be the best way, doesn't it?

To Daretodream from Walkunafraid: I think so. Best we plan it properly, but it's killing me. And that screen wasn't frozen at all, you wicked girl!

But too quickly the memories of our time together faded. Within days my throat swelled to the extent that I could hardly swallow. The next day, it felt as if I were swallowing scalpel blades. The following day my nose blocked. When would the Mark come? Soon, hopefully. If I was unlucky enough to need medical attention, I needed the sickness before the influenza symptoms disappeared. And two days later, there it was. I looked into the mirror and bumps rose on my arms, my flesh recoiling from the vile purple stain that had oozed outwards from the centre of my cheek. Luckily, thanks to my dark skin, it was nowhere near as livid as the ones I'd seen on beggars, but it extended almost as far as my jaw. I visited the rest room every half hour to smother on facebase. That evening I found an even bigger blemish smeared across my thigh. Gross.

> To Walkunafraid from Daretodream: The Marks are here, two of them, one on my cheek – just my luck – and they're freaking huge. But facebase totally covers them. And my throat's agony. Hope to come into work tomorrow but in case I don't get to talk to you for a few days, remember that I love you and don't regret a single thing that happened.

The next day, Mac gazed at me, his expression tender. I shot him an annoyed glance. What if someone noticed? Then without warning, nausea overcame me and I vomited in the toilets. As I raised my head, the cubicle span. I clung to the toilet bowl to steady myself. Slowly, I rose to my feet but the spinning continued. Oh no, not here, not now. How would I ever make it back to the office? Relax. Take it slowly. Apply more facebase. The dizziness eased and I tottered back, but the bones in my legs had turned to rubber.

"Kit, I don't feel well," I croaked.

"Don't come any closer. You may have contracted a virus outside. I'll call a health worker."

"Stupid girl. She's so stubborn. I kept telling her to take sick leave. She hasn't been feeling well all week." The harsh tone of Mac's voice made me want to cry, even though I knew he was acting. It was the last thing I heard before I collapsed into a chair. I was only vaguely aware of the health workers, covered in masks and gowns, zipping me into a bag. While one wheeled me away on a trolley, I heard another saying, "I'll need you all to leave the office for five minutes while I spray it with disinfectant."

I felt as if a flashing neon sign was pointing at me: Unclean! Unclean! The next few days passed in a blur. I drifted in and out of sleep, losing track of time.

"You can come out now, Caia," an unfamiliar voice urged.

"I don't want to." I wanted to stay in the comforting cocoon of the IsolationPod.

"Now, come on. Take it slowly."

I tottered to the restroom, looked in the mirror, and released a sigh. The facebase was still intact. There was a faint shadow on my cheek where I'd sweated, but no-one had been close enough to notice. I smeared on a fresh layer. I swallowed, grimaced, and shuffled back.

"What day is it?"

"Saturday. You've been in isolation for five days," said the health worker. "Your virus load is still higher than I'd expect, but you shouldn't be contagious any more. Your time outside suggests that you contracted influenza but the symptom pattern isn't a hundred percent consistent." Her eyes lingered on my face for a second longer than felt comfortable. I swallowed. I hadn't realised they'd assess my virus load. "If you don't feel better in a day or so, come back and we'll try and identify the specific virus."

I took a TravelPod back to the residence; walking was too much effort.

"Hey, kitten, where have you been?" said Uma.

"An IsolationPod. I got an influenza virus outside."

"Eeuw." Uma, Von and Mika shrank into their seats. To them I was unclean too.

To Walkunafraid from Daretodream: They let me out. I'll be back at work on Monday, but can I see you before that?

To Daretodream from Walkunafraid: I'll be alone from 20:00 to 22:00 tonight. Come over.

It seemed to take me forever to walk the short distance to his residence. I had to remind myself how to walk. "How can you look so hot and so sick at the same time?" He grinned, and then chucked my chin. "How are you?" "Better now I've seen you. But honestly? I feel like shit." I followed him into the leisure room, then he crushed my body against his. Woow. Even here, knowing that someone could burst in on us at any time, this felt so right. We kissed until, breathless and wheezing, I had to draw away, and burst into a fit of coughing. He lifted me up and carried me to a seat. As he knelt by me, I squeezed his hand, as if by letting go he'd disappear.

"Sorry, too much," he said. "It gets better. You'll probably have good and bad days for the next few weeks. Anyway, you've covered the Mark well. Which side is it?"

I pointed.

"Really?" He looked closely. "I can't see anything. Do you want a drink?"

"Vitaboost, if you've got any."

He went to the kitchen and returned with a large glass. "So, me and you. We still OK? You forgiven me?"

"Forgiven what? I started it." I giggled.

"Wasn't sure if you remembered. You were absolutely smashed."

"I remember everything. And I'd do it all over again if I could."

His mouth went to my throat, his lips moving down towards my breasts. The forbidden feeling stirred, and my stomach lurched.

"Sorry, I'll have to stop. I feel sick."

"Huh, charming. That's not good for a guy's ego." He winked.

"The health worker told me to rest and avoid unnecessary excitement. I don't suppose she imagined this."

"How about an unexciting hug instead?"

I buried my head in his chest and inhaled the smell of him.

"Can I take this shirt back with me? I need to have

something of you."

"Mmm, nice idea. Only if I can take yours."

I ripped mine off and put his on, it was enormous on me. I hugged myself before tucking the shirt into my pants, rolling up the sleeves. At the sight of him shirtless, I flung myself against him and kissed his bare chest. Oh, he was beautiful. He groaned, his breathing accelerating. This time he pulled away.

"I've unleashed something wicked in you, haven't I? If you do that any more I'll explode." He stood up. "Let me put something else on."

Once he'd left the room I breathed slowly and deliberately. The nausea was back with full force. What was I playing at? Surely I could control myself better than that?

"Have you managed to contact the surgeon?" I asked.

"Yeah. You have to meet her at 1051 Eastern Boulevard, 22:00 next Friday. She's expensive though. ¥2000 per Mark."

"Four thousand? How are we going to afford it? I don't have that much."

"I've taken on some extra work. I'm going to edit the Knowledge Fountain at weekends. I'll resist the temptation to put the truth in it." He winked. "I've already got three thousand. I should get two hundred in the next week. Give me your details and I'll transfer the money."

"Guess we won't need it any more when we're out of here."

"Exactly. I went to the health worker and got some antivirals, told them I was coming down with something. It's the first of my stash of things to take in spring."

"Fantastic. I've already started collecting fruit seeds, and I ordered extra toothpaste and brushes."

We chatted about escape and the things we planned to take with us, and I left in an optimistic mood, but it soon faded. That night I held his shirt against my face, drinking in his scent, but I couldn't recapture the feeling of him next to me.

As the sickness faded, my discontent grew. The sickly harsh fluorescent Citidome lights repelled me. I craved the flicker of sunlight through cloud and the golden glow of firelight. I wanted to see trees randomly placed and shaped, not in neat rows. I remembered the happy faces of the villagers at the dance. I heard Anna telling me that love was worth more than Citidome comforts. Then I remembered something else. Those girls, looking at Mac. Daisy's head thrown back in laughter. Losing him to someone else would be worse than never being with him at all. So much for a perfect new life. The flames of hope flickered and ebbed.

***

It was Friday night on Eastern Boulevard. In the quietest part of the Citidome, a woman emerged from the side entrance of a building. I stared at her; was she a CE? No – she had no disc on her cheek. Glancing around, I pointed towards my face. The woman inclined her head and walked back inside the building, holding the door open. I followed her down an unlit corridor to a room – obviously a private clinic – and let out a slow, unsteady breath. The woman locked the door behind us.

"Payment first," she said, a thread of steel running through her voice.

I handed over my DataBand.

"Show me the Mark."

I wiped my face and pulled my pants down to expose my thigh.

"Two Marks? You've only paid for one."

"¥2000 per Mark, we were told."

"No, it's ¥4000 per Mark."

I gasped. She was ripping me off – I was sure of it – but what could I do? "I haven't got that much."

"In that case I can only do one. And your 'friend' didn't mention that you're dark-skinned. The ultralight causes temporary pigment loss; I'll have to give you a special cream."

"B-but –"

"No buts. You have to appreciate the risks I take. I could lose my job. I'll do the one on your face; you can hide the one on your thigh. Use facebase. Message me when you've raised the extra money, then delete my details." She proffered her finger and I took her details. "Now, sit down. I need to be quick."

I slumped to the chair and closed my eyes. Would this hurt? I felt a pleasant coolness – she was wiping my face – but then came a sharp burning, like hundreds of pinpricks in quick succession. The health worker worked efficiently. Pulse after pulse of ultralight wiped the shame from my face. Fifteen minutes, it was all over.

"That was quick. Are you sure you can't do my leg now? I'll pay you a thousand now, the rest as soon as I can."

"Huh, I don't do anything without the money upfront." She sprayed my face and applied a wad of fibres. "I've uploaded the aftercare instructions on your DataBand. It'll be red for a few days. Your skin tone might be lighter where you've been treated so you'll still need facebase. Here's some cream to fully restore the colour. Now hurry out by the way you came in."

I tiptoed outside, seething with injustice. I checked my DataBand. Twenty past ten. I couldn't go back to the res now, too suspicious. Von had seen me earlier without a pad on my cheek; no-one would legitimately be discharged from surgery at this time. Idly, I wandered around the streets, alive with weekend parties. Game Zones and clubs glowed enticingly. Should I call Mac, see if he'd keep me company? No, we were supposed to be playing it safe, not being seen together in public. Besides, I had neither the energy nor the inclination for dancing. But how could I be inconspicuous all night?

Ah, a performance was about to begin at the movie theatre. I paid my entrance and tried to doze in my seat, though the noise, dazzling lights and 3D images penetrated my brain even with my eyes closed. Citidome movies were light on plot and heavy on action, and explosions and the acrid smell of burning flesh filled the theatre, leaving no room for thought. Two movies later, the Citidome refused to sleep.

Now, what else could I do? Steam rooms and hot tubs were out of the question since I had to keep my legs covered. A massage wouldn't be possible either. I had a manicure and pedicure, a haircut, and then inspiration struck. A blissful session in the Float Zone loosened my tension. Finally, it was morning. I ambled back to the residence in the hope that everyone had left for the exercise centre. But Uma was still in the middle of her morning stretches.

"Woow, what happened to you?"

"A mole. It changed shape so I had to have it removed." I'd already prepared the lie. "It must have been while I was outside. I wasn't careful enough with sunscreen. So unfair; we only had one sunny day."

"I didn't notice a mole."

"That's the wonder of facebase."

"Euw, first an infection and now a mole. I'm never leaving the Citidome." Uma shuddered. "Anyway, I'm late for my workout. Join me?"

"No, I'll give it a miss today. I'm still wiped out from the influenza."

How long could I keep this up? How many near misses would I get away with?

To Walkunafraid from Daretodream: Come over now if you can, everyone will be at the exercise centre for an hour.

Five minutes later Mac arrived. I spilled out the story of the surgeon.

"What am I going to do?" I sobbed.

"What a crook. I'll try to find someone else. We'll raise the cash; don't worry. Put a heat dressing on it for now; say it's a muscular strain."

A sound from the door jolted us apart. Mik had returned early.

"Am I interrupting something?" He frowned at my tear-streaked face and dressing.

"Just a work debriefing. She's had a mole removed. It changed shape and she's been imagining it was something sinister," explained Mac.

Mik made a sound somewhere between a snort and a sniff, went to the fridge to get a vitaboost and slouched on the sofa, flicking on the media console. After ten minutes Mac said, "I'd better go to the exercise centre myself. I'll see you on Monday. We'll start playing racketball again when you're up to it."

"Did I get in the way of you and your friend?" Mik taunted.

"Friend? Don't be silly; he's just a colleague." I knew my words were too sharp, too hasty, and was sure Mik didn't believe me, but what could he prove? I'd have to work harder at avoiding him.

I spent the weekend indoors, slumped in front of any media show the others chose to watch. On Sunday evening I removed the dressing. No traces of the Mark remained and a liberal covering of facebase hid the lingering redness. It was only after another day that the redness subsided and I saw with a stab of horror that my skin was several shades lighter. I applied the cream and listened to the information that came with it. Oh no, it could take several weeks for the pale patch to match the rest of my skin. I ordered extra supplies of facebase. The pale patch wasn't as noticeable as the purple but anyone with half a brain could guess the truth. I still bore a Mark of shame.

I cried until my head throbbed. So much for the Citidome being a safe haven. I was unclean, Marked, an outcast. I'd been so stupid. I should have stayed in that freezing, foreign world while I had the chance. I could no longer be a part of this one.

CHAPTER - 13

Newsfeed: Escapees interned.
In a new crackdown on escapees, two people were arrested fleeing from the Citidome yesterday, and have been sent to outdoor correction camps.

Had we missed our chance? Had escape really been a pipe dream? Gradually normality returned to my life but it was a normality I no longer wanted. I tried to recapture the images of my and Mac's time together but they were hazy, blunted by harsh reality. Even seeing him became a torture. Perhaps it was paranoia, but I was certain that Jana was giving me funny looks. The only things that kept me going were the messages from Mac.

To Daretodream from Walkunafraid: You looked pale today – are you still sick? I sleep holding your shirt against me, wishing you were in it, or even better, out of it.

To Walkunafraid from Daretodream: still some nausea but I can live with it. What's hardest is the sickness in my heart. I sleep with your shirt too and imagine you beside me, inside me. Being without you is agony.

To Daretodream from Walkunafraid: You're turning into a very bad girl. I can't believe you said that!

To Walkunafraid from Daretodream: I made myself blush!

The illness lingered. For the next month, barely a day went by without me having a dizzy spell, and more than once I fainted in the toilets at work, but said nothing. I didn't want to face a barrage of uncomfortable questions at the health centre. I started preparing for escape, collecting useful objects and medicines, had the expensive dental treatment that would ensure my teeth never decayed – prioritising it over removing the Mark on my thigh – but I couldn't believe that escape would ever happen. I performed my day-to-day tasks sluggishly. Occasionally I caught Mac's eye, his furtive winks still precious, but these flashes of happiness were too short-lived. Had I really once caressed the soft, curling hairs under his shirt? Perhaps I imagined the whole week.

To Daretodream from Walkunafraid: My last-ever week at the Pleasuredome's due next week. I might not get the chance to message you. You going to be OK?

To Walkunafraid from Daretodream: Yes, course I will. Lucky you; I'll miss the Pleasuredome. What's your favourite thing there?

To Daretodream from Walkunafraid: You're going to think this is really childish but I love going to the zoo.

It didn't surprise me. I'd get through the week by picturing him there. Or so I thought. On Monday, Jana called me into the private office.

"I'm not stupid," she said in a muted voice. "Kit asked me to keep an eye on you because he's worried about you, but I've worked out what's going on. Something happened between you and Mac outside, didn't it?"

"No, he just worked me too hard." But treacherous heat flooded my face.

"You stupid girl. I said the two of you shouldn't go out together. Look, Caia, I like you. I like Mac. But at this rate, one of you will be forced to leave the team and I don't want that. Anyone who's vaguely observant can see the signs."

"What signs?"

"Whenever he walks in the room you look up then look down too quickly. Your lips part, you start fidgeting with whatever's on your desk. Sometimes your face flushes like it's doing now. And you've looked lost all day since he isn't here. I don't want to know what's going on, but end it now, or I'll be forced to say something. Forget him."

Forget him! That was like forgetting to breathe.

I could see the chasm of depression opening up but couldn't stop myself from slipping deeper into it.

To Daretodream from Walkunafraid: I'm back! Good week, but I missed you like mad. What's new?

To Walkunafraid from Daretodream: Bad news. Jana's on to us. She gave me a warning. I don't think she's going to do anything about it but we'd better be ultra-careful. Don't even look at me more than you have to. I'll be in the lab a lot next week, which should help.

To Daretodream from Walkunafraid: Oh crap. I'll try and focus on office work. Maybe we should think of going sooner, but I heard that security's still high. Better if we can stick it out another month or so. I'm having my teeth done tomorrow. I'll keep my mouth closed for a while; don't want her noticing we've both had them done. Keep your spirits up.

To Walkunafraid from Daretodream: Huh, the

Citidome has starved my spirit.

As days turned to weeks it became increasingly difficult to be Caia, the conscientious Ministry worker and cheerful resmate, as if they were roles in a movie and I'd forgotten the lines. Mik's contempt became more open by the day.

"Hey girl, you look like shit. Get yourself a permastraighten at least," he sneered.

I feigned interest in banalities, was witty and anecdotal about work but my worthless life oppressed me. I got into a habit of digging my nails into the smooth flesh of my inner arm until they left raised red crescents. I needed to concentrate my pain, focus it into a physical form where it would heal. Eventually even Uma commented.

"Has your fashion program malfunctioned? You've worn that outfit for three days in a row."

I hadn't even noticed, changing my uniform each evening for the first garment to hand, forgetting to send them back for sanitization.

"Come on kitten; we need to get you a new set of nails. Those ones are ragged."

I allowed Uma to take me for new nails. It didn't cheer me up.

To Daretodream from Walkunafraid: No smile today? Kit wants my input on your one-year assessment. At this rate I'll have to say 'Must try harder'.

To Walkunafraid from Daretodream: Sorry, just feeling grotty.

Then I made a mistake in tuning one of the instruments, which caused a week's batch of data to fail its quality control criteria. Kit called me for a private meeting.

"What's happened to you? It's not like you to be careless, and you're not as productive as you used to be. Where you used to be eager you're now passive. Do you not enjoy the job any more?"

"It's nothing, just a lingering tiredness after that influenza I caught."

"I can't help noticing that you hardly talk to Mac any more. Did you not get on when you worked outside? I've heard him speak quite harshly to you."

"No, there's no problem with Mac. He's very efficient. The two of us work well together." I paused, seeing Kit's frown. "He's too much of a perfectionist though. When we were outside, sometimes I wanted to stop work early but he wouldn't let me."

Kit sighed. "I'll give you the day off tomorrow. See a health worker and make sure the infection has fully passed. And on Monday you'll be working in biofabrics."

"What? But I love working here!"

"Then prove it to me. Pull your weight in biofabrics and we'll transfer you back."

To Daretodream from Walkunafraid: What did you tell K today? He gave me a rocket for pushing you too hard. Clever. What do I have to do to get a smile out of you these days? I'm still trying to find another surgeon to do your Mark; I've got another thousand.

To Walkunafraid from Daretodream: Nothing to smile about. I made out that we don't talk much at work any more because you were too hard on me. But he's transferred me to biofabrics. And I've got to see a health worker. What are we going to do?

To Daretodream from Walkunafraid: We've got to get out of here, soon. I'll start asking around and checking the gates.

I told the health worker I was well but felt unhappy, and answered all the questions indifferently.

"Since there's no obvious reason for your depression, I assume the cause is chemical, possibly due to your recent illness," she said. "I'm prescribing mood enhancers and a course of therapy."

I didn't take the pills. A pill couldn't blot out Mac, as if he was some imbalance in my brain. I dragged myself to the therapist, his room heavy with the stagnant stench of misery.

"When did you first start feeling unhappy?" he asked.

"Since I had the infection."

"What did you think of the outside?"

"I hated it. All I can remember is the cold. I never want to feel cold again."

I stared at the walls, wondering how many hurt and hopeless words had bounced off them, and endured the interrogation. Yes, Mac and I got on well. No, I had no inappropriate feelings for him. The therapist had nothing useful to offer. How could he?

To Daretodream from Walkunafraid: What's it like in biofabrics? It's crap at work without you. We've got a skinny graduate with no sense of humour. I've been running round the dome at night, trying to suss out the gates. I heard security's getting more lax again. I'm working on a plan. Will let you know when the time's right.

To Walkunafraid from Daretodream: I hate it. They're nice enough people, but I can feel their eyes on me, wondering what I've done to get myself transferred. I can't stand living like this much longer. I had my health insurance assessment this morning and my premium's shot up. My body fat's gone up to 28%. More fat control food. It's because I can't exercise. I feel like a blob.

To Daretodream from Walkunafraid: You could never look like a blob. I want to run my hands over every one of those curves. It's the rest of them that are freaks.

In the shower, I stood so my thigh faced the wall. It wasn't unusual for one of the others to wander into the restroom while I showered. At least for the first weeks after the illness they kept their distance, fearful of infection. Now I wore a heat dressing, saying I had a muscular strain. To perpetuate the lie, I couldn't play racketball with Mac, the only way I could see him. And he still couldn't find another surgeon.

While spring started to warm the outside world, my misery deepened. And still nothing from Mac. He must have been having second thoughts about escaping because of the heightened security. Oh, what did it matter anymore? I was losing the ability to feel anything. I stopped replying to his messages, trying to close the door in my heart. What was the point in making myself even more unhappy, craving something I couldn't have?

Then a message made my heart thud.

To Daretodream from Walkunafraid: Time to get out of this prison! Apparently the most corrupt guard in the Citidome's on duty on gate 4 at the moment. Come round tomorrow at 08:00 am. Wear comfortable clothes: a leisure suit and running shoes are probably best.

I threw everything into my bag, and programmed my RestPod to wake me at 6:00. But that night, my fantasies about our new life spiralled into a frightening vision. I was at the village dance, watching Mac dance with Daisy. She grabbed his hand and they ran out of the hall together. Only at 7:30, did I realise that I couldn't do it. I couldn't risk life on the outside without Mac. But I could live on the inside without him.

To Daretodream from Walkunafraid: Where were you?

167

To Daretodream from Walkunafraid: Are you getting these messages? Why won't you even reply?

He came to the res, of course. Uma was in, so we couldn't talk, but his eyes met mine. I glanced to the floor, and saw from his expression that he knew I'd read the messages.

"How about a game of racketball soon?" he said.

"Yeah, maybe. I'm a bit out of condition," I said.

"You need the exercise," Uma said.

I requested a change of residence; Mik was still looking at me suspiciously. Maybe if I moved in with others I could come up with a feasible lie for my Mark, a birth deformity perhaps.

To Daretodream from Walkunafraid: Veez, what sort of sick game are you playing here? I've had enough. I don't know why you're not replying, but I can't wait much longer. I'm going soon, with or without you.

And life would have continued its endless, hopeless trudge, if it hadn't been for one stupid, careless moment. I'd had a shower, and came back to my room, to find Mik sitting in my chair, scrolling through pages on the screen projected from my DataBand. My throat tightened. How could I have been so stupid? I never left my Documents switched on! How much had he read? I tried and failed to swallow, and clutched the towel against my chest.

"I knew you were hiding something." He lunged towards me and grabbed the towel, leaving me naked in front of him, my Mark exposed. I folded my arms across my breasts.

"Thought so. You had one on your face as well didn't you? That was no mole. You're busted, freak."

"No!" I darted towards him, tried to grab my DataBand but he held it out of my reach. The commotion roused Uma and Von, who stared open-mouthed at my naked body.

"Euw, you've got so fat!" squealed Uma and then gasped as her eyes dropped to my thigh. "You're Marked! How could you? It was that hairy freak, Mac, wasn't it? And you carried on living here, contaminating us."

"I'm calling the CEs." Von tapped his DataBand. "You're creeving disgusting!"

"No way, I'm getting the citizen points," said Mik, brandishing my DataBand. "I found her out."

I stared at them, their faces twisted with contempt, my mind and heart racing. Could I buy their silence?

"Please don't report me. I'll pay you anything, transfer all my citizen points. That's more than you'd get for reporting me. I've already requested a change of residence. I won't bother you again."

"No way! You fat, repulsive freak," said Mik.

His words sent an explosion of adrenaline coursing through my body, white hot, fusing all my feelings into a solid block of rage, as if the monsters from Jem's VirtuGames had taken control of my body. With a burst of speed I didn't think myself capable of, I leapt at him, clawed at his face, wrestled my DataBand from his hand and threw it across the room. He cried out, his hand flying to his cheek. Uma and Von stared, motionless.

"She's scarred you!" Uma gasped.

"And I'll do it to the rest of you unless you all take off those DataBands," I hissed. I was shaking now; molten lava cascading through my veins. But these were empty threats. I couldn't take them all on. My eyes darted around the room, searching for inspiration. Then I had it. I grabbed a facial spritz from the shelf and brandished it as if it were a stun gun. "This has got acid in it; I got it from the laboratory. Do you know what acid does to skin, Uma?"

Uma gulped, and shook her head.

"It burns right through it, and leaves hideous scars. One squirt in your face, and everyone will think you're Marked. You'll never work again. So, DataBands in this drawer, and stand in the corner." I seemed to grow larger with each word.

As Uma, Von, and Mik, faces even paler than usual, removed their DataBands and dropped them into the open drawer, I couldn't resist a smile. But panic pushed it aside. Blood was pounding in my temples; I couldn't think. What next? Clothes, DataBand, supplies, find Mac. If he was still here. It was five days since he'd sent me the message about leaving. I pulled on my leisure suit, the nearest thing to hand. Still pointing the spray bottle towards them, I jammed on my running shoes, fastened my DataBand to my wrist and picked up the bag of supplies I'd collected. But Mik hadn't given up. As I made for the door, he pounced on me, wrestled the spray bottle from my hand and grabbed my wrist.

"You think you're getting away that easily?"

But by now I was beyond fear. Must escape, must fight, but how? Jem's VirtuSlam – what did he do? I curled my free hand into a hard ball, turned and smashed it into Mik's face. I heard a sickening crunch, then a flood of scarlet gushed from his nose. He let out a cry and slumped to the floor. I shook my hand – it stung – and raced to the entrance.

"Grab her!" Mik shouted.

"I'm not touching her," said Uma.

Without turning, I ran outside, leapt into the nearest TravelPod and headed in the direction of Mac's residence, calling him as I drove. Please answer, please answer. After ten rings the panic mounted. What would I do on my own?

"Hey, I was in the shower. You got my message? You're coming?"

"What message?" My voice came out in gasps. "Mik found out everything. He's reporting me. I'm in a TravelPod heading for your res."

"Shit ... I'll be out in a minute."

Within the minute I'd reached his residence to find him wearing his Ministry uniform, carrying two backpacks and two thick coats that looked suspiciously like the protective ones from work.

"You really didn't get my message?" he said, unsmiling. "I was going today whether you came with me or not."

"No." I rubbed my hot, red knuckles. "I thumped Mik. Might have broken my hand."

"You did *what*? Move over; I'm driving. And crouch down; we'll have to hide you. Your ID's probably being circulated around every gate by now. This is going to be tricky."

I shuffled across and folded myself into the narrow footwell, allowing myself a smile. Finally, my small stature was good for something. He covered me with the coats, plunging me into darkness. Then a heavy weight forced the air from my lungs – he must have put the bags on top of me too. I tried to take the deep breath I needed but couldn't. Wrapped in my tiny cocoon, unable to see, my leg already cramping, the short drive to the gate seemed endless. The TravelPod lurched to a halt. I held my breath. What was happening? Voices. Muffled fragments of conversation filtered into my ears: authorisation … Ministry experiments … mission isn't on my log … urgent … problem with the sensors.

The passenger door opened. I stiffened, a rigid ball of fear. The weight shifted above me.

"Just supplies for my mission." Mac's voice. The sound of the bag being opened.

"OK, number two, all yours."

The vehicle started to move! Could it really be so easy? A chink of light pierced my vision. I saw Mac's hand, heard his voice.

"He's given us a rugged TravelPod. I'm driving to the shelter, but he's still looking. I'll have to wrap you in the coat and lift you across."

"OK." My heart hammered against my ribs. We'd never get away with this.

"Oh shit, he's waving me back."

The vehicle stopped. Mac opened the door. The chill of the outside air. Fresh panic thudded through me. What was happening? Slowly I raised my head, peered through the window. Mac was intent in discussion with the guard, showing a screen from his DataBand. My eyes darted towards the open shelter; presumably that was the rugged TravelPod, about five metres away. Could I? Clammy with perspiration, I rolled to the driver's side. I inched my way out until I was crouched on the dry earth, hidden from view by the vehicle. Muted conversation from the gate. I peered across; neither was looking my way. My leg muscles tightened, preparing to run. My eyes scanned the short distance that lay between me and freedom. Fear-filled needles prickled my skin. The ground was strewn with stones and gravel; how could I scuttle across without making a sound? A distraction, that's what I needed.

What was that sound? I raised my head at the cooing noises from the other side of the TravelPod. Pigeons! I picked up a stone and hurled it toward them. The frantic flapping of wings.

"What was that?" The guard's voice.

"Look, a reddish-brown animal, over there. Is it a fox?" Clever Mac. A fox from outdoors had got into the Citidome from the shuttle exit last month and caused widespread panic; they carried disease.

"Hang on, better check. Wait here a minute."

Seizing my chance, I scurried to the shelter, opened the TravelPod door and crouched inside the footwell. An anxious few seconds. What if Mac didn't follow? A thud over my head – the coats and bag! Another thud – a driver.

"Well done." Mac's voice, hard, terse.

The TravelPod set off, accelerating faster than I'd known was possible. And in an instant, we were free. No time for regrets or farewells, we fled the Citidome, an uncertain future awaiting.

CHAPTER - 14

Newsfeed: dissident on the run.
Caia 031954 has been identified as a subversive thinker, is wanted for assault, and is presumed to be in hiding in Sigma-2. She is a Ministry worker and is Marked. Five hundred citizen points will be awarded to anyone with any knowledge of her whereabouts. Two hundred points will be awarded to anyone who obtains her DataBand: it is believed to contain illegal information.

"Oh no, look." I raised my head from under the coat. "They're already on to me."

"But the guard didn't see you," Mac said. "It'll take them a while to connect your disappearance to mine. Veez, we're lucky to be out at all."

I shrunk from the animosity in his voice. "How did you get past him?"

"Used my Ministry status; said it was urgent, that one of the sensors had failed on our outdoor studies and I needed to fix it today. I'd faked an authorisation, given him Kit's contact code but with one incorrect digit. If I'd have got the corrupt guard, like I planned, we'd have been fine." The temperature around me seemed to drop with his every accusing word. "But this one checked it; that's why he called me back. I could tell he wasn't the sort to be bribed. I was trying to talk my way out of it when you pulled your stunt with the birds."

"But won't he chase after us?"

"Fifty-fifty chance, I guess. Does he admit he screwed up? With any luck he'll cover himself by not logging it at all. But there's the matter of a missing TravelPod. How's he going to explain that? Anyway, it's not like we have much choice, is it? We've got to assume they'll be after us at some stage and keep going. You keep a lookout. We'd better take our DataBands off."

We removed the bands, deactivated them and put them in the bags. I kneeled on the seat, staring out of the back window but already the gate had receded from view and there was no sign of any pursuers. But my pulse refused to slow. Surely someone would come after us? When we reached a junction of roads, we stopped for Mac to set the destination on the navigator he hauled from one of the backpacks.

"I'll take the minor roads." His voice was disconcertingly unemotional, his attention focussed on the road network.

We crossed the main road, turning onto a road so unused that grass and weeds grew from the cracks in the tarmac. The silence was punctuated only by the noise of the TravelPod against the potholed road and the sounds of our breathing. Why wouldn't he talk to me?

"Gonna tell me what happened?" he eventually said.

"Mik read the history I'd been recording. I had to attack him to get away."

He groaned, then shrugged. "We can't go back anyway so what's it matter how much trouble we're in? Except – did you put in details of the community?"

"Not locations ..." I put my hands to my head, then winced – my hand still stung. "But if he read that bit ... it doesn't take a genius to work out it'll be near Upsilon-2 or Tau-2. He might not have. He could only have been reading it for five minutes at the most."

He sighed. "Great. Just great. How's your hand?"

"Still sore." I squeezed my knuckles and winced. "But I can move it. Guess it's just bruising. Those bags were much heavier than mine. Is that all supplies?"

"Yeah, everything on Daniel's list: changes of clothes, towels, light tubes, salt, vinegar, detergents, toothpaste. There's a tonne of medical supplies: antivirals, antiseptic lotions and creams, painkillers. I even managed to steal two coats from work; you try cramming one of them into a work bag."

I laughed, the clenching terror in my stomach loosening. "I remember Dal saying he couldn't find a coat last time he went into the minus-twenty room. I've got a few things but nowhere near as much as that. You really don't think they'll find us?"

"They can only detect the identity chips that track the TravelPods if the engine's switched on. Better not to drive all the way to Ashford. It's about 100km from here. Daniel suggested we go halfway in the TravelPod, then hide it out of view of the road and walk the rest. Someone from the village can come and remove the chip."

"Walk 50km? How long will that take?"

"I don't know; two or three days I guess."

"Three days? That's madness!"

He spoke as sharply as I had. "So what's the alternative, brainiac?"

"Veez, I don't know. How can you be so freaking logical? We've just run out on our lives, with my name on every newsfeed! And now you're telling me we have to walk for three days? Where will we sleep?"

As my voice rose, his face contorted and one hand grasped my thigh.

"I don't care where we sleep!" he yelled, his voice raw. "I'd sleep on the roadside if I had to. I wanted this; I'm glad it's happened. I thought you wanted it too. I don't care how hard life is out here. I want love and truth and freedom and you, or at least I did until you started ignoring me. Veez, Caia, what have you been playing at? This would have been a lot easier if you'd have turned up last week, like I asked you to."

"I know. Sorry." My voice was small.

"Sorry? Is that it? I don't get you. Even now, you're only coming with me because you have to, aren't you? If you don't want me any more, find your own way to safety."

"Course I want you; you must know that. I just couldn't look at you. It was like seeing the best candy in the world each day and knowing I couldn't have it. I don't know … I've been in a sort of depression. I kept reading about escapees being arrested. I just didn't have the guts to go through with it." How could I tell him I didn't trust him not to find someone else?

"I planned it all last night; I was going without you. Then I sent the message; one last chance. Why wouldn't you even reply?"

"I thought that if I didn't see you again, life could get back to normal."

"I never thought you had it in you to be so creeving selfish." He shook his head, his anger replaced by a heartbreaking disappointment. "What about my life? Didn't you care about my feelings?"

"Huh, you'd be fine without me. You never doubted we could do this. Look at you at that party, so confident, talking to everybody. I'll only hold you back ..." The rest was lost in choking sobs.

"Do you really not get it yet?" Now his voice was the vulnerable one. "You think I'm this fearless guy with all the answers but I'm not. I'm just a boy in love for the first time. And right now I'm confused and hurt and absolutely terrified."

And that's how we were for the rest of the drive: all babbled reassurances and spilling out the misery of the last months. Eventually Mac spotted a copse.

"Looks like a good hiding place. Brace yourself; I'm going off-road." The TravelPod lumbered its way through an overgrown field. He drove behind the trees and stopped the engine. I leapt out of the car and gulped the cool air, gazing around in disbelief.

"We're free!"

He caught me in his arms, lifted me into the air and spun me around until we were both dizzy. Then he crushed me against him. I grasped at him, my mouth finding his, ravenous for the taste of him. My hands pulled at his clothes, desperate to feel his bare skin.

"What, here, now?" he said, eyebrows raised.

I nodded. And we coupled there and then, among a bed of bracken. It was hurried and uncomfortable but I didn't care. I was desperate for release and as I reached it I screamed.

"Hang on, I think I've escaped with the wrong girl. I remember a prim girl who kept holding back and said that passion was a dangerous emotion."

"She's gone. You corrupted her. And it will be dangerous if we don't move soon." I laughed. The sun peeked through fluffy cotton candy clouds and my spirits soared. We really were free!

"Better get going, I guess," he said.

"I can't believe no-one came after us."

"Let's not take anything for granted. We've got to get there first. Cross-country would be safer and more direct but the navigator won't let me do it that way; we'll have to follow the roads. We'd better walk in the grass verges."

We made slow progress, hampered by the weighty backpacks and the need to constantly look over our shoulders.

"Wish I hadn't brought these coats now," he said. "I'm sweating. I'm going to have to take it off."

"Me too. But what does a bit of discomfort matter? I feel alive again."

I wasn't the only one with renewed vigour. The land had awakened from the winter sleep of our previous visit and the hedgerows, cheerfully coated in white blossom, crackled with scurrying sounds of life. Birds, mostly brown; others large, black and menacing, filled the air with a glorious tumult of sound.

"Listen to that, living creatures in the wild." I murmured. "I wonder what else is out here?"

But all we saw on the ground were the remains of previous incidents – a flurry of feathers, various droppings, a disembowelled rabbit. We marvelled at glossy white flowers, the trees feathered with the bright, fresh green of spring foliage, and the coconut scent of a spiky shrub studded with yellow nuggets of flowers.

I stopped in my tracks and grasped Mac's arm.

"Look over there! The forest floor's completely blue!"

At first I thought I was hallucinating, but as we approached I saw that the ground was carpeted with a cobalt mist of flowers. I took in the smooth, grey trunks of the beech trees, bursting with thick clusters of heart-shaped leaves. The sun lit them from behind, causing them to glow lime green, and dappled light fell onto the mass of blue. There was no sound apart from the whisper of the leaves above.

"Nothing I've seen in the Pleasuredome comes close to being as awesome as this," Mac said.

Gradually, our strides matched each other's and we fell into a companionable silence.

"You haven't said anything for ... must be at least five minutes," I said. "That's a record for you."

"You saying I talk too much? I'm getting used to the fact that I don't have to." He grinned. "No more intense, hurried conversations. We can actually relax with each other."

But it was hard to relax when we could never drop our guard. Eventually we left the minor road and turned onto a road heading northwest. I glanced over my shoulder and saw the dark shape of an approaching TravelPod, almost silent despite the pitted road surface.

"Quick, hide!" I hissed.

We dropped to our knees and crawled through a narrow gap in the hedgerow. "Block the gap," whispered Mac. We grabbed armfuls of fallen twigs and undergrowth to cover the opening.

The TravelPod passed by, then stopped about 100 metres up the road. The sound of voices came closer.

"Lay down," Mac mouthed. I pressed myself into the base of the prickly bush, needle-like thorns jabbing into my side. He lay on top of me, supporting his weight on his elbows.

"Are you sure it was here?" A male voice.

"I thought so," said a second man.

"I can't see anything. Must have been an animal."

"No, it was definitely two humans, one short. It had to be them. Has to be worth a look."

I held my breath, as if its sound might alert the men to our presence. The crunch of footsteps grew closer. Mac stiffened. Someone kicked at the bushes.

"Don't see how they got through this," said the first man and then let out a cry of pain. "Veez! That freaking plant stung me!"

"Let's note the co-ordinates and come back with protective clothing. They won't get far."

We stayed in hiding as the footsteps retreated. I heard muted conversation, but only caught a snippet: "... community must be around here." I raised my head after a minute. The TravelPod had disappeared.

"Did he kick you?"

"No, just missed." Mac's mouth was set tight. "So they're on to us. Best not risk the roads any more. We'll have to go across country." He pointed to a decrepit wooden gate at the corner of the field. "Run to that gate and keep going in the same direction if the ground's clear."

I ran across the uneven land, avoiding rocks, the dense profusion of undergrowth impeding my progress. Beyond the field lay a seemingly endless array of other fields, each separated from the next by the savage hedgerows. Eventually my burning lungs forced me to stop.

"Do you actually have a plan?" I asked between gasps.

"Sort of. They'll assume we carried on in a North-West direction so I'm going South-West, to put them off the scent."

"They seemed to think we were headed for a community around here."

"Yeah, that helps. Doubt they'll search for too long; most citizens are scared of the outside. I'm not surprised. I think that plant stung me, too. Look at my hand." His palm was covered in red, angry bumps.

"Must be poisonous." I rubbed his hand, now hot and swollen. "Looks like it's only localised though. Oh, we're hopeless out here."

"But we can do it. It's just going to take longer."

I took strength from his determination and for the rest of the day we battled through shrubs and undergrowth. Some hazards were easily surmountable, others more daunting.

"Huh, a river. What now?" I said.

"Oh, crap. We'll have to wade across. To follow it would take us way off course. Here, hop onto my back."

He took off his pants, shoes and socks, threw them and our bags to the other bank and crouched down. I wrapped my arms around his shoulders, securing my legs across his waist when he stood up.

"Did I ever tell you you're amazing? Is it cold?"

"Freezing." He winced. "And you're heavier than you look."

"Hope you're not calling me fat." I swatted his hair.

"Wouldn't dare. And get it into your head – you're not fat."

Within an hour, my legs smarted where the barbs of vegetation had ripped through my now-ragged leisure suit. But what were a few scratches when my heart soared at the riot of nature at every turn? Apart from a stop to eat a nutribar, we walked without respite until the sun dipped low in the sky and we noticed an abandoned barn.

"Guess it's early evening. We could walk for a bit longer but we might not find shelter. What do you think of that as a ResLodge?" asked Mac.

"Looks good to me."

The barn was empty except for a few clusters of hay. A scuttling made us both jump.

"Mice, or rats?" I asked.

"I'd rather not think about it. Not up to much, is it? Not a RestPod in sight." Oh, I loved him. How could he keep so cheerful? But the strain behind his eyes wasn't fooling me.

"Makes student accommodation look like luxury. How about a HayPod?" I suggested. We gathered the hay to make a bed.

"Natural homemaker." He winked. "When we have our own home, you can make the bed."

"Watch it. I was about to offer you a foot rub, but I might change my mind."

"I think it's your duty, after I carried you over all those rivers."

"My all-conquering hero." I took off his shoes. His feet were icy. I took them between my hands, rolling them and blowing on them. Although now April, the warmth of the day had dissipated. We'd zipped the coats together, making a cocoon, and huddled inside. As darkness fell, we ate nutribars, shivering as the chill nibbled deeper. I felt something crawling across my face, screamed, then realised it was a spider.

"You won't last five minutes out here if you're scared of spiders," he teased.

"See how you like it." I grabbed a bundle of hay and shoved it down his shirt. He retaliated tenfold, and soon we were wrestling on the ground, shrieking with laughter. Euphoria turned to exhaustion and for those last waking moments, the outside world seemed a safe and happy place.

I woke early with an aching back and the disorientation of waking in an unfamiliar environment. Oh, but there he was, warm against me. I moved my hand to his chest, and he rested his hand over mine. We're together. A stab of happiness. I took in our surroundings. The barn, its beams coated in a lacy shroud of fibres strung with pearls of dew, was an enchanted palace to my optimistic eyes.

Mac roused and broke the blissful moment. "Better get going; we need to get further away."

It was a reassuringly uneventful day and, by late afternoon, we were back on course and reached a village.

"Fantastic, there might be a community who'll take us in for the night," I said.

"Hope so. I can't believe we've walked so far without any signs of life."

But the village appeared to be abandoned, the cottages empty except for a chilling presence of a skeleton in an upstairs room. The interiors had been stripped of any comforts, but we were grateful for the shelter and fell into each other's arms with the relief of a day without threat.

"Perhaps we should spend the day here, coupling," I said the next morning.

"Wasn't last night enough for you?" he said. "But it might be no bad thing to hide here for a day. I could work out where we are from the Navigator and plan a route. We could top up our water from that river. Besides, look outside." I looked and groaned. A fine drizzle fell from the leaden sky. "And we should stop calling it coupling. No-one uses that expression outside the Citidomes."

"What should we call it?"

"The guys at Tau-2 taught me a lot of expressions. The one you'll like is making love."

"Mmm, nice. Let's make love all day."

It wasn't one of my better ideas. A day in the damp cottage with nothing but a bed of plants and nutribars for food soon dampened our spirits. The following morning looked no more promising.

"I suppose we ought to get moving," said Mac. "We might make it as far as Bakewell if we set a good pace. This road seems the most direct. Look, it has a ditch running beside it – we could walk along the bottom. What do you think?"

"Yeah, don't think I could face another day in here. A nice hot bath, that's what I'd like."

Because I was determinedly looking down, the smaller details caught my eye – the moss and lichen that clung to the rocks, the dead leaves, decaying logs. It was the untidy side of nature that the Citidomes didn't show us and was the only interesting diversion in an increasingly difficult day. The drizzle intensified to persistent rain, soaking our pants – at least the jackets were waterproof – and turning the ditch into a thick, sludgy bath of mud that clung to our shoes.

"It'll take forever at this pace." Mac said. "Let's take our chances on the road."

And so we began our climb into the mist-shrouded hills of the Peak District. I wiped my wet face and smiled at Mac's expression of grim determination, his wavy hair flattened against his head.

"This isn't how it should be," I grumbled. "Where are the rainbows and the pots of gold? The fanfares and trumpets?"

Eventually the rain dwindled to a beaded mist but by then our sodden pants clung to our legs and the jackets dragged us down. We trudged onwards with dull determination, willing the journey to be over as soon as possible. I began to feel lightheaded, beyond tired, beyond hungry and beyond cold, almost ready to abandon myself to fate.

"Get down, there's a light." Mac's urgency shook me from my sluggishness. Seeing a beam coming from an approaching TravelPod, I leapt into the ditch, then heard a sickening thud and muffled cry as Mac fell in. The TravelPod drove on without stopping. I raised my head and saw him wince.

"Oh no! Are you OK?"

He shook his head, agony etched into his expression. "I turned my left ankle; can you look?"

I bent down and lowered his sock. "Oh no, it's already puffy. Can you stand on it?"

He stood up, wobbled and immediately sat down, his face tinged with grey, a sinister pallor even worse than his usual colouring.

"I think you might have broken a bone."

"Shit, Caia. W-what are we going to do?" His voice spoke of defeat, his assurance evaporated.

"You must be able to hobble if you lean on me. Crawl out of the ditch."

He crawled out. I hauled the bags out and he leaned on my shoulder but it took us forever to progress a few steps.

"We'll never do it at this pace; it'll be dark soon." His eyes scanned the immediate surroundings. No sign of shelter.

"It might be best to wrap you in the coats and hide you in the ditch for now. If I'm quick I might be able to get help out to you. I'll take my DataBand. We can't be far from Ashford now, and they have a TravelPod, don't they?" I said, surprised by my new strength. For so long he'd led and I'd followed. Time for me to take charge.

"Guess so. But if you can't find anyone to come out tonight, at least find shelter for yourself."

With no intention of spending the night without him, I zipped both coats around him, gave him a nutribar, painkillers and anti-inflammatories from the backpack, and left him with the last of our water supply. Finally, I pulled branches from the hedge and covered him in an attempt at camouflage. Armed with the navigator, I memorised the co-ordinates and turned away, not wanting to say more in case I burst into tears. I walked with fresh urgency, breaking into a laboured run, impeded by the heavy clothes. Without him by my side, the anxiety of the journey increased to a stomach-twisting fear. In the gloom of the fading light, dim shapes scuttled ahead of me on the verges, each causing me to jump. Were they rabbits, and did they bite?

Darkness descended more quickly than I'd anticipated. But soon cottages peppered the road, light glowing from some of the windows. A sign read, "Welcome to Bakewell." Oh no. I'd hoped to get to Anna's, but now realized I'd have to gamble on a stranger being generous enough to help us. Would they report me? But why would they? What use were citizen points out here? The thought of Anna's warm crackling fire made me reckless, and I knocked on the door of the first house that appeared to be occupied. An elderly woman answered, huddled in a blanket.

"Sorry to disturb you, but I'm on the run from the Citidome

and I need someone to –"

"Sorry, too risky," she said, not looking me in the eye, and slammed the door.

So much for the welcome we'd had from Anna's community. I tried the next lit house. A man of indeterminate age, wearing a patched jacket and dirty jeans, scrutinized me warily and listened to my garbled story. When I finished, he smiled.

"It's too dark to rescue your friend tonight, but look at you; you're drenched. Come in; you can stay the night. We'll get your friend as soon as it's light."

"But I can't leave him on his own all night!"

"You haven't got much choice, I'm afraid. It'll be pitch black out there in half an hour; we don't have any way of lighting our path. He'll survive it."

Guilt twisted my guts. How could I leave Mac on his own?

"I'm telling you, it's too late," the man said, "and even if you did find your way in the dark, you'll do him no favours by staying out with him. You coming in or not?"

Defeated, I followed him into a warm cottage, similar to Anna's. Inside was a woman, maybe in her late thirties, and two boys, a few years younger than me. How strange to see them living with adults, not in a development centre. Both boys were good-looking though one had an unpleasant drip from his nose and sores on his face. Was he seriously ill? I didn't like to ask.

"I'm Bob," the man said. "This is Jean, my wife, and our two sons Jim and Mark."

"I'm Caia. Thanks for letting me in. I've been walking for three days."

"Look at the state of you," said Jean. "I don't have enough hot water left to offer you a bath, but we'll find summat for you to wear and we'll try and dry your things in front of the fire."

I followed Jean upstairs and rubbed myself down with a towel. Cosy in tattered fleece pants and a top that Jean called pyjamas but looked like a leisure suit, I returned downstairs and crouched in front of the fire. Bob was an escapee, but Jean was born in Bakewell. We spent the evening exchanging life stories, the sort of conversation that would be engrossing if Mac was with me, but I couldn't tear my thoughts from him – cold, wet and in pain in the ditch. I reached for my DataBand, wondering if I should send him a message, but Bob warned me against it.

"Too risky. They may well be tracking it. Jim can take the trolley out first thing tomorrow. He's not City born, so his fingerprints won't register if anyone stops him. There's been a few CEs around here lately."

"What would happen if they found you? Surely they wouldn't take you back after all this time?"

"No idea. But people have disappeared from the town before; no point in taking chances." Bob shrugged, increasing my anxiety. Had we been hopelessly naïve in assuming that once we survived the short-term search we'd be safe?

When the others went to bed, Jean pulled out a large, stuffed object and some blankets, all smelling of damp and the all-pervading wood smoke.

"You can sleep on this, lovey; it's filled with hay. Goodnight."

How could I sleep, knowing that Mac couldn't? What if something happened to him? But somehow sleep found me, and the next thing I was aware of was a knock on the door and the guilty realisation that it was past dawn.

"Jim's ready to go," said Jean. "Best set off as early as possible."

Jim held the handles of a wire trolley, filled with straw and covered with blankets. He was a taciturn boy, and I struggled to hold a conversation with him.

"What do you do during the day, Jim?"

"Work on the farm, mostly."

"Really? How old are you?"

"Fifteen. Been working there since I was ten."

"Didn't you have any education?"

Jim shrugged. "I can read and write a bit, add up. What else do I need?"

"Nothing, I guess," I said, though the answer saddened me. I'd been halfway through my diploma at fifteen. Thousands of years of human advancement had resulted in this. The only way that humans could live in freedom was to regress to primitive living.

Our pace was fast – I was edgy and constantly expecting to have to jump into the ditch – but no TravelPods passed. I checked my navigator.

"This is the right place. Ah, there he is." Behind the camouflage lay an inert huddled figure. "Mac?" I said.

He didn't answer. Terror spiked through me. I clambered down and shook his shoulders. Nothing. Then he moved his head. My jaw slackened. But when he looked at me his eyes were unfocussed, his lips colourless.

"Hey, gorgeous," he croaked, his breathing fast and shallow.

I knelt beside him and rubbed his icy cheeks. "This is Jim; he's going to take you to Bakewell. Can you stand?"

"Don't know." He tried and failed to move, his eyes closing once more.

"We'll have to lift him. You take his arms, I'll get his feet," said Jim. I took Mac's blue-tinged hands and squeezed them. He didn't squeeze back. I shot Jim an anxious glance.

"Mum'll get a health worker out to him," he said.

Once we'd crammed the bags into the trolley with Mac on top, his legs dangling over the sides, Jim camouflaged the contents with broken branches and draped the blanket to cover him. We started our return trip, each shriek of birdsong causing me to jump. The outside seemed a hostile land, laden with hidden traps. At least the sun was shining. It was the glint of sunshine reflecting from the approaching TravelPod that alerted me to its presence, giving me time to jump into the ditch. I held my breath. Jim broke into a fit of coughing. I felt certain he was putting it on.

"What's that on your face, boy?" A female voice.

"Got a dose of the pox off me brother."

Fragments of muttered conversation: "not too close" … "contagious"

"What's in your trolley?" A different voice.

"A dead body. Birds were just about to peck out his eyes. Wanna see?"

"What are you doing with a body?"

"What d'you think? I was out looking for firewood and rabbits, but there's a hell of a lot more meat on this."

As I suppressed my nausea, I heard more mutterings:

"Freaking savages." Then a loud, clear voice. "Is the body male or female?"

"A bloke. Youngish."

"Step away from the trolley."

Dizziness overcame me.

"Don't touch him!" the female voice. "What about the kid's pox?"

"Shit, yeah ... but don't we have to fingerprint him?"

"Veez ... let's think. Press the pad onto him, then use the disinfectant spray."

I heard the familiar synthesized voice. The synthesized voice: "Identification: Mac 022852."

"We need to confirm he's dead."

I stiffened, preparing to pounce. They weren't taking Mac away from me. Would Jim help? Could we fight them off? My hand felt around me, tightened around a jagged stick. Not much of a weapon but better than nothing. But the talking continued.

"We can't risk taking his pulse; the kid'll have touched him. Didn't you see the spray when he coughed all over him?"

"Check his breathing? Look, it leaves a mist against the screen."

"Genius. You do it. Kid, take the blanket off."

I held my breath, hoping against hope that Mac was sufficiently conscious to do the same. Another explosion of coughs. Don't overplay it, Jim.

"Veez, certainly looks dead." Silence. "No, nothing. That's one down. Hey, kid. You seen anyone else? A girl?"

"Nah, just him. He whiffs a bit. Reckon he pegged it a day or so ago," Jim said.

The world was still spinning when I heard Jim's voice, "You're safe to come out now."

I stumbled onto the road. This time the coughing was Mac's.

"Didn't know I could hold my breath that long," he rasped.

"Christ, Citidome folks are stupid." Jim's smile transformed his face. "Not you, them. Why did they have those daft plastic circles on their cheeks?"

"It marks them out as CEs – correction enforcers," I said.

"And it lets them jump the queue in the Citidomes. What's the pox?"

"Dunno. I just remember Dad telling me: they're all scared of us, and squeamish as hell. Terrified of catching disease. Tell 'em summat to make 'em squirm and they back off like a shot."

"Clever." I breathed more easily, while trying to decipher Jim's strange vocabulary. Would I ever be as resourceful as this boy?

When we returned, Jean drew in her breath. "He doesn't look good, lovey. His pulse is racing and I don't like the sound of his breathing."

"That sounds serious" I swallowed.

"We need to get him looked at," Bob's expression was as grave as Jean's. "I'll find the health worker in town. Caia, why don't you carry on to Ashford? There's a path goes right aside the river. They've got their own TravelPod; send someone to fetch him. Tell 'em it looks like pneumonia."

"Pneumonia?" I exaggerated each syllable of the unfamiliar word, to fix it in my brain. "He couldn't d-die ... could he?"

"We'll know more when we get a health worker. Now shift yourself."

Alone again. So much for our triumphant arrival. I trudged through Bakewell and was disappointed; it was a depressing, empty shell of a town. Buildings, presumably once businesses, lay open to the elements through gaping doorways. I easily found the riverside path. Pink, yellow and cream feathery flowers lined the route, but my knotted stomach made it impossible for me to fall under their spell. Soon the stone cottages of Ashford came into view. I was home.

Home. Would this village become home? And, most importantly, would Mac come back to share it with me?

CHAPTER – 15

I pounded on Anna's door.

"I don't believe it! Come in, sweetheart." Anna gave me a crushing hug. "Where's Mac?"

"In Bakewell. Walking for days ... broke his ankle ... too dark ... had to leave him in a ditch all night ... he might have pneu-pneumon-ia." The words came out in a mixture of sobs and gasps.

"Jesus Christ. Is anyone after you?"

"Could be, but they think Mac's dead." I gave her a garbled explanation.

Anna looked at me and smoothed out the crease that had appeared between her brows. "Leave it to me; you look shattered. Give me the location, then run yourself a hot bath. I'll leave some food out for you."

I scuttled upstairs and surrendered to exhaustion, luxuriating in a full, steaming tub. As a slick of dirt spread from my limbs, warmth seeped into my body, but didn't loosen the tension in my muscles. I stayed in the water until my skin wrinkled, then dried myself quickly with the rough, tattered towel and dressed. No hair serums, moisturisers, facebase, or deodorant. Guess I'd get used to it. I went downstairs and ripped into the bread and cheese Anna had left. The door opened and in walked Anna and Daniel.

"Where is he?" I jumped to my feet.

"Don't worry, we've sent Alex to get him," said Anna. "He's a health worker. Now, how about you telling us the whole story?"

"Not until you tell me how serious pneumonia is."

"Let's not panic." Daniel said. "People coming from the Citidomes have hardly any natural immunity. If he spent the night outdoors in the rain, that'll have put further stress on his immune system. It could be one of any number of

189

infections: influenza, bronchitis, pneumonia. Without imaging media it's hard to diagnose. How long have you been outside?"

"Four days, but he was OK yesterday. I shouldn't have left him –" My panic rose again.

"We caught it early, then. There's a good chance he'll pull through. Tell us all about the escape."

Pull through? So it was possible that he'd die? I told the story as succinctly as I could, but Daniel's frown deepened with every sentence.

"What exactly did your resmate read?"

"I'm n-not sure, but possibly the story of our trip here in January." I hung my head. "But they don't know the location. And I've got my DataBand."

"Thank God. Did Mac bring his?"

"Yeah, but they're deactivated."

"Good. And they should have recorded Mac as dead, so he's safe. Thank God for that kid's common sense; can't believe the CEs didn't check his pulse. But two of them … they only travel in pairs when there's a high alert. We'd better keep you indoors for a couple of weeks. They're not likely to waste resources looking for you for longer than that. That OK?"

I nodded, feeling bleak. As Daniel talked of an induction week to our new life, unfamiliar words like butcher, baker, dairy and tannery washed over me, drowned out by the sentence that reverberated in my head: "He should pull through." Then came a knock at the door. A sparse-haired man of around fifty muttered something to Daniel. He followed the man out of the house and they returned, carrying a body. Mac. Anna rushed to my side and put a hand on my shoulder. What weren't they telling me?

"He's alive, just," said Daniel. "We need to get him in a bed."

"Put him in mine; first on the left," said Anna.

We followed them upstairs. Mac's colour hadn't improved and his skin was coated in a sheen of sweat. He was unconscious, his breath coming out in rasps.

"Hey, Caia. I'm Alex," the new man said. "Mac's ankle isn't broken; it's a bad sprain. But he has mild hypothermia and some fluid on his lungs, which most likely indicates pneumonia."

"Why will no-one talk straight to me? How serious is it?"

"Hey, no need to panic. Yeah … it's serious, but I looked in his backpacks. He's brought the most advanced antibiotics and antivirals I've ever seen. I've given him both, to cover all options. He'll need plenty of nursing over the next few days until he's out of danger. Hey, I can see you're in shock, so I'll give Anna the instructions."

Out of danger? I lowered my face to kiss Mac's cheek, and stroked the short, bristly hairs on his chin.

"Don't leave me," I whispered.

"Caia, I'd like to examine you too," Alex said. "Are you feeling OK?"

"Grotty throat, bit like the influenza I had after last time." I swallowed with a grimace, and surrendered myself to Alex's examination, involving a weird instrument with earpieces and a cold metal disc, which he pressed against my back and chest.

"Common cold. Most people get that." He smiled. "Nothing to worry about; it'll go in a day or two; if it doesn't I'll give you some antivirals. There's a fair chance you'll get an upset stomach too, but I'll keep an eye on you. I'll pop by in a few hours to check on Mac. Hey, don't cry. He looks like a fighter to me."

After Alex and Daniel left, Anna's composure crumbled. At the sight of the tears streaming down her face, I fell against her and soon we were a mess of sobbing. Anna was the first to pull herself together.

"Come on now, sweetheart. This isn't helping our Mac, is it? We need to get warm liquids down him every few hours. I'm going to make some tea, get a hot water bottle and boil up some soup. Why don't you get into bed with him? His temperature's still too low; bet the warmth of another body would help."

I crept under the covers, pressing myself against Mac, willing my heat, my life force, into his body. Anna returned with hot drinks and a kind of rubber bag she called a hot water bottle. Between us, we propped him up and parted his lips. When he swallowed, we both sighed with the achievement. It was hours before he regained consciousness.

"My breathing hurts," he moaned, a child's voice, then burst into a fit of coughing, as if he wanted to expel something and couldn't. Eventually, exhausted by the effort, he coughed a blob of something thick and green into a square of cloth held by Anna. I gagged.

Over the next few days, he lapsed into fever, with few lucid moments. I rarely left his side, watching as Alex pummelled his back, forcing him to expel the disgusting gunk that was apparently mucus. On the fourth day Alex smiled for the first time.

"Looks like he's over the worst."

"Messed up our big entrance, didn't I?" Mac croaked with a wink.

"That was so gross. You wouldn't believe what you coughed up."

But we had no chance to be alone. Anna never stopped fussing around us. And Alex and Daniel were the first of a steady stream of visitors.

"Good news," said Daniel. "Daisy managed to find the TravelPod. We're well pleased; we can trade our old one with another community for some livestock.'"

"That's brilliant." I smiled. "How many communities are there around here?"

"Three under my leadership. Twelve within a ten-kilometre radius of Bakewell. Beyond that, we don't know. By the way, I hope you wouldn't mind living with Anna for now? Eventually, we'll fix you up with a house of your own."

"Our own house? I never expected that. Do you turn many newcomers away?"

"Yeah, plenty. We can usually tell within a couple of weeks whether new people are going to fit in. We ask about one in four to leave. They get here with no practical skills and aren't prepared to lower themselves to do tasks they see as beneath them, especially if they had high-status jobs in the Citidome."

Like us. The thought gave me a twinge of fear.

"Around half the people who come here leave of their own accord," Daniel continued. "Seem to think there'll be something better round the corner."

"You needn't worry about us. We'll do whatever you want."

"For now you'll both be assigned to farm work. Don't look so scared – we'll build you up gradually; you especially, Mac. You'll be weak for a while yet. And your skin won't have much resistance to the sun. Caia, you should adapt more easily, being dark."

Our next visitors were Daisy and Mary, holding a strange concoction in a bottle.

"I brought you this, it's soothing for coughs," said Mary.

"Caia, if you don't come out soon I'll start hounding you until you do. I need to see another face on an evening apart from Mary's." Daisy's eyes twinkled, then she nodded to Mac. "And you malingering git, get yourself out of bed."

"Daisy seems like a good laugh," croaked Mac after they'd left.

"Hmm," I said without conviction. "I'm never sure when she's being serious."

"Hey, come here."

I lowered my face and we kissed until the spear of jealousy melted away, the unfamiliar rasp of his stubbled chin leaving my chin raw.

By the weekend, Mac was able to sit up in bed, but the slightest effort made him cough and I refused to leave his side. On Monday, Anna returned to her work in the weaving shed, and finally we had the privacy I craved. A delicious smile tweaked his lips.

"Perhaps we could see what it's like to make love in a bed, when we're both sober?"

"You sure you're up to it?"

"Only one way to find out." His hand caressed the length of my body, my limbs tensing with longing. And the rest of the morning was all about entwined limbs and murmured voices, exploring each other, discovering what gave us pleasure. When he needed to rest, I lay my head on his chest and listened to his heartbeat, touching the points where his pulse flickered under my fingers, stroking the hairs on his chest. The fear and anguish of the last months dissolved. When we heard a knock on the door, we struggled to pull apart, my skin tacky with perspiration. I flung my clothes on.

"Wonder how long it'll take to lose the fear?" Mac said. "I can't help thinking it's someone coming to drag us to a correction centre."

I looked out of the window. "No, it's Alex."

"Look at your throat, it's glowing scarlet. I'm sure he'll guess what we've been up to."

"Is it this good for everyone?" I grinned. "I'm surprised anyone ever does anything else."

By Wednesday, Mac was able to walk downstairs for dinner, and Anna had a new mind-bending piece of information.

"Did Daniel mention changing your name? Most escapees here take on a traditional name. It's partly for security, but you could see it as something symbolic, a new life."

"So that's why everyone has such odd names." I said. "Ooh, I love that idea, shedding the old me. I never much liked the name Caia anyway." Memories of reading *Wuthering Heights* widened my smile. "I want to be Cathy!"

"Cathy of the anti-Mind Values? Suits you." Mac smiled. I'd told him every detail of the story on our long, long walk. "Shall I be Heathcliff?"

"Only if you want to stand out like a sore thumb. Cathy used to be a common name, but there was only ever one Heathcliff, and the idea's not to draw attention to yourself." Anna chuckled. "How about Michael? It was the name of the guy I was with – I always liked the name."

"I like it," we said together. How strange. For months, his name was ever-present in my mind, and now I'd have to replace it with a new one. Michael … Michael. I rolled the name around in my mind, fixing it there. It fitted him well, more complex, more substantial than Mac.

"Now, what about a family name?"

"A what?" My head span with yet another strange concept.

"People outside the Citidome have two names: one's their given name and the other their family name, which they take from their father. But since most of us arrive here without a family, we choose one, usually related to the jobs we do. Mine's Brewer, and I'd be honoured if you both took that name too."

"Cathy Brewer. Ooh, that's lovely. So much nicer than

Caia 031954."

"19th March? You were eighteen last month? You didn't say," said Mac

"I didn't celebrate. This time last month there didn't seem to be much worth celebrating."

And so, in an instant Caia and Mac ceased to be, and our new incarnations, Cathy and Michael were born. By the weekend, Daniel and Alex agreed that we could leave the house. The prospect of socialising worried me.

"Daisy and Mary seem friendly, but everything here's so different, I'm not sure how to behave with them," I said to Anna.

"It's only natural to be overwhelmed," she said. "God knows I was. Don't be afraid to admit you're scared. Everyone will understand. You don't have to keep anything hidden any more."

Saturday evening brought the social, which involved the two nearby communities.

"First we buy drinks," Anna said. "Only water for you I'm afraid, Michael. Alex's orders. Oh, you haven't had your token allowances yet. I'll lend you some."

She gave us a handful of shiny metallic objects, silvery in the middle with an outer gold ring. The words '1 euro' were imprinted on one side. Following her lead, I poured a drink from the selection of bottles on the table and dropped a coin in the box.

As the evening went on, I circulated while Michael had only the strength to sit. My anxieties eased with each sip of wine.

"Hey, Daisy."

"How's Michael doing? Great new names by the way."

"He's improving each day, though I think he'd rather be dancing." We grinned at Michael, sitting in the corner, a blanket around his knees, being fussed over by a gaggle of older women.

"Is it what you expected?" Daisy asked.

"It's exciting, apart from housework, but I'm still disorientated. I can't quite believe it's real, that this is my life from now on."

"Bit different from your Citidome job I guess?"

"Yeah, I was a Ministry scientist. I loved my work. Being with Mac, sorry, Michael, is amazing, but I'll miss the work. I'm not an outdoors type. I'm an academic."

"Me too. Believe it or not, I was an IT whizz at the Citidome, top job and all, but now all I get to do is repair DataBands. Getting the chip out of the TravelPod last week was the most exciting thing I've done all year. And you've turned up at the start of summer and outdoor work's gonna rule for the next few months."

"At least it's warmer than last time we came. And the people are lovely. The worst thing at the moment is that everything's so uncomfortable, especially the beds. I'm finding it hard to sleep without my RestPod."

"It takes a week or two. Believe me, once you work on the land you'll sleep like a baby. And I bet you'll enjoy having a man in bed, once he's up to it." Daisy sniggered, causing my hand to cover my burning cheek. "Takes a while to shake off the Shittydome brainwashing, huh? I was like that at first. I freaked the first time I did it, back inside."

Ah. I wondered why such a beautiful BodyPerfect would leave the Citidome. "Did you get the Mark?"

"Yeah, but it's not on my face. She pulled down her collar and I understood why she always wore high-necked tops. "They found out anyway. Lost my job, had to move into a hostel, hours of counselling at the Correction Centre. Eventually I escaped and stumbled on this village. Six months afterwards I started seeing Peter. And when I first saw his body – let's just say I was madly in lust."

Once Daisy had explained what lust meant, I couldn't believe she felt it for Peter. He was older than us – mid-twenties, perhaps more. I guess you could call him ruggedly handsome but that carroty hair colour did nothing for me. Nor did the bulk of him.

"He's the one over there, right?"

"That's right. Built like a bull isn't he? Biceps like grapefruits. Men out here really are men, not like those effeminate BodyPerfects. And women become women. My monthly bleeds were never regular until I came here. Talking of which, femicups are a thing of the past. You'll need a supply of rags to wash out. And then there's body odour.

Guess you still think we all stink."

Not wanting to offend her, I shook my head. In truth, my sense of smell had never been so assaulted as it had in the last week, from the pleasant aromas of wood smoke and blossom, to the dreaded toilets, kitchen waste and odours that emanated from everyone. I'd been grateful for my blocked nose. But now I understood why. After several days without deodorant and the realization that daily showers were an extravagant waste of water, this morning I'd been repulsed by the smell of my own armpits.

"Nice try, but you're not fooling me. Give it a month and you won't even notice."

"Hey, Cathy, fancy a dance?" Peter had joined us. I looked at Daisy in alarm.

"It's OK; we dance with each other." Daisy said. "As soon as he's fit, I'll dance with Michael."

With that disturbing image in my mind, I danced with Peter. He danced well, but for the whole dance his eyes never left my breasts. It left me with a mixture of queasiness and embarrassment, as if I were standing naked before him. Surely this couldn't be acceptable behaviour? When the dance was over, Daisy was talking with Michael. I saw Mary standing alone and joined her.

"Having fun?" she said.

"Yeah, but can I ask you a question, in private?" She nodded. "Is it normal for a man to stare at your breasts?"

She laughed. "In your case, I should think it's hard for a man not to. Do you mean Uncle Peter?"

"Er ... yeah. Uncle?"

"My mum were his older sister. Don't look so worried; he shouldn't stare, especially when he's with Daisy. He's got a reputation for it though – wandering eyes. Wandering hands, too. Don't mention it to her."

After that perplexing information, Mary told me a rich collection of stories about the villagers, half of which she seemed to be related to. And new people kept joining us.

"Hey Cathy, my brother's dying to meet you."

"Cathy, come and play Truth or Dare. Not that Shittydome show, the real game."

Soon I was part of a group of people, laughing so hard my

stomach hurt. And by the end of the evening I realised I'd finally found what I'd always been looking for. A peer group in which I belonged. And yes, it was a strange peer group, whose language and behaviour I didn't always understand. But it was mine. I was home.

And then came the day of perfection, the day I'll never forget. It started with the swings. I dragged Michael by the hand to the playground.

"Look, they swing up and down. I saw the children playing on them yesterday when Anna and I went to the wash house."

We sat on one each, I started it with my feet, the way I'd seen the children doing, and soon we were flying through the air, thoughts of our old life flying away with every swoop and soar.

"Ha, I'm going higher than you!" I shrieked.

When we could take no more, we staggered off, giggling, and tried the climber set. Was it really possibly that I was reliving my old fantasy? Could I finally have a happy childhood? Eventually, we climbed through a patchwork of meadows inhabited by grazing sheep, marvelling in the construction of dry stone walls that had endured for centuries without collapsing.

"Lean against that wall," I said. "You need to rest."

"You're getting more bossy than Alex. I haven't coughed once today."

"Remember yesterday?"

"It was the tanning liquid that caused the coughing fit. It reeked. What did Robert call it, brain soup? Weird that an animal has just enough brains to tan its own hide."

"I don't know what freaked me out more: that, watching the cow being chopped up or James telling us how he decides when it's warm enough to sow barley by dropping his pants and sitting on the soil with his bare backside." We giggled at the image.

"Milking the cow had to be high on the gross-out list."

"Yeah, I don't feel the same about drinking it after that. I'm not keen on Peter; he gives me the creeps. But everyone else is lovely. It's been the most surreal week of my life, but the best."

We linked hands and carried on walking until we reached

the stunning viewpoint of Monsal Head.

"I need to rest," Michael gasped.

"I knew you'd overdone it. Sit on the wall."

"Looks comfier over there." He dropped to the grass and looked to the sky. "Come on, join me."

I lay down beside him, the long grass brushing against my cheeks.

"Drink it in, Cathy. It's ours. The whole of the outside world! It's all ours!"

As the sun cast its last long shadows of the day, I almost couldn't contain that happiness; it felt as if it would burst right out of me. Life had come full circle. Childhood had been enchanted, but too short. My first taste of adult life had shown me how meaningless and mundane Citidome life was. Now the magic had returned and my world brimmed over with treasure to unearth. At this moment, with the early evening sun, soft and low in the sky, bathing the hills in golden light while incandescent red clouds illuminated the horizon, it was hard to imagine that anything bad would ever happen to us again.

CHAPTER - 16

Michael limped in at six o'clock, face glistening with sweat, pink from sunburn and smeared with dirt. He bent almost double, groaning and rubbing his back. His hair was matted and standing out in all directions.

"Mmm, I like you when you're sweaty." I ran my hands under his shirt. "How was it?"

"Tough, but fun. We made hay. You wouldn't believe how they do it – by hand with a long-handled tool called a scythe. Luke swung it from side to side as if it weighed nothing, but when I took it – hell, it weighed a tonne. We let some chickens loose to follow us; they eat all the insects that turn up under the swathes. I was terrified I'd accidentally cut their heads off. How was your day?"

"Tough but fun sums it up for me, too. Daisy and I planted out two hundred runner bean seedlings, as well as lettuces, and beetroot. She gave me heaps of gossip, and the time flew by. Funny, damp soil feels lovely between your fingers, and I love the smell of it, but – ooh – it was good to prise off those heavy boots."

"Bloody uncomfortable, aren't they?" I grinned. Michael was picking up the colourful local language at quite a rate. "You got a blister?"

"Yeah, a huge one on my heel. Daisy said our hands and feet are going to take a couple of weeks to toughen up. And my back's killing me – you owe me a massage. But you get a sense of accomplishment, don't you?"

"That's how I felt. It's nothing like a Ministry project that'll take years of reports and approvals processes to get implemented. At the end of each working day here, you really feel you've made a difference."

It was the theme of our first working weeks: discomfort, dirty fingernails, but at the same time, there was something about this way of living that felt so … right. Our learning curve was steep. By the end of May, we could write with a feather and ink, ride horses, milk cows, snare rabbits and catch fish, as well as identify edible and poisonous plants. But there was more to learn than the practicalities of life. It seemed that there were more than four seasons; the landscape changed weekly. I could spend a happy hour watching the progress and changing shapes of clouds across the sky. The children taught me to skim flat stones across the river and make them hop. So many simple pleasures to enjoy.

As spring turned to summer, relentless heat scalded the land and water became precious. At the weekend social, the air hung heavy with the fetid odour of inadequately washed bodies.

"You can't stand Michael dancing with Daisy, can you?" Mary said.

"No ... it's crazy, I know. I feel like I've known you and Daisy forever, and I'd trust you both with my life. It's just ... these last three months – they've been the happiest of my entire life. And I guess part of me thinks this is too good to last. I can't believe I'm not going to lose him."

"We don't hit on each other's partners. That's one of the cardinal rules around here."

"Hit on?" Mary explained another foreign expression. Mary puzzled me. Her understanding of relationships was so much more advanced than mine, and yet she had no man of her own. "What about you? Don't you like anyone?"

"I like Vincent." She smiled at Vanessa's handsome brother. "But he's Marked, and if I get Marked, Shin won't want me any more."

I sighed. Mary still spent every market day with the Citidome trader. "But you can't trade yourself forever."

"I keep telling meself that, but there never seems to be a good time to call a stop to it. You've got to admit, Shin's a useful contact."

I couldn't deny it. Without revealing our new identities, we'd learned through Shin that news of Mac's death had been widely circulated, and that Caia – already I thought of her as a separate entity – was also presumed dead. Daniel warned me to be on guard, that the newsfeeds might only be propaganda, and that people may still be out looking for me. But our new incarnations refused to believe it, and for those enchanted early weeks we enjoyed our new lives without the spectre of the Citidomes intruding into our happiness. Mac, the rebellious boy, had been replaced by Michael, the man whose strength had grown with each passing week. We'd reached a level of intimacy that Caia the girl would never have believed possible. And so we reached the pinnacle of the village working life – the harvest season.

"Gathering nature's bounty; there's nothing like it," said James, the farm manager.

"That's poetic." I smiled. "But I do feel part of something special, part of a grand team effort. I love the way everyone sings while they work."

"We've done that for years; takes your mind off the screaming pain in your back. Just wait until you see the barn dance and the festival. It's grand – a celebration you won't forget in a hurry."

The warm breeze caused the golden wheat and barley to ripple like the wave pool. I was sorry when the stiff stems fell to the blades of the scythe but delighted as they rose again, pyramids of sheaves rising proud on the land. But grains weren't the only pressing demand – each day vegetables burst into ripeness and demanded to be picked. The small, nimble fingers of the children picked peas and beans from the pods. Milk production was peaking and extra hands were recruited at the dairy for cheese making. I approached my week on the rota with trepidation – Peter ran the dairy.

"Start by stirring that vat of milk," he said, standing too close, as usual.

I goggled at the huge vat; there must be over twenty litres of milk in there. Peter added a liquid and left it. Magically, after a couple of hours, I uncovered the pan to find it transformed into solidified curds.

"Now you have to separate the curds. Shift over, I'll show you." Peter demonstrated how to filter the curds and wrap them in a cloth. "Let's see if you've squeezed hard enough."

He put his hands over mine and tightened them, his stale breath hot on my ear. As he drew away, his hand brushed against my breast, where it lingered. I stiffened and spun around. Peter winked. I suppressed a shudder.

"What do we do next?" I said, with only a slight waver in

my voice. How should I react? Should I tell Daisy, but what could I say? No doubt Peter would deny it.

I said nothing. The next day, Peter's hand pressed into the small of my back as I finished cleaning the vat.

"Nowt wrong with a bit of fun, you know." He grinned.

"I have plenty of fun of my own, thanks," I said in what I hoped was a cold-but-firm voice.

He muttered something that sounded like, "frigid bitch," leaving me tense with anxiety about where his hands would go next.

I agonised for the rest of the day. Was this what Mary had meant by wandering hands? Surely this wasn't acceptable behaviour? I told Michael, that evening. He formed his hands into fists and leapt to his feet. "The bastard!"

"Don't –"

But without letting me finish, Michael marched down the street and hammered on the door of Peter and Daisy's house, me following.

"Wait, Michael! Don't go doing anything stupid," I shouted.

I was too late. When Peter answered the door, Michael's fist smashed into his face. "Keep your hands to yourself in future," he growled. Peter staggered backwards.

"What the hell's going on?" said Daisy.

"Ask your lecherous creep of a boyfriend," Michael muttered.

Peter had recovered and was about to lunge for Michael. I flung myself between them.

"Daisy, get Peter inside. We'll go home; come round later and I'll explain."

"What did you do that for?" Michael said, shaking his hand.

"I don't think you'd come out well in a fight with him, and what's the point in making enemies?"

"I want him to know he can't get away with it. Daisy should know, too. He's got a reputation, y'know. She deserves better than that scumbag."

"Oh, God. I thought you were going to say, 'Take your hands off my girl' or something. I've become your property, haven't I?"

"Yeah, guess you have." He grinned. "But it works both ways. Don't tell me you wouldn't have smashed Daisy's face if she'd groped me."

I squeezed his hand. He knew me too well.

Daisy arrived ten minutes later, her expression grim. "What's going on? Peter says that you" – she pointed at me – "flirt with him all the time, then flinch when he comes within a few metres of you. I know you're new, but you must realize that's not on."

"He said what?" I told her the whole story.

"I see." Fine lines scored her forehead. "Well, I'd better go. Peter's got a split lip."

Daisy left, and nothing more was said, but it fractured our friendship, and I wished I'd kept my mouth shut.

"Daisy's in a strop because deep down, she knows you're right," Mary said. "Best say you can't work in the dairy any more. Say the smell makes you nauseous."

"It wouldn't be a total lie. I've been queasy a lot lately, especially in the morning."

"It's probably the heat," she said, but gave me a peculiar look.

"Daisy said she didn't fancy playing cards tonight. She's still being off with me," I said to Michael. "And Margaret's not spoken to me since. Only Mary believes me. I should've kept quiet."

"Leave them to it; they'll come round. From what I've seen, family loyalty clouds all judgement. James says Peter's always tried it on with girls in the dairy; they put up with it because he's so good at his job. I heard giggling coming from the dairy this morning. Reckon he's fooling about with Vanessa now. Daisy must know."

"That's what Mary says. But why won't Daisy believe me? Families, couples … I'm starting to wonder if they're such a good idea. Are all relationships based on dishonesty? Is this why Mind Values were introduced?"

"Me and you … we're a good idea, aren't we?" He winked. "Don't lose faith. Maybe we expected too much. Maybe there's no perfect way of living. How much honesty was there in the Citidome? How many secret loves and desperate citizens struggling just to be themselves?"

"I guess so. Think I'll go to bed. Don't know why, but I'm wiped out."

"Lightweight," he teased, then become serious. "You do look tired, though. Maybe you should see Alex."

I chewed on a nail, wondering if I should tell him that I vomited again this morning. What was happening to me? While he was sprouting new muscles every day, my body was letting me down. Had I contracted a virus? I swallowed my fear, tried to match the output of the others, but my energy levels kept on plummeting. Then the following day I fainted in the field.

"Let's go to my surgery and have a look at you," Alex said.

Alex's 'surgery' was the spare room of his house. Only the metal cabinet and a handful of books hinted at its function.

"I had the TJB virus seven months ago," I said. "Could that explain the vomiting?"

"It's not likely to be that. Any other symptoms?"

"Not really. I've put on weight but I suppose that's because of the different food. There's something I wanted to talk to you about though. I've missed two monthly bleeds. I guess it's to do with the change of diet, but will they come back?"

Oh no, what had I said? Alex was smiling in the indulgent way that villagers did when I said something stupid.

"I've never come across it in a Citidome girl, but you could be expecting a baby. Hop onto that bed and take off your clothes below the waist; I'll take a look."

A baby? I stared at him, open-mouthed. In my shock, I forgot to feel embarrassed by the examination of my intimate area.

"Yep, you're pregnant all right. Congratulations."

Pregnant? I had a child growing inside me? But I didn't want a baby. I'd barely learned how to live out here myself.

"I'm only eighteen." My voice was flat.

"Margaret was only seventeen when she had her first."

This did nothing to reassure me. At twenty-four, Peter's twin sister seemed middle-aged and rarely came to the socials. I couldn't be a mother. I wanted to be young and free.

"When will the baby come?" I said, dread rising like bile in my throat.

"It takes nine months from conception. You're probably two to three months already so that'll be – let's see – mid to late February."

"But how ... surely you don't operate here?"

"You don't need an operation."

"So how do you get the baby out?"

When Alex explained, I shrieked. "No way – a baby can't come out of there!"

"Bit of basic biology the Citidome doesn't bother to teach, eh?" He opened a book and explained the reproductive system to me. "You'd be surprised what the human body's capable of. It's not as frightening as you think. I've delivered ten in the area. Go home and rest. It'll take a while for it to sink in."

But it wouldn't sink in. I could hardly see through the mist of terror. By the time Michael returned, my head was throbbing from crying.

"Daisy said you went off with Alex. What's happened?" He spoke in gasping bursts; he must have run home.

"We're having a baby." My voice was a croaky whimper.

He grasped my hands, his mouth gaping as if unable to form the words. "A baby? Christ."

I bit my lip. It wasn't the reaction I'd hoped for. But when he spoke again, his eyes were twinkling and a smile had crept across his face.

"A baby. Me and you. That's fantastic! I didn't think it'd be possible. But you always were more of a woman than the skinny freaks in the Citidomes."

"Easy for you to say. You don't have to have it growing inside you and then push it out of your body!" The tide of panic rose again.

He pulled me against him and, gradually, his solidity steadied my breathing.

"You are pleased though, aren't you?" he asked.

"Not really. It's too much responsibility. I want to carry on being young."

"We'll muddle through." I saw the flicker of doubt on his face. Then he smiled and put his hand on my stomach. "I can't believe there's a person in there. Remember how you felt when they took your daughter away in the Citidome? Just think, we'll have our own kid to look after. A proper family, the way it's meant to be." Then without any warning he dropped to one knee. "Cathy, will you marry me?"

I gave him a look that was half-frown, half-smile. "Am I missing something? Isn't marriage something that died out over a century ago?"

"Something Mum told me ... some couples here have a ceremony in the church. Means nothing in any practical terms, of course, but it symbolises two people's lifetime commitment to each other. Plus it's a good excuse for a party."

"In that case, how can I refuse?" I laughed. "Of course I want to make a lifetime commitment to you. But to a whole new person ..." I shook my head. "I'm not sure I can do it. I can barely look after myself."

"There'll be plenty of people to help us. How difficult can it be? So we might drop him on his head a few times? I've heard that babies bounce. Hope he doesn't get my mouth and nose."

Soon we were giggling and, as the news settled and took root, we thought beyond the short term.

"Hope he or she's like David, Dora and Matt and not those weird, mousy kids at Little Longstone," Michael said.

"They're just shy." I defended Helen and Paul, who blushed whenever they saw us, suspecting the thirteen year-old girl had a crush on Michael.

"Hey, maybe if it's a girl, Matt can be her boyfriend."

"Slow down! I wonder if he or she'll ever meet her half-sister." For months now I'd nursed a dream of contacting Suna when she was older and encouraging her to escape. By the end of the evening I'd persuaded myself I wanted a family of our own. But why couldn't it have happened later? Couldn't I have had more of Michael to myself before this new invasion?

Anna cried when we told her. Even Daniel overcame his usual reserve and hugged me. "That's fantastic. I'd love a self-sustaining community, but it's an impossible dream. So few people can reproduce naturally these days. Did you know that in the history of our community, only two other Citidome-born women ever conceived, and that was over sixty years ago."

"Really?"

"Yeah. Village-born women have borne children to Citidome-born men but not the other way round. We desperately need new blood, new genes. We have to look after you from now on. No more land work or riding for you, young lady. And extra tokens for food. Plenty of eggs, milk, meat, and vegetables."

I wouldn't be allowed to work any more? What would I do all day? Leaving the land work I'd once dreaded now seemed an almighty wrench.

Over the next few days, I learned more than I wanted to about pregnancy and childbirth.

"I can't imagine the skin on my stomach stretching that much," I said.

"Try having twins the size of Margaret and Peter," Kate chuckled. "Heartburn for nine sodding months. And talk about stretch marks; me stomach still looks like streaky bacon. By the end of it me ankles were the same thickness as me calves."

Everyone competed to lavish me with gifts and advice; I'd become the most important woman in the village. But I soon became lonely during the day, missing the banter of the land work. I offered to help the older villagers with the pickling of shallots and cabbage. I loved the pungency of the hot, spicy vinegar, but everyone insisted on me sitting down the entire time and, eventually, I felt more of a burden than a help.

The confinement had only one advantage. With little to occupy me, I read voraciously, borrowing books from everyone in the community. I devoured books indiscriminately, from Hans Christian Anderson to Flaubert to Catherine Cookson. I thrilled in trying to guess the twists of the plot and adored glimpses into new worlds, new lives. I preferred fiction written by women. I loved the intimacy of the voices, the thoughts and emotions expressed through the written word. After a lifetime of suppressing emotion, these books became my building blocks for understanding relationships.

Then I started to explore the factual books and my life became more enriched by the day. This was the rounded education I'd always wanted. I even found a history of State

11, or the United Kingdom as it used to be called. It ended at around 2030 but I learned about kings and queens, prime ministers and wars, including the Great War mentioned on the churchyard memorial. It sounded horrific, the war to end all wars. Presumably bioterrorism didn't exist then. Wars aside, it didn't seem such a bad world in which to live.

"How many hours a day are you reading?" Alex asked during one of his regular visits.

"I don't keep count, but at least nine, I guess."

"That's too many. You'll ruin your eyesight. Did you ever have vision correction surgery?"

"Yeah, two years ago."

"So what do you think will happen when your eyesight fails next time? Some of the older villagers are almost blind, but there's next to nothing I can do. Keep the reading down to four hours a day or less."

"You're kidding? What do you expect me to do all day?"

"You can have short walks as long as you don't go far on your own. But would it be too much to ask for you to just rest?"

Rest? I hated resting. Hours of having to put my feet up and do nothing. But evenings brought a stream of visitors.

Any progress with the great name debate?" Daisy asked.

"No." I grinned. Michael and I couldn't agree on a name. "I'm still on Scott for a boy, Emily for a girl. Think I've talked Michael round on Scott but he hates Emily. But his taste in girl's names is ridiculous. We've had Madonna, Bathsheba, Drusilla."

"Christ, keep him away from books. They say you know what the baby looks like when it pops out."

I frowned. "From what I remember about the breeding centres, babies don't look like anything much." In reply she smiled, but I noticed a strain behind her eyes that wasn't there yesterday. "Hey, what's up?"

"I thought I'd surprise Peter in the dairy this morning and caught him tongue in lung with Vanessa." She sighed.

"For heaven's sake, Daisy, why do you put up with it?" I said.

"In case you hadn't noticed, there's not much choice of men around here. You got the best one. Besides, who'd look at me?"

"What do you mean? You're gorgeous!"

"Huh, in the Citidome maybe. Not here. I knew Peter had the hots for you. So do half the men here; don't tell me you haven't noticed. No-one can keep their eyes off your boobs. Peter's said more than once he wished I wasn't so flat chested."

I blinked. The definition of beauty must be tipped on its head here. I'd noticed it in the case of Michael – when he worked on the field without his shirt you could practically hear the collective dropping of female jaws – but not in myself.

"Have I still not managed to convince you you're the hottest woman on the planet?" Michael said later. "Yeah, I know they all want you. Scares me a bit."

"Scares me too, when all the girls look at you with their mouths open."

"Do they?" He appeared genuinely surprised.

"It makes me angry. All those normal people in the Citidomes being made to feel ugly. So-called beauty – it's meaningless. It's just about conforming to other people's standards. It's what's on the inside that counts. I wish I could show them what's out here. But how can we? If we posted what we know on the Truth Exchange that it's possible to live happily outside, people would escape in droves. This village would be deluged with escapees. It'd wreck everything."

"In the message she sent me years ago, Mum begged me not to tell anyone, for that reason. But we've got to do something, haven't we? We've got to at least let some of the people in there know that there's an alternative way of living. Since you became pregnant, I realise it even more. All those so-called overweight people in there – they're exactly what we need. Communities like this have no future unless there's new blood."

As we talked, I saw the old flash of intensity in his eyes and realised that giving birth wasn't the only challenge ahead. We'd never be free of the Citidomes. The memories couldn't be folded up and forgotten. We had a mission to help people like us: the rebels and misfits still trapped.

CHAPTER - 17

An unearthly sound in the night woke us with a start. It sounded as if the sky had split in two and, before we'd fully roused, a blaze of light illuminated the room.

"What is it?" My voice trembled.

"Dunno. It sounded like an explosion. I'll look through the window."

Michael peered into the blackness of the early hours.

"There's no sign of anything other than sheets of rain lashing at the window."

Another, louder crack, so intense that the air in the room appeared to shake, made us sit up in time to see a forked flash of brilliant white dancing across the sky.

"What was that? It looks like the sky's broken!"

Together we watched our first thunderstorm. How could nature be so furious, so unpredictable? The next morning we marvelled at the freshness in the air and the break in the oppressive humidity of the past month. The change had been sudden, violent and miraculous.

So summer gave way to the mellow tones and aromas of autumn. The wet October showed us the full ferocity of nature. The river in Monsal Dale became a raging torrent, which flooded the valley. I took short, daily walks to explore the changing landscape, and found a new perfection that only this season could bring. It was sad to see the trees mournfully shedding their final glory, but fun to kick piles of leaves, sending showers of gold, burgundy and rust flying in the mist. And the trees and hedgerows gave me new, gleaming treasures – from ruby red haws and hips to acorns, conkers, beechnuts and chestnuts. I loved these walks – nothing but the rustle of my footprints on the leaves, the steady pace of my breathing and the wind against the trees.

Over on the farm, Michael was harvesting the beans he sowed, drying and storing them for winter. But the land, once stripped of its harvest, had to be prepared for winter crops and the rain turned the soil into thick clods, which were impossible to work with.

"I wish I could do more to help," I said to Anna. "Now the days are shorter, Michael's having to work weekends too."

"It's always like that at this time of year," Anna said. "A race against the weather. Don't feel guilty. What you've got in there's worth more than any harvest."

"I guess so." I rested my hands on my convex stomach. "But sometimes it feels like my body no longer belongs to me. I'm just a baby-bearer, a symbol of hope for the village. Oh, I didn't tell you. I've been having these kind of sinking, fluttering feelings. Alex said that's the baby moving. Isn't that exciting?"

"Bloody miracle, isn't it? Do you want it to be a girl or a boy?"

"A girl," I said with conviction. "Girls are the future out here. There'll always be men coming from the Citidomes, but we need village-born girls to reproduce."

"You're putting your feet up and relaxing more these days."

"Yeah, funny, I don't feel the need to be on the go the whole time. I'm enjoying the presents. Look what Kate brought me." I held up two thick cardigans, the work of the knitting circle.

"She's having to let out your wedding dress," Anna said. "You've grown more than everyone expected."

"I'm going to be the fattest bride in the world," I said with a grin. The wedding was scheduled for a week on Saturday, by which time most of the land work should have been completed and the villagers would be desperately in need of a party. I knew the timing made sense, but I wish I could have looked slimmer for the big day.

"I see Michael's getting you well stocked for winter."

As he hauled in another load of logs, slippery from the rain, I smiled at his arms, biceps visible through the long sleeves. Michael was now positively rugged. His hands were thickened with the calluses of a working man, his body harder and leaner than before. He'd never looked better.

"Burnt any more meals lately?" Anna teased. Last month, we'd greeted the death of one of the older villagers with mixed feelings. I'd miss the loveable old curmudgeon, but he'd left a vacant cottage, which was now ours, another advantage of our soon to be married status. But looking after ourselves was harder than we'd imagined. Luckily both of us were happy to live in a state we called casual and Anna called squalid. Heaven knows how we'd cope with a baby.

"No, and we've finally mastered mashed potatoes. But could you light a fire for us?"

As Anna produced a flame on her first try, I wondered if we'd ever get the hang of it. Naked flames weren't allowed in the Citidome; Uma's friends used the electric hob to light illegal cigarettes. In the village, each household was provided with a metal stick, which had to be struck against a knife to produce a spark.

As the temperature plummeted and the rain persisted, I became increasingly happy to be confined to the house, restricting trips outdoors to the weekly movie showings and social evenings, and a visit to the market every two weeks with Michael. I adored market days, which transformed Bakewell from the ghost town I found on my first visit.

"Hey you two, can I walk with you?" Mary caught us up.

"Yeah, haven't seen you for ages. You OK?"

"Actually, I've got something to tell you, but you mustn't tell anyone. I'm pregnant."

"You're kidding!" I squealed. Oh, this couldn't be more perfect. As well as stressing about my own ability to cope, I worried about my child growing up without friends. The youngest village child, little Matt, would be almost four when my son or daughter was born. Besides, Margaret, Matt's mother, hadn't exactly been friendly with me since the incident with Peter. The thought of sharing the experience with Mary was a comforting one. But she didn't look thrilled.

"That's brilliant news," Michael said. "So why the big secret?"

"Only Alex knows. I'm terrified to tell Daniel. Luc's not going to want me any more; we're all going to have to do without luxuries."

"But you're going to tell Shin, right?"

"I ... guess so. But not today. He was going to raid the medical stores. We need some more of them eye drops for

215

Frank and he's bringing enough antivirals to see us through the winter – he doesn't always come out if it's snowing. And this week I were gonna ask him for some infant formula milk."

"I don't need it. I'm going to try to breastfeed. And James is taming some wild dogs, just in case I can't. He reckons that their milk's the closest to human milk." I held my excitement in check, pleased that Mary would have to give up the trading. I loved the luxuries, but I'd sacrifice them at a stroke for her not to have to do this. Soon, we reached the market.

"Hey, Cathy, good to see you," said a Bakewell resident from behind a trolley of produce. "It's really showing now, isn't it? How are you feeling?"

"Not bad, thanks. No more morning sickness, thank God. Hmm, what have you got there?"

"New cheese recipe. Wild garlic and herbs. Fancy a taste?"

"That's fantastic." I turned to Michael, "Shall we buy some?"

"We could, but we've only got twenty tokens left over if we're saving ten for the weekend. And I fancy that fish paté."

It was a typical market dilemma. We were interrupted by a high-pitched voice shouting, "Mac!"

I clutched his arm. Who knew his old name?

"Don't look," he whispered. "We'll wander away and maybe they'll think they were mistaken."

We turned to leave but a hand tapped Michael on the shoulder.

"Hey, Mac, you hearing impaired all of a sudden?"

"Mei, I don't believe it!"

Mei? Wasn't that the girl he used to like in Tau-2? He greeted her in the Citidome manner. Tall and thin, she had the steely eyes and pale hair of Uma. I instantly disliked her.

"You grew up." Her eyes ran up and down Michael's body. I moved closer to him.

"This is Cathy." He put an arm around my shoulder.

Mei's eyes darted to the swell of my stomach. She took a step backwards, then raised her tattooed eyebrows at Michael.

"Woow, you've broken a lot of rules haven't you?"

"Cathy's from the Citidome too," said Michael, and turned to me. "Remember me telling you about Mei?"

"Yeah." My voice was icy. He tightened his grip on my shoulder.

"So you finally made it out?" she said. "We wondered what happened to you."

"They moved me to Sigma-2. We got out in April. Sorry, did you know that they caught Hal? They put him in a Correction Centre. He reported you as dead but I guess he was trying to protect you."

"Yeah, I guessed." She rolled her eyes. "He broke back in one night to steal supplies for trading. Hang on, let me get this straight." She stared at me, her eyebrows furrowed. "You're from the Citidome and you're ..." She nodded towards my stomach.

"Pregnant. Yeah."

"Woow." It appeared to be all she was capable of saying, her eyebrows raised almost to her fringe.

"I'm sorry about your friend." Guess I ought to be friendly. "It must have been awful out here on your own."

"Yeah, but we'd already split up by then. Once it was just the two of us, we drove each other mad." Did I imagine it, or did she shoot Michael a glance that was loaded with meaning?

"Where have you been?" he asked.

"I've been in a few different places around here; can't settle."

"Where are you living now?"

"The other side of Bakewell, but I'm looking to join a different community. Where do you live?"

"Ashford. You're welcome to walk back with us after market, see if you like it," said Michael.

"Thanks, that'd be amazing. Is it OK if I stay the night? Otherwise I'd have to walk back in the dark."

"Yeah, why not? Be good to catch up. We've got a bit of shopping to do but meet us here in an hour."

"That'd be great. See you later."

"Don't I get a say in this?" I hissed once she'd gone.

"Sorry, but I thought she might be useful. Remember what we've been talking about – a plan to help people escape from the Citidomes? She knew so much; she'd have some good ideas."

"And you thought I'd just nod my head and say yeah, why not invite the girl you used to have the hots for?"

"But that was years ago. And I didn't have the hots for her, not like I do for you. If you don't like her by tomorrow morning, we won't introduce her to Daniel, but I think you will."

I sighed, remembering how generous Bob and Jean were with their hospitality when we were on the run. I had no reason not to invite her. Daniel would be glad of another young person in the community. But I didn't like the way Michael and Mei laughed and reminisced about student life as we walked home. Only as we approached the village did the conversation change to something that interested me: our growing interest in contacting the Citidomes.

"What do you think?" Michael persisted. "Surely we could link in with the Truth Exchange, get messages to a selected few?"

"I guess so," she said. "But I daren't use my DataBand out here. Do you?"

"Haven't used it since we arrived. Our leader, Daniel, keeps them all, for security."

"Yeah, ours does the same." She didn't seem to share Michael's enthusiasm. Thank God. Maybe he'd lose interest in her.

"Nice village," she said. "Woow, what a beautiful church."

As the evening progressed, I increasingly resented Mei's intrusion and hoped she wouldn't want to join us. Perhaps I could have a quiet word with Daniel. I tried to be generous, recognising the jealousy monster I thought I'd tamed. But Mei was impossible to like.

"What's that weird flavour?" she asked, wrinkling her nose at my chicken casserole.

"There are wild mushrooms in it, home-made wine and some herbs I picked." I raised my chin.

"Fantastic, isn't it? Our favourite recipe. Cathy's a much better cook than me," Michael said.

"How can you eat like this? Don't you have constant indigestion?"

"Well yeah, it's an acquired taste, but surely you're used to it by now?" I narrowed my eyes, stung by the criticism. "You've been living outside for over year now haven't you?"

"Yeah, but I don't like the food much."

She didn't seem to like anything much. Was this really the fiery rebel who'd inspired Michael? He must have liked more than that in her. Maybe he was lying about the physical attraction to protect my feelings. She had a kind of elegance that I could never achieve.

"Your hair looks great," I said, looking at her smooth, flat hair. "Guess it was naturally straight?"

"Yeah, lucked out, huh? I see your permastraighten's grown out." She frowned at my curls. "Tough break. You could use some serum."

"What work are you doing in your community?" Michael changed the subject.

"They always want me to work on the farm. It's not what I expected."

"What do you do?" Michael asked. "I loved the buzz of cutting the wheat at harvest time."

"Oh yeah, I tried that." She scowled. "It half killed me. I did a bit of everything."

"Are you at the Chatsworth community?" I knew that they grew most of the wheat around here.

"Yeah, that's the one. But let's not talk about wheat; I'm sick of the sight of it. D'you have any alcoholic drinks?"

"Yeah, mum's made some cider. Try some."

"Ugh, it's sharp."

I swallowed my increasing irritation, noticing that Mei's disparaging comments about the cider didn't stop her from draining the glass and asking for more. "You've got quite a few luxuries haven't you?" she said. "This cottage is lovely. It's nicer here than Chatsworth. Do you think your leader will let me join you?"

"Depends if you're willing to do the jobs you're assigned," I said, no longer worried about appearing welcoming. "Everyone has to do land work at some stage, whether they like it or not."

"Guess so." She scowled.

"But with winter coming, there's plenty of other things to

do." Michael's voice was encouraging, and he described our plans for a biopolymer manufacturing laboratory. My jaw tightened. I was already stinging with disappointment that my pregnancy wouldn't allow me to work with hazardous chemicals. If she took my job, I'd be furious. As for what else she might be planning to take, I couldn't bear to think of it.

"Now that sounds like my sort of work." Mei smiled, looking only at Michael. "Seems like you're way more forward-thinking than the other places I've been. How many other Citidome escapees live here? Young ones, I mean? I'm dying for intelligent company."

"There's around fifty in the three communities, and quite a few under thirty," Michael said.

"That many? Any recent escapees? Ones whose brains haven't stagnated yet?"

"A few."

"That's what I was hoping for. By the way, I keep meaning to ask. Cathy … strange name."

Before I had a chance to stop him, Michael explained. "Yeah, we chose old names from books. I'm Michael now. Cathy was Caia."

Fresh fear gripped me. Something about Mei's barrage of questions while only giving vague information about herself was disconcerting me. Surely she knew that most communities largely consisted of Citidome refugees? And most people in the Chatsworth community had changed their names. Did she really live there? Anna had told me that the Chatsworth community was in trouble because there were no women there between the peak childbearing ages of 16 and 30. Mei must be in her early twenties. Perhaps they discounted her because she was from the Citidome. And why had we never seen her in the market before? But why would she lie? Had she been asked to leave another community?

I tried to dispel my worries; Michael didn't seem unduly suspicious. He was a good judge of character. But perhaps Mei's smiling eyes and heart-shaped face had clouded his judgement. While alcohol cast a warm glow over them, their conversation becoming increasingly exclusive, I sipped at yet another cup of bitter herbal tea. It burnt my tongue.

By the time we went to bed, Mei was almost paralytic from the amount of cider she'd drunk. Michael laid her on the sofa and covered her with coats.

"You were quiet; didn't you like her?" he whispered once we reached the bedroom. He slurred his words.

"No." My voice was a harsh rasp. "In case you didn't notice, it wasn't much fun for me, listening to you exchanging all those stories of your student days that I couldn't join in. And why did she ask so many questions about the community?"

"Course she would, if she wants to join us." He frowned, but his face softened. "Sorry, didn't mean to leave you out." He squeezed my hand in a gesture that refused to console. "Guess it's not much fun when we can drink and you can't."

I turned away from the warm fumes of alcohol on his breath. Soon, the sound of his snoring increased my irritation. The presence of Mei in our home seemed to grow and twist beneath me. I analysed and reanalysed her words, and increasingly found them riddled with inconsistencies. But just after I thought I'd never sleep, the pressure on my bladder woke me. I sighed – another annoying consequence of pregnancy. It wasn't yet too cold to venture outside and since I never got over my horror of urinating into a bucket, I tiptoed through the living room to take the chilly trip across the yard. Mei's snores caused my hands to clench into fists. Why had she lied? Why had Michael laughed so freely and drank so much?

Making my way back across the room, I stumbled, almost tripping over something – Mei's bag. Motivated by instinct, I opened it but instantly began to close it. What was I expecting to find? Then my attention was caught by an unmistakeably familiar glow – a DataBand. I lifted it out and stared at it. Hadn't Mei said she'd handed hers to her community leader? And why was it activated? It was easily traceable.

Unless ... my throat tightened. Was Mei in contact with anyone in the Citidome? Had she been back? Her hair was too perfect – not a single split end. And that white trim on her top – surely that should have been greyed by repeated washing? But how could she have returned to the Citidome without being sent to a correction centre? Maybe Daisy could hack into the DataBand. I took it upstairs, hiding it under my pillow and spent the rest of the night awake, my mind spinning with the possibilities. Was Mei a trader? Or worse, a spy? Should I tell Michael? No, he wouldn't believe me. The wait for daybreak had never seemed longer.

As the sun rose I dressed silently. Michael stirred and yawned.

"Hey, gorgeous. What time is it?"

"Only six-thirty. My back's killing me so I'm going to get up and feed the chickens. You go back to sleep."

I ran to Anna's house and hammered at the door. Eventually Daisy appeared in pyjamas.

"Christ, where's the fire? Have you any idea what time it is?"

"Sorry, it's an emergency. I found this on a girl that's staying in our house. She's been asking questions about escapees. Can you hack into it?"

"Shit. Yeah, these used to be easy; should take about ten minutes."

Our noise woke Anna. I told her the whole story while Daisy worked on the DataBand.

"I think you're worrying unnecessarily, sweetheart," Anna said. "Are you sure you're not just jealous because it's an old friend of Michael's?"

As promised, nine minutes later, Daisy raised her head, her face ashen.

"You're in deep shit. She sent two messages, one at 11:30 yesterday, the other at 21:30."

I scanned the words.

Have located two escapees from Sigma-2 and one of them is carrying a child! Am spending the night in Ashford, so I might get more information. Meet me there tomorrow?

09:00 tomorrow sounds perfect.

"Oh no!" I was going to be sick.

"Don't just sit there; we need to move. We have to get her out of the village, us too. They've got our location and our new names. But why me?"

"Michael … they knew each other in the Citidome. He was chatting to her about recent escapees."

"Bloody idiot. Thought he'd have more sense. Oh well, no time for that now. First we should destroy this so they can't trace it."

"You two get over there. Tell Michael. I'll tell Daniel," said Anna.

Daisy attacked the DataBand with a kitchen knife, then submerged it in a glass of water. "That should have wrecked it. Let's go. We'll need weapons."

Still numb, I took the knife and rope and together we ran to the house. We had less than three hours to find a hiding place. And then what? Michael and Mei were upturning cushions.

"It's got to be here somewhere," Mei muttered.

"Looking for something?" My voice froze the room. As Mei turned around, I waved the slashed DataBand. She took a step forward, but Daisy leapt towards her, grabbed her arm and twisted it behind her back.

"Knife, Cathy," said Daisy.

I placed the blade against Mei's neck.

"One move and I'll slit your throat," I hissed. I might by accident, if not intentionally, my hands were shaking so violently.

"Have you gone mad?" asked Michael.

"We've destroyed your DataBand so you won't be able to contact your Citidome pals," Daisy snarled in Mei's face.

"She's turned us in," I glared at Michael. "CEs are on their way."

"What?" He staggered backwards.

At that moment, Mei caught me off guard, jerked my arm and knocked the knife from my hand. But as she made a lunge for it, Daisy launched herself on her. Michael joined the fight and soon had her pinned to the floor.

"You treacherous bitch!" he roared.

"Grab her hands. I'll tie them up," said Daisy.

Daisy and Michael tied Mei's hands behind her back and bound her ankles together.

"There's no point," Mei spat the words at Michael. "They'll find your freak girlfriend anyway. Turned out she was on their priority list even before the pregnancy. Illegal record keeping, assault … But pregnant? They'll hunt her down like a rabbit."

"You poisonous …"

"You're all deluded," Mei sneered. "This isn't living. It's survival, no more."

There was nothing to do but wait for Daniel, and the question hung between us like a cloud about to burst. Why had Michael trusted Mei? Terrified to voice the thought, I gazed out of the window. No sign of anyone. What time was it? How far away could we get before the CEs arrived?

Michael glanced at Mei, his forehead furrowed. "Why?"

"I couldn't stand life out here." Her voice was laced with venom. "You remember how we all used to be in Tau-2. All I wanted was answers to all the questions we used to talk about. I wanted to meet intelligent people, but where are they? All that goes on here is struggle and hard labour. Within a month my brain had turned to mush. What are you doing here, Mac? You're wasting your brilliant mind. You'll never find the truth here."

"Yes I will," Michael said, his eyes flashing. "And I've found something more important. Love and friendship."

"Huh. You've gone soft in the head." Her rosebud mouth twisted into a sneer. "I saw this place for what it was: an intellectual graveyard. Once Hal disappeared I couldn't stand it, wanted to get back in. Then a trader told me that escapes have doubled this year and the authorities were keen to find recent escapees, people that'll still be remembered, and make an example of them. Through him, I struck a deal: if they didn't put me in a Correction Centre, I'd find other escapees. So far we've caught twenty. Generally I go to towns and ask questions. Seeing you was a stroke of luck. But I'm kinda puzzled. I heard on a newsfeed that you were dead."

"I thought we were friends." Michael said with a shake of the head.

"You've forgotten. There are no friends in the Citidome."

Then, in a swift movement, Daisy grabbed the knife from the floor and plunged it in and out of Mei's stomach. Mei screamed and clutched at herself, crimson oozing between her fingers. Before I had time to process the horror scene in front of us, Michael took the knife.

"Jesus, Daisy. What d'you think you're doing?" he said.

"What can we do? We've got to get rid of her before she talks to the CEs. In her messages, she didn't give any names, just two escapees." Her voice dropped and she glanced at me. "One pregnant."

"Shit. Yeah ... you're right. But if you're doing a job, do it properly. One stab wound's not going to do it." With that, Michael plunged the knife into Mei's chest. A gasping sound came from her mouth and she lost consciousness. I slumped to the sofa, overwhelmed with dizziness, and pressed my hands to my eyes. When I released them, Daisy was checking Mei's pulse.

"That's done it."

No-one moved. Daisy and Michael stared at each other, as if trying to get the other to confirm what they'd just done. I returned my gaze to the red stain oozing across the carpet. My home, tainted with Mei's blood. My home, a murder scene. Then Michael directed his gaze to me and opened his mouth to speak.

"Cathy, I –"

A pounding on the door stopped him. We looked at each other.

"Must be Daniel." Michael said. "I'll get it."

Michael had barely opened the door a fraction when they burst in. Two men, the discs on their cheeks identifying them as CEs, armed with stun guns.

"Quick, out the back!" Daisy's hand grabbed mine and dragged me from the room, to the sound of shouting and struggle. And then we were running down the backstreets, leaving Michael behind.

"To the barn." Daisy's breaths came out in gasps. "We'll get the TravelPod."

"B-but … Michael!"

"We've got to save you."

"No!" I screamed and wrestled my hand from Daisy's grip. Then a ringing slap took my breath from me.

"Sorry, I had to do that. You were hysterical. Cathy, think logically. Daniel's onto it. We have to hide. It's you they're after."

I couldn't think any more. Daisy took my hand once more and soon we arrived at the barn.

"Wait there and I'll see if I can find out what's happening."

I slumped against the side of the barn.

"I saw Mary; she got me the key. They're turning the village upside down, looking for you. I'm going to take you away from here."

"What about Michael?"

"Dunno, there wasn't time. Come on."

"But where?"

"West, I think, the further away from the Citidomes the better. For God's sake, Cathy, get moving."

And before I had time to protest further, Daisy had bundled me into the TravelPod and set off, wrenching me away from everyone I loved.

CHAPTER – 18

Melancholic wreaths of mist shrouded the hills as we drove westwards.

"You can't take me away from Michael!" I yelled. "What if he's been hurt, or recaptured?"

"For God's sake, you're not thinking this through. CEs aren't usually armed with anything stronger than Stun Guns. Mei's messages didn't name you. She said there were two escapees; two people ran out of the room. Michael's officially dead; he should have been deleted from the system. If you go back, they'll link him with you. And ..." Her voice dropped. "There's no going back now. Once the safety of the village has been compromised, Daniel will probably ask you to leave anyway. Your only chance of ever coming back is to disappear for a while until they stop looking."

"W-will he kick Michael out too?"

"From what Mei said, it's gonna be you they're after."

"But where? And for how long?"

"No idea. I'll work that out as soon as I find signs of life."

"But what about Michael? I have to be with him! And what about our wedding?"

"Weddings can wait. And as for Michael ... I know how heartless this sounds, but right now you can't think of him. You have to think of yourself and" – she tapped my stomach – "what's in there."

Heartless was the word. She and Michael had just committed murder. And while part of me had wanted to plunge that knife deep into Mei's treacherous heart, I knew I didn't have it in me to take a human life. The image of the blood on the carpet wouldn't leave me. I pressed my hands to my eyes, as if trying to blot it out.

"B-but other recent escapees? Will they capture other people?"

"Might do, but there's not that many apart from me, and I'm here now, aren't I?"

Gradually the shock subsided and I took in the hills, even larger and more majestic than the ones we'd seen on our first trip. Soon we entered an opulent town with awe-inspiring architecture but, again, gaping shop fronts blighted the centre. But I couldn't enjoy the new surroundings. My mind was whirling. Was Daisy trying to appease me or did she know what she was talking about? Would Michael really have been deleted from the system or would he have merely been recorded as deceased? Even if they didn't identify him as an escapee, would the CEs punish him for Mei's death? Worst of all was the anger that was bubbling inside me, anger directed at Michael. He'd always had flawless judgement. But one look at the girl he used to like, and all common sense had abandoned him. His carelessness had destroyed our safe haven.

"Breathe slowly," Daisy said. "This town doesn't look very promising, and it's a bit close to home. We'll keep going."

"I don't know about this. I'd rather go back."

But Daisy ignored my protests. After another hour, we crossed on a stone bridge overlooking what looked like an artificial river, and she stopped abruptly.

"Oh wow, look at that!"

I looked along the ancient waterway. While one side had been left to nature, evidence of man-made structures remained, crumbling wooden defences forming a straight edge to the waterway, and an overgrown path running parallel to the water. Trees lined the route, the backdrop of hills completing a beguiling picture. But it was what sat in the centre of the picture that had caught Daisy's eye. A long, thin vessel, multicoloured with layers of paint, was tied to the bank. I grabbed Daisy's arm.

"Look, there's smoke coming from that little chimney," I said. "Do you think it's occupied?"

"Must be. God, that could be perfect, if we can persuade them to take you."

"What – live on a boat with complete strangers?" My panic rose again but before I could stop her, Daisy marched across to the bank and was soon on board and knocking at the door. A spare-framed man with milk-white skin, his red beard stretching to the base of his neck, emerged, brandishing a shotgun, then lowered it.

"Can I help you?" he asked.

While Daisy explained our plight, a curvy, mahogany-skinned woman came out of the cabin. I could hardly take my eyes from the striking couple, especially their hair. It hung halfway down their backs, in matted coils. They wore homemade clothes, all patchwork, as colourful and offbeat as their home.

"Pregnant, and from the Citidome?" The man scratched his beard.

I tried to swallow but a knot had formed in my throat. Had we been too trusting?

"If you feel it's too much of a risk, we'll understand," I said.

"It's a risk all right. The whole State could be out looking for you." The man raised his eyebrows and looked at the woman.

An iron band tightened around my chest. The whole State?

"Don't scare the girl, Kell. Of all people, we should help them, and you know it," the woman urged, and then smiled. "Sorry, he gets jumpy. I'm Dee, this is Kell."

"I'm Cathy."

"Guess we'd better take you," Kell muttered.

"That's sorted then." Daisy drew her hands together. "So I'll come and get you in, what, two weeks?"

"Y-you're not coming too?" I swallowed. She planned to leave me with strangers for two weeks?

"I can hardly leave the TravelPod here, can I? I'll take it back and find out what's going on. They might well be looking for me, too. But that's not your problem."

"But we won't be here in two weeks' time," said Dee.

"You don't know how the canal folk work?" Kell said.

"Canal?" I frowned.

"This waterway – there's a whole network of them. We transport goods up and down the country in exchange for food."

"So how will I find you?" Daisy said.

"Hmm, kinda hard to say," said Kell. "We come and go wherever people want us to. But to be honest, I don't think it's going to be safe for Cathy here to go home until after the baby's born. They'll lose interest in her then."

I frowned. Why was my pregnancy such a big deal to the Citidome? I'd have imagined it would gross them out too much for them to come near me.

"But I'm not due for another three months! You can't seriously expect me to stay away from Michael for three whole months?"

"I dunno; this is such a safe place, away from roads," said Daisy with a hopeless shrug. "It's not a long time in the grand scheme of things."

"B-but –" I started.

"Cathy, we'll look after you. I promise. Maybe your Michael can come and join us." The warmth in Dee's voice made me trust her. "We could send you a message."

"How?"

"Christ, you do have a lot to learn. You don't communicate electronically?"

We shook our heads.

"OK, let's think … Daisy, about a kilometre down that road is a town called Macclesfield," Dee said. "Take the first left and you'll find a small community. If Michael stays there, we can pick him up next time we're passing. If there's no-one there next time we pass, we'll leave a message."

"OK. I'll tell him."

Feeling helpless, I said goodbye to Daisy, and found Kell scanning the surroundings, as if expecting a marauding army of CEs.

"We'd better get on the move, then we can talk," he said.

He took my hand to help me aboard. Next he unravelled the ropes and as the wood-fired engine chugged into life, I explored its narrow, cosy cabin. The smell of damp pervaded the air and varnished timbers had evidence of rot, but it felt like a home. On every wall hung works of art made from natural materials – woven grasses, sea shells, and dried flowers mounted on fiberstone. Doors from the kitchen and living area led to a bathroom and two bedrooms. But I couldn't stem the flood of tears. Would I ever see Michael again?

"Hey, don't cry." Kell put an arm around me. "We meant what we said about keeping you safe."

"And here's someone else you should meet," said Dee, emerging from the bedroom with a large bundle.

I gasped at the sight of a cheerful, and most importantly, healthy-looking baby who gurgled and smiled.

"That's why I insisted we should help you. You're the only other pregnant Citidome refugee I've ever met. This is Harry. He's six months old."

"He's gorgeous!" I said, proffering a finger for the baby to hold. His tiny fingers grasped mine, sending a shudder of yearning through me. "You're from the Citidome too?"

"Yeah, we left around a year ago. I realised that I might be pregnant, so we had to make a run for it. And when we found a community – Hest Bank, which is where we're going next – they suggested we take on the boat until Harry was born. The couple that used to run it wanted to retire. But mostly, it was for my protection." Her voice dropped. "I have to warn you, Cathy. The authorities target sick or injured people, and pregnant women, for capture and return to the Citidome. They parade them as warnings – you know the sort of thing – if you run away you'll end up like this. And in their view, pregnancy is the most freakish fate that could befall a citizen – your stomach gets so big. You need to be careful."

"It's really that bad?"

Their grim expressions told me that it was.

"So why did you stay on the boat after you had Harry?" I asked.

"It's a lifestyle that suits us: no-one else's rules to obey. We get to be part of a community when we choose, but without getting too bogged down in their internal politics. The scenery changes all the time; it's perfect. We're taking flour to a community on the coast on this trip. Bet you've never seen the sea."

"The sea! I've always dreamed of seeing it." The pressure in my chest eased. For now, at least, I was safe. "Why are you transporting flour? Don't they grow their own wheat?" I asked.

"No, most of the north don't. The land's only suitable for cattle and sheep. That's why the State farms are concentrated in the southeast. And then there's the problem of milling. No-one along the network's self-sufficient; we can transport stuff over hundreds of miles."

"Interesting," I murmured. "Our community's pretty self-sufficient."

"Really?" And they quizzed me on every detail of our village. Part of me tensed, remembering Mei's relentless questions. But this seemed different, a genuine curiosity.

"This trip's going to be an eye-opener for you. We'll have plenty of chance to chat. The Lancashire canal has no locks," Kell said.

"What's a lock?"

"It's a gate that changes the water levels according to the lie of the land. But none of them have been properly maintained for over a hundred years. Once we got stuck there for a week trying to repair one. That's why we don't get out your way. The canals heading east are full of locks. Some don't work any more. So you end up with satellite communities like yours."

"Satellites?"

"Yeah, little clusters of communities, with just local trading networks."

"I never realised there was any other sort."

"Most of them are the other sort. You'll have to give us the names and locations of your communities; we're trying to fill the gaps in our map." Kell switched on a DataBand and projected an image of State 11, covered in symbols. I gasped.

"How can you use your DataBand here?"

"Don't you know how to delete the personal details and scramble the tracer signal?" Kell raised his eyebrows as if this were the most obvious thing in the world. "I guess you're not part of Out There, either?"

I shook my head.

"You really are out of it, aren't you? Look, this is the Out There base. Only people with this passcode can access it. We use it to share knowledge, news about the Citidomes, ways to do more than just survive in this godforsaken land. Spread the word. We're looking to form links all over the country."

I goggled at the titles – tips for harvesting oats, basketry, fish farming, making paper, methane digesters, and growing cotton.

"How can all this be going on and us not know about it?"

"Because you're not on the canals. Look." Kell returned to the image of State 11 and started to explain the symbols to me: locations of Citidomes, large and small communities, most close to the canal network. I reeled. Maybe a few weeks away from Michael wasn't so unbearable. Daniel would welcome me back with open arms when he realized what useful contacts I'd made. With our DataBands operational once more and this shared knowledge base, winter didn't seem so daunting any more.

I had to admit that if any aspect of being ejected from my home could be considered lucky, I'd fallen on my feet with Kell and Dee, and we soon became friends. I was astonished by how slowly the boat travelled, barely exceeding running speed, but soon appreciated the advantages of the leisurely pace. Kell and Dee insisted that I sit with my feet up and as I looked out of the window, waterside wildlife provided non-stop distraction from the rat that was nibbling at my stomach: herons, dragonflies, a fleeting, thrilling glimpse of a kingfisher – an electric-blue shimmer against the branches. But best of all was the chance to spend time with Dee and little Harry. He was a beautiful baby, his colouring similar to mine – a perfect blend of Kell and Dee – with enormous brown eyes.

"I won't lie to you. Giving birth tears and hurts like hell," Dee said. "One was enough for me. And I never lost that weight I put on. Took six months before I could see my feet again." She had an irresistible laugh: half snort, half squeal. "But I managed to breastfeed for three months until my milk dried up." She went on to describe breastfeeding in graphic detail.

"The idea of my nipples producing milk still freaks me out," I said.

"It did me, but women used to do it all the time. Want to hold him?"

"Yes, please."

Harry was surprisingly heavy. But as I bounced him on my knee, he giggled. My heart wanted to burst. Never had anything felt more natural. I could do this! But only if Michael was with me.

We reached Hest Bank, a village on the Lancashire canal,

and moored the boat. Though the village was an attractive mixture of white-painted and stone cottages, I barely noticed it, my eyes drawn to the sea.

"Can we go right up to it?" I asked.

"Of course."

"It's not blue." I was disappointed to see that the colour of the water was closer to black, with silver flecks where the light bounced off it. But, on reaching the beach and hearing the roaring and grumbling of the water, I gasped. "It's like standing on the edge of the world. Listen to the sound of the waves. All that power."

"That's why a strong community formed here," said Kell. "All the villages have electricity from wave power."

"Is the water cold?"

"Take your shoes off and try it. We'll wait here; take as long as you like." Kell and Dee smiled like indulgent parents. I abandoned my shoes and ran to the sea, shrieking first as my feet squished in the wet sand, then again when I made contact with the glacial water. I strolled along the beach, inhaling the salt air and listening to the crashing of the white-capped waves, while screeching gulls circled overhead. If only Michael had been with me, it would have been a memory to treasure.

We spent the evening at a gathering of the Hest Bank community, one of the largest in the region, with forty-five inhabitants.

"I'd like to introduce a new friend, Cathy," said Dee. "Cathy, this is Fin, the community leader."

Fin, a sandy-haired man of around forty whose good looks were marred by a deep circular depression on his cheek, gave me a look of concern. "Cathy, I need to tell you something. I used to be a CE in the Citidome."

"Really? Oh ..." I said as realisation dawned. "You removed your disc."

"Yeah, it was one of the reasons I escaped. There's more to them than a mark of status; they transmit your voice to a central control with a voice recognition system. Anyone who says the word backup gets immediate reinforcements sent out. It's a great system, but it ensures that no-one in the Correction Unit can ever say a word out of turn. You never know what else they're listening to. Eventually I felt so oppressed by it I tore it out and escaped."

"Ouch. Bet that was painful."

"It was." He traced the outline of the scar with his finger. "But there were other reasons I left. I didn't like some of the things I was asked to do." His eyes – the colour of autumn leaves – bore into mine. "A girl became pregnant. I had to arrange for her to be displayed as a freak in the Pleasuredome." His words thudded in my ears. A freak? "They kept her in a cage, naked, for people to laugh at. Like an animal in the zoo, but they treat the animals better. When she was ready to give birth, they cut it out of her and left her to bleed to death." His voice lowered. "Keep your head down until it's born, won't you?"

Nausea rose in me. I'd kill myself rather than allow that to happen. The evening gave me more unpleasant food for thought. Only one of the community – a prematurely aged woman called Lita – had given birth in the last ten years – and she had four children.

"Isn't that exhausting?" I asked.

"Like you wouldn't believe, but I need to have as many as possible. The only other woman here of childbearing age died last year ... giving birth." She flushed and looked away, obviously realising the tactlessness of her words. "The community needs to reproduce. And when they're adults I'll have to send two of them away in exchange for someone of the same age from a different community to mix the blood lines."

As the evening went on, any illusions I had of bringing our child into an idyllic world were shattered. Communities still faced endless difficulties and few had been established as long as ours. No communities were self-sustaining; they needed trading arrangements and a regular influx of Citidome escapees to boost the active, working population. And even if I wasn't captured and got back to Michael and survived childbirth, would I then become nothing more than a baby-making machine?

The conversation turned to the Citidomes, and Fin was able to confirm some of my suspicions.

"I once saw a CE injecting something into two people

who'd been caught having sex," I said. "Was it the TJB virus?"

"Yeah." He nodded. "They do it as a precaution in case one of the couple aren't already Marked. We had to make people believe that everyone who did it got the Mark. And we had to make the consequences of the Mark as dire as possible. But it's nowhere near as bad as people think. Scientists are still experimenting with new virus forms, trying to make it more debilitating. There's too much of an illegal trade in lasering Marks at the moment."

"Christ – so evil," I muttered.

"At first the authorities wanted to tag sexual deviants – that's what they call them – like the RedTagging for subversive thinkers, but it tends to be easier to discover subversive thinkers. So they developed the virus."

"So they do tag subversive thinkers? I've heard of RedTags but never seen them." I said.

"That's because a RedTag's a life sentence. The tags have a polymer disc on either side, attached by a bar that goes right through your earlobes. They're heat sealed – you can't pull them out. If they ever recapture you, you'll be tagged, tortured if they think you have any information – mostly something that'll make you look less pretty, because to them, that's the ultimate punishment – then taken to one of the correction camps on the outside. And if by some miracle you escape that, the tags have trackers."

I shivered. "Are these the outdoor correction centres they're putting the Marked in now?"

"Yeah. They've been around for decades. Brutal places. Who do you think does all the manual work outside the Citidomes – waste disposal, food production and the like?"

"Never thought about it. But presumably the authorities know about communities like ours. Why don't they do anything to deter us?"

"Because we don't cause them any trouble. They don't want everyone inside to know how good it is out here. They especially don't want evidence of healthy outsiders. It's when they find one that they consider," – Fin lowered his eyes – "deformed, that they display them."

"So if we helped other people escape, we might destroy

everything." I said.

"Biggest controversy we have," Fin said. "Some of us think we have to do something to get more people out here, others think it's best not to risk antagonising the authorities."

"What do you think?"

"I'd do anything I could to help people escape."

"You'll have to meet Michael. We've been talking about co-ordinated escape plans."

Michael would have loved the evening. He and Fin were so like-minded: men with a mission. I chatted to other community members and glowed with what I'd achieved today. But just as I was thinking that the disaster of Mei would end in triumph, I noticed Fin, Kell and Dee in heated discussion, Dee's head nodding in my direction. What were they saying about me? As soon as I approached, they stopped talking.

"Ah, Cathy," Fin began. "Kell and Dee will be moving on tomorrow morning and we all think it's best if you stay with us until after the baby's born."

"Oh, that's kind of you ... but surely I'd be safer on the boat?"

"In some ways yes, but now, with winter approaching, and it being your first winter, it's not such a good idea. We need to think of your baby."

I widened my eyes. "B-but what about Michael?"

"Kell and Dee will leave a message for him at Macclesfield and give him our co-ordinates. A few other canal boats travel up and down; he should be able to find us. I'd love to meet him; sounds like we'll have a lot to talk about." His face softened. "Don't look so frightened; I have a cellar in my house that I've converted into a bedroom. The trapdoor's hidden. A CE would never even suspect it's there. I'll take care of you, Cathy."

Dee's eyes wouldn't meet mine and I couldn't hide my feeling of betrayal.

"I trusted you. What am I – some sort of unexploded bomb that you want to get out of your hands as soon as possible?" I snapped.

"No, it's not like that, honestly." Dee's words were too hurried. "In fact we all want to keep you; we're just trying to decide what's the safest thing for you."

But the whole exchange had made me uneasy. And I couldn't shake the feeling that my safety wasn't the only thing on their minds.

CHAPTER - 19

In my first few days in my new home, I had no cause for complaint. My cellar bedroom was more comfortable than it sounded and had an electric light. Every member of the community came to visit me. Fin was fascinating company and the Out There knowledge base compelling. But it couldn't distract me from the fact that my wedding day had been and gone. And as well as the desperate physical, as well as mental, longing for Michael, I missed my friends. And more than that, I missed my house, and the entire village. It was something I'd come to understand, how a place can touch us in a special way, retaining part of us in the fibre of its buildings. Attachment. Surely it was part of what made us human?

"What are you reading about today?" he asked.

"Building an ice house. Fascinating."

"Did that myself," he smiled. "We need one, all the fish we eat. Talking of which, I've made a crab salad for lunch."

Yes, I liked Fin. I wondered why he wasn't in a relationship. He was a good-looking guy, in a less obvious way than Michael. Because of a scar, his face wasn't one that caused women to drool, but it was a good face, with a warm smile and eyes that crinkled at the corners.

"You look a bit down," he said. "Missing Michael? I'm sure he'll be up here within the week. Makes sense for you both to hide out here."

Missing Michael was an understatement. As well as the lingering anxiety there was an aching void inside me. Strange how quickly I'd adapted to having another body in the bed. Each morning I woke in a state of disorientation, looking for him. And being confined to the house all day soon became claustrophobic.

"Can I really not go for a walk?" I asked.

"Maybe when the first snow comes; it tends to block the roads so no-one leaves the Citidome then." Fin said. "Remember, I know how the CEs operate. Trust me, now they know you're pregnant, they'll be scouring the country for you. I've made an exercise routine for you to do in the house. You need to keep up your fitness."

A chill passed through me. "But how will we know whether it's a CE at the door? There's always people coming and going."

"Have you never noticed? Villagers have a coded knock." He rapped on the table in a recognisable rhythm. "If we hear anything different, you'll be straight down to the cellar."

It did seem a secure arrangement. I could access the trapdoor to the cellar in seconds. With a faded rug on top, it was undetectable. So why didn't I feel secure?

"Fin ... I've been thinking. I appreciate everything you're doing for me, but when Michael gets here, I think it's best I go home before the baby's born, maybe in late December. Surely no-one from the Citidomes will be out by then. You see ..." I paused, wondering whether to continue. But I had to voice the thought that had been gathering momentum. "I don't like to say this, but people die in childbirth. There's a chance I might not survive this. The doctor in our area has delivered ten babies. I bet there's no-one else in the country with so much experience. And ... if these next few months were my last, I'd want to spend them with the people I love. You see, my friends in Ashford – they're my family."

"I see." A flicker of disappointment passed across his face. "Well, I certainly wouldn't want to keep you here against your will. We'll talk about it when we get word from Michael. But for now, put that over-active imagination of yours to rest. Put your feet up and treat this trip as a learning experience. From what you've said, it sounds like your community is so hell-bent on being self-sufficient that they don't do much else."

"You've got a point. I can't believe what Mei – the woman who betrayed us – did, but I can partly understand her frustrations with the outside. We were driven outside partly by a thirst for knowledge. I thought we'd find the answers here. And I've been happier than I ever thought possible, but

I'm further away from the truth than when I was inside the Citidome."

"The truth?"

"Oh, you know. About the Citidomes, who controls them, whether the rest of the world has them, that sort of thing."

"You mean you really don't know?" He frowned.

"Know what?" I blinked.

"OK, tell me what you do know."

"I've realised that a lot about State 11 doesn't make sense."

"Such as?"

"The currency. The coins we use here; they're from Europe. Geographically, we should be in Europe. But our accents are different to the village-born – American, I think. And the currency we used in the Citidomes was Yuan, which seems to be Chinese."

"Huh. I assumed everyone outside knew." He shook his head and strode to the bookshelf, pulling down a thick folder. He returned and handed it to me. I frowned at the contents, which seemed to consist of a collection of inexpertly bound sheets of handwritten fiberstone. "Read this," he said. "It's the original records of the founder of this community. It'll explain everything better than I could."

Genuine history! My hands were shaking so much I could hardly hold the papers. I squinted. The writing was almost illegible at first, but gradually improved. Even a hundred years ago, the art of writing seemed to be dead.

1st January 2071

My name is Jake Benson. As the first elected leader of the Hest Bank self-sufficient community I intend to keep yearly records of our activities. But since I've lived through the most momentous years in our country's history, years that saw the death of a once-great nation, I feel it necessary to record my personal account of the events. I graduated from Liverpool University in June 2065, two weeks before the Thebula attack wiped out the city. Luckily I was at home in Hest Bank with my parents and two sisters when it happened. No-one could quite believe the estimates of the dead. The country was plunged into a state of emergency, overseas aid arriving on a daily basis, since it was unsafe to enter the cities. The world held its breath. Then came retaliation. The images of the horrific aftermath of the neutron strikes on the Middle East will stay with me forever. People spoke of nothing but apocalyptic horror and the end of civilization.

Then a miracle happened. It was as if the world had become a giant playground. Fearful of being the next to fall victim to bullies, countries started to huddle together in gangs. Alliances were formed that even a year before would have seemed unthinkable, nations that had traditionally been enemies united in fear. The United States of Central Asia was the first, followed by the United States of the Orient. The USA teamed up with Canada and the Central and South American countries to form the imposing United States of the Americas. Peace had broken out. There was talk of United States of Africa and Europe, but no-one answered the question everyone wanted to know; what would become of the citizens of the UK?

I lifted my eyebrows. According to the Knowledge Fountain, the various alliances were already in place by then.

Just as we were starting to think about emigration, Citidomes started being constructed at a record rate, with the ultimate intention of the entire population living in them. I wondered where the money was coming from. The UK economy had never recovered from the crash that followed the London Flood Disaster. It seemed an obvious question for newsfeeds to address but no answers came. I messaged the shows myself but received no reply. But few people questioned; we were living in a state of terror and were desperate for protection. My parents remembered the horror of the London floods, and were enthusiastic about the idea of moving.

Then came the big announcement: the United

Kingdom had ceased to exist. Parliament had been dissolved. The Royal Family had been despatched to Australia. We were to be renamed State 11 of the United States of the Orient.

Naturally we were all staggered. How was it possible that a country that once ruled most of the world could cease to be? We waited for news of riots and protests but none came. Our newsfeed presenters were all replaced by Chinese ones. The news was all positive: the United States of the Orient were delighted to welcome us. My parents' fear – that we'd all be forced to speak Chinese was soon dispelled. A beautiful female presenter assured us that all would continue as normal: English as the first language with Chinese taught only to a selected few as the second language. We had our first broadcast from our new president, Wei Tian.

I dropped the papers.

"The USO?" I murmured. "Isn't that on the other side of the world?"

Fin turned around. "You had no idea? The reason we speak with American-accented English seems to be because it's the internationally recognised form of the language. Did you never question why some people studied Chinese?"

"I studied it myself. Yeah, I asked what the point was. They told me that only the most advanced children got to study Chinese, that it was a huge privilege. It was the ultimate intellectual challenge and would stretch my brain. It seemed a reasonable explanation. After all, what was the point of all those mathematical equations?"

"It was a privilege all right – you'd probably have got sent out there in time. They like to cream off our intellectual elite."

My eyes widened and I read on.

Throughout the confusion I could only think – why has everyone accepted this without question? But it soon became obvious: fear. I was, by then, living in Wigan. One day in the town centre, someone furtively pressed a note written on fiberstone into my hand. This in itself was surprising – written notes were antiquated, even to my parents. When I read it I was intrigued. "Say no to the USO," it said, and gave details of a meeting to take place that week. Naturally I attended. But, as soon as the meeting had convened and the speaker introduced himself, dozens of uniform-clad oriental men burst into the room, firing weapons more advanced than anything I'd ever seen. Being near the back, I managed to escape. Needless to say I was too frightened to question any further.

In December 2065 I was offered a job and a home in one of the newly constructed Citidomes but declined it. By then I had a job I loved at a Centre for Alternative Technology. However, in October 2067 the entire company were forced to relocate to a Citidome called Gamma-1. We were given little information about its location. I made specific enquiries as my mother had recently lost the use of her legs following a road accident and I didn't want to be far from her, but all I was given were vague reassurances that it was "not far."

Once I saw it, I was awestruck by the sheer beauty and grandeur of the Citidome. As a scientist, I was given Sector B accommodation, which offered me luxury quite unlike anything I'd known before. Until then I'd been renting a flat with my work colleague. The only puzzling aspect of the Citidomes was the number of people living together; never less than four. Couples were forced to share with others, a move that wasn't popular.

For a single man, however, life seemed easy and stress-free, until some unpleasant truths emerged. We weren't allowed to travel outside the Citidome except for emergencies. I messaged my family but received no reply. Soon, I became cynical about the Citidome's intentions. I'd been a politically active student and remember in my second year seeing an illegal pamphlet called "A Blueprint for a new Society", which described a so-called ideal society, housed in

Citidomes, that championed independence and non-attachment as the key to fulfilling one's potential. Citidomes started to bear an increasing resemblance to what I remember of the pamphlet.

Mind Values, which had been nothing more than a cult, a so-called ideal for living, began to be enforced and personal relationships became discouraged. The first ominous sign was the declaration that marriage was no longer legal. I started to meet up with others who had doubts about the way the Citidome was manipulating us, but we had to meet in secret as we noticed another phenomenon: the sudden disappearance of people, usually anyone who'd rebelled against the Citidome rules. A month or so later, all outside communication ceased, most sites became blocked and we were trapped.

In September 2070, early one morning two armed guards burst into my room. I was marched to the Citidome gate where a few of my friends had already been rounded up. Three trucks were parked outside and we were marched into them, with the news that we had been expelled from the Citidome as 'subversive thinkers' and were going to be relocated to the USO to join the Army. At this news, one guy attacked one of the guards, who retaliated by randomly opening fire. As we saw the bodies of our friends falling, my colleague Dave and I ran for the outside. We hid until the lorries left, then realised that we had no idea where we were. Dave's family had been wiped out by Thebula so we decided to head back to my family home.

"So that answers the question of where some of the missing millions went." I whistled. "Shipped off halfway around the world."

"Read on, you'll see what happened to the rest," said Fin, his voice dense.

I noticed with surprise that there were few cars and lorries on the road – of course they'd been in decline for years and the new TravelPods were gradually replacing them – but the number of vehicles of any description was still astonishingly low. A walk along the tracks to the railway station brought another shock. There were no longer any passenger trains. After a day we found our first outsider, who told us that since the relocation of most of the North West was two-thirds completed, the train network had been reserved for freight travel. There was no public transport of any description. We had to complete the journey home on foot. On arrival, we found a deserted village. Soon we discovered a local farmer, who told us the horrific story of the village.

The younger people had been offered Citidome places first, in 2068, and my sisters had left then. The disabled and elderly, including my mother, had been taken to a special care unit in an unknown location soon afterwards. I never saw any of them again.

"Oh, hell." I swallowed.

The remaining people had been relocated to Citidomes in stages over the year. The farmer had been told to relocate to the South where he'd work on a giant-scale State Farm. When he refused, he was told that it was compulsory; all public services, trading and water supply would cease on 30th December 2070. Despite this, he decided to stay in the village. His wife and daughter stayed with him. Meeting him – a man with a vision – persuaded me to stay and help him realise his dream of a self-sufficient community. He realised that the Ministry would take his stock and equipment so he took the best of his herd and half his sheep and hid them in the hills. He tinkered with his tractor to make it run noisily so it wouldn't be seized. While he could, he bought spare parts for the tractor, a plough, a harvester and all the seeds he could lay his hands on. He learned everything he could about arable farming. The only thing he lacked was labourers. The only other village residents were a couple in their sixties, who'd refused to be relocated to the special care unit.

It didn't seem much of a community but the alternative was to turn ourselves in and join the army, and the challenge of self-sufficiency was a more appealing adventure. Our first priority was the water supply, something on which I'd become an expert – my graduate project had been to create a rainwater plumbing system. I converted as many houses as I could and scoured the towns for spare parts. I hoped in time our community would grow.

We travelled into nearby towns for looting expeditions, collecting anything that could be of future use, and met two men and a woman who agreed to join our community. Ayaz and Nadeem were born in Syria but had been living in the UK since infancy. They told me that everyone who was not UK-born had been forced to repatriate, but they no longer had family in Syria and had no desire to live there. Amazingly, people had taken very few possessions with them. Our new friends told us that people were allowed one suitcase each weighing no more than 30 kg. We amassed vast supplies of useful commodities and stored them in a manor house in the village, which had become our warehouse.

I put down the book with a thud. "Special care units? Sounds like only the young and fit were chosen to relocate to the Citidomes. And how many people were forced to repatriate to their country of origin?"

"Chilling, isn't it?" Fin said. "I did my own research afterwards and discovered that at the time of the relocation, there were ten million registered disabled people and another ten million over the age of seventy. There were also about seven million immigrants – people who weren't born here. I imagine that none of these were wanted in the 'New Society'."

"So many disabled people? All sent away? To the USO?"

"I guess that only the subversive thinkers went to the USO. They were young and fit. They could at least be used in the Army. I heard rumours that the others went to Australia. I did some reading about that, too. It's a vast, underpopulated country. Historically it belonged to the United Kingdom, as State 11 used to be called. It was originally used as a colony for our prisoners. My guess is that it became a dumping ground for unwanted people."

"Oh yeah, Jake mentioned the Royal Family. Were they the kings and queens I read about in the history books?"

"Yeah, I've never understood their function. As far as I could see they didn't actually govern the country, but they lived in huge palaces."

"Do you know anything else about the pamphlet – what was it – *Blueprint for a New Society*?" I asked.

"No, but there's something sinister about its timing. Look again."

"Huh? It was produced before Jake graduated; he read it as a student ..." I scratched my head.

"That's right, and he graduated just before the Thebula attack. That means that there were plans to put us all into Citidomes before Thebula. The ultimate aim of Citidome wasn't to protect but to control."

I took a minute to let this sink in.

"So the Thebula virus attack wasn't the reason for the Citidomes; it was just an excuse to start this project?"

"Exactly. It seems that the USO took advantage of a national disaster to seize a country and treat its citizens as nothing more than laboratory animals, to see if their theories of social control worked."

"The whole thing was planned? I can't believe it. So what'll happen in the future? What if they decide the experiment has failed? Is there any way back now?"

"How can there be?" said Fin.

Neither of us spoke.

Oh, where was Michael? My head was bursting. I needed to share this with him. Finally, I understood the origins of the Citidomes. But it brought me no comfort. Over the next week I struggled to process the information. I read each year's record, and became so immersed in the story of the developing community that I felt I knew each of the original residents. I read of running tractors on ethanol, constructing stills, failed harvests and the revival of the canal network.

"Those early years must have been tough," I said.

"Especially the fear that the USO army would find them."

"Yeah, I'm amazed they didn't," Fin said. "There's mention of cities being firebombed, but only those affected by the Thebula virus attacks. I guess it was a way of disposing of all the decomposing bodies. Perhaps once they had all their lab rats in place, they no longer worried about those left on the outside. The Citidomes don't get a mention until 2073 when the first escapee arrived."

Over the week, I devoured the records as ferociously as I had any novel. Jake's vision for the community had been far-sighted. In 2119, at the age of 72, Jake recorded his last entry.

This year has seen a record influx of fifteen arrivals, and all for the same reason: they bear the mark of the TJB virus, the sexually-transmitted virus that has suddenly appeared in the Citidomes. Interestingly, these people have not all hailed from the same Citidome. It seems that movement from one Citidome to another is uncommon so I'm surprised that the virus has spread so quickly. Has it been deliberately introduced? It beggars belief, but it seems that they're now outlawing sex. Whatever next! I'm more convinced than ever that the world has gone mad and I was right to set up this community. I look upon the fifty-two residents of our twin communities with a sense of satisfaction and intend to pass on the task of record keeping, hoping that I leave my records in good hands.

I closed the book sadly. I'd miss the old man. The records continued on a DataBand; presumably by then they'd learned to make them untraceable. As I discussed each new gem of information with Fin, I grew to enjoy his company more and more. We discussed all aspects of the community's history except for one statistic. There had been 34 births since the records began, of which three were stillbirths, three women died in childbirth, and two children died in infancy. There'd also been eight reported miscarriages. The odds for a successful birth weren't good.

And as the second week passed without word from Michael, the now-constant knot in my stomach grew and tangled. Someone must have got my message by now. So why no word from anyone? Michael was safe ... wasn't he?

CHAPTER – 20

The first non-coded knock came at the end of my third week.

"Cellar – now!" Fin hissed.

I bolted down the stairs. Could it be Michael? Or … I held my breath. Footsteps pounded the floor above me. The trapdoor remained closed. I sat in the total blackness, holding my head. The sound of slamming doors told me that this wasn't a friendly visit. But Fin didn't open the trapdoor, even after the noises had gone. Silence. Had he been taken too? Surely not. He'd lived here ten years; he wouldn't be of interest any more. The trapdoor couldn't be opened from the inside. I curled up into a ball on the bed. As the time passed, my terror rose like bathwater. Was this my fate, to be trapped forever in a dark cellar? My rational voice calmed me. A villager came to the door with fresh eggs every morning; she'd surely check on me. My internal debate was still in full flow when a chink of light pierced the gloom.

"You're safe to come out now; they've gone." Fin's voice – was he there all along?

I crept upstairs, screwing up my eyes against what seemed like blinding light.

"CEs?" My voice was small.

He nodded, took my arm and led me to the sofa where he knelt beside me. Oh hell. What now?

"Sorry, there's no easy way to tell you this. Someone from your home village tipped them off that you were here."

My blood turned to iced water. "W-what? Who?"

"They didn't say. Now, calm yourself. Hyperventilating won't help anyone. Come on, in, two, three, four." He talked me through my breathing until it steadied. "Cathy, it's going to be OK. Lita just came to give me the all-clear. They've spoken to everyone in the village. Everyone gave the prepared lie: that you'd been here but we didn't want you endangering us, and that we sent you south."

I breathed. In, two, three. Out, two, three. "Why south? Isn't that where I came from?"

"You came from the south-east. No-one in their right minds would believe you'd gone further north in winter."

Nothing made sense. Who would betray me? Did Michael even get the message? Then, the most sinister thought of all, could I trust Daisy? Her words – you got the best one – echoed in my mind. Since Peter's fling with Vanessa, her relationship with him had deteriorated even more. With me out of the way, Michael would be available for her.

"I have to go home!"

"Oh, Cathy, you know that's suicide. The canal people come by quite often; there'll be a message soon."

As my tears started to flow, he drew me into his arms and I sobbed against his shirt. He stroked my hair and I surrendered to his comfort, wondering whom I'd ever been able to trust.

The second suspicious knock came just days later. This time my incarceration lasted only around five minutes. From what I could hear, no-one entered the house. But when the light returned, Fin's expression was even more grim than it had been the first time.

"Cathy …" He held out his hand. Soon we'd assumed our respective positions for the giving and receiving of bad news. And this time Fin didn't seem to know where to start. He swallowed, then cleared his throat. "That was one of the canal people. They picked up a message for you at Macclesfield, from your community leader."

He paused.

"Please, Fin. It can't be any worse than I'm imagining right now."

"I-I'm afraid it is. Apparently one of your friends tipped off the guards; they were harassing the villagers all the time. And the leader doesn't want you to return because it puts them at too much risk. And …"

"And Michael? What about Michael?" My voice rose to screaming pitch.

Fin took both of my hands and clasped them between his. "I'm so sorry. He was killed in the scuffle with the guards on the day you ..." A rising noise filled my ears, drowning out the words I didn't want to hear.

And my world shattered into a million glistening shards.

I became aware of the ceiling. I was lying on the sofa, Fin bathing my hands in warm water. Why were my knuckles bleeding? I sat up and looked around. A broken mirror. Did I do that?

"I'll need to bandage them. Don't worry; your reaction was hardly surprising. I've made you some warm milk with plenty of sugar. Good for shock. Here, drink up." He brought the mug to my lips and I took the milk.

"Your home's with us now. And I'm going to do everything I can to make sure it's a happy one."

Happy. Happiness was a state I'd only been allowed a brief glimpse of. All that now remained for me was existence.

I didn't cry. Not once in those early days. I ate but tasted nothing. I slept occasionally. My heart kept beating, for all I willed it not to. I rose every morning, performed my exercises, bathed when Fin reminded me to. What did it matter any more? I was aware of Fin's presence, but only vaguely, as if he were a breeze on an otherwise calm day. We soon fell into a domestic routine. He cooked for me. In return I washed his clothes and cleaned the house. Strangely, it was in those mundane moments that I missed Michael the most. Washing the dishes would remind me how Michael used to add too much soap and flick foam at me.

And that's when I realised that Michael hadn't left me, not really. He was in my thoughts, in my blood, and most importantly, in the new life I carried inside me. In our short time together, we'd gathered so many memories. I relived them daily. Thoughts of hot summer afternoons temporarily blotted out the present. Days so hot we had no energy to do anything. We'd wander over to the grassy banks of the river, and lay under the shade of a tree, our feet dangling in the river. Blissful afternoons, when we did little but tickle each other with long grasses. When I was happy just watching Michael breathe. I could have spent eternity there.

"Cathy, they caught some salmon this morning. I'm going to cook it for our dinner. You're going to love it." Fin's voice dragged me back to reality.

My first nightmare came a week later. Dreams had been a mystery to Michael and me. The programs of the SleepPod controlled the brainwaves so we never had them. We both had our first one on the same night. The dreams didn't match, nor did they make sense – just random, mixed up people and events. But this one was different. I was lying in a bed, the sheets soaked in blood. The blood kept oozing from underneath me – where was it coming from? At that point I woke up, clammy with sweat. I had it again, the following week.

"You've been through a lot; your mind's still trying to process it all," Fin explained. "That's what dreams are: a sort of mental spring cleaning. Time's a great healer."

But I didn't see how time could fix this huge, gaping hole in my heart.

The first snows came in mid-December.

"Come and have a look, Cathy. You wouldn't believe that all this could fall from the sky in such a short time."

Who was talking? Each day Fin assigned a different person to sit with me and 'raise my spirits'. By now they were merging into one. I heaved my body to the window. Pavement was indistinguishable from road. The entire landscape had been obliterated by a thick, suffocating white blanket. I turned around and sat down without comment.

"Quite a sight, isn't it?" said Relentlessly Upbeat Woman.

I didn't respond. I hadn't spoken since that day. What was the point? All I needed was to push this baby out then I could succumb to the gigantic, overwhelming gloom that had enveloped me. As if to remind me of my reason for existence, the baby kicked. I winced. Why wouldn't it give me any peace?

"Oh my God, he kicked, didn't he? Can I feel?" She put her hand to my stomach anyway. One of the villagers had told me that because I was carrying the baby high, it was definitely a boy. I couldn't decide whether or not I was pleased. Girls were the future. And would a young replica of Michael comfort me or torment me, a daily reminder of what I'd lost? At that moment, Fin entered the room with a mug of hot milk and sugar – the one thing that gave me pleasure – and gazed at me with that tender expression he always wore these days.

"Here you go, Cathy, love." As ever, he held it to my lips. I looked into his warm eyes, and wondered if I'd ever be able to love again. Fin was certainly worthy of love. He was much older than me – thirty eight. But he seemed fond of me, if the whispered endearments when he thought I was taking a nap were anything to go by.

The Cheering Up Cathy campaign gathered momentum as Christmas approached.

"New year soon, new start." Fin drew me closer to him. He'd taken to putting his arm around me on an evening, to make sure I stayed warm he said. I didn't have the energy to resist. "You're so young still. Michael was your first love, that's all. You were what, seventeen when you met him?"

I nodded.

"Seventeen's nothing. Cathy, you have more than fifty, sixty years to live. I lost my first love, too."

His breath was warm in my ear. I shifted away. I knew where this was leading. It would be so easy to allow myself to be carried away on the tide of his affection. But a memory of Jem flashed in front of me. Fin was a good man. It was unfair to give him false expectations.

"I'm tired, need to sleep," I muttered.

The gifts started next.

"Cathy, love. Look what the villagers made for you." I raised my eyes to see Fin proffering a cream-coloured cotton garment. He shook it before me with a flourish.

"It's a smock, for the Christmas party."

I forced my lips upwards in acknowledgement. Bloody Christmas. All I heard these days was cheery talk of festivities. I felt bleak. Apart from Fin, none of the villagers had become my friends. My lack of communication didn't exactly help. I could feel sympathy for me draining away by the day. I didn't want to make the effort to get to know new people; I'd had good friends. Or so I'd thought. I fingered the smooth fabric. At least it would be nice to have a garment that fitted; these days I lived in one of Fin's huge sweaters. Anna had explained to me the significance of the season, and the village traditions. Anna – what about Anna? How was she coping? Didn't she want to see her grandson? How could they all have abandoned me so easily? Did Daniel take a unilateral decision not to allow me back? I thought that villagers voted on important decisions.

I survived the parties by retreating into my own world: the fantasy world I'd created where Michael still existed. On Christmas morning he'd turn over lazily and draw me into his arms. We'd make love, feed the chickens and then drink Anna's wine for breakfast. I'd always fancied wine for breakfast: it sounded so deliciously decadent.

Instead, Fin greeted me with a mug of milk and sugar.

"Merry Christmas, love," he said, planting a kiss on my forehead, his standard morning greeting these days. "I've brought you a present."

I opened the small box and my lips parted, almost allowing a sound to escape. Inside was a beautiful gold cross and chain. I'd never seen anything like it. My eyes filled with tears. This was the sort of gift I should be getting from Michael.

"Hey, darling, it wasn't meant to make you cry." Once more his arms enveloped me. "Now, how about trying on that smock? Party time later."

I put on the smock and frowned. It was well-made and disguised my hideous bump. Was Fin really going to allow me to go to a party? He'd barely let me out of the house since the day on which time stopped. But by now I'd achieved non-verbal communication with him and he smiled.

"Of course you're not missing the party. There's six inches of snow out there. No-one could possibly drive in that."

I went to the party but the scenes of glee only heightened my despair. Seven days later there was a New Year party. My stomach tightened at the memory of Michael's res party: that chaste kiss on the cheek that so electrified me. Was it really possible that only a year had passed? I felt like I'd lived several lifetimes since then.

The kiss that Fin gave me at midnight was anything but chaste. My lips remained defiantly closed, denying him access.

"Sorry. Stupid of me to rush you. But you look so beautiful tonight."

Huh. I'd never felt less beautiful. My hair was as rough as a bird's nest; I never bothered to wash or comb it. The black circles under my eyes told of my sleeplessness. My body felt like it no longer belonged to me. My breasts were so enormous that my bra no longer fitted. And as for my stomach, the skin was as taut as a drum. Surely it would split soon.

Things with Fin were in danger of spiralling out of control. I had to say something, to stop this now. I opened my mouth to speak, but nothing came out.

"Cathy, you really ought to sit down." It was Lita, the community's young mother. I followed her. "Coming on to you, was he?" My eyes widened. I nodded.

"If he's giving you grief, just say the word," Lita said. "I know what his game is."

I frowned.

"Gene pools. Bloody obsessed, he is. He'd love it if everyone under forty was knocked up."

My frown deepened.

"Katie was the first, must be going on for ten years ago," Lita continued. "Had two of his brats, then he traded one to another community. She did a bunk with the other one. Then of course there's Graham, my three-year-old. Oh, didn't you know he was Fin's? You see, he wants the communities to be self-sustaining, but you have to mix the bloodlines around, trade people across villages. Kids are a great trading commodity, you know. He sent my Jon away." Her face clouded over. "Only guy I ever loved, but he was my second cousin. Can't have inbreeding, so he chose a Citidome guy for me. Bastard left me after our third. Don't think nappy-changing was what he had in mind."

My mouth fell open but Lita continued before I could say more.

"Fin must have been wetting himself when you turned up: new blood, and a young breeder too. Don't look so scared. He cares for you; I can tell. But he cares more for what's in there." She patted my belly.

Then her eyes rose to my throat. She tapped the cross and chain.

"Did he give you this?"

I nodded.

"You're definitely in favour then. He gave me one once."

I stared at her, not caring whether it was true or not. What did it matter whether Fin loved me for myself or my bloodline? I didn't love him. What future did I have anyway? At least here I was safe. Without Michael, why not stay with Fin and become a brood mare?

And life continued its torpid state until the second week in January, when the third suspicious knock rattled the door. I trudged to the cellar. Nothing could be worse than the last visit. But this one was different again. The sound of people entering the house. Raised voices. I crept up the stairs to hear better. Then the unmistakeable sound of a baby crying. Kell, Dee and Harry! Oh, I wanted to see them. But my spirits dropped almost as soon as they'd risen. How could I be sure who my genuine friends were? Had they struck a deal with Fin, traded me and my baby to the community? I waited for the trapdoor to open but it didn't. Fear gripped me; why didn't Fin want me to see them? I knocked on the trapdoor. The voices stopped. I knocked harder. Then daylight flooded my vision and I found myself looking at Kell.

"Cathy, what the ...? Take my hand."

I climbed out and stared at each person in turn. Fin was staring at his boots. Dee's expression was one of horror.

"What the hell's going on, Fin?"

"It's the only way to keep her safe. CEs are swarming all over the place. And we care for her. You know one of her own friends betrayed her, don't you?"

"Yeah, I'd heard that much." Dee said, with a sympathetic glance in my direction. "But what about the guy who'd been looking for her?

"What guy?" I found my voice at last.

"Someone from your community. He's been trying to find you, the guys from Macclesfield said, but Fin here told him you'd moved on."

"What was his name?"

"Sorry sweetheart, they didn't say. A guy with a beard."

My shoulders drooped. Daniel. But why was he looking for me? A terrible realisation gripped me.

"B-but, what about everything else you said? That I'd been cast out, that Michael was dead?"

"Fin! Did you lie to her?" Dee tilted his chin, forcing him to look at her.

"She's one of us now," Fin muttered.

"Christ, Cathy, I'd have never left you here –" Kell began.

Then Fin dropped to one knee. "Cathy, I did it all for your own good. You've been happy here, haven't you? Safe? Secure? I can take care of you better than anyone else can. Me and you, we'll be a great team. We'll –"

"Kell, Dee, get me out of here, now." I screamed.

And with that I was whisked from the house that had become my prison.

CHAPTER - 21

As the boat chugged into life, I shivered.

"Put this fur around you, sweetheart," Kell urged.

"You haven't been here for months," I murmured, my voice heavy with accusation.

"Yeah, that wasn't planned. We got stuck at a broken lock near Oxford. I'd been worried about you," said Dee. "Cathy, I'm so sorry. Didn't want to leave you, but Fin can be pretty persuasive. He got us paranoid that by keeping you, we'd endanger you and ourselves. I'd have taken the risk, but with little Harry here ..."

"I knew he was obsessive about new blood." Kell rubbed his chin. "He tried everything to get us to stay last year. But I never thought he'd stoop so low."

"S-so, everything Fin said to me was a lie? Michael might still be alive?" My voice was high with hope.

"Don't get too optimistic." Kell said. "There's been no sightings of anyone answering Michael's description." He sighed. "Truth is, I don't think they ever delete anyone from the system, just mark them as deceased. And besides, if he killed their spy, they'd have retaliated. And those stun guns – they can turn them up you know. They don't just stun."

But the fact remained that they wanted me back at Ashford. Course they do, a bitter voice in my head snarled. Everyone wanted this new life, whose presence I increasingly resented. If I could have cut it out of myself I would have. If I'd lost Michael, I needed to share the burden of this child with Anna, Alex, Daniel, Mary ... and Daisy? Could Daisy have betrayed me? Someone did. That seemed to be the only true thing that Fin had told me. But Daisy's only motivation could have been to have Michael to herself. Please let Michael be dead or captured, rather than with her.

I realised we were going north. My eyes widened. Where

were they taking me?

"We have to get to the end first. How do you think we turn the boat round?" Dee smiled. "But then we'll take you back to Macclesfield, see if there's been any word from your community. But there's been a fair bit of snow. They might not have been across for a while."

"I need to get back; the baby's due in less than a month. Please, Dee. Alex is the only person I'd trust to deliver my baby."

"Hmm, experience counts for a lot. Well there's not a lot we can do, but maybe we'll talk one of the Macclesfield lot into taking you across. They're good people; they have a few horses. Not that a horse ride's such a great idea in your condition."

"I have to." My voice rose.

"It'd be best," Kell said. "The woman who delivered Harry wasn't up to much."

As the boat continued its gentle trundle, my thoughts turned to the future.

"How can I bring up a baby?" Tears welled in my eyes. "I'm eighteen and three quarters and I feel like my life's over."

"Hey, look at me. You can do it. It's not like he's much bloody use." She flicked Kell's beard with obvious affection. "We're friends now, right? You can always come to us for a break if it gets too much."

"New blood … Fin told me all about the way the Citidomes started," I said. "Michael would have been staggered. He wanted to set out on some sort of mission to help people escape and settle into communities that needed new blood."

"There's a few of us thinking along the same lines," said Kell. "Things have got really bad this winter. We'd normally hear of a few escapees each month but, since October, nothing."

"Have you seen any CEs?" I asked.

"We tend to keep a low profile – God help Harry if they recaptured us. But I haven't heard of many since the snow came."

We approached the town of Macclesfield, rows of redbrick terraced houses coming into view. We moored the boat and made for the inhabited part of town. The streets were deserted.

"It's not as pretty as Bakewell or Buxton," I said.

"No, they don't have a lot of natural resources," Kell said. "They make good use of Citidome waste, and they're amazing hunters. Christ, Cathy, run!"

He grabbed my hand, but I stumbled and let go. Running was impossible in my condition. A flurry made me turn around to be confronted by a man with a familiar uniform – a CE. Before I had time to scream he'd pointed his stun gun to my temple.

"You gonna come quietly or do I have to use this?" he snarled.

My throat tightened too much to allow any sound to escape. I looked for Kell and Dee but they'd disappeared. Of course. They had to. There was little Harry to consider. My mind flailed. Would they be able to rescue me? Must buy time. I doubled up, grasped my stomach and dropped to the floor, writhing as if in pain. A jolt through my head stunned me into oblivion. I was only dimly aware of being dragged to the road and shoved into a TravelPod. When my awareness returned, a second CE – a female – was pressing an instrument to my earlobe. Searing heat sent my hand flying to my ear. The lobe was completely covered by a hot plastic disc. No, no, no! My mind roared. The female started the engine.

As we left the town behind, I looked over my shoulder, but no army of rescuers materialized. Plan … need a plan. But what about the RedTag? Wherever I went, they'd track me. Think, Cathy, think. No, I wasn't Cathy anymore. The RedTag had marked me as Caia, the eternal Citidome misfit. I couldn't let them imprison me. Not now I knew there was a chance, however remote, that Michael was alive and that Daniel wanted me back. I had to try something, anything. Guess they wanted me alive rather than dead. Could I attack them? Mik … his nose. I scrunched my fingers into a fist, aimed it at the driver's face. But her reactions were too quick and deflected my blow. She stopped the TravelPod, the second CE grabbed my wrist, and inputted a code into the instrument that had RedTagged me.

"Feisty little savage, aren't you? " Her voice was laced with scorn. "This'll calm you down." She took my other wrist, held both together, placed the instrument against them and out shot a barbed polymer wire, which bound them together. I twisted my hands, trying to free myself from the tendrils that were gnawing at my flesh. But struggling only tightened the wire. I let out a cry of pain. Beads of blood encircled my wrists. Defeated, I let my hands fall to my lap. For the first time, I felt alone. Alone and scared.

"Gonna calm down now, are you?"

"Wh-where are you taking me?" I whimpered like a rabbit caught in a snare.

"Not the correction camp. Not yet, anyway. You're going back to Sigma-2 first. Veez, it really is our lucky day. There's a huge reward for hauling you in: two thousand citizen points before the birth and a thousand after."

"B-but why Sigma-2?" We were a long way from Sigma-2, a two hour drive. Why not take me to the nearest one? Fin's words returned to me, images of having my baby cut from my body and being left to die assaulting my brain. I spread my hands over the mound of my stomach. It tightened under the cold clutch of dread.

"Gotta let the people who used to know you see what you've turned into." The man spat at me. "Then we're gonna show you on *Vile Bodies*."

I gasped. Vile Bodies? Is that how people thought of me?

"You're gonna give birth live on air. The whole State's gonna watch you tear up – see what the outside's done to you." He swiped a disparaging hand at my breasts and stomach.

"That's sick." Nausea engulfed me.

"You're the sick one, freak," the female sneered. "And don't think there'll be any health workers to help you. That thing's gonna burst right out of you ..."

A rising noise filled my ears, drowning out her words. No medical assistance? She couldn't be serious. My chest constricted – was I having a heart attack? Maybe I could will it to happen. Death was my only escape route. I couldn't go back to the Citidome. Around me was silence, except for the sound of my own jagged breathing. Perhaps if I screamed,

thrashed about, they'd be forced to kill me. But my baby –
this life so precious to the outside world. What would happen
to my baby? No, I had to escape. I swivelled in my seat
again. Guess Kell and Dee weren't going to come to my
rescue. How could they? How could they fight off two CEs
armed with stun guns and with access to back up?

"Let me out! Let me out!" My frenzied mind could think
no more.

"You're really getting on my nerves." The male fired the
stun gun once more. This time the stupor was welcome.

We began to climb into the hills of the Peak District. I
remembered climbing the hills with Michael, him dropping to
the ground and declaring that the outside world was ours. It
didn't seem to be on my side now. Fierce crosswinds meant
that the TravelPod travelled at little more than a crawl,
intensifying my agony. As I gazed at the horizon, a swell of
nostalgia for what already seemed the distant past overcame
me. Were those few months to be the sum total of my
happiness? So dulled were my reactions that I barely stirred
when the TravelPod stopped. Although it hadn't snowed for
over a week, the hills were still carpeted in white. A mound
had fallen from the hillside and was blocking our path.

"Shit; this is gonna take some clearing." They exited the
TravelPod, taking two shovels from the back. I tried the
doors. Locked of course.

As I watched their endless, monotonous shovelling of
snow, a fresh wave of panic overcame me, so powerful I was
drowning in it. In my head I was back in the Citidome.
Crowds of people were chanting, "Vile Body!" Uma, Von
and Mik were in the front row, my WorkMates too: Dal, Ren,
Jana, Kit. They laughed and pointed. I couldn't move my
legs. And then my stomach split, clean in two, and there sat
the baby. The crowd roared. And still no-one helped. And
blood … blood was everywhere.

I lifted my bound hands to my face. It had to be rescue or
death – the alternative was unthinkable. Maybe I could end it
myself. Think, Cathy, think. The windows were ETFE –
that'd never break. Maybe the control panel? One jagged
piece of plastic could do it. I pounded my hands against it.
But the female CE had seen me. She opened the door and

slapped my face.

"Trying to get out, are you? Forget it, freak. You're RedTagged, remember. Wherever you go, they'll hunt you down." Stunning me once more, she shut me in.

I could never be sure what happened next – the stun gun had dulled my senses – but I heard a thud against the side of the vehicle, and the shouts of the male CE: "Backup!"

I rubbed my eyes. The female CE had disappeared. But what was this? Two – no, three figures appearing on horseback. One was launching long, narrow missiles from a strange weapon. One flew through the air and narrowly missed the shoulder of the male CE, who was now running away. One of the men continued to project the missiles, the other two dismounted. But who were they? With their long, straggly hair, beards and ancient weapons, they looked like something from a primitive civilization.

"Cathy!"

I looked up. How did they know my name? And then I saw him. Michael! But it was a barely-recognisable Michael, his fringe blowing into his eyes, and half of his face lost to – oh God – a beard. It made him look years older. I placed my bound hands to the window.

Michael and the other man spread their bags on the ground, checking their weaponry. While the unknown man battered the door from one side with a hammer, Michael shot at it and tried to lever it open with what looked like a poker from a fireplace. Noise filled my ears. Bang, crash, smash. I watched the other man pursuing the second CE. It was soon over. The CE, stumbling through the snow, was no match for the horseback man whose aim was perfect. Soon the man dismounted and joined the assault on the TravelPod.

The battery of blows continued. I put my hand to my tagged ear. The CE's words reverberated in my ears. They'll hunt you down. That's what Mei had said, three months ago. I'd lived in fear ever since. Even though I'd found Michael, I'd never be able to have what I wanted: the family life among the people I loved. My chest tightened. Was it possible for a heart to literally break? Tears flooded down my face.

Then everything happened at once. The sudden shock of

icy air. The driver door was open! Then hands reached out for me. Michael's hands. Paralysed, I allowed myself to be hauled across the seats. And then I fell into his arms. I buried my head in his chest, breathing the refuge of his scent, absorbing him.

"T-tracker." The choking intensity of emotion had made me incoherent.

Michael held me at arm's length, as if reminding himself what I looked like, and then the significance of my words sunk in.

"Oh hell." His eyes darted to his companions.

"There's only one thing we can do." One of the men reached into their bag of weaponry. Only at that point did I notice the female CE lying beside me, one of the missiles, which were constructed from sticks and feathers, protruding from her back. The man extracted a kitchen knife, sliced through the wire, releasing my hands, then raised the knife to my ear. "Sorry, it's the only way. I'll be as quick as I can."

Before I had time to work out what he meant, I flinched at the cold of the blade against my ear. Oh no. He wasn't …

"Hold still, sweetheart," Michael urged.

My ear burned, white hot. I clenched my teeth.

"Shit, it's not as sharp as it should be."

I tried to ignore his increasingly frantic sawing motions, focussing on Michael's arm around my shoulder, but my legs liquefied. All was pain. The agonizing process seemed to last forever. Finally, I saw him toss the disc, together with my flesh, into the TravelPod.

"Pinch it; should ease the bleeding."

I reached for the place where my ear used to be and gasped. Half of it was missing. I clutched at the warm, raw flesh and reeled at the flood of warm, sticky liquid. When would the pain ease? Blood dripped from between my fingers, merging with that pouring from the CE, a crimson stain on melting snow.

"For God's sake, don't just stand there," said one of the men. "Back up's on its way, remember. Get her out of here and we'll cover your tracks."

I looked up at the horse and then down to my stomach. I'd learned how to ride a horse in my first month in the village, but I hadn't been pregnant then. How would this be possible?

"In front, I think." Michael and the two men helped me onto the horse.

"Good luck," said one.

Michael shook each by the hand. "Don't know how to thank you guys enough. We'll be over to see you when the baby's born."

And with that, Michael jumped on the horse behind me, enveloped me in the extraordinary cape he was wearing, which seemed to be composed of hundreds of rabbit skins, held me against him with one arm, took the reins with the other, turned and headed back towards Macclesfield.

"Wrong way?" I murmured.

"Don't worry, we're heading home. A few hundred yards up here there's a bridlepath. We'll take the cross-country route back."

Home. Was a word ever more precious? But would the Citidome ever allow me a home?

"What's with the beard?" I murmured.

"Thought I'd try a new look. Like it?" I tensed. I hated it. But I recognised the old familiar teasing in his voice.

"You think I'm having that tickle my face every day? Think again," I said with a lightness I couldn't feel.

"Truth is, after you went, none of it seemed to matter," he said. "And there's been no traders out, so I thought I'd save my stash of razors. What's with these?" His hand brushed my breasts. "They're even bigger."

"Yeah, can you move your arm higher, so it's just underneath them? Ah, that's better. Not bouncing up and down so much."

I felt the low rumble of his laugh. "Tell me how fast I can go. Don't want to make it too uncomfortable for you."

The horse broke into a trot and I soon realized that comfort wasn't going to happen. With one hand still pinching my screaming ear, I placed the other on the front of the cracked, ancient saddle to steady myself. The jolting from below couldn't be good for the baby.

"No faster than this," I groaned.

We carried on in silence. So little of this situation made sense, I hardly knew where to start with the questions.

Michael found the bridle path and its uneven surface forced us to slow our pace. Only then did his voice break.

"Christ, Cathy, I've been looking for you for months." He kissed the back of my head. "I'm never, ever letting you go. Where were you?"

"Hest Bank," I murmured.

"But I went there! The first person I saw said there'd been a girl but she'd left. I insisted on speaking to the village leader, Fin, I think his name was. He said you'd gone off with a man, to Merseyside. Didn't believe him. Never thought you'd leave me ... been searching every day."

The pieces of the puzzle clicked into place. The second suspicious knock. The canal people who didn't enter the house, just left the devastating news. It must have been Michael.

"I was there, with Fin. I was in hiding in the cellar."

"What, you mean he didn't tell you? He kept you there? But why?"

"I patted my stomach. "He wanted this."

"Shit, Cathy. I'm never letting you out of my sight from now until the baby's born."

"It's hopeless, Michael. They're going to find me. Once back up arrives, there'll be CEs crawling all over Ashford. They were going to put me on *Vile* –" My words were drowned in tears.

"Don't cry, sweetheart, please don't cry. I'll die myself before I let anyone else get you."

My tears tingled, icy against my face. I leaned against him, drinking in his warmth and solidity.

"That bleeding's not slowing down much, is it?" He drew to a halt, dismounted, took a square of fabric from his pocket – the handkerchiefs we'd never needed in the Citidome – and scooped up a ball of snow in it.

"Hold this to your ear. It might help," he said.

I pressed down hard. As ever, he'd been right. The cold didn't take away the pain but numbed it to a bearable level. And my thoughts started to clarify.

"Daisy ..."

"Bloody marvel, she is. Getting away so quickly ... saved your life, no doubt about it."

At the admiration in his voice, my stomach clenched.

"Tipped off the guards …" My voice faded.

"How do you know about that? You mustn't blame Daisy. She feels terrible about telling Peter. They've split up –"

"Peter? Can we go back to the beginning? What happened after we ran away?"

"The CEs were so keen to get you, all they did was stun me and went chasing after you. But they set off in the wrong direction. Daniel sent me away from the village on horseback, to a disused pub up in the hills for a few weeks. Daisy joined me there later that day. We were there for a couple of weeks. By then, the first wave of CEs had left, but the village was still like a bloody fortress. Daisy and I found out from those canal guys, Kell and Dee – nice people – that you were in Hest Bank. We went back home to find out where it was. Daniel said it was too far and forbade me from going. Everything seemed normal for a while. I guess Daisy didn't see any need to keep it a secret from Peter. But I couldn't rest. Daisy and I went to Macclesfield every day, left messages for you. It was while we were out that the CEs came back, offering everyone rewards in exchange for information. And that's when Peter told them. As soon as I found out, I took the horse."

"P-Peter. Figures." I muttered. "So what was the great reward?"

"A jar of coffee." Michael sniffed. "Peter's been thrown out. Gone to a community twenty miles away."

"B-but us?"

"Oh yeah, there was talk of that too. Hell of an argument. They put it to the vote. It was tight, but seems like we've got a lot of friends there."

My body relaxed. Then another spike of anxiety pierced my brain.

"So you and Daisy … been spending a lot of time together."

"Yeah … Hey, this isn't going where I think it is, is it? You don't seriously think …"

"Well, why wouldn't you? She's gorgeous. Look at me. I'm a huge, bloated mess, CEs chasing me, about to saddle us with all this responsibility." My rant accelerated. "And what about Mei? Let's not forget how this started. There you were, all night, drinking, laughing, talking about old times. Don't tell me you didn't, just for a minute, wish you were back there, with her?"

"Cathy, don't!" His voice was a strangled cry. "I didn't think that, even for a second. Every minute since you've been gone, I've tortured myself, knowing that it was all my fault; that by trusting Mei I lost the most precious thing in my life. How can you think I'd ever look at someone else?"

"I've been petrified of losing you since that first night. That's why I didn't come with you the first time you asked. I thought I was getting over it, until ... this."

"Now can you see why they banned love in the Citidomes? It's so messy; it's easier to control us if we're not screwed up by it." His grip intensified. "Christ, Cathy, I get it though. Jealousy. When you told me about Jem's dying words to you ... it killed me."

I slumped against him.

"Cathy, I've got so much to tell you. I've got to know the Macclesfield guys pretty well. And you'll never guess what I've found out about the Citidomes."

Too tired to talk any more, I listened to him telling me the things I already knew. Then his talk moved to some sort of alliance he wanted to form. His words washed over me. I no longer cared about missions or alliances or the Citidomes. I just wanted my old life back.

The snow against my ear eventually melted, a stream of pink water trickling down my arm. To detract from the pain I focussed on the sounds around me. Michael's impassioned voice. The clatter of the horse's hooves. Branches, groaning against the wind. My chattering teeth. But it was impossible to ignore the physical. For all the discomforts of the past months, nothing could compare to the screaming pain in my ear, the cold gnawing at my flesh, my bouncing breasts, a rising nausea and a worrying cramp in my lower regions that I tried to ignore.

Finally, I recognized the rooftops of the village that had sheltered us, offered us a haven and were now welcoming us home. As we reached the bridge, Michael tethered the horse, and helped me down. I clung to him. Ouch – the insides of my thighs were screaming.

Then a new stab of pain made me forget about anything else.

"What is it?"

"A … stitch. Oh, no … pain in my back … moving round to my stomach. Ooh." I took a deep breath, and as my eyes met Michael's, we both paled with realisation.

"Oh hell. I think the baby's on the way."

CHAPTER - 22

My beloved village hadn't changed at all. But there was no time for happy reunions. Michael helped me off and pounded on Alex's door.

"Cathy!" Alex flung his arms around me. "We'd almost given up hope. Hell, what's happened to your ear?"

"She got RedTagged; someone cut it." Michael's words hurtled out at an almost unintelligible speed. "And the baby's coming."

"Oh God." Alex darted forward. "Cathy, how often are the pains?"

"I had one a few minutes ago but nothing since."

"OK, come on upstairs, Cathy. Michael, tell Daniel. We need to put the village on high alert."

I followed Alex upstairs and lay on the bed.

"They'll find me ..." I whimpered.

"Put it all out of your mind," Alex soothed. "All that matters now is you and our baby."

But I couldn't put it out of my mind. *Vile Bodies*. I was vile, a freak, a hideous warning to others. But oh – if the baby came now. I could save my baby.

"It's nearly a month early, Alex."

"Don't think about the timing. Everything's going to be all right," Alex said in a way that did nothing to convince me. "Any more pains?"

"Nothing – was it a false alarm? Ooh no, here's another – ooh – that wasn't bad."

"Let's have a look at you," he said, helping me off with my pants. "Hmm, you might have a while to go yet. Let's see to that ear first. I'll need some ice."

I lay alone, my vile body exposed, a slab of meat on the butcher's table. Then I heard knocking downstairs, voices, followed by running up the stairs. It sounded like half the village had arrived. Anna was the first to rush in, followed by Daisy.

"Oh, sweetheart, I can't believe it."

Both garbled incoherently and smothered my cheeks with kisses. I allowed their words to wash over me like warm summer rain. But they couldn't distract me from the ordeal that awaited me.

Alex returned. "Daisy, could you hold this ice pack to her ear? Cathy, I'm sorry, there's no way this isn't going to hurt."

Anna stroked my hair as I winced, first at the sting of ethanol being applied to my ear – or what remained of it – followed by bite after bite of a needle. Alex was sewing me together as if I was one of the toys we made for the children's birthdays.

"Daisy, we'll have the ice again," Alex called. "Keep changing the dressing until the bleeding stops."

The intensity of the pain of the stitches had been so great that I'd bitten into my tongue, the taste of blood metallic in my mouth. Then a thrusting pain from below took my breath away.

"Another one?" Alex asked.

I nodded.

Alex examined me again and drew in his breath.

"I'll need to get myself prepared. Don't look so frightened; I'll be back in a few minutes. Anna, Daisy, can I have a quick word? Cathy, take hold of the ice pack."

More voices downstairs. Another pain – ooh, sharper – was followed by a gush of liquid running out of me. It didn't seem to be the enormous rush of liquid of waters breaking that Alex had described. Perhaps I'd urinated – gross. Oh well, I left my dignity behind the minute I became pregnant.

More activity on the steps – Michael.

"How are the pains, sweetheart?"

"That last one was a bad one, and I think my waters broke, but at least it took my mind off my ear." I managed a smile for him.

"Cathy … He threw himself onto the bed beside me and his lips claimed mine. Our kissing had a new urgency, as if we knew that this may be the last time. But the beard tickled. He still didn't look like my Michael.

"Michael, do something for me."

"Anything."

"Go home and get a shave." If anything went wrong, I wanted to see his face properly, one last time.

"Bossing me around already." He chuckled. "You're so beautiful."

"No, I'm not."

"You're the loveliest woman I've ever seen." He ran a hand through my hair. "No-one will notice your earlobe. Now your hair's longer and curly, you can't see it anyway."

But I hadn't been talking about my ear. I meant my vile body. A body soon to be degraded by childbirth, as well as the Mark that still stained my thigh. In the eyes of the Citidome, I'd always be hideous, deformed, ugly. What should I do? Give myself up once I'd had the baby? Go somewhere new with Michael? But what was the point? I was the most wanted woman in the State. Tracker or no tracker, they'd find me eventually. Better for everyone if I wasn't here. Give the village my baby, the new blood it needed, then go. Maybe back to Fin; I didn't care about endangering him. Give Michael the chance to be safe, to live a normal life.

As if reading my thoughts, Michael said, "Every entrance to the village is being guarded and we're about to board up this house to make it look unoccupied. Then we'll bolt it from the inside. You're safe, sweetheart."

Safe. I'd never be safe.

He slipped out of the room. Another flurry of footsteps. Mary, rushing over to hug me. "You'll be OK. Everything's under control." But she didn't look me in the eye.

The sound of banging distracted me from another wave of pain. Alex returned, armed with a bag and a large book.

"How are the pains now?"

"Stronger, and some liquid came out."

"Your waters have broken. Baby's on his way."

He was really coming now. I'd expected this moment to be exciting, but all I felt was tired. The energy had been sucked from me, the warmth, the life, and soon, my baby. No, mustn't think like that. Must get my baby out. He was the future.

"I want to sleep," I said to Alex.

"It's OK to close your eyes if that's what you want to do."

But hardly anything happened for another half an hour apart from the noises from outside. Michael came back, fresh-faced and irresistible.

"That's more like it." I traced his jaw.

"Good, because I'm not moving from your side now." His voice was tense.

Outside I heard raised voices, downstairs the opening and closing of doors, the low tones of anxious conversations. And then everything started in earnest. Ripples of tightening pains rolled through my stomach, increasing in strength and frequency, propelling my whole body into agony.

"I don't want to lie down any more; I want to squat or walk around."

"Sorry, this is the only way I can do it," Alex said.

Wave after wave of torture seized me with decreasing respite and sweat soaked the sheets. I'd had enough of the pain and lost all sense of time. How long had I been like this? How long would it last? I felt as if two people had their hands around my stomach – one squeezing, the other pulling. I grasped the bed sheets and pulled my knees to my chest. A blazing inferno consumed my insides. I screwed up my eyes and shouted, "I've had enough!" When I opened them, vision blurred from sweat, I saw only Michael's concerned brown eyes.

"Nearly there, sweetheart."

Then Alex's voice. "You're nearly ten centimetres dilated. Soon you'll feel an urge to push and then I'll tell you what to do."

He was right. I felt an overpowering urge, but followed his instructions to alternately push and stop and pant. How could this be a natural process? Never had anything felt more unnatural. Pain followed pain with increasing rapidity, until I felt a tearing down below and screamed. A cry from Michael and Alex.

"Cathy, I can see the head!"

I squeezed Michael's hand so tightly that I must have hurt him. I raised my back, pushed with all the force my shattered body could muster and felt something pop out of me. It was over. A wonderful ease overcame me. I sank back into the pillow.

"It's a girl!"

I heard a small, high-pitched cry, then someone took the baby away. My job was done.

"Can't she hold her?" asked Michael.

"Just need to check her over."

"She looks perfect to me. Christ, Cathy, you're incredible. Glad you had to do that and not me." Michael beamed, but his eyes were shining with unshed tears.

I tried to raise my head, to at least see the baby, my gift to the village. They were all beaming: Anna, Daisy, Mary. Oh, the love in that room. The walls seemed to expand, unable to take the emotions contained in its small space. A thrill passed through me. All those BodyPerfects, striving for immortality but, in losing touch with the most basic human instinct, they'd lost the ability to reproduce. Michael and I – we'd produced another human being. I'd achieved my immortality. I looked down at my deflated but still distended body – still freakish – then noticed the redness seeping out on the sheets between my legs. So much blood. Too much.

"What's happening?" Michael tried and failed to steady his voice. Alex handed a tiny bundle to Anna. What was wrong with the baby? Why couldn't I see her?

"It should stop once she delivers the afterbirth. Come on, Cathy, one more little push."

But I didn't push. What was the point?

"Come on Cathy, push!" Alex's voice became more insistent. "Anna, we really need to stop this bleeding. Massage her abdomen. I need to check my books."

Anna rubbed my stomach, and as my body relaxed and weakened, I became enveloped by an overwhelming sense of calm and a strange detachment, as if I was a spectator at the scene. So this was how my story ended.

"Cathy, sweetheart." Ah, it was Michael. "Can you manage a little push?"

I shook my head.

"Cathy." Michael's voice had risen. "You have to. You might bleed to …" A sob caught in his throat, blocking the word.

Then came a louder, terrifying thumping at the door – it

sounded like someone was trying to break it down – followed by a huge crash. The thundering of feet on the stairs.

"Play dead," hissed Michael.

Play dead? Surely it was only a matter of minutes anyway? My eyes had time to scan the room before Alex covered me with a sheet. Would the scenes of grief convince them? Or would I spend my final moments bleeding to death in a TravelPod?

The footsteps came to an abrupt halt.

"She's dead." Alex's voice – hard, terse.

"D'you really think we're that stupid?"

The sheet was torn from me.

"Veez the blood."

"Check her pulse."

"You do it."

A sigh. Icy fingers shifting against my wrist.

"Nothing." The sound of crying – loud, harsh sobs from Michael, softer, female weeping.

A pad against my finger. I heard my old name for the last time. "Caia 190319"

Retreating footsteps.

"N-no pulse?" Whose voice?

More fingers – this time warm – against my wrist, pressing down, hard.

"Shit, no. I'm so – oh, hang on. Christ, it's faint. No wonder they didn't find it. Cathy, can you hear me?"

I blinked and nodded.

"Anna, carry on massaging her."

Michael's face was once more above mine.

"It's OK, Michael. I'm not scared." My voice seemed incapable of rising above a whisper. How strange. This isn't what I expected at all. I'd been scared of a painful death but this was peaceful, like someone dimming the lights. A gentle slipping away into oblivion. How long would it take?

"Cathy, you can't leave me and our little girl. Look at her."

"No." I found more power to my voice. "Don't want to see her … too hard. She'll be loved. She'll be safe. It's the best way … the only way."

"B-but, we can go other places. So much to discover."

"Come closer," I whispered. He leaned over me until his

head was in front of mine. I raised my hands – such an effort – and cradled his face in them, drinking in the eyes I adored. "I don't need to discover any more. In your eyes I can see it all. Love, beauty ... and truth."

His tears splashed onto my cheek.

"Of course!" Alex's voice. A book slamming. "We need to put the baby to the breast."

"N-no."

Alex ignored me. I screwed my eyes shut. Someone lifted my jumper; I shivered at the sudden chill. Then – oh – a warm weight on my breast. A tingling on my nipple made me open my eyes. And then a miracle – the baby began to suck. I was feeding my daughter! Sensation welled up inside of me, so overpowering I felt I might burst. Oh, she was beautiful, pink-faced with a velvety crown of dark hair. I inhaled her sweet, milky scent and marvelled at the smooth perfection of her newborn skin. Of all the incredible things I'd experienced, nothing could compare to this. This little girl didn't think my body was vile. The all-consuming love was almost too intense to bear. In that ecstatic moment, I felt something soft slip out of me.

"Is that it?" Whose voice was that? I couldn't distinguish them any more.

"I think so. Look, the bleeding's slowing down."

At Alex's insistence, I fought the urge to sleep, raised my head and drank the glass of water he forced on me. What was happening now? Then Michael was beside me, beaming. "Look at you two. That's a hungry girl we've got."

"B-but, you really think that's it? That we'll be safe from now on?"

"God knows. Cathy, I should never have put you through all this. I should ... I should have kept you safe in the Citidome." Michael's voice wobbled.

"You think I'd exchange a lifetime of safety in the Citidome for what we've got here? And Michael ... I know what it means now."

"What, sweetheart?"

A sudden clarity struck me. "That's what we'll call her."

The baby had stopped feeding and lay contentedly against my breast. Then she shifted her head and opened her eyes.

Big, brown eyes. Michael's eyes. I kissed her forehead, beckoned Michael forward, and kissed him too. With our heads locked together, I spoke to my daughter for the first time.

"Hello, Joy."

ACKNOWLEDGEMENTS

I'm grateful to so many people who have supported me in this journey, but the biggest thank you goes to my husband, Gerry. Thanks for your constant love and support, for putting up with my turbulent moods and for making me smile even on a bad day! My dogs, Poppy and Jasmine, also helped by taking me for a walk every lunchtime.

Two friends have always been on hand for critiques, edits and sometimes just to listen to me rant! Thanks, Sue Johns and Diana McGarry; I couldn't have done this without you.

The Word Cloud online writing community have been enormously helpful to my development as a writer, and I'd like to mention three: Alan Rain, Sophie Jonas-Hill and Abi Cocks. Your critiques were sometimes painful, but they made the book better. I'd also like to thank Debi Alper; your professional manuscript review was invaluable, as has been your support since.

My family are incredibly important to me. Thanks, Mam, for everything. Dad, I wish you were here to see my book in print; I know you'd have been bursting with pride. Thanks, Alex Harrison and Steve White for all the encouragement, support and laughs.

I'd love to thank all the friends who've encouraged my dream, but it'd take too long and I'd run the risk of missing someone out and causing offence. Instead I'll give a special mention to Fiona Worner, Sheila Alexander, Alison Broughton and Sharon Numan. To Mel Numan, thanks for helping me find the perfect day job. As for the rest of you; you know who you are! Writing can be a lonely occupation and I'm grateful for the respite you provide.

Last but certainly not least, a huge thank you to Peter Buck and the team at Elsewhen Press for your belief in my novel, for your support and for advising me at all stages of the publication process.

Elsewhen Press
an independent publisher specialising in Speculative Fiction

Visit the Elsewhen Press website at elsewhen.co.uk for the latest information on all of our titles, authors and events; to read our blog; find out where to buy our books and ebooks; or to place an order.

Elsewhen Press

an independent publisher specialising in Speculative Fiction

Jacey's Kingdom
Dave Weaver

Jacey's Kingdom is an enthralling tale that revolves around a startlingly desperate reality: Jacey Jackson, a talented student destined for Cambridge, collapses with a brain tumour while sitting her final history exam at school. In her mind she struggles through a quasi-historical sixth century dreamscape whilst the surgeons fight to save her life.

Jacey is helped by a stranger called George, who finds himself trapped in her nightmare after a terrible car accident. There are quests, battles, and a love story ahead of them, before we find out if Jacey will awake from her coma or perish on the operating table. And who, or what, is George? In this book, Dave Weaver questions our perception of reality and the redemptive power of dreams; are our experiences of fear, conflict, friendship and love any less real or meaningful when they take place in the mind rather than the 'real' physical world?

Dave Weaver has been writing for ten years, with short stories published in anthologies, magazines and online in the UK and USA. Jacey's Kingdom is his first published novel. He cleverly weaves a tale that takes the almost unimaginable drama of an eighteen year-old girl whose life is in the balance, relying on modern surgery to bring her back from the brink, and conceives the world that she has constructed in her mind to deal with the trauma happening to her body. Developing the friendship between Jacey and George in a natural and witty style, despite their unlikely situation and the difference in their ages, Dave has produced a story that is both exciting and thought-provoking. This book will be a must-read story for adults and young adults alike.

ISBN: 9781908168313 (epub, kindle)
ISBN: 9781908168214 (272pp paperback)

Visit bit.ly/JaceysKingdom

Elsewhen Press
an independent publisher specialising in Speculative Fiction

A LIFE LESS ORDINARY
CHRISTOPHER NUTTALL

There is magic in the world, hiding in plain sight. If you search for it, you will find it, or it will find you. Welcome to the magical world.

Having lived all her life in Edinburgh, the last thing 25-year old Dizzy expected was to see a man with a real (if tiny) dragon on his shoulder. Following him, she discovered that she had stumbled from her mundane world into a parallel magical world, an alternate reality where dragons flew through the sky and the Great Powers watched over the world. Convinced that she had nothing to lose, she became apprenticed to the man with the dragon. He turned out to be one of the most powerful magicians in all of reality.

But powerful dark forces had their eye on this young and inexperienced magician, intending to use her for the ultimate act of evil – the apocalyptic destruction of all reality. If Dizzy does not realise what is happening to her and the worlds around her, she won't be able to stop their plan. A plan that will ravage both the magical and mundane worlds, consuming everything and everyone in fire.

Christopher Nuttall has been planning sci-fi books since he learned to read. Born and raised in Edinburgh, Chris created an alternate history website and eventually graduated to writing full-sized novels. Studying history independently allowed him to develop worlds that hung together and provided a base for storytelling. After graduating from university, Chris started writing full-time. As an indie author, he has self-published a number of novels. *A Life Less Ordinary* is his third fantasy novel to be published by Elsewhen Press. Chris is currently living in Borneo with his wife, muse, and critic Aisha.

ISBN: 9781908168337 (epub, kindle)
ISBN: 9781908168238 (336pp, paperback)

visit bit.ly/ALLO-Nuttall

Elsewhen Press

an independent publisher specialising in Speculative Fiction

ARTEESS: CONFLICT

JAMES STARLING

Arteess: Conflict is the first in a new science fiction series where much of the action takes place inside a game. But surviving the game is not child's play. We learn of science, betrayal, power and progress – from the perspective of innocent, but nevertheless accomplished gamers.

Created as an experiment into the nature of time itself, the virtual world of Arteess exists, in the near future, as a private digital realm. A full-body virtual reality experience where the talented, the shrewd and the lucky are invited to participate in an international war zone of nomadic factions. We are introduced into the world of Arteess alongside the Shard squad, a group of friends specialising in conflict arenas. Though each member possesses unique talents, they are ultimately defined by their personalities, their own personal battles and the moral choices they make in the consequence-free virtual environment.

Surrounded by sociopathic technicians, facetious pilots and a potentially insane commander, they must carve out a place for themselves while surviving the onslaught of rivals and the antics of the rest of their own faction.

James Starling is, by any definition of the word, a gamer. From the mean inhospitable streets of a lovely little community nestled deep within the Devon coastline, James finds himself caught between two distant generations. Dragged along with the modern and the technological, he revels in the virtual environments and endless community entertainment of this millennium's gaming scene. However you view it, he's certainly caught up in the rush of gaming to the point where it's become a bit of an obsession.

Bridging the chasm-like void between literature and gaming, James brings together both the disturbingly amusing black humour of the gaming community, and the focus, scope and monumental scale possible within modern literature. He's quite fond of the end result… *Arteess: Conflict* won the Silver Award in the Teenage Fiction category of the 2013 Wishing Shelf Independent Book Awards.

ISBN: 9781908168306 (epub, kindle)
ISBN: 9781908168207 (240pp, paperback)

Visit bit.ly/Arteess-Conflict

Elsewhen Press

an independent publisher specialising in Speculative Fiction

TimeStorm
Steve Harrison

In 1795 a convict ship leaves England for New South Wales in Australia. Nearing its destination, it encounters a savage storm but, miraculously, the battered ship stays afloat and limps into Sydney Harbour. The convicts rebel, overpower the crew and make their escape, destroying the ship in the process. Fleeing the sinking vessel with only the clothes on their backs, the survivors struggle ashore.

Among the escaped convicts, seething resentments fuel an appetite for brutal revenge against their former captors, while the crew attempts to track down and kill or recapture the escapees. However, it soon becomes apparent that both convicts and crew have more to concern them than shipwreck and a ruthless fight for survival; they have arrived in Sydney in 2017.

TimeStorm is a thrilling epic adventure story of revenge, survival and honour. In the literary footsteps of Hornblower, comes Lieutenant Christopher 'Kit' Blaney, an old-fashioned hero, a man of honour, duty and principle. But dragged into the 21st century… literally.

A great fan of the grand seafaring adventure fiction of CS Forester, Patrick O'Brien and Alexander Kent and modern action thriller writers like Lee Child, Steve Harrison combines several genres in his fast-paced debut novel as a group of desperate men from the 1700s clash in modern-day Sydney.

Steve Harrison was born in Yorkshire, England, grew up in Lancashire, migrated to New Zealand and eventually settled in Sydney, Australia, where he lives with his wife and daughter.

As he juggled careers in shipping, insurance, online gardening and the postal service, Steve wrote short stories, sports articles and a long running newspaper humour column called *HARRISCOPE: a mix of ancient wisdom and modern nonsense.* In recent years he has written a number of unproduced feature screenplays, although being unproduced was not the intention, and developed projects with producers in the US and UK. His script, *Sox*, was nominated for an Australian Writers' Guild 'Awgie' Award and he has written and produced three short films under his *Pronunciation Fillums* partnership. TimeStorm was Highly Commended in the Fellowship of Australian Writers (FAW) National Literary Awards for 2013.

ISBN: 9781908168542 (epub, kindle)
ISBN: 9781908168443 (368pp paperback)

Visit bit.ly/TimeStorm

About the Author

Katrina Mountfort was born in Leeds. After a degree in Biochemistry and a PhD in Food Science, she started work as a scientist. Since then, she's had a varied career. Her philosophy of life is that we only regret the things we don't try, and she's been a homeopath, performed forensic science research and currently works as a freelance medical writer. She now lives in Saffron Walden with her husband and two dogs. When she hit forty, she decided it was time to fulfil her childhood dream of writing a novel. *Future Perfect* is her debut novel and is the first in the *Blueprint* trilogy.